About the author

Neil McLocklin was brought up in Dorset and enjoyed visits to the Purbecks and Corfe, something he continues to do with his wife and family. He has enjoyed a career in business consulting and real estate but has written a number of books in a diverse range of genres, mainly written on his commute to London. *A Nation in Ruins* was the first to be published and *A Nation Beheaded* is the sequel, following the fortunes of the Bankes and Harvey families through to the end of the first and second Civil Wars and the execution of Charles I. The final book in the trilogy will take the characters into Oliver Cromwell's rule as Lord Protector.

A Nation Beheaded

VANGUARD PAPERBACK

© Copyright 2024
Neil McLocklin

A CIP catalogue record for this title is
available from the British Library.

ISBN 978 1 80016 971 5

Vanguard Press is an imprint of
Pegasus Elliot Mackenzie Publishers Ltd.
www.pegasuspublishers.com

First Published in 2024

Vanguard Press
Sheraton House Castle Park
Cambridge England

Printed & Bound in Great Britain

I would like to dedicate this book to my six children who provide so much joy but also worry and pain as they go through life's challenges. I hope that they will read it and enjoy history in the future as much as I have in the past, and that it provides them with some comfort to know that the challenges of today are not so different from the ones of yesterday.

"I go from a corruptible to an incorruptible crown, where no disturbance can be, no disturbance in the world." – King Charles I on the scaffold before his execution

Chapter One

Lies, Deceit, Quarrels and God's Gift

August 1610, Hinchingbrooke House, Huntingdon

The two boys, both armed with wooden swords, chased after each other through the pine trees and undergrowth of the woods on the Hinchingbrooke estate in Huntingdon. The older boy, thirteen and a head taller, led the way, and soon had outrun his playmate who suffered from a limp. He hid behind a tree trunk that had the added protection of a holly bush at its base and jumped out on the unsuspecting younger boy of eleven years, pointing his sword at his chest.

"Surrender or I will cut off your head," the elder boy demanded.

"I surrrrrrrrender," the younger boy stuttered, but as the older boy lowered his weapon, his opponent slashed his sword into his ribs.

"Aw—that hurt. You lied," the elder boy shouted, holding his side, but the younger boy had already run off and was heading back to Hinchingbrooke House.

It did not take long before he had been caught up. The boys continued to walk up the drive, past the lake and towards the Tudor mansion, which was the home of Robert Cromwell, the father of Oliver, the older boy. It was a great privilege for the family to be hosting sixteen-year-old Prince Harry, the eldest son of King James, who had business with Oliver's father, having been granted considerable authority by the King. He was a dashing young man, skilled in both horsemanship and sword play, and the talk of royal courts all across Europe for his looks, his charm and as heir to the prized throne of England. He was the hero of his younger brother, Charles, whom Oliver had just been playing with. The younger prince received little attention from his father, but his brother Harry made up for this in part, always having time for his sibling, although young Charles lacked many of the characteristics and abilities of the dauphin. Prince Harry knew Robert Cromwell had a son of roughly Charles's age and so had invited him along, recognising that he had few opportunities to play with other boys. As Oliver was the only boy in his family he was equally as excited by the prospect of a playmate. But over excitement meant that the occasion to play did not start well after Prince Harry had given them wooden swords and sent them into the woods. Prince Charles insisted on playing his brother as a character and that Oliver should be a Spanish prince, but Oliver had no desire to be a Catholic or a Spaniard. He wanted to be an English knight.

"Englishmen against Englishmen, this is not possible," Charles declared when they had started to play earlier.

"Why not? If the King is not just then the knights will rise up against him and take away his crown."

"But the King is appointed by God!" declared Charles, but Oliver had already run off.

The boys dragged their swords as they made their way to the house with two royal guards stationed on its giant oak doors which had been left ajar.

"My brother is going to be the greatest King this country, no, the *world* has seen. He will make this country the strongest and most powerful and promote our faith across Europe. You will see."

"And if he is a good King and follows God's will then his subjects will all serve him well." Oliver smiled at the young prince.

As they entered the house, the younger boy suddenly swung his sword around shouting, "Off with your head," directing his wooden blade at the neck of his playmate, but Oliver ducked just in time, and the weapon decapitated a china vase of summer flowers standing on a pedestal . The vase smashed on the wooden floor, the crashing sound reverberating around the vestibule. A moment's silence followed as the boys looked at each other with dread. The two guards looked in but decided not to intervene as the sound of voices and footsteps could be heard from within the house. The governess was the first to arrive, immediately followed by the head of the household staff; neither were known for having a sympathetic approach to children. The governess was first to speak.

"What a mess. Who did this?"

"He did it," Charles declared, pointing to a dumbfounded playmate.

"Well Oliver will clear it up then, whilst I escort you back to Prince Harry," the governess declared.

"But he is lying. It was he who attacked me with his sword and knocked the vase over."

"Princes do not lie." And the governess led the prince away, leaving Oliver to the wrath of Mr Jakes.

7 July 1648, Swanage, Isle of Purbeck, Dorsetshire

Colonel Tom Harvey was riding his horse Lightning at barely a trot in the drowsy sun through the Isle of Purbeck back to his home in Swanage. The summer had been cool all through June, but had warmed up during the last week, and this was a day when the sun scorched the fields along the limestone ridge to his south. The cattle and sheep stood or lay lifelessly under the few trees that provided shade. To the north were the wilting woods at the base of the chalk ridge of Nine Barrow Down as he trotted slowly in the drowsy summer sun. He now could see the blue sea ahead, reflecting the sun in a thousand jewels across Swanage bay. He knew Camille, his French wife, and his one-year-old daughter, Emily, would be in the house he had built overlooking the spectacle. The Isle of Purbeck was his home; he knew every square foot of it like his own hand. Most of it was owned by the Bankes family but managed by his father on their behalf. It was not in fact an island but a peninsular bordered by water on three sides: the English Channel to the south and east, where steep chalk and limestone cliffs meet the sea; and by the marshy lands of the River Frome and Poole Harbour to the north. The entrance to the Isle had been guarded by Corffe Castell, owned by the Bankes family which had been the heart of the community and this land, his playground as a boy. In the army he had seen much of the country and he could think of nowhere that compared to the beauty of this small patch of Dorsetshire. But so much of it had changed in the last ten years. He had been so happy back then as a boy, working with his father and family, and enjoying the company of his friends which included the Bankes children, especially John who was his age, Francis Trew and Joseph Cobb. But whilst the Purbecks were idyllic the rest of the country started to pull itself apart. Prince Harry had died from typhoid two years after the visit to the Cromwells and it was the ill-prepared Charles who had succeeded his father as King. A cocktail of religious, social and political differences between King Charles, Parliament and other interest groups in the nation fuelled the tensions which ultimately had resulted in civil war. The Parliamentary 'knights', in the form of Oliver Cromwell's New Model army, rose up in a bloody conflict against the King who was backed by his cavalier lords, the Royalists. Tom and his friend Francis Trew had been attracted to the new social ideals of the Levellers, hoping for a world where wealth was more equal, and everyone would have a patch of England to call their own; where people had a right to land and a say in how the country was governed. This cause had been championed by the Parliamentarians and so they set off to battle in 1642, expecting to be back by Christmas. That was a festivity Francis did not see for he lost his life at the battle of Edgehill and was the first of many friends Tom would lose. He soon realised that it was a fantasy fighting for the ideals he had signed up for, but Cromwell provided training and opportunity for anyone in the New Model who showed aptitude for advancement which was at least a step forward. Tom's brawny physique and being six foot tall made him a formidable pikeman on the battlefield, but he was intelligent and understood the need to use his mind, living the words of his mentor back in Dorsetshire, the retired Captain Cleall: 'in the confusion of battle, it is a plan that gives you the edge; not the sword.' He almost lost his life had it not been saved by John Bankes, now a Royalist opponent but found himself being promoted to a sergeant and then a lieutenant. As an officer he was faced with the appalling prospect of orchestrating a siege on Corffe Castell, the place that had been his home and within which had been trapped his wife Camille, many of his friends as well as Lady Bankes and Captain Cleall. He devised a plan that did take the Castell, and rescued Camille with hardly any loss of life, but amongst those who did die was his friend Captain Cleall. He had been promoted to Captain for masterminding and leading the execution of the victory at Corffe, but Parliament then ordered that the Castell be slighted, and commanded him to oversee the destruction, something that still haunted him at night.

Tom was a man of status and authority now, still only twenty-seven but responsible for the army and public order across Hamptonshire and

Dorsetshire. Sometimes the level of responsibility he had and the decisions he had to make made him shiver but at those times he would ask himself: *what would Captain Cleall have done?* The question would soon reveal an answer, as if the Captain were riding by his side trumpeting the causes of justice and integrity. He had also lost another guide, Colonel Bingham, the Puritan alderman who had caused so much harm to Tom and his Corffe friends when they were young but who had mellowed over time. It was the war that had helped the alderman reframe his views on the world, with more understanding and compassion mixed with a drive to reflect God's glory in the effort and toil you bring to the world, rather than material possessions. The alderman was the son of a ship's mate but had reached political and military levels of influence that would be the envy of any aristocrat. He showed a path for Tom to follow, one that no longer held any resentment towards the wealthier classes. It was a path that Tom literally followed for it was the Colonel's retirement from the army when he became Member of Parliament for Shaftesbury that resulted in his promotion from Captain and taking over his responsibilities.

He continued to spend a lot of time away from home with his regiment of over one thousand men having bases in Poole, Salisbury, Winchester and Southampton. Camille very much resented his time away. She went crazy when he first declared he was joining the army at the start of the war six years ago, and in hindsight, he saw she had been right. Home by Christmas he had promised. It was three years before they saw each other again as he fought in battles all across the country and then when he did get assigned to a regiment in Dorsetshire it was to siege Corffe Castell. And of course there was the rest of the Corffe community that he had to be reconciled with. Yes he had ended the siege that had brought so much suffering to the community, but it was the likes of Tom and Francis who had turned their backs on their home in the first place, following dreams of social and political reform and a better life. Well so far this had only resulted in a worse life for most of them, and the loss of loved ones for others. Tom's father, William Harvey, had never said such things to him but he suspected he thought as much, having argued forcefully that he should not leave his family in the first place and refusing to fight to protect the Castell. He had just ridden through Corffe village beneath the ruins of the once formidable guardian of the isle, that had withstood many a siege through history, but was now under attack by the ivy creeping through its broken walls and the carcass of the Bankeses' former home. The village houses had been patched up, but the repairs to the church had come to a halt the year before when the money Lady Bankes had provided dried up, so folk were still forced to climb the limestone ridge to Kingston to worship God at the church there. En route many would ask themselves why God seemed to be punishing them in such a way; the suffering and loss of life, no church or castell and now food shortages and escalating prices.

Things had certainly not turned out as Tom had expected, but he was just a small cog in a big machine. If he had not gone to war there would have still been a war, and there would have still been a siege of Corffe, but perhaps much longer and bloodier and he would not have been able to bring it to an end. He had always done what he thought was best and prayed every day for God's guidance. Although not a Puritan, he had learnt a lot from Colonel Bingham and believed in many of the Puritan principles, especially the glory of good through hard work. And his hard work and commitment had been rewarded for now he had a status and lifestyle Camille and he could not have dreamed of, and he was continuing to use this for the good of everyone. But there was also something else that vexed him and continued to drive him. He wanted justice for all the pain and hardship that he and all of England had suffered. That meant bringing the King to justice for, in Tom's eyes, he was to be blamed for it all. He knew this was a feeling shared by many in the army, but he was uncertain where the commanders, Fairfax and Cromwell, stood on the issue. They both kept their thoughts to themselves when the future of the Monarchy was discussed. Even less clear was what Parliament's position was with many representatives apparently supporting the Monarchy but Tom sensed the time was coming for people to take their position whilst the King remained imprisoned in Carisbrooke Castell on the Isle of Wight. He could actually see the island on the horizon of the sea as he made his way into Swanage Bay. A short boat trip could bring the tyrant here and he could face the wrath of the army, Tom thought.

Away from the politics it was the everyday folk that had suffered and one was John Anderson, a man closer to his father's age but Tom had known all his life. He had a small cottage on the Bankes estate at Worth and the right to farm several strips of land, but also had laboured for larger holdings and at the quarry at busy times. After the first year of the war with the closure of the quarry and the general economic hardship locally closing other opportunities to earn money, he joined up to fight, not for any political view but just to earn a living. He had heard a Royalist force was gathering to make an assault on Melcombe, and so he set off and joined leaving his wife to tender the strips of land at home. During the assault, his first taste of battle, he was shot both in the leg and arm. He was lucky to survive but had his arm amputated and now walked with a limp, having little to offer any work that did exist locally. Tom had just travelled through the market square in the Corffe village, and saw him there with a beggar's bowl. Tom had given him a couple of coins and offered him a ride on the back of his horse up to Worth, a diversion on his route but the poor man would have taken hours to walk back with his limp. Having left him with his grateful wife, Tom pondered how he could help the poor man and his family. An idea was starting to emerge in his mind, but he would have to discuss it with Camille first.

He was getting closer to home and he was looking forward to seeing his family after another few weeks away. He loved his wife and his little girl with all of his heart and Emily amused him so much. Camille was expecting their second in four weeks' time and had been grateful for a cool summer. He prayed for a boy but was thankful to be blessed with such a wonderful wife and daughter already. Camille resented Tom's absence and suffered from loneliness. Her parents had returned to France when the war broke out and so she had no family locally. She had been the maid to Lady Bankes and during the Castell siege had developed a strong relationship. With Camille's elevated status they had remained friends, but she was now living in a modest house at Kingston Lacey, near Wimborne twenty miles away. At least Camille now had a housemaid of her own, Nella, who was just seventeen. She had lost her father in the war and her mother died shortly afterwards, leaving Nella alone in the world. Camille heard the story and offered her the position and she was a godsend for she was not only a good maid and great with Emily but good company for Camille. Nella had a wicked sense of humour and kept everyone amused.

As he left Swanage Bay, with its hamlet of fishing huts, nets and boats, he rode up the hill to his home, two storeys high and made from local stone, quite imposing from close up but from afar it seemed to blend into the landscape. He dismounted and tied his horse to a ring on the wall as the door was flung open, and Camille ran out with Emily.

"Mon amour," she cried

"Papa, Papa!"

Tom grabbed Emily and simultaneously hugged and kissed Camille.

"It is good to see you both."

Tom removed his bag and jacket from the back of his saddle. Nella came out and greeted her master with a curtsey and Tom asked her to water Lightning. Then he took his family down to the beach. He stripped off to his breeches and ran into the water to cool off, before returning to play with Emily in the shallows. Camille loved watching the two of them play, as she sat on the sand shaded by a parasol. The fishing boats were returning from their daily catches trailed by shrieking gulls, and their womenfolk were salting fish and mending nets under a canvas shade further up the beach. She could feel her baby's kick inside her, joining in the fun. Why could not every day be like this?

The family returned to the house, and Nella had prepared a simple meal of fresh crab and garden vegetables. Emily was bathed and put to bed whilst Nella cleared up before leaving the couple to talk.

"There is always so much to do, and I am feeling so tired in this heat, Tom,"

"It must be difficult, but not many more weeks now," he replied.

"If only you were not away so much."

"I do wish I could be here more; you know that Camille, but I have responsibilities all across the two counties. And I am afraid there is not good news, my dear." He had been dreading telling this to Camille all the way home and had decided it was best to come out with it at the earliest opportunity.

"What is it now Tom?" she asked, in a tone that was already cooling

"The war looks like it is about to restart. The King has conspired with the Scots to invade, and Cromwell is leading an army North."

"No, no, not again. I will not let you go."

"It is not planned that I do go. His army has already left and I am sure in a few months it will be all over. Why they just cannot bring the King to justice and string him up I do not know. If there is no King there is no King to fight for."

"A few months you say, Tom. Do not give me any more false promises, Tom. The last time you said a war would be over in a few months and I did not see you for three years."

"This time it is different. I am sure I will not be going to Scotland but…" He paused and she spotted his hesitancy.

"But what Tom? Tell me what you have to say," she said, the tempo and volume of her voice increasing.

"But we have intelligence to say that Royalists will simultaneously co-ordinate risings in the South."

"So you *will* be fighting, Tom. No, you have done too much already."

"I am an officer and I must serve and obey my orders, Camille, and I need to see this through to the end. The Royalist's cause must be defeated and the King brought to justice."

"Whose orders? Those aristocrats in Parliament? The ones that do not even pay the wages of their soldiers. What are you fighting for, Tom? Even you have realised that the ideas of the Levellers were just a charade to get young men to sign up to be cannon fodder for those politicians. And what do you get in return? They do not even pay your wages. Well, you can be a labourer on any farm around here and at least get paid. We need the money, Tom. How am I supposed to run this house, pay Nella, buy food and wood? Have you seen the cost of food: bread, pork, even cheese? Prices are going sky high."

"I know, Camille."

"No you do not. You have no idea. I think I should return to France and away from this chaos."

"I am buying food for a thousand troops every day. Anyway as the last resort we have the Castell money." Tom had been paid fifty shillings as a reward for devising and executing the plan to take Corffe Castell. "You mean the blood money. We will never use that. You should have never put us in that situation. Every day my resentment to every shilling of that money grows," his wife replied.

"Fairfax and Cromwell have assured us and all the troops that all back salaries will be paid next month. It was a condition of Cromwell taking the army North."

"Yes I am sure it was. Those good-for-nothing rich Parliamentarians were no doubt shitting themselves when they heard the Scots were coming, but they do not have the decency to pay their soldiers who brought them already so many victories. How are their wives coping, not to mention the widows of the ones who were lost in Parliament's name? Cromwell and Fairfax had better live up to their word, or I will march up to London and tell them exactly what I think about them." She paused for breath, and as she did so a feeling of compassion mellowed her temper slightly.

"Where will these uprisings be, Tom? As a colonel you will not be fighting in the front line, will you?"

"I do not know, my love. We do think they will be minor skirmishes at best as our troops are so well drilled and equipped, and I will be careful."

"Careful to you is high risk to others. Promise me Tom, promise me, think of Emily and this one," she said, patting her stomach.

"I will, I promise."

"And when do you have to go back?"

"The day after tomorrow and that is stretching it beyond what I should."

"I do not want to argue Tom. Let's make the most of this precious time," and she kissed him lovingly, her hand brushing his cheek.

"Camille, I think I can find John Anderson a position in the garrison at Poole, but he will need to brush up on his numbers. Would you mind spending some time with him to help him. He just needs to be confident on all the basic additions and subtractions. He tells me he has not done much since school"

'You are always thinking of others, Tom. We cannot help everyone, but yes, Tom. I know the poor man needs help. I saw him in Worth last week and he was so melancholic. He feels hopeless as he thinks he has lost all ability to keep his family."

"I have known him all my life. He always was whistling or singing and had something positive to say but his injuries have sucked the life out of him. He has no family to support him and his wife. We must do something."

7th July 1648, Kingston Lacey, Wimborne

Colonel Coke had struggled to regain his status and position after his failure to take Corffe Castell three years earlier. He had returned to London where he still had oversight of the enforcement militia that ensured the increasing number of Puritan rules that were passed by Parliament were complied with. He continued to define these in his own way and focused on merchant and aristocratic excess for he knew they could easily pay penance to him directly rather than burden the judiciary system. This role kept him in an acceptable lifestyle and he had saved enough to invest in a plantation in the New World where the slaves were now providing him with a healthy return. He also had acquired a house in the newly developed square of Covent Garden, at a significantly discounted price as he exploited the distress of a Royalist aristocrat being punished for supporting the wrong side in the war. But he felt he could do more for the Parliamentarian cause as he saw it, and so he was delighted when he was offered a new role by the Parliamentary leaders. The Royalist lords who had fought for the King had been punished by death or imprisonment but more often by having their lands taken away. Now Parliament needed money fast to pay for the debt of the war, including paying for the salaries of the standing army and so it was felt more sensible to give back the lands to the gentry but impose fines on them which they could pay from working the land and disposing of assets. This meant that the burden of producing money quickly would be shared amongst the gentry and would be more effective as long as there was a big stick to ensure they paid promptly. This would be where Coke fitted in for he would now be responsible for ensuring the debts were paid by the Royalist gentry in southern England and had power to impose penalties if they were not. He would be paid 2% of late debts he recovered and 5% of fines he imposed. He found it difficult to hide his joy when he was offered the position. He would ensure the Royalist pigs squealed with their financial repayments, and then make them squeal even more. He already had a reputation that made him feared across London and now that would be extended across nearly half the country. He loathed much of the aristocracy for so many of them measured him against the legacy of his infamous father and made no secret in how wanting they thought he was. But who could live up to Sir John Coke, for whom the church bells tolled across the land in celebration of the passing of his Petition of Rights which he crafted and steered through Parliament. His father's legacy, if written down, would have been as long as his arm and in contrast his own reputation was as a drunk in the whore houses of London after gambling the family fortune away. Ironically, he had found some salvation as a Puritan enforcer in the years before the war, building up a strong militia and informant network across the capital. When the war came Parliament wanted to deploy his men in the field, made Coke a colonel and sent him to Dorsetshire to besiege and conquer Corffe Castell. With five hundred men at his disposal he wrought havoc on the community in Corffe as a revenge for his treatment as a young man by the villagers when his father owned the Castell. But the bitch Castell owner and defender, Lady Bankes, was a formidable opponent, and with just forty or so men, held the Castell for nearly seven months before he was relieved of his command. But now he could taste sweet revenge again on his lips for the Bankes name was right at the top of his list of Royalist debtors. Another visit to Dorsetshire was in order.

The lodge house at Kingston Lacey, near Wimborne in Dorsetshire, made him smile as he approached on his horse at the head of a troop of five mounted men. The bitch had lost so much already with her Castell now in ruins and was now living in this humble abode. *Let's see if we can push her a few more rungs down the ladder*, he thought. He ordered one of his men to dismount and knock at the door, a maid opened.

"Colonel Coke to see Lady Bankes," the man said. The door was closed and then a moment later reopened and there she was, his old foe, her hair greying and her face ageing, but still with that air of aristocratic status and standing defiantly, which riled Coke.

"Coke, I thought we had seen the last of you. What do you want?"

"I am back as I believe we have unfinished business," he said with confidence and some glee in his voice that worried Lady Bankes. She was joined by John Bankes behind her, looking a little dishevelled.

"Have you met my son, Captain John Bankes?"

"Captain of what? A defeated force that fought for a King locked up in Carisbrooke?"

"What is your business?" John asked.

"You can invite me in and I will declare it in the quiet of your home, or I can pronounce it out here."

"We have nothing to hide; what are you here for?" Mary asked, not wanting to give Coke the pleasure of eyeing up her home which she was sure he would turn to his advantage. Just the thought of him in her parlour made her stomach turn.

"Well I am surprised that you treat a representative of Parliament with such inhospitality, but as you wish. I have here two documents: one is my authority as Parliamentary Bailiff for War Fines. This gives me the authority to oversee payment of these fines and impose penalties for non-payment or irregularities."

John and Mary looked at each other and both could see the anxiety in the other's face. John stepped over and reached up for the document from the Colonel, still mounted on his horse. He skim read it and nodded to his mother.

"Then this document I will leave with you. It is an account of your debt and your payments, as well as the fine I have imposed. I am sure you will be pleased to know that I prioritised the review of your debt and yours is the first fine I have imposed since my appointment." He handed the document to John, who took it and walked over to his mother.

"We have paid all the debt payments, every quarter."

"You will note from the document that the quarter days for payment are 25 March, 24 June, 29 September and 25 December. Your last payment was made on the 25 of June, and for that I am imposing a fine of two hundred shillings. The fine is due for payment within one month of the default, which is now two weeks away. If the fine payment is not made there will be an additional fine, and so the process goes on."

"This is ridiculous. It was a mistake that the payment was a day late. A genuine mistake. And the fine is disproportionate. How was such a number derived?" Lady Bankes asked.

"I have the power to determine the fine and believe it will ensure such mistakes will not occur in the future."

"Well, your fine will be paid, and so I bid you farewell Coke," Mary replied, and guided John inside before closing the door. She was determined not to give him one more second to relish the pleasure of his new position and the power he had over her and her family.

They heard the horses leave behind the door and Mary was already gathering her thoughts.

"I will not let that evil man have the better of us," she said to John.

"But what can be done? How do we raise more money? William Harvey says most of the tenants are struggling to survive. There is a shortage of labour and prices are going up on everything, food, timber, wool."

"Send for William and we can work out a plan."

The next day William Harvey arrived with his estate ledgers and sat down at the dining table with Mary and John to review the situation. William was always meticulous in his record keeping and his books showed all the rents and licence fees from tenants' houses, the mill and taverns, land, fishing and hunting rights, as well as the livestock and all the assets in the Bankeses' estate. Mary had her own book of accounts, but she just kept details of the summary totals from her estate manager's books, as well as a summary of the expenditure from her housekeeper's books. This was something she had always done for Sir John Bankes had been away so often leaving her to oversee the estates. Her book gave her a good overview of the family's financial situation and particularly reassurance during these challenging times. The three of them went through the books, line by line, and wrote down all the ways to realise money from the estate in order to pay Coke's fine in two weeks' time. The list included offering tenants a discounted price to buy their holdings, selling livestock, and increasing rents. But few items on the list would realise value in two weeks and most were unpalatable. They agreed to put their energy in selling as much livestock as possible but were not hopeful. They agreed to reconvene in a week's time. Mary said that she would also write to George and Elizabeth Coke, brother and sister of Colonel Harry Coke. They could not be more opposite in character to their devious, plotting brother and although she knew both had very little to do with him, she hoped that they may be able to soften his desire to make the Bankes family suffer so much.

Chapter Two

Conflict and Prayers

Battle of Surbiton, Second English Civil War 7th July 1648

The Duke of Buckingham, George Villiers, was the epitome of the Cavalier Royalist, both in style and temperament. His long hair, dashing looks, the fine pelt of his hat, a distinguishing French style, and his highly polished boots, as he sat mounted on his steed, all were made to exude gallantry. His dedication to the Crown was not surprising given his godfather was the King, and since the assignation of his father when he was not yet a year old, George had been brought up in the royal court. The first Duke of Buckingham had been a close companion of both King Charles and his father, King James, and now his son, George, sat saddled on his charger under the command of the Earl of Holland, amidst a force of five hundred Royalist rebels on the borders of Surbiton Common, west of London. The plan was to exploit discontent amongst the people across the country, who were struggling with increased food prices and the aftermaths of the Civil War, and seize towns in advance of an invasion by the Scots, who would return the King from his imprisonment as Carisbrooke Castle on the Isle of Wight, and grant back his power. Of course there was a price to pay: the Scots wanted their Presbyterian faith to be accepted south of the border, but they could worry about that later. George and the Royalists had gathered the day before at Banstead Downs and had initially seized Kingston bridge and then the town. But Lord Fairfax was quick to respond, for every tavern in southern England was abuzz with the plan which had been repeatedly leaked by over enthusiastic Royalists. Word of the anticipated uprisings spread nationwide, as people asked would the nation divide again and would the war start over, after just two years of a fragile peace. Lord Fairfax was well prepared, having already sent Cromwell and ten thousand New Model army troops north to face any threat from the Scots. It did not take him long to respond to the Kingston threat either, as he dispatched five hundred men from Windsor to Kingston, five troops of horse and three companies of foot. And here on the common is where George awaited his first real battle, with his younger brother, Francis.

George was just twenty years old, and he had taken part in a few early skirmishes when he was just fifteen, under the protection of Prince Rupert, but more as an observer. As the tide turned against the King he had been taken for his protection to the continent, and a relative in Florence, but had returned after Naseby at the age of eighteen, to find his lands had been confiscated by Parliament. Friends lobbied on his behalf and he managed to get his estate returned, largely on account of him being so young during the war. But now he was a man of age and ready for battle. He had mastered swordsmanship for the last ten years in the King's court and could ride as well as any man. Today would be the day that his name would become known amongst Royalist circles as a hero of the King's cause. Next to him was his brother, Francis, a year younger , who had shared the same upbringing and outlook on the importance of today in their destiny. Both were eager to fight and prove their skills against the approaching Roundheads all dressed in red tunics, leather breastplates and their turtle helmets readying their pikes and muskets. They seemed of equal number overall although fewer horses, but George knew that they would not be able to match his swordsmanship and he was ready to put it to the test. The Royalist had no need for colourful dress. Their attire was of far superior quality, they had upbringing on their side and this would surely prevail with such even numbers. The Roundheads had drums and marched in line to the beat as the morning sun revealed itself from behind a band of cloud. The Royalist's plan was simple, charge with cavalry into the foot soldiers and cause as much havoc as possible. The power of horse and blade would prevail. They did not need to form a line to charge, just set off together with as much pace and fury as possible. And when the enemy foot were within one hundred yards that is exactly what they did, George spurring his horse on ferociously. With half the ground made, half the opposing line knelt, anchoring pikes to the field and projecting them towards the charging Royalists, whilst the other half stood firm and shouldered their muskets.

Along their lines, flashes could be seen as powder ignited and puffs of smoke emitted from the barrel of each one, before the musketeer started to hastily reload the priming powder and the balls from pouches strapped around their chests. It took time to reload, and George knew that they did not have time, but to his left a Royalist rider went down, hit by one of the musketeer's shots, and then he felt a shot sear through the side trim of his hat. The bigger threat was the pikes and this was a question of who would hold out. Two or three pikes working together could easily bring down a charging horse, but a charging horse could jump the pikes and trample the pikemen in its path. The moment of truth was rapidly coming, and he could already see some panicked movement as musketeers sort to get out of the line of charge and reposition themselves, but what would the pikemen that he was now racing towards do? He could see them clustered on the ground, four pikes between them, bracing themselves for the impact. George decided to give them something else to think about and with a roar lunged his sabre forward to his right. It had the desired impact, for it was the foot soldier on the right who first dropped his pike and rolled out of the way of the charging horse, but the other three remained steadfast as his horse started to jump over the line of defences. In mid-flight, George felt the sudden reflex of the beast between his legs and realised that his horse had been speared by at least one of the pikes. The animal landed on one of the pikemen in a scene of carnage as its legs gave way, and George was propelled twenty feet beyond the line. It took a moment for him to gather his senses, and the adrenalin brought him to his feet, sword still in hand. Behind him, the line had been broken at the expense of his horse, as he saw Francis and then two other Royalists jump over the bodies that George's charge had created.

Pikes are unwieldly, and it took several moments for the Roundheads to realise that there were three horses with mounted swordsmen cutting through their line, whilst musketeers were still hurriedly trying to reload. George joined the fray, and his sword found first blood in the back of a pikeman, a split-second realisation that was the first man he had killed, before a musketeer tried to smash him over the head with his musket. George saw it coming out of the corner of his eye, ducked and then followed up with his sword cutting much of the man's arm off, blood spewing everywhere. The three mounted Royalists had taken two or three enemy out each, but then another musketeer was charging at Francis ready to bludgeon him with his gun. George cried out but it was too late, and the world seemed to go into a slow-motion nightmare, although it was very real, as his brother's head was smashed from one side and his body fell to the other, still strapped to his horse. George's legs seemed to be bogged down in treacle in response, but with all his effort he sliced through the musketeer foe and used his fallen body as a launch to jump on the back of his brother's horse. He grabbed the reins in one hand, with sword in the other. His arms steadied his brother's limp body, and he spurred the horse away from the pikemen and further behind their lines. There was a copse of willow trees centred around an oak about fifty yards away, and he headed for it.

"Francis, stay with me, I will get you out of here," he pleaded but there was no response from his brother. A musket ball whistled passed his head, and a pike was lunged at him but he parried it with his sword.

In the copse he jumped off the horse, pulled Francis down on to the ground to the base of the giant oak tree and splashed his face with water from his flask. To his relief his brother started to come around, but he was still very dazed. Above the sounds of the battle, cries of men appeared to be getting louder. They were being followed.

"Francis, we need to get out of here; can you get up?"

"Eh, what happened? I think so," replied Francis and George helped him on to his feet and leant him against the oak tree, whilst he gathered the reins of his horse, but as he did so Roundheads started appearing amongst the willows and bracken, first one, then another, five in total, one with a pike, the others with swords. The pikeman looked battle hardy and twice George's age, and his smile betrayed what he thought about the odds. He lunged the pike at George who sidestepped it which maddened the pikeman. He pulled the pike back and stepped back ready for another attack whilst two of his comrades moved forward with their swords. George was too quick for both providing a cut across the arm of one who pulled back holding his wound with a bloodied hand. The other swordsman paused for a moment to see his colleague, opening up an opportunity for George to attack and the Duke lunged his sabre through the leather tunic and into the chest of his foe. The man's face froze in pain and as George twisted his blade and pulled it free, blood spewed from the man's mouth, his legs crumpled and he fell to the ground. But as he did, there was a yell and a

the rein with his other hand and felt the wound and his bloodied fingers found a hole. He had to ride to safety and find help.

An hour had passed, before an exhausted half dazed George found the estate he had been aiming for, a friendly family where he could find sanctuary. But he had lost a lot of blood and was losing consciousness. Adrenalin had taken him this far but now his body felt limp and the landscape was blurred. He could make out somebody in a field, picking flowers, and he cried out before his horse came to a stop, as the reins slipped from his hands, and his body fell to the ground.

Kingston Lacey, 10 July 1648

Mary Bankes was in her bedroom, sat at her dressing table with its silvered mirror and had just finished her letter to her daughter, Alice, who lived in London. She signed and sealed it and was now ready for bed. She looked in her mirror and could see how time and pain had honed her face, her blue eyes a shade darker, now that she had reached the age of fifty. Her eyes still sparkled, but the surrounding wrinkles testified to her years and her red brown hair that was losing the battle with the streaks of grey, despite the dye she used to maintain the colour. She had brushed and curled it to give her locks more body but physical ageing cannot be held back forever. For a woman time seemed to be crueller than for men, many of whom seemed to just refine with age as had the loves in her life both with more years than Mary. She was in her new home at Kingston Lacey just outside the town of Wimborne in Dorsetshire positioned on the banks of the River Stour. The Bankeses had plenty of land north of the town, but only this modest house built in a simple Jacobean style with the air of a hunting lodge in a setting of young beach trees, saplings mostly, and a few outbuildings and stables. The rents from the farming tenants, and the revenues from the hunting and fishing nearly all went to pay the Bankeses' fine imposed by Parliament on the family for siding with the King during the war. And now she had the additional fine imposed by Harry Coke who seemed to have a personal vendetta against her and her family which she did not understand. It would be several more years before the fines would be paid unless they could start to sell Purbeck stone to the London market again. That was their only hope, but in the meantime the family resided in this lodge house, whilst their homes in Middlesex, where Mary had been brought up, and London had also been sold to pay down some of the Parliamentary debt. The family mourned their loss of status but outwardly were resilient and rarely showed it.

She knelt by her bed and began to pray. She needed to be strong and needed God's guidance and the fortitude her faith provided to bare all of the worries of the children on her shoulders. She first prayed for the soul of little Bridget, her daughter who died at the age of eight last year from smallpox. A mother's grief for the loss of a child is the ultimate test of one's faith and she had asked God so many times why she had been taken from her. But ultimately it was her faith that ensured her belief that she would be reunited with her little one again and enabled her to be strong for her other ten children. She thanked God for each of them. Half of them had grown up and left home, but still she was worried about them all like any mother would do. As soon as she had addressed a concern with one, something would happen to another. Her main worry at present was her eldest, John, who still lived at home, and was struggling to find his way in the postwar world. His drinking habit and melancholy was a large part of her letter to Alice. John took up a large amount of her prayer for she was at a loss of what to do with him. He was her favourite and she was so grateful that he had survived the war, but it had taken its toll on him and she knew he suffered at night from flashbacks and nightmares of what he had experienced. There was no time clock ticking for young men to be married as there was for women, but she wished her son John would show some interest in settling down. She was convinced love would reinvigorate him, and give him something to live, or in his case, fight for. He missed so much the camaraderie of the army, leaving a big gap in his life. Estate matters at Kingston and Corffe bored him and he did not know what to do with his life but he showed no inclination or interest towards the fairer sex. As she prayed for him, an idea was planted in her mind. She should send him to London to find business for the quarry and position it as a mission to help the family defeat the Roundhead fines. She thanked God for the idea.

Two of John's siblings, Elizabeth and Jane, were also uppermost in Mary's mind. They lived with Alice and her husband, Sir John Borlase, in the capital, both young ladies being introduced to society by their elder sister. Now Alice was a mother of two and she was eager to help find suitable husbands for her sisters so they could be as happy as she was and put her mother's mind at rest. If a young lady did not find a husband by the time she was twenty, there was a strong risk of her being left on society's shelf. But Alice was well connected and had already found a match for another sibling, Mary, and what a pairing for she had married Sir Robert Jenkinson, an acquaintance of theirs from Oxford who had aspirations to become a Parliamentarian, and Sir John was championing his cause. She prayed that they would find suitors and happiness in marriage. Her other son, Ralph Bankes, was working in London as a lawyer following in his father's footsteps and wrote to his mother frequently about society in London and his plans for the future. He was ambitious and determined to make his name, and Mary had no worries on his count. That just left Jerome and Edward and their two younger sisters Ann and Arabella at home in Kingston, but they were all playful children and eager to learn so life was never dull at Kingston.

Mary's energy and fortitude were still what the outside world saw, but alone here in her bedroom she would weep and grieve not only for the loss of her child, Bridget, but also her husband, Sir John, and her lover, Captain Cleall. She now prayed for them both and also for her reunion with them in the afterlife. The children left little time for Mary to think about herself, but in the quiet of the night or when she went out riding alone, she yearned for the men in her life. She had loved both and in different ways and she relied on both to be a light in her life. But now she lived in the shadow of grief with both men buried beneath the ruins of Corffe Castell, leaving behind big holes in her life that time did not seem to fill. She was grateful that she had loved twice and thanked God for this gift; firstly her husband whom she had wanted to love and grown very much to love over time, and Captain Cleall, whom she did not seek to love but it happened anyway. She knew many people, particularly woman of status, who never experienced love, or worse still, found themselves in nightmare marriages and being treated very harshly.

She took a deep breath, holding off a yawn, as she continued to pray. Her body was going through life's change. She felt more tired and had to dig deeper to rise to the everyday challenges and often struggled to focus.

She was a woman of status and fortitude, and that was inbred in her and would not be taken away, but she prayed for continued strength. She had kept the family together but as she grew older her dreams were fading but filled by memories of her family and the wonderful life they had had in Dorsetshire. The family picnics and society hunting parties and deer stalking with guns, horses and excited dogs were all distant memories. That life had been shattered by the war, for it was not only the Bankes family that had suffered but Mary's social circle of aristocratic families. Many husbands, sons and heirs had died and those on the Royalist side were all facing huge fines or worse with some being tried and executed for treason. Many others had fled the country. With the destruction of wealth and status there was a ripple effect on the lower classes as long serving household staff and estates workers found themselves without income at a time of food shortages and increases in prices. Her prayers now turned to these people, the communities in Dorsetshire that she knew were suffering and asked for guidance on how she could help them. The quarry came to her mind again, and she felt God was again giving her a message. This gave her hope and she went to bed with some comfort.

12 July 1648, Weymouth Dorsetshire

John Bingham was sitting in the chamber of his new bank that he had opened in Weymouth reflecting on the achievement of his third operation after Poole and Lymington. From a business perspective it made sense, for the power base in the county was changing. The old establishment was on the decline, with families like the Bankes, Cranbornes, Welds and Digbys being on the losing side of the war, the symbols of their wealth and influence at Sherborne and Corffe having been slighted and left in ruins. Bingham's bank was playing an important role for Parliament as those Royalist aristocratic families faced penalties for their role in the war, debts which were paid into his safekeeping and were used to fund the army expenses and wages of the soldiers in the Dorsetshire Parliamentary regiments. The twin boroughs of Melcombe and Weymouth had suffered much during the war, with the loss of hundreds of lives as the opposing forces battered each other from different sides of the harbour, but this is why Bingham considered it a good time and place to invest. The towns would rebuild and that required funding, and Bingham's bank would be on hand to capitalise from it. The Weymouth harbour had been surpassed by Poole which had been unscathed by the war largely due to the strong defences that Bingham had commissioned as its alderman, and it was now able to accommodate larger vessels than its westerly neighbour. Unfortunately Poole had suffered from an outbreak of the plague at the end of the war which was a setback, but the port was now thriving again. This taught Bingham not to have all his eggs in one basket, and the Weymouth bank was part of that plan.

The banker knew the town well and saw that it was in a good position to supply trade to the whole of West Dorsetshire and could benefit from trade to Newfoundland and new settlements in Massachusetts. It also had local quarries where Portland stone had been produced prior to the war, but these were currently closed as there had been little demand to build new homes or churches during the conflict. Fighting had started again with skirmishes up and down the country and there was talk of the Scots invading. However, Bingham could see little fight left in the Royalist campaign and was confident in the New Model army's victory, which would bring an inevitable focus on rebuilding the destroyed buildings across the land, and for that people would need stone. His bank in Poole had flourished on the back of the Newfoundland cod trade and even more successful was the Lymington enterprise where the salterns provided much of the country with the salt that preserved the traded fish as well as the meat that fed that armies on both sides of the war. Rebuilding the nation with Portland stone would be the foundation for this bank's success.

Bingham believed that God provided him with commercial opportunities which he had to exploit not for his own benefit but for His Glory and the expansion of the Puritan movement. He had planted the first such church in Poole nearly twenty years ago, and his power and influence had enabled new churches to be established in many towns across the shire, but his commercial expansion would enable this momentum to be maintained. He had retired from his military position as Colonel of the regiment that protected Dorsetshire and Hamptonshire but had become the Parliamentary representative in the commons for Shaftesbury in the north of the shire. He had lost his wife Frances two years ago but had remarried the previous month to a fellow Puritan, Jane, who shared his drive for promoting Puritanism. It was a marriage of convenience to follow their shared conviction but they made each other happy and so all in all things were looking hopeful.

His clerk knocked and opened the door and announced the arrival of his expected visitor.

"Mister Giles Strangeway to see you, Sir."

"Ah, Mister Strangeway. It is good to see you; please take a seat. Can we offer you a drink?"

"Not for me, let's get down to business if you please," the gentleman replied. He was a man in his thirties, dressed in a blue satin tunic with gold buttons, a large white lace collar, and black breeches and stockings. A gold medal dangled from a ribbon around his neck which intrigued Bingham. His brown eyes looked around the sparse chamber as he took a seat opposite Bingham's desk. Bingham had been acquainted with the gentleman before, when he was member of Parliament for Melcombe and Weymouth prior to the war, but the conflict had resulted them being on opposing sides.

"Well, I received your letter, Sir. It seems like you would like to mortgage Melbury House. For what purpose may I ask, Sir?"

"To pay the dammed fine of ten thousand pounds that Parliament has imposed on me."

"Ah I see. And the worth of the House?"

"With its lands it would provide sufficient cover I am sure."

"What income does the estate produce, Sir?"

"I have my books here. In normal times, eight to nine thousand pounds, but since the war, more like six," and the man pulled out a leather-bound book from his satchel and handed it to Bingham. The banker opened it and skimmed through a few pages and with the benefit of a magnifying glass his ageing eyes were still skilled at seeing the patterns in any set of accounts, even if they were poorly set out like these.

"Ah, I see you also own a quarry," Bingham stated.

"Yes, here is Portland, but not much use as there is no market for stone these days."

Bingham was making notes and calculations in his own book as he went through the accounts.

"But that will change, Sir. It seems like they were producing a profit of five thousand a year before the war. Mister Strangeway, could I make a different proposal to you?"

"Why not? Let's hear it."

"The bank makes an investment into your quarry. We will loan you say half the fine, five thousand pounds, in return for a half stake in the future profit from the quarry. We will then lend you the other five thousand pounds, in return for a payment of one thousand pounds out of your income from the Melbury estate over the next seven years, leaving you with at least five thousand pounds to live on each year and you will have the opportunity to grow that income back up to the pre-war levels."

Strangeway frowned as he pondered the proposal.

"So you will lend me money on the quarry even although it is not producing anything?"

"Yes but I would require to have authority to install a manager to change that situation. I am sure we will soon be able to start production again."

"We have a deal, Mister Bingham," and Strangeway stood up to shake the banker's hand. The Royalist landowner left happily with the unexpected proposal, whilst Bingham smiled to himself. The re-building of the country would have to start soon with so much destruction of towns, mansions, churches and even bridges, and they would all need stone. He could see God's hand at play and was sure that this opportunity would open doors to advancing the Puritan cause in ways that would be revealed by the Lord in due course.

14th July 1648 Wareham, Dorsetshire

The penalty was due to be paid in six days' time. Mary and John rode to Wareham where they had had agreed to meet William Harvey and review progress in gathering the funds. Berthed at the quay was a ship with its cargo doors wide open having its grain unloaded by stevedores dripping with sweat as they toiled in the heat. The granary clung to the quayside, its pulley screeching with the labour of hoisting bags of grain up to the labourers inside, accompanied by the cry of gulls circling above eyeing the cargo in a fishing vessel moored a few yards upstream. Mary and John tethered their horses outside the tavern on the quay, greeting William who was waiting for them apprehensively. The estate manager had arranged the use of a back room, which the landlord was pleased to oblige as he would welcome any custom. The light from two sets of tallow candles on either wall was supplemented by a small window on to the taverns rear yard. In the centre of the fusty room was a bare wooden table with six seats. Drinks were ordered, the doors closed and the three got down to business.

"I sold a couple of cows and a small flock of sheep. That raised thirty shillings. The prices I got were low but times are hard. But it is a long way short of what we need. I am sorry my Lady but we had no time as you know to sell any land and folk just have no money," William Harvey reported.

"And we have just raised twenty-five shillings and that was from selling a good horse," John added

"I am sure you did your very best William, but we are barely halfway to paying the fine," she said. She pulled out a pouch from her riding bag, took a deep breath, and she lifted a piece of her jewellery from it. Her hand opened to reveal an exquisite gold chain with a large emerald that reflected the light of the candles in its green magnificence. "John I want you to take this to Poole and get a good price for it. It should be worth far more than the penalty and so will also provide us with some money to sort ourselves out. If you cannot get a good price in Poole then go to Lymington where the salt merchants do not know what to spend their money on."

"But that is the necklace that Father brought you."

"I know John. He gave it to me when Bridget was born which makes it even harder to let it go. But what am I to do with it? I hardly have cause to wear it and your father would be the first to say it should be put to good use, if it means protecting the family from that rogue, Coke. It is a necessity to sell it, so take it John, please."

She passed the necklace to her son.

"Once you have got the best price, then deposit the money in Bingham's bank and ensure it is credited to the repayment account."

"Yes Mother," John said, seeing the sense in his mother's words, but knowing that this was very hard for her. A moment of silence passed, as

John pocketed the jewel, Mary dabbing her eyes, before finding an inner strength to direct the two men again.

"But we now need to work out a plan to make more money so we can pay off this debt faster and get Coke off our backs and bring some hope and prosperity back to our lands and the community of the Purbecks. We need to open the quarry again, and it may require some investment which the surplus from the necklace may provide. What do you say William?"

"That would be wonderful my Lady and would surely be a blessing from God for all the folk around here if it could happen. Before the quarry not only provided jobs, but also pride for the community. People everywhere knew that churches and the best houses in London were being built from Purbeck stone. It put us on the map. But is there demand, my Lady?"

"I have heard from Alice that people are returning to the capital and that a few people are starting to build houses again. We need to find out William and promote Purbeck stone in the capital, for I suspect people have even forgotten about what wonderful stone it is. John, once you have deposited the money, I want you to ride on to London, stay with Alice and between you, Sir John and Ralph, find some business for the quarry. Purbeck stone is the finest and if people are starting to spend money they need to know that they should have it for the floors of their hallways."

"That sounds like a plan, Mother," John replied enthusiastically, with the prospect of a mission of some sort away from the drudgery of Kingston. It was not the army, but a task to help the family defeat Coke.

"And William what do we need to do at the quarry in preparation for an order?"

"We need to make sure there is no flooding, but also we need to repair the wharf at Swanage for the ships to pick up the cargo. It was battered in the storms last winter. Nothing too major. The quarrymen, stone masons, cutters and marblers will need to be hired again, but most are still in and around Corffe, labouring or doing whatever they can to earn a crust. They will be delighted to be rightfully employed for what they do best. My Lady this will be the best news we have had since the war started."

"Let's hope so. I will travel over there with you to Swanage to see what needs to be done and then I can also see Camille. John, you had better make haste as the time is ticking on that penalty payment."

sudden charge by the man with pike in hand directly towards George, who just saw him in time to parry the pike with his sword and simultaneously step out of the way, but that did not stop the drive of the shaft which carried on an impelled itself through the chest of the still dazed Francis and into the oak behind.

In vain George jumped to his brother's aid, but his lifeless body just gushed blood down its tunic already pooling around as it was pinned to the tree. The horror of the death of Francis fired George into action. He had no time for remorse and turned with vengeance in mind, his first victim being the pikeman with his blade piercing the man's throat, before he kicked him out of the way. The three remaining men, one severely injured, faced him, but George could see fear in their eyes.

"I can and will kill all of you; I am the Duke of Buckingham and a master swordsman," he said assertively, "You have killed my brother and you will pay with your lives."

The Duke lunged at the man on the right, slicing his sword arm, and pivoting to parry a strike from the roundhead in the centre of the group. Another turn and his sword clashed again with such force that it sent the opponent's weapon flying. He faced the men again, now two wounded and one unarmed.

"I said I would kill you all, but if you ensure he is buried, here beneath the oak tree with a cross to mark the spot, I will let you go, and I will ride away."

The men looked at each other in turn and the wounded one nodded. George took steps backwards, not letting his eyes off the Roundheads, until he was at the foot of the oak tree. He lowered himself slowly until he was head-to-head with his brother, and then kissed him gently on the forehead, an eye still on the enemy.

"Goodbye Francis. I will always love you. I will see you in the next life," he whispered and then jumped up and bounded to his horse a few yards away, mounting it with one jump, and spurring it off out of the copse. The battle was still raging as he rode in parallel with the line, minded to try and ride around and then re-join, but he could see it was not going well for the Royalists. Any lingering desire for more battle vanished when he felt a sharp pain in his left shoulder. He had been hit by a musket ball. He released

Swanage, 14th July 1648

Tom had returned to his command and Camille was left to fend for herself with little money and many more worries. She had been visited by John Anderson three time over the last week to help him with his numbers and she was pleased to do that, although the recent summer heat and her heavy pregnancy meant that it was tiring. But today she had been pleasantly surprised by the arrival of Lady Bankes. The hot weather had continued and the two of them strolled along the beach, whilst Emily had an afternoon nap. They talked about the prospect of the war erupting again, which had been confirmed by the news pamphlet that the peddlers had brought to both Wimborne and the Purbecks. The Scots had invaded and Cromwell was leading an army to meet them. Mary told Camille about her recent visit by Colonel Coke and the financial pressure the family were under, but that she and John had just met up with William Harvey to plan how they could make some money to pay back their debt faster and get him off their back. They hoped to reopen the quarry, and she had just left William who was working on what needed to be done whilst John would travel to London to determine what business there was. She also talked about her children and the worries she had for all of them in this world of war, political turmoil, and rising prices. She was a woman of fortitude who rarely shared her fears with anyone, but Camille had been her lady in waiting before her husband's rise in status and her own financial challenges. Back in those days, Mary found that Camille had a very wise head for someone so young and she was very sensitive and had good intuition, so they would often talk together whilst Camille attended her hair or dress. They had also spent seven months together in the Castell's siege, a stressful time that brought tensions between them but a shared experience that would bond them together for life.

On the way back from the beach, halfway up the path that led up to the Harvey's house, Camille suddenly cried out in pain, bending over and holding her bump. Mary comforted her and said that sometimes this happened in the final weeks, but with a second and then third contraction she became worried, and said she was going to get help.

She rushed up to the house, burst through the door and shouted, "Nella, Nella."

The housemaid came through from the kitchen.

"I think your mistress is going into labour. Can you get a messenger to Doctor Phelps in Wareham and ask the same messenger to continue to the garrison at Poole to notify the master? Then I will need two bowls of hot water and some towels, and some help. Have you any experience in childbirth?"

"No my Lady."

"Well, you are going to get some now. I will go and help Camille now but be quick. You will also need to mind Emily when she wakes."

Camille was still sitting on the path taking deep breaths when Mary returned. She supported her with an arm across her back, and then led her slowly up the path, stopping every time she contracted and then again for a breath. They reached the porch of the house just as Nella caught up with them, in a sweat from her run.

"Will Spinney is on his way. He rides the fastest of the folk here," she said breathlessly.

"I am not sure there is much time," and just to reinforce the point, Camille's waters broke.

"I will need that hot water with all haste," Mary directed Nella. Mary helped Camille up the stairs to her chamber, as she started to moan more frequently.

"I think the baby may be coming soon, Camille. My last couple were very fast too. Let's get you ready."

She helped her undress other than her night shift and washed her when Nella brought the water, who had also brought a draft of something in a mug.

"What is that? Mary asked

"Some herbs my mother always told me helped with pain."

"Well I think you are going to need all the help you can get Camille so I suggest you take it."

Camille did as she was told, but another wave of pain tightened her face and body, as you bent over and clung to the bed. Mary and Nella felt helpless until the contraction abated and Camille fell back on to the bed.

"Where do you feel most comfortable? How about keeling on the bed?" Mary asked wiping Camille's forehead.

"I do not know. I think I will lie down."

Mary was praying that the doctor would be here soon. Whilst she had given birth eleven times, it was not the same helping to deliver another's. The responsibility seemed almost overwhelming. What would she do if something went wrong? She put those thoughts aside and comforted Camille. She remembered the importance of breathing in a regular pattern and counting the time between contractions. Everything seemed to be happening so fast. The pain would overwhelm Camille as she cried out in agony and then she would try to recover before another wave came. Mary held her hand and felt for her wishing she could share in the ordeal but knew there was little she could really do. In the intensity of it all, time was lost but then Mary could see that the baby was coming.

"Camille, the baby is coming. Please let it come at its own pace. I will help it out and push when I say."

Camille groaned in pain, and then screamed, as she tightened her muscles, whilst Mary helped her, praying at the same time.

"Camille, now rest for a moment please. You are doing fantastically well. I can feel the baby. The head is coming. I think the next push will do it."

Nella gasped with excitement, and took a glance, giving a nervous smile to Mary. A few moments passed, and before Camille pushed and screamed again.

"That is it, Camille. You are doing really well. The baby is coming," she said, as Mary carefully took hold of the baby's slippery head and shoulders and working with Camille's pushing, eased the newborn into the world. She knew she had to help the baby to breathe, so she wiped its nose and mouth and then sucked out the fluid. Time was precious. She patted the baby's back, and it seemed to do the trick, as it coughed, took a breath and started to wail. Mary felt overwhelmed with relief as much as joy, and tears came to her eyes as she admired God's perfect gift, the little hands and perfectly formed face. Oh what a wonderful sound to hear that cry. She wrapped the baby in a small blanket, its cord still attached, and handed him to Camille.

"Camille, you have a wonderful boy. Tom will be so happy."

Camille was half dazed, but the bundle brought an instant smile to her face, with Nella peering to see the little one's features.

"Nella I will need some string thread to tie the cord and a knife to cut it off please, and some more hot water if you do not mind."

"Yes my Lady. You were magnificent. I mean both of you were. I will remember this day for ever, seeing the gift of life for the first time. I will be back right away."

"He is beautiful, Mary. Thank you so much," Camille said. "Look he is opening his eyes." The baby had quietened down and seemed at peace in his mother's arms, eyeing the world for the first time.

"You did all the hard work just now and not forgetting the last nine months. And it was marvellous to be here. Let me clean you up before any of the men arrive, and perhaps you might want to give him some milk."

"Yes, I will try," and it did not take long before the baby latched on, leaving all three in a state of bliss, reflecting on God's grace and the wonder of life.

A few hours later, Mary presented Tom with his son, William Harvey, named after the baby's grandfather. He was over the moon with joy, and thanked Mary, then walked into the bed chamber to see Camille. Doctor Phelps was just packing up his things, and confirmed baby and mother were all well.

Whilst Camille rested upstairs, Nella had made up a supper for everyone, serving it outside on a table in the garden; mackerel, crab, mussels, cheese and bread, and wild strawberries with wine and ale. William Harvey senior and his wife, Elizabeth, their son Danial and his wife Rose came over to celebrate the new arrival. A fine time was had by all, including some singing, before the family and friends bade farewell, leaving the couple with their new born.

"How have you made something… someone so perfect? I love you absolutely," Tom said, kissing his wife on the forehead as they admired their new son wrapped in a baby blanket.

"We must ensure there is a better world for him and Emily; no more wars, no more hunger, people living in harmony, hopefully a new King."

Yes, a better world for his children would continue to motivate and drive Tom.

"And some time together as a family, please," Camille pleaded.

Chapter Three

Love and Enterprise

11th July 1648 Sir Edward Mansfield's estate Clyveden Reaches in Buckinghamshire

George Villiers, the Duke of Buckingham, came around his eyes squinting in the light as his senses came to life finding himself in a wonderfully comfortable bed and in a grandly decorated chamber with the sun flooding through a large window, partially opened. He could hear the birds twittering outside, and sensed it was a glorious summer's day, but knew not whether it was morning or past noon. He sensed a pain in his shoulder and realised that it was wrapped with a blood-stained bandage. Elsewhere, he sensed aches and pains throughout his body and he tried to recollect what had happened to him and how he had arrived there and indeed where there was. Snippets of a battle came to his mind but nothing he could piece together to make sense. He turned his head and found snoozing in a chair next to his bed a young lady who looked peaceful in her rest. She was of fair complexion, her delicate face framed by brown locks that were shoulder length and he thought she would be of similar age to himself, perhaps eighteen or nineteen. She had a petite frame and was wearing a modest navy dress that suggested a Puritan gentlewoman, rather than the silks and swags of the women of court. George's movement aroused her.

"You are with us, thank the Lord," she said with a warm smile and some glee in her voice.

"Where am I and who are you?" he asked.

"You are at Sir Edward Mansfield's house and you must continue to rest. You have been in a fever for two days and have lost a lot of blood. You have a wound in your shoulder, and Doctor Hawkins removed this." She picked up a musket ball about half an inch in diameter from the table next to her. She spoke in a soft tone, sounding angelic to George in his dazed state.

"And you, who are you?"

"I am Sir Edward's goddaughter and the person who found you, or maybe you found me. You fell off your horse not far from me in the grounds at the front of the house whilst I was picking flowers."

"Well it appears like I fell from hell into heaven. I thank you and I must thank Sir Edward and then be on my way." He made an attempt to raise himself but was bombarded by pain from different parts of his body.

"I am so thirsty," he said, the frustration evident in his voice. The young lady helped him drink some water from a cup that was also on the bedside table.

"You are going nowhere, my Lord. You need to rest and build up your strength, and let your arm heal."

"You are forceful for one so petite. How long have I been here?"

"Two days. I agreed with Sir Edward to nurse you and I have watched over you as you tossed and turned and talked nonsense in your feverish sleep. At least the fever has gone. God knows what other damage has been done for your body is black and blue."

"What do you know about my body?" he asked with a hint of a smile

"Enough to know it needs healing and that is what I am here for. I had to change your nightshirt for it was soaked." She blushed. "I am your nurse and as I said you need to rest and you have no say in the matter."

George thought about being undressed by the lady before him as she provided him with the sweetest smile. He was glad for her kindness and attentive care.

"And you did not tell me your name."

"My name is Mary, and I know you are the Duke of Buckingham."

"Please call me George."

"Of course, George, and first we need to get you some food. I will be back shortly. Do not move."

Mary left her patient, taking with her the bowl of water and cloth she had been using to mop his face. Yes, she saw him as her patient for she had not only found him and then got the help to bring him to the house but had sat by his side day and night since, mopping his brow through the fever, holding his hand and comforting him as he cried out on several occasions in a state of delirium. And he was the most handsome patient anybody could wish for. She had spent hours just admiring his facial bone structure, his perfectly formed head resting in a nest of wild curly long hair, even his earlobes and Adam's apple. But she had longed to see what she imagined as the twinkle of his eyes and the warmth of his smile. Her desire had just been met and although she had only received a glimpse of a smile she could see so much in his eyes. He was a man of action and passion.

It was not a coincidence that he had made his way to Clyveden for Sir Edward had known George ever since he was a boy and so he knew it would be a safe haven from whatever battle he had been fighting. Sir Edward, now in his late sixties, was too old for all the politics of the last ten years and always had said anybody was welcome in his house, as long as they came with good intentions. That is one of the reasons Mary had always enjoyed her summers in his company for he just respected people for who they were, not for what flag they flew under. He was a gentle man with time for anybody, but especially his goddaughter whom he loved as much as her own father did, for he had no children of his own. Mary had been coming to stay at Clyveden for a couple of weeks in the summer with him ever since she was little. The death of Sir Edward's wife, Ann, two years ago had hit him hard and having his god daughter to stay was a tonic for his mood, even although he was not a person who would drown in melancholy. He always saw the bright side of things and there was always something to do in or around Clyveden. But he was now in the twilight of his life and the loss of Ann after nearly fifty years of marriage was always going to be hard.

Sir Edward had told Mary that George was the King's godson and had been brought up in the court as a man destined to be of significant power. He was a man of considerable intellect but also flamboyant in nature and wooed by many women in the court. He was a Royalist through and through and had obviously been fighting for that cause at Surbiton as news of the defeat there had spread to Clyveden the day before. He was an important figure in the uprising fighting against her father's forces, for she was Mary Fairfax, daughter of the Commander General of the Parliamentary forces, Lord Fairfax. What would her father say about her nursing one of his biggest enemies? She felt he would be compassionate enough to understand the need to nurse such a man, but Mary's interest in the Duke of Buckingham had moved beyond the perspective of a nurse. Inside her she felt an insatiable need to know more about her patient and befriend him. Then what would her father say? At least the Royalist revolt had turned out to be a complete failure as more news spread, and so perhaps there would be no more fighting and her father would not feel threatened by such a friendship.

More worrying to Mary was what would the Duke of Buckinghamshire think of her, a simple Puritan girl from York, compared to all the ladies of the court? They were glamorous, with beautiful silk dresses and well connected – yes connected in Royalist circles in the upper echelons of English, if not European, aristocracy. Yes her father was a Lord, but that was nothing compared with a Duke, and he was the wrong type of Lord, fighting against everything George Villiers stood for. She then pinched herself. What was she thinking? She did not even know the character of her patient and so why was she putting herself through this self-imposed inquisition? The truth was that she had rarely had the opportunity to meet young single men of any type or description, and now this handsome man who in her mind seemed so perfect had literally dropped into her lap. The more she nursed him the more she sensed he was hers, right or wrong.

She returned to the room with some bread, cheese, slices of ham on a plate, a jug of cool, fresh water and a goblet, and set about cutting the food into small portions and feeding her patient. He captured the scent of her perfume as she leant over him. They made small talk, as he asked how long she had been at Clyveden, who else was resident in the house and what she had been doing over the summer. But he soon tired and then went back to sleep whilst Mary reflected on the conversation before she also nodded off as tiredness caught up with her.

"Francis, Francis," George cried. He had awoken, soaked in sweat, as he pieced together the reality of his memory of the death of his brother. A tidal wave of grief hit him, mixed with guilt as he realised he had left his brother's body on the battle field. "Francis, Francis. No, no, please no."

Mary awoke, instantly rose and attended her patient, mopping his brow, but then saw the tears flooding from his eyes.

"What is it George?"

"My brother. My little brother. Francis is dead. Killed by the bloody Roundheads."

"I am so sorry." But her words seemed to be worthless and there was nothing she could do to relieve the pain that she saw in his eyes. She held his head to her chest to help comfort him. She felt for him and wished she could do something more whilst relishing the closeness of her patient.

"I left him there, his body with a pike through his chest. I just left him there, leant up against the trunk of an oak tree. Not even a Christian burial. I must go back and find him," George blabbered.

"George, you cannot go anywhere. I will talk to Sir Edward and perhaps he can send people to find your brother. I am sure he would have been buried somewhere."

"That would be a comfort, Mary. Please do as soon as you can."

Mary left the room, and went to find Sir Edward, who sent two men to investigate what had happened to Francis, and returned with Mary to George's room, to express his condolences.

"My men have left with all haste to Surbiton to make enquiries. They should be back this afternoon. I am not sure there is anything else we can do, unless Mary writes to her father, Lord Fairfax," Sir Edward replied.

"You are the daughter of Lord Fairfax, the commander of the men who killed my brother," George stated, with venom in his tone.

"War has two sides of course, but Mary obviously had nothing to do with the death of Francis. However, her father, if anyone, has the power to find out what happened to your brother's body."

"Hopefully your men will provide news, Sir Edward. I am not begging any favours from a rat like Fairfax. I am surprised that you house his daughter under your roof."

Sir Edward started to reprimand his guest for what he had just said but Mary was already running out of the room. How could be so ungrateful and spiteful she thought to herself. A gentleman on the outside, so handsome, but beneath the veneer he was everything she despised in so many men. She went to her bed chamber and lay down spinning in a mix of emotions ranging from anger to despair, as she wept. But time passed and her tiredness unveiled itself and sent her into a deep sleep.

It was not until early evening that Mary awoke, and she joined Sir Edward for dinner. Sir Edward advised Mary that the Duke of Buckingham had apologised to him for what he had said and would be grateful if he could also apologise to Mary on his behalf. But Mary decided that he should wallow in his regret, if indeed it was sincere, until the next day before she would see him again.

It was early afternoon the next day when Mary decided she would take him his lunch and tentatively opened the door to find her patient asleep. She thought about backing out, but George stirred and before she could do anything his eyes popped open, and he greeted her with a warm smile.

"My wonderful nurse has returned. I am truly sorry for what I said. Sir Edward has told me how you nursed me day and night and for that I am truly grateful."

She walked over to him. He was looking better, sweet-smelling and his colour had returned.

"You are looking much improved and for that I am thankful but you obviously have a blinkered view on the world. There are many people who are not interested in the politics of this nation and just want to be good Christians and loving neighbours to each other. I have said as much to my father whom I love with all my heart. He has always been an officer in the army, fighting for and protecting this nation, and I can tell you that he wants to bring this war to an end as much as anyone."

"But he fights against the King, the man anointed by God to be our monarch," George replied.

"I am not going to talk politics. If you want to, I will have to leave."

"I am sorry, I will not talk about it again. Tell me more about the daughter of Lord Fairfax."

"There is not much to tell, your Grace, I mean George. I am Mary, twenty years of age, and I delight in everything in God's natural world."

"Well Mary, I am truly thankful for the care you have given me. Sir Edward told me it was touch-and-go. I have lost my brother Francis, and I need to get well enough as quickly as possible to see his grave. Sir Edward has discovered that your father's men did provide him with a Christian burial and for that I am grateful as well. Will you help me mend? I am sure your sweet smile is perhaps the best remedy for my aches and pains."

She blushed and smiled as she realised he was complimenting her.

"Well let's see if we can sit you up," she said, and she put both arms around him, lifting his upper body, and repositioning the pillow to be a support, breathing in the scent of his body as she did so, surprised by the tingle she felt in her stomach.

Poole, Dorsetshire 20th July 1648

Colonel Tom Harvey had brought John Anderson to Poole on the back of his horse. The town had escaped any significant action during the troubles of the war due to the parliamentary garrison stationed there and the stone wall that protected it built by Colonel Bingham, the governor of the Borough. But then it had been inflicted by plague at the end of the war and was only recovering and starting to thrive again. As they entered the Borough's gates the masts of the tall ships along the quay could be seen above the roof tops of houses, taverns and artisanal workshops within the town. Tom had nearly one hundred men garrisoned here with a converted warehouse providing beds, a mess and washrooms.

It was in the heart of the garrison building that Tom stumbled on Captain Arthur Morris, the son of a Yorkshire minister who Tom had entrusted with all the planning and sourcing of provisions for his entire regiment spread across the two shires. The Captain was slight in build, shoulder length hair and emerald-coloured eyes. Tom suspected would not be the best man to have by your side during battle, but he knew that he was the man you'd want on your side when it came to ensuring that your army was amply supplied, well-fed, watered and armed – far better than your enemies could ever hope to be.

"Captain!" Tom exclaimed as he caught sight of Morris. "This is John Anderson, the man we spoke about. He'll be helping you with the provisioning and supply of our regiment."

"Pleased to meet you, John. I could certainly do with some help," the Captain replied cordially.

"Thank you, Captain. You can see I have some physical limitations but I will do everything I can to help you," John Anderson, grinning with enthusiasm.

"Well let's get going John," the Captain said leading the way.

"And Captain, John will need a horse to source provisions," Tom said, smiling to John.

"Of course, Colonel," Captain Morris replied with a nod.

Tom couldn't help but smile as he watched John's face light up with delight. A horse would allow him to overcome many of his limitations and also give him the opportunity to visit his wife in the Purbecks from time to time. Tom hoped to hear the familiar whistling and singing that had once characterised John before the war, returning soon.

Sir John and Alice Borlase's House, London 24th July 1648

John Bankes had arrived at the house of his sister the day before, having successfully completed the first part of the mission his mother had given him. He had been offered a fair price for his mother's necklace by a Poole merchant, but something inside him said that he could do better, which proved to be the case when he stopped at Lymington. The town was famous for its wealth built upon its salterns and providing salt across the country and even to Europe. The war had increased demand as meat and fish were cured to feed the armies on both sides, and the merchants grew richer. He had bumped into John Bingham, the banker and former rival to the Bankes, who had led the forces that sieged and conquered Corffe Castell, but had since helped his family manage their post defeat predicament. He had welcomed John into his bank and hearing about his mission introduced him to two wealthy merchants in a tavern, both of whom had the benefit of a couple of glasses of brandy, and both took a fancy to the necklace. John managed to get them to bid against each other, and finally closed at a price of seventy-five guineas. He was delighted, for it was far more than the cost of the debt fine and thought that the surplus could be invested in opening up the quarry and repairing the wharf at Swanage. He had deposited the money and set off to London.

Ralph Bankes had just arrived at the house and warmly greeted his brother. They had not seen each other for several months and Ralph had matured into a fine-looking London gentleman, who was obviously doing well in the practice of the law, although still only eighteen years of age. He had his mother's blue eyes and bronze-red hair, which was curled and worn shoulder length. He was dressed in a style that nodded to a Puritan leaning, with a small collar, and charcoal-grey tunic, but there was no mistaking the quality of the cloth.

When John remarked on this, Ralph replied, "When in Rome, John. Most of my clients are Puritans and I have to at least look the part."

John had already explained the situation to Sir John and Alice, and he quickly brought Ralph up to speed. The four of them discussed how they could relaunch the Purbeck stone quarry business in a city that had suffered significantly during the war. Many of the aristocracy had left the capital in the lead-up to the war, those that were named the 'Leavers'. The 'Remainers' were typically sided with the Parliamentary cause and a significant portion of them were Puritans whose preference was for houses that were large but without the lavishness of design that would require marble-looking stone. During the war, people felt so uncertain and money was so tight nobody was building anything and even if they wanted to the masons and craftsmen had all been enlisted into the New Model army whilst the workshops that were used to produce timbers or craft stone had been repurposed to manufacturer weapons and ammunition. The ending of the war had seen escalating prices and shortages of labour, as well as much of the aristocracy being fined, like the Bankeses, for siding with the King. On top of that, plague had reappeared in Southwark, and this was a big concern for the city residents and was another reason to keep many people who had left the city at the start of the war away. The measures that had been successful to contain the disease before the war had been redeployed as that part of London was put into quarantine again. News of the start of new conflict with the Scottish invasion but as close to the capital as Kingston and Surbiton was the final straw that would make any other family give up relaunching a luxury stone business but not the Bankeses.

"We have to find some clients from somewhere to get the quarry going. If people can see the quality of the stone then others may be interested as well. It is our only chance to get Coke off our back before he strips us of all our assets. We also owe it to the people of Corffe and the Purbecks. They are really struggling now the Castell is no longer providing work for many, on top of the challenges from the war," John said.

"I believe we also owe it to our own family. Mother does not show it but has been really hurt by the loss in her status," Alice added.

"I have recently started to work with a merchant from Antwerp, who is looking to build a house in London. I think we could show him some houses which already have our stone, using your connections, Sir John and Alice. We need to make him think that this is the fashionable London style. I mentioned it to him, and he was minded to use marble from Italy," Ralph interjected.

"Well, I know a few very grand houses we could show him and Purbeck stone is as good as any Italian marble,." said Alice and her husband offered to take him to Westminster Hall, where the floor was Purbeck stone.

"When I was at Basing House, during the war, Indigo Jones was there. He is the architect favoured by the King; he designed the Banqueting Hall and the Queen's House at Greenwich. Perhaps I can track him down and he would surely have some advice."

The next day, John found himself knocking on the door of the famous architect who was living in an annex to Somerset House. He was shown into a parlour by a manservant, and there in a chair looking out of a window on to the river was the great master himself, now in his seventies with a bushy beard and long hair, all grey and in a slightly unkempt state.

"Captain John Bankes for you Sir," the servant announced.

"And who is John Bankes?" the old man grumbled.

"Your humble servant, Sir. You may recall we met in Basing House."

"Terrible business that. Cromwell smashed that wonderful mansion into smithereens. Devastation. They had to drag me out. Naked I was. Wrapped in a blanket. The pounding, the destruction, I will never forget it, or forgive it."

"I have come to seek your advice, Sir. My family owns the quarry which produces the Purbeck stone that has been used in many buildings in the capital. We are hoping that the time is right now for the capital to start rebuilding and whether you knew of any projects or people who would be interested in the stone so we can reopen the quarry."

"I am the King's Surveyor of Works, you know. But God knows where the King is, and there certainly has not been any work in London for five years or more. What a worthless title would you not agree? I know your stone and would warrant it as good as any. I lived and worked in Italy in my early years. That stone of yours is as good as any Italian marble."

"Would you be able to confirm that to a merchant from Antwerp we know who is considering building a new house?"

"Happy to, anything to get some building started again in the city. I also recall that St Botolph's church is planning a small extension. Maybe some custom there."

"Thank you, sir, you have been very helpful."

By the end of the week the Bankes family reconvened and it seemed that their plan was coming together. With the comfort of Indigo Jones's recommendation, the Antwerp merchant had placed an order for delivery in January of the following year, as had another acquaintance of Alice's. John had followed up the tip on St Botolph's church and discussions were ongoing. John could not wait to return to Dorsetshire with the news but before he did, he wanted to pay one more visit.

Colonel Coke had taken over a small house off the Strand as his headquarters for his enforcement operation, and more recently had employed two bookkeepers to keep track of the Royalist debt. He was surprised when his servant announced to him that there was a John Bankes to see him. The visitor was shown into his study, which was a poorly laid-out room, with mismatching artefacts and furniture.

"Mister Bankes, take a seat," the Colonel said, stressing the 'Mister' and pointing to a shabby chair in the corner, whilst he remained seated in his own throne size mahogany chair behind his desk. "What can I do for you?"

"I trust that our accounts are now all in order," John said.

"I believe they may well be, now you have paid that fine. I trust that you will be able to make all future payments to the correct sum and on time."

"Of course, but I wanted to know what you have against my family."

"I have nothing personal against your family, I am just upholding my duty to Parliament."

"How many debts for Parliament are you responsible for, Colonel?"

"I do not recall, but what is it to you."

"I am informed it is seventy-eight, yet of all those debtors I understand that you visited Kingston Lacey three days after you were appointed, which, allowing the travel time, must have meant that you left straight away as if your life depended upon it."

"You were in breach."

"A minor infringement. One day late. I know for a fact that others had significant payments overdue."

"What are you trying to say?"

"I will ask you again, what have you against my family?"

"Mister Bankes, I have better things to do with my time than be questioned by Royalist scum. But be assured that I will do everything in my power to see that you and your bitch mother are kept in a position worthy of your rapidly declining status. Guards!"

John was taken back by the insult. He stood up, and had his hand on his sword, wanting to make the Colonel apologise, but two guards had already entered the room.

"Mister Bankes is leaving. See him off the premises."

"Nobody insults my mother, Coke. I will ensure you apologise for that."

The guards escorted John away, and the Colonel summoned Captain Bulldock into his chamber.

"I want you to go down to Dorsetshire, the village of Corffe and around Wimborne, and find out any information about the Bankes family that might be of interest to me. I am sure they are planning something. There was too much swagger in that man's attitude. Do not return until you have discovered what it is."

28th July, Sir Edward Manfield's Estate Clyveden Buckinghamshire

George had taken a couple more days to recover before he could get up and move about, although still in pain. He insisted on seeing his brother's grave and so Mary accompanied him in a carriage to Surbiton, with the Duke in disguise, wearing a priest's tunic and with his hair tied up within his biretta hat as warn by the clergy. They talked much of the journey and she discovered that he was a man of good character, very much interested in her although he had much to share about himself. He had lived a much more exciting life than Mary had, having travelled extensively across Europe. He was not arrogant or aloof but was always charming to her. He was in a sombre mood, given the circumstances of the journey, but was grateful that he was accompanied by somebody so sensitive and supportive.

Since they had returned, George's bruises had healed and an exercise routine meant that he announced that he would be leaving in a few days' time. He had learnt that the Royalists were regrouping in Cambridgeshire and he was determined to be with them. Mary had spent the better part of every day with George, mainly in the parlour talking as the fierce heat of the July summer made it unpleasant to be outside. She had found him charming and fascinating for he seemed to know about everything, but at the same time he was interested in Mary in a way that nobody had been before. As an only child she had lacked the companionship of people of her own age, but George was making up for it. She seemed to connect with him on many subjects and found it very natural to be in his company.

It was now the day before he was to leave and he received a visitor, Lady Martha Brooke, who had heard of his brother's death and had come to express her condolences. She was a lady of the court, and arrived in an elaborate carriage, with a poodle for company. Mary and George were walking together at the front of the house when her carriage drew up and her footman jumped off the back to open the door. She stepped out in all her glory, fanning herself and looking around the building with her low-cut red dress oozing passion and matching the rouge of her lips. She saw George and gave him a dainty wave before walking towards him under the cover of a parasol provided by her footman protecting her pale skin from the glare of the sun.

"George, I am so glad to see you. I have been so worried about you."

"Martha, and it has cheered me to see you," George replied, taking her hand and gently kissing it, a gesture in which the recipient appeared to revel.

"And who is your friend, George? Please introduce me."

"Of course, Mary Fairfax, whom I owe my life to with her skills as a nurse. Mary, may I introduce you to Lady Martha Brooke."

"My pleasure your Ladyship." Mary gave the new guest a gracious bow of the head.

"Nothing to do with the General Fairfax I hope,' Martha replied, ignoring the gratitude and compliment that the Duke had bestowed on her.

"The very same General is my father, my Lady."

"George, this cannot be true. In your hour of need you turned to the daughter of you avowed enemy. Well, that is funny."

"Martha, at the time I had little choice in the matter, for I had fallen to the ground awaiting death's door to open, but God sent Mary like an angel to save me."

"Well God moves in mysterious ways, that is all I can say. It appears we must give you the benefit of the doubt, Mary and I am grateful for what you have done for my George."

Mary had taken a dislike to this woman before she had even stepped out of the carriage, but every time she opened her mouth the aversion to her intensified. She could not have been any older than herself, but she had mastered the craft of using every word to put down her enemies, which she had obviously decided Mary was, even before the disclosure of her father. The 'my' George was her declaration of war, a battle Mary felt ill prepared for. At that moment she knew it was a battle she wanted to fight and that she had true feelings for George. But how to fight a woman with so much confidence and gander, and presumably knowledge of gentlemen and how to entice them—and who, it would appear, had a significant head start?

"Before going into battle, you must prepare, Mary. Preparation is everything." The words of her father came back to her.

"May I propose the two of you go for a walk so George can show you the estate and you can catch up with each other, and then Sir Edward and I will meet you in the cool of the house with some drinks," Mary suggested to them both. Martha seemed to think it was a wonderful idea, George perhaps less so but he went along with it anyway. Mary needed time to think and prepare and made her way back to the house. She needed an ally and knew where to find one in the form of Sir Edward.

"Ah, there you are my dear. How are you today and how is your patient?"

Sir Edward had been reading in his library where Mary found him.

"He is walking with a Lady Martha Brooke. I think he knows her from the King's court. They seem to know each other well."

"You like him, don't you Mary?"

"Yes I do and I do not know what to do about it. My father would be furious and now George is being swooned by this glamorous courtier."

"What do you want to do about it?"

"Keep him here, nurse and love him and let nobody else near him."

"Oh my dear that is not going to happen. The Duke is a man of adventure and ambition, and it would be wrong to tie him down, even with love and comfort. He will be leaving to continue to fight for the Royalist cause shortly and I do not believe you can do anything to stop him."

"I know he wants to, indeed has to leave but I am worried he will be wooed by Lady Martha and her like, and just forget about me, or even worse, get arrested or killed in battle."

"Yes, but love must prevail over all of that. If he is worthy of your love and trust, he will have no eyes for other women and will fight for you even more than his King, which will give him the strength to return safely to you, it just may not be for some time."

"Do you believe that Sir Edward?"

"I know this to be true, Mary, from my own love for Ann. I was, shall I say, a little cavalier as a young man but when I met her nothing else mattered."

"Can I just ask for one more day with him, alone Sir Edward? I am sure Lady Martha would suggest staying here for the night, but can we find a reason why she cannot?"

"I am sure we can think of something."

It was not long before George and Martha returned from their walk, seeking relief from the heat of the day. George introduced Sir Edward.

"Welcome to Clyveden, Lady Martha. Have you travelled far?"

"No I am staying with friends at Hughenden. My family home is in Suffolk."

"Ah, Sir Robert Dormer's place. I knew him well. So sad. He was killed at the Battle of Newbury I recall."

"Yes, I am staying with his son, Charles, who is the heir to the estate."

"Ah yes, I recall young Charles. He has done well to retain it in these times. Under normal circumstances I would offer you dinner and you would be welcome to stay overnight, but as you can see our house is humble compared with Hughenden, such a wonderful place. Clyveden only has four bed chambers, and there are currently ongoing repairs to the floor in the only spare room."

"Oh, of course I understand. My main reason to come was to make sure George was well, which I am delighted to see he is, and I am sure he will visit me at Hughenden. I have tried to talk him out of going off to find more battles to fight, but George will be George. He will carry on fighting for the King's cause until all the Roundheads and their generals are put in their place." She caught Mary's eye with the tail of that sentence, and Mary sensed it also implied the daughters of the generals also being put in their place.

Lady Martha left shortly after that, and Sir Edward disappeared for a nap, leaving George and Mary in the parlour.

"Is she your lady?" Mary asked.

"Lady Martha? No, not at all. We have known each other for a long time as she and her family spent a lot of time at court."

"She definitely has feelings for you."

"Maybe. She is rather assuming, but she is just a friend and other than that not my type."

"What is your type?"

"Somebody more genuine, somebody who can care for me and nurse me… somebody more like you Mary."

Mary flushed. She could not believe what he had just said. Her heart jumped and there were butterflies in her stomach. He came over to her, held both hands and looked into her eyes.

"I have fallen in love with you, Mary."

"But I am Lord Fairfax's daughter."

"Love can conquer such difficulties, I am sure."

"But you are going to leave in a few days to fight my father's forces."

"Yes, I am a Royalist and will fight to the end. But I will now have even more reason to fight for my cause for if the war ends and the King is given back his God-given power this will enable us to be together."

That evening they dined with Sir Edward. The conversation flowed but for Mary she felt it was shadowed by George's pending departure. She should be overjoyed about his declaration of love, but that made his leaving harder to bear. How could she learn to live without him and would he just forget her? When dinner finished, Sir Edward announced he would retire. George invited Mary for an evening stroll. It had been a glorious day and the sun was providing a perfect finale with a smooth collusion of sky-burst reds and yellows flowing into the calm of the darkening sky. Mary wanted to take George down to the River Thames which bordered the fifty-acre estate and where Sir Edward had built a stone structure, covered in honeysuckle as a resting and viewing place. Mary knew the path there like the palm of her hand and took George's hand to lead the way, a gesture that seemed the natural thing to do and it was returned with a warm smile from the Duke. They walked through parched bushes and knee height scorched grass along the path of dry cracked mud and stone. Behind them the Tudor house stood high on the treeless escarpment, illuminated on one side by the setting sun, its brick chimneys lined up in rows reaching up to the sky. George and Mary sat and watched the silvery water of the Thames gently flow past. On the far bank, willows seemed to bow before them and dip their branches into the river, whilst on the near side, the water pooled and was gilded with lilies. The whole scene was serene as nature prepared for night. The songbirds made their last tweets leaving behind an intense quiet, in which every sound was amplified in the tranquillity of the evening: a kingfisher's high pitched trill as it retired for the night , the chirp of a cricket in the grass, their own breath. The gentlest of breezes kept the warm air fresh, and both George and Mary could sense the magic of the universe as Venus provided the first twinkle in the east, before other stars joined in amongst the moonless velvet curtain of the sky.

George broke the quiet.

"Half of me wishes I was not going in the morning."

"I wish it was more than half," Mary replied but there was nothing more to say or needed to be said as they absorbed the moment together, one of perfect harmony with nature which seemed to be staged for them with an air of expectancy, and a sense of oneness. The perception of the boundaries between themselves and all else disappeared. They were at one with the rest of the universe as their senses become alive to what they could see, hear, smell and feel in the natural world. Time elapsed but neither knew how much as they immersed themselves in the sensation.

"It is mystical. I have not felt like this before," Mary said, looking at George, their eyes meeting, and George taking her hand.

"Me too. So many sensations, I feel so alive."

They were both engulfed by it, no longer thinking about tomorrow and George's departure, nor any other thoughts, as they entered a state of elation and contentment, thrill and desire.

"Mary, will you lie with me, here now, in this magical moment, under this wonderful sky?"

Without replying, she rose up from the bench and she untied the laces from the front of her shift, revealing the curve of her breasts. She dropped her skirt to the floor and stood with her open shift, revealing her silky legs and barely disguising the form of her naked body within.

She came to him.

Chapter Four

Barley, Dreams & Treachery

Barley Fields, Kingston Lacey Estate, 15 September 1648

John Bankes looked up at the sun setting in the west, the silhouette of the treeline at the edge of the field like foot soldiers facing the fireball of battle. But it was the sickle rather than his sword that was John's weapon in his battle today as he wiped his brow and looked around at the fallen enemy; sheafs of barley that were being tied together by the women and children who stooked them up into what appeared to be barley tents spaced out across the field. It was tradition for the landowners to join the harvest periodically through the collection season, and today John had joined the mowing formation of William Harvey, Daniel Spear, and two men from Kingston. They formed a line as disciplined as any in battle, stepping and cutting in unison, to avoid the risk of scything each other, and covered from one end of the field to the other, before returning along the next section of barley. The mowers had finished their last run to complete this field and in perfect time Lady Bankes had arrived with jugs of cider.

John enjoyed the camaraderie of the harvest, indeed it was one of the few estates tasks he did enjoy but it was gruelling work especially on warm days like today. Looking at the harvested field provided a sense of achievement, and it also took him away from his despair and the brandy that pre-occupied him at home.

The last sheafs had been bound together so the five men, Mary Bankes, Elizabeth Harvey, Jane Spear, Elizabeth Hardy, and the Bankes children formed a circle as was the custom in Dorsetshire. John as the most senior male walked to the centre of the circle with a sheaf of barley, which he held high above his head. All the folk in the circle in turn bowed and quietly mumbled the words, "We have him.". The second round of chants was lounder, and the third event louder, until the final "We have him" was greeted by a great cheer from them all, laughter and joy. The cider was shared out and the precious harvest was toasted, for everyone there knew how important this harvest was when food was in such short supply.

16ᵗʰ September 1648, Wareham, Dorsetshire

The tavern on the quayside at Wareham was full of people with six ships moored on the River Frome. Captain Bulldock knew to gather the intelligence about the Bankes that Colonel Coke had requested he need a place in the heart of the Bankes estate, but one where he would not stand out and people would not be suspicious of him. This tavern was perfect for the traders and sailors equalled the local labourers who had come in from their toil in bringing in the harvest. Bulldock had rented a room for the night and was tucking into a ham pie, a knife in one hand, washing it down with his second jug of ale. He was looking for a local amongst the crowd he could talk to in order to provide Coke with the intelligence he was after. It did not take him long to spot a promising prospect, a man who obviously enjoyed a drink but was being shunned by the groups of people he tried to join. Bulldock invited him over and offered him a drink which he enthusiastically accepted. The Captain had to put up with slurping, belching and farting as he tried to understand the man's broad Dorsetshire dialect. It appeared the man collected from local taverns piss which was used in the dyeing process for wool in a workshop in Wareham and he carried with him the stench of his trade. No wonder he was not popular. A second jug of ale gave Bulldock the confidence to probe more and he discovered that there was a lot of talk about the Bankes family reopening the quarry they owned on the cliffs at Worth Matravers in the Purbecks. People were hoping that the market for the stone had recovered in London and this trade would bring back some prosperity to the Bankes family and the local community.

Kingston Lacey Estate, near Wimborne in Dorsetshire, 29 September 1648 – Early Hours of the Morning

John Bankes awoke in a sweat; darkness filled his room, the embers from his fire having long ago died. He had returned from London the previous month and was back into a routine of life on the Kingston Estate which he loathed and after his recent mission he had started again drinking too much brandy and suffered from a poor sleeping pattern. He lay awake and relived the same memory that he had just dreamt and replayed the horror that had awoken him as the ghosts of his dream seemed to moan with the wind wafting down his chimney. In the darkness he replayed the drama of the musketeer taking aim at him and the smoke that signalled the deadly lead ball was on its way. Time had slowed, for yes, he could make out the ball leaving the muzzle of the gun. It was coming straight towards him and there was nothing he could do. His horse was taking him towards the shot and although his brain signalled to his hands to pull the reins to his left away from the trajectory of the gunshot, he knew it would be in vain. The musket ball had his name written on it, and fate would bring to an end his short life now, on a field in Hamptonshire amongst so many others on that day. There would be nobody there to grieve for him and his body would be left for the crows to feast upon. Time had almost stopped as he awaited the inevitable impact of the shot and the journey into the unknown afterlife. But in that split second the quiet of the inevitable was broken by another cavalryman and his horse crossing the line between John and the musketeer. In an instant time restarted and the pace of the battle all around John boomed. And in that same instant the cavalryman shrieked and fell forward in his saddle as the musket ball destined for John found another target.

"No, no!" screamed John as he realised that his friend and mentor, Colonel Sandys, was the victim.

John sat upright in his bed, the memories of the Battle of Cheriton whirling around the darkness in the room. It took him a moment to work out where he was and that it had just been another flashback. As he came around, he recalled the hours before Colonel Sandys being shot, as dawn had broken on a frosty late March morning on Bramdean Common, near Cheriton, just west of Winchester. His cavalry had come out of the historic city the day before and had been manoeuvring though-out much of the cold and murky night having been informed that the Parliamentary force of some 8,000 men were intending to sneak past Lord Hopton's Royalist army.

Since their remarkable victory at Roundway Down in Wiltshire the summer before, the King's men had been on a roll of success, moving west into Hamptonshire. The Parliamentary forces under Sir William Waller now sought to reclaim the south-west, but Hopton caught wind of the plan and the forces were now facing up to each other that morning. John Bankes was positioned on a ridge north of a wood from which the Parliamentary forces were emerging. He was mounted on his horse next to the cavalry chief and friend Colonel Henry Sandys, and the regiment's commander, Lord Hopton. They were watching as a thousand or so Royalist musketeers under Colonel Appleyard were charging into the wood, whilst guns on the ridge had sent barrages of cannon balls over their heads, into the trees that were just starting to spawn their leafy coats. Smoke amidst the heavy great sky and the cries of men, cannon and breaking timber filled the air.

The battle continued and it had been difficult to see how it was faring. John recalled feeling somewhat surplus as there was little cavalry could do in a battle amongst trees. His horse had been restless, and his stomach churned, for the fear of battle had been barely watered down by the experience of combat over the last few years. Captain Cleall, his family's friend who had guided him through his first battle at Edgehill and a veteran of many conflicts, had told him that he was just as fearful at every battle, but that you needed to channel that fear into decisive aggression that would give you an advantage when it comes to the one-on-one situation, amidst the stench and guts of the battle.

John recalled some of the conversation that preceded his engagement in the fighting.

"I think we are making progress," Lord Sandys had said, as more Royalist musketeers entered the wood.

"I think you are right Henry; I can see some of the enemy retreating out of the rear of the tree line," Lord Hopton had replied.

"What next?" Lord Sandys had asked.

"We should maintain our defensive position on this ridge. As long as we hold them back that is enough for now. They were planning to get around us and we have stopped them and that is mission accomplished."

"Agreed, we need to maintain what we have gained," Lord Sandys had said but he had hardy finished his words, when they could see Royalist foot soldiers streaming out of the wood towards the flanks of Parliamentary horse on the left.

"What are they doing?! Stop them; they will have no chance against the cavalry," Sandys had ordered but to no avail, for it was too late. Muskets had been fired as hordes of men with long pikes were charging towards the Parliamentary flank of cavalry men. The Parliamentarians had been regrouping in a hedge-lined field and started to turn their horses to front the Royalist foot soldiers coming out of the woods. They were struggling in the surprise and confusion with some Parliamentarians being shot in their saddles, and a few horses were rearing. But the Parliamentary commanders could see what was happening and had reacted quickly, sending in the London lobsters, an elite unit of cavalry, equipped in suits of full-length plate armour, to deal with the danger.

Despite Hopton and Sandys' plan to stay put and hold their position, there had been no option but to join the fray and the cavalry had been sent to try to regain the initiative and save the Royalist foot. That is when the musketeer had almost killed John, but it was Colonel Sandys who was hit by the ball that John could see coming towards him as the musket flashed from its breech. John had ensured that the musketeer would not be taking the lives of any more Royalists as he charged and sent his sabre into the man's chest, but then turned his horse back to where Sandys lay. The musket ball had hit him just below his collar and the wound was pouring blood. John had dismounted and torn a length of cloth from his own shirt with his sword to act as a bandage and contain the bleeding. The Colonel was still alive, but he was in poor shape. John feared a broken arm as well, for he had fallen badly. He had managed to lift the Colonel on to his own horse and then lead the horse away from the chaos of hand-to-hand fighting, musket fire and with cavalry from both sides out of formation and fighting sword to sword. He found a gap in a hedge that lined the field of conflict which provided cover for him to retreat back to the wood. He had given his friend water and hidden him in a cluster of hawthorn. Part of him had wanted to return to the battle, but he had been determined not to lose another friend and one who had taken the musket ball targeted at him. He had decided that his best course of action was to get his friend to a safe Royalist base where a doctor could treat him. Winchester would have been closest but the Roundheads now blocked that road, so he decided to ride north, to

Basing House. The House had been under siege for many months but had been relieved as Waller rallied his men for the Parliamentary surge west. Using the cover of the wood to leave the battle raging behind him, he set off as quickly as he could, mounted behind his wounded friend. Basing House had been one of the icons of the Tudor reign, but few would have thought so when John finally made it there. There were already two doctors there who had been summoned as soon as there had been a respite in the siege to attend the wounded within the House which had suffered from months of bombardment by the Parliamentary forces. John found a bed for his friend and ensured he was attended to by one of the doctors, but the prognosis was not good. He summoned Jane, Henry's wife, from their house at Mottisfont, near Romsey. John, Jane and the Colonel's eldest daughter, Hester, stayed with Henry night and day for a week, but to no avail, for the wound had been too much and he had passed away on 6th April 1644. John had only known him for a year but had built up a great friendship in that short period of his life, and the man's death haunted him on many a night.

John lied back down in the dark. He had lacked a father figure all his life, with Sir John Bankes spending so much time away at court. He yearned for the comfort of male companionship to fill the gap and that was one of the reasons that attracted him to the army. The army would make him a man he had always thought and so it had. Even before the war he had risen to the challenge of the training and very much enjoyed the camaraderie he found amongst the cadets. The war had been horrendous with the death of his own countrymen on both sides and the destruction of his nation, but it had given him experiences which had toughened him and provided him with the skills to lead men. The army had provided father figures amongst those in the ranks especially in the form of Captain Cleall and Henry Sandys, both in their forties and of his father's age. But without the army and with his father and both his mentors dead, he was lost. His mother said that he should find a wife. But this was a whole area he felt very uncomfortable about and the truth is that he felt no inclination or feeling towards women at all, and he did not know why that was. He had discussed this with Henry Sandys who thought that he had just been in the army fighting for so long that he had forgotten the joy and pleasure of female company. Whilst they were at Winchester, he took John to his house at

Mottisfont to meet his wife Jane, and other members of his family including Hester, who was eighteen at the time. It was his encounter with Hester that made him decide that he lacked the education of the social norms with aristocratic women. He recalled Tom Harvey seeking his advice on courting Camille many years earlier. Who was he to give advice, but was it not easier for the lower classes? They seemed to just let nature play its part and families and etiquette did not get in the way. He did go for a walk with Hester, who was indeed a very agreeable person. She was fair in complexion, had her father's twinkle in her eyes and he was sure that most men would find her very attractive. The conversation was stilted for John could only talk about the war and she seemed to twitter on about flowers on the estate at Mottisfont, something he had little interest in. John was pleased when he was riding back to Winchester and was asking himself why the encounter had been so difficult for him, a question that whirled around his mind again in the early hours of that morning in Kingston Lacey.

6 October, the Vyne Estate, Hamptonshire

The Vyne was one of the principal country estate houses in Hamptonshire, located near Sherborne St John in the north of the county. It had been transformed from a cluster of medieval buildings into a Tudor palace by the Sandys family, with a wonderful lake, surrounded by trees from which leaves of red, gold and bronze swirled around the colder autumnal air. Lord Fairfax now rented it as a convenient base from which he could command his army in the south and London, as his wife did not like the dirt and bustle of the capital. His daughter Mary Fairfax had left Sir Edward and returned to the Vyne House some weeks ago. She was a very different person on her return, the day after George Villiers had left Clyveden and the best night of her life. She had told her mother that she'd had a very pleasant time with Sir Edward as always and had met a number of interesting people but she would not be drawn any further despite some questioning by Lady Fairfax. At night, she struggled to sleep as she realised what she had done and how she felt. It must be love, there could be no other word for it. All she had for certain was that incredible memory of their time together by the river, the scent of his body, the passion of their love making and the harmony of the universe as they lay in each other's arms looking at the stars in the night sky. It had seemed that nature had laid on a stage for George and Mary to come together. It was early morning before they returned to George's room and made love again before falling asleep wrapped up together until daybreak a few hours later. The morning sun started to lighten the room and they listened to the first tweets of the birds as they announced the arrival of the new day, the first day of the rest of Mary's life, which would never be the same again.

"I love you, Mary. You are a wonderful person who has nursed me and last night took me to heaven and back. I absolutely love you," George declared.

Mary rested her head on her arm and looked into his eyes.

"I love you too, George Villiers."

At that time Mary could not have been more content. She had broken all conventions of a lady of her status and upbringing, but it was just the right thing to do, the natural way to show how much she loved him, trusted him and cared for him. He made her feel beautiful because he was beautiful, and the way he made love to her made her feel like a goddess. She had wanted to stay in that moment for ever, for she feared what life would be like without George and how could she survive. How would their love transcend what ordinary life would bring? She knew he had to leave on that last day, but she clung on to him dreading letting go. But as the room brightened and the birds became more vocal, she knew she had to retire to her own room before the household awoke.

She had recalled those memories numerous times over the last few weeks but rationality had started to return and with it endless worries. George had left and she wondered whether she would she ever see him again? He had promised to write and had given her a passionate kiss in the stables before setting off. But then Mary thought of all the things that could happen: a musket shot in another battle, arrest and being tried for treason or her own father banning any liaison, all equally probable. She could even be with child.

She was in the library of the Vyne house, such thoughts swirling around as she tried to read a book of poems, when she heard the trundle of a carriage outside. It could not be her parents who were in London and not expected back until the weekend. She got up and walked to the window to see a footman jump down from the carriage to open the door and for Lady Martha Brooke to get out, with a poodle in her hand. What did she want? Mary felt a moment of panic. She was not dressed to receive Ladies from the court. But then did she care. She recalled the advice of Sir Edward when she encountered Lady Martha at Clyveden, and that the most important things was love and she was sure George loved her. But she still had not heard from him. Had he written to Lady Martha and not her? Did she have news of him? Perhaps bad news? Had he been injured or killed?

She received her guest in the large drawing room and offered her tea.

"I used to visit this house when the Sandys owned it. I knew Hester well," Lady Martha said.

"It is still owned by them," Mary replied.

"Oh, so you just rent it," Martha said in a disparaging tone. "Have you heard from the Duke of Buckingham?"

"Not since he left Clyveden shortly after your visit."

"Me neither, but I am sure he will write to me as soon as he is able to. I have heard he was fighting in St Neots and I am assured he was unhurt but escaped with other Royalists to regroup."

"I am pleased to hear that. I am worried about him."

A maid arrived with the tea, and there was a long silence between the guest and her host whilst it was served.

"I think we should be clear, Mary. The Duke of Buckingham, George, is mine. Everyone in the court acknowledges that we are destined to be together. We just need this war to stop and then the King to return and he will give us his blessing."

Mary felt a moment of uncertainty. The confidence of Lady Martha in what she said was compelling, but she had to be strong, stand up for herself and believe in the love and trust she had for George.

"I am sure George will find love and know what is right for him and will seek the King's blessing at that time."

"Yes, and that is a union between my family and his, through our marriage."

"Are you engaged?"

Mary thought she would tackle her head on.

"Ah, no not exactly, but that was always the intention. Everyone knows that."

"Does that include George? He did not mention that to me, even after your visit, Lady Martha."

"Of course. Why would he disclose his intentions to the daughter of his sworn enemy?"

"Yes, why indeed, unless he had feelings for her?"

"Feelings for you? How could he? Look at you, a plain girl from an unknown family in a rented house. You would not last a single day in the royal court."

"And what court is that?"

Lady Martha opened her mouth but closed it before she could respond.

"I suggest, Lady Martha, that you return to the court, if you can find it, and wallow in your self-centred narrow view of the world, whilst the rest of us, including George, adapt to the new reality of the real world. Frankly, if you are any representation of the royal court, my father is right, we will be better without it."

Lady Martha got up and left without a further word spoken.

8 October 1648, Severn Star Tavern, Aldwych, London

Two soldiers sat inconspicuously in the corner of the crowded tavern, the air a concoction of smoke from the tallow candles and the clay pipes that many of its patrons were puffing as they indulged in their gin and ale. Few would have dared to be so boisterous if they knew Oliver Cromwell, the commander of the victorious New Model army and leading Parliamentary figure was one of those soldiers behind his disguise. He was there to observe everything that happened in the tavern that night, although just with his right eye for the patch over his left was the final touch in his masquerade. His large nose had a slight orange hue in tone, shadowed by the brim of his hat, a battle-worn trophy from a cavalier gentry, adorned with ribbons that were the mark of an officer if worn on the arm but foot soldiers collected as mementoes. As he sipped his tankard of ale, the flashback to his childhood days in Huntingdon when his playmate that day had been Prince Charles and it reinforced his view of the boy who was now King. He had been lied to back then and he was here to find out if Charles Stuart continued to lie.

A lot had changed in the lives of both Oliver and Charles Stuart since the day they played together. Cromwell's family had fallen on hard times and the future for Oliver as he emerged into adult hood had been bleak. Indeed, with not much more than a small farm to sustain his family and local affairs to occupy his mind he became melancholic but then had found his faith, which transformed his life. He trusted in God to guide him, which gave him the confidence to make a name for himself, first politically as a member of parliament and then militarily, all within the last eight years, and now he found himself as one of the most important influential and powerful men on the Parliamentary side. His meteoric rise up the military and political ladders reconfirmed in his mind that God had plans for him which in turn strengthened his character and will.

In the meantime, the Prince had grown up to be King after his elder brother had died from typhoid fever, and Charles succeeded his father to the throne in 1625. But he was barely prepared for the throne as his father mourned the loss of Prince Henry and could not be bothered to invest in training another heir, especially when there were other more enjoyable pastimes at court. When Charles became King, as a staunchly religious man, he cleaned up the vices of his father's court and otherwise spent much of his time collecting artwork, hunting, and with his family having married Henrietta Maria, sister of the French King Louis XIII.

The King was insulated as a boy and had continued to be so as a King, travelling rarely and certainly not mixing with ordinary people. Much of his reign was in conflict with Parliament. A war with Spain was a disaster and Charles offered Parliament no explanations of his foreign policy yet demanded that they fund it. He was also at odds in religious terms, as Parliament, with Cromwell amongst its ranks, was increasingly being influenced and populated by Puritans whereas the sympathies of the King were with the traditional High Church view of ritual and the Book of Prayer. The King suspended Parliament for years but found he could not raise taxes without it. And when he recalled it, the Parliamentarians had so much pent-up frustration that they would spend their time focused on drawing up a list of remonstrances against the King. Charles's contempt for Parliament was such that he would not even read their grievances. He believed in the Divine Right to rule of the King and as such he believed he should only answer to

God. The antagonism increased between King and Parliament, but it was the latter that realised the power of the printing press in this confrontation. Pamphlets were regularly printed making the case for the Parliamentary position and fuelling fear and discontent by making out that the King was a Catholic sympathiser and would use the Irish to help re-establish popism in the country at the will of his Catholic Queen. Cromwell was in the midst of this, having become a member of Parliament and seeing the two sides divide to irreconcilable positions before the King in August 1642 raised the Royal Standard in Nottingham, a declaration of war against the Parliamentary forces. Later that year the English Civil War started when the forces first met at Edgehill and continued fighting across the country with different shires and towns declaring for different sides, and often switching sides, with brothers fighting brothers, fathers fighting sons, friends fighting friends over a period of four years.

It had been Cromwell's New Model army with good training and proper supplies, and officers appointed based on ability rather than upbringing that caused the decisive blow as the Battle of Naseby. Shortly afterwards the capture of the King had caused the Royalist cause to peter out. The King had been in his custody for nearly two years now. Cromwell had spent more time with him in Windsor and Maidenhead. He had almost fallen under the charm of the King whom he had allowed to retain some semblance of royal courtship, servants, entertainment and hunting. He had been moved to see the reunion of Charles with two of his children, Henry and Elizabeth. At the time he could see no future other than one with the King, who would need to repent and agree to the demands of Parliament as well as the army which was now in a powerful position. The previous year there had been much disagreement between the army, as the Royalist threat had reduced, and Parliament, struggling to pay the backlog of wages for the soldiers. Cromwell and Fairfax, the leaders of the army, backed its cause, despite being Parliamentarians. Their men had not only not been paid but had also been radicalised by the Levellers, and it was only by marching the army ever closer to London that an agreement had been reached with Parliament.

Having the King in his custody had strengthened Cromwell's hand, but it had been better for him to try and work with Parliament with the King out of reach and so he arranged for him to be put under the protection of Sir

Thomas Herbert on the Isle of Wight in Carisbrooke Castell. This would prevent the King and Parliament negotiating directly and side lining him. He would channel negotiations with the King but he had been frustrated by the King's refusal to entertain a future where Parliament had as much say in running the country as the monarch. Indeed, the King had lied throughout negotiations, secretly agreeing to a deal with the Scots behind his back which resulted in the latest outbreak of war. Cromwell and Fairfax had to lead their army north to counter the Scots, whilst pockets of Royalist uprising occurred in many parts of the country. They were all badly planned and fizzled out with the defeat of the Scots by Cromwell in August at Preston.

Cromwell had just returned from the north and was staying at Windsor when he heard through his spy network that the King had written a letter to his Queen and that it was coming through London secretly in a saddle without even the rider knowing. It was on its way to Essex but the rider was to call in a tavern in Holborn where the horse would be refreshed and the message in the saddle removed and diverted to the Queen. Cromwell had decided to investigate the matter himself for few could be trusted even on the Parliamentary side as there were so many differing views on what should happen to the King. With his disguise he could see first-hand if the King's treachery was real. This time the consequences would be severe.

Outside the tavern, Cromwell had stationed men observing the tavern and its stables to the rear. In a street nearby a guard of thirty New Model army cavalry awaited orders, under the command of Colonel Henry Ireton, a man who had led Roundheads at Naseby and other battles to victories in the name of the Parliamentary cause. He had been a moderate and had advocated a constitutional Monarchy and so was a man that people would listen to if what Cromwell's spies had informed him were to be true. Ireton also happened to be Cromwell's son-in-law, having married his eldest daughter, Bridget.

The tavern door opened and some patrons observed a man with a large hat and darting eyes make his way through the crowd and over to the soldiers. He whispered something into the ear of one, who then nodded leading to all three men getting up and finding their way back through the crowd to the door. An oil streetlamp provided the soldiers with a view of the scene outside and Cromwell waved to another man standing on the opposite corner. It was the signal he had been waiting for and the man turned around and waved behind him. The sound of hooves on cobbles immediately followed and in no time at all the street was chock-full of cavalry horses and mounted Roundheads with swords drawn. They made their way to the stables and formed a cordon around the four doors, one of which was open with a horse being led inside by a startled stable boy. The rider, who had just taken his pack from the horse's back and was on his way to the tavern door, was stopped in his tracks by the ring of horses. His face displayed his anxiety as he asked the Colonel at the centre of the horses had he done anything wrong.

"We would just like to ask you a few questions," the Colonel responded, and he nodded to another cavalryman who moved his horse forward to the stable and took the rein of the rider's mount from the stable boy. The Colonel quizzed the messenger about where he had come from, and what he was carrying, learning he was on his way to Colchester in Essex with a letter from the Isle of Wight. He pulled out the letter from his messenger's satchel and showed that address to the Colonel. Meanwhile two other cavalrymen had dismounted and had removed the saddle from the sweating steed that had brought the messenger. The saddle had been turned upside down and the two men were running their fingers over every stitch, before one cried, "Here it is!"

He pulled out a knife and severed a few more stitches before his fingers could pull out a tightly folded piece of paper in the form of a small square with a red wax seal on one side. The soldier passed his find to the Colonel.

"Ah so what have we here? It would appear that you are carrying more than you let on."

The messenger looked dumbfounded.

"I swear that I know not what that is or how it came to be in my saddle," he pleaded.

Cromwell and his two colleagues from the tavern observed what was happening from the edge of the ring of horses. It seemed like Cromwell's spies were right about some kind of conspiracy. He watched with eagerness as his son-in-law opened the seal and read the contents while shaking his head. He read it a couple of times before he looked up and made a slight nod in Cromwell's direction which was the signal. The King was up to his tricks again and this must be the last time.

It was not long before Cromwell was mounted on a horse, having removed much of his disguise, and riding alongside Colonel Ireton on their way back to Windsor. The Colonel was clearly in a state of some shock.

"You were right, General. The King cannot be trusted. I have the proof in my bag. The letter has the King's seal. It is a message to his Queen asking her to raise a Catholic army against England, an alliance of French and Irish."

"The traitor. After so much suffering how could a so-called King contemplate such treachery that would lead to more bloodshed and foreign troops into this country. An alliance of Catholics against Protestants." Cromwell muttered the words but could not conceal his anger.

This was worse than Cromwell had dared to fear, but his son-in-law was even more distraught. Ireton had been backing a compromise solution, a constitutional monarchy, that would bring the country back together again, but he could not contemplate a king who would form an alliance against his own country to save his throne. With the evidence in his pocket, Ireton would make a strong case to the other Parliamentarians and military that the only solution was to bring the King to trial. Cromwell recognised that this was a dangerous course of action but it would appear to be what God wanted. Cromwell always believed that God would show him the way. God's will was starting to be unveiled. Once the way had been shown then Cromwell would use all his leadership skills to execute God's will as effectively as possible as he had done in organising and training the New Model army. Tonight, the Lord had provided evidence of the King's treachery to put Ireton on a course to bring the King to justice. Cromwell would let Ireton and the other Parliamentarians debate and discuss this, and if it was God's will then there would be enough support for a Parliamentary declaration to put the King on trial. The crime would be treason, something that was unprecedented, and the only penalty for such a crime was death.

Westminster Hall, London 28th October 1648

In a side room a group of Puritan Parliamentarians had gathered along with Colonel Coke to discuss moral enforcement within London. Thomas Goodwin, a Puritan minister and member of Parliament, chaired the meeting. He frequently preached by appointment before the Commons. There were ten members in total and these had been the men that had driven the more radical measures passed by Parliament including the banning of festivities over Christmas and Easter in favour of peaceful time to reflect on God's grace. Coke, with reference to a large book he held in front of him, reported on the number of arrests and the charges that been made for breaches of various laws, largely related to gambling or excess alcohol, for drinking was not banned but only allowed in moderation.

"Thank you for your report, Colonel. Gentlemen, anything else to discuss?"

"If I may, I would like to make a suggestion," Coke offered, which resulted in a raised eyebrow on Goodwin's pointed face.

"Whilst we have laws and guidance on moral behaviour and excess in how people live, we do not in where they live. Before the war, this City had a building boom of lavish houses to the west with extravagant decoration and a wasteful use of materials. There are signs of new development starting again and is this not an opportunity to rein some of this in and promote more modest buildings?"

"An interesting idea, Colonel. What do others think?"

There was nodding and supportive comments before Coke added, "It would be easy to enforce, with a ban of certain materials like stained glass, marble or Purbeck stone, and it could be applied to houses, churches and meeting houses."

"Well, I will take counsel from a wider group and we will discuss further at our next meeting in November," Goodwin said, concluding the meeting.

The Vyne Estate, Hamptonshire 30th October 1648

Mary Fairfax's own room was on the western side of the house without the morning sunlight and it felt cold and dark in the autumnal day. Her fears and doubts have intensified for it was two months since she had last seen George and no word or letter since, despite her prayers and longing.

She had heard that there had been fighting at St Neots in Cambridgeshire and across Essex but the Roundheads had quickly defeated the Royalists. Colchester had defiantly stood up to the Roundheads, with the benefit of a large gun that had been named Humpty Dumpty from the walls of the town, but after a month the Parliamentary cannons pummelled the ramparts until the walls fell down and with it the Royalist last hopes, as the defenders were rounded up and imprisoned. Had George been amongst them? Was he dead, or had he forgotten her, both unthinkable prospects. As time had passed, she knew now that she was not with child, something that she had worried about but part of her was now disappointed.

Finally, today she had received a letter and when one of the servants handed it to her she struggled to hide her excitement. She had kept it in her shift pocket and brought it up to her room, where it rested on her dressing table, and it had been the best part an hour now with her just staring at it and thinking what it would disclose. Where had the letter come from, and whose handwriting was it? So much rested on the contents of what was inside and she was still preparing herself for whatever it was. She finally broke the seal and found two pages within, focusing immediately on the signature first: "Yours forever George." It was from him and he was hers forever. She took a deep breath holding the letter to her chest and then started reading it.

"My Dearest Mary,

I am truly sorry that I have taken so long to write to you, but I have been on the run almost from the moment I left you. I am now in the Netherlands staying in the court of Mary Princess Royal, who, I am sure you will know, is now Queen to William, Prince of Orange and the United Provinces of the Netherlands. It is only now that I am here, I have been able to write to you, and I hope this letter will find you with all haste.

I have not stopped thinking about you ever since we parted, despite the challenges I have faced since then. I will not go into detail, but our cause is lost for the time being, after we lost battles in St Neots and Colchester. Your father's forces are greater in number but I also accept are better equipped and more disciplined. We will learn from this and regroup on the continent and ensure the King's cause is not lost. But other than that, I am well thanks largely to my wonderful nurse and her care, although my heart yearns for her company.

I am assuming you have not disclosed our relationship to your father. I am at a loss on how to resolve this. We are like Romeo and Juliet, lovers from feuding families, but I am determined that our end is not a tragedy. I have decided to write to the King for his counsel on how to bridge this divide and ensure that we can see each other again. I have been thinking about coming back to England and bringing you to the Netherlands, but I know you would miss your family too much. I fear if I surrendered and put myself at your father's mercy I would end up in the Tower. Despite my heart's desire, our relationship is too important to me to risk it in any way and so we must act with caution. Let's see what the King says.

In the meantime, I have every precious memory of our time together at Clyveden, and those days and especially that last night, which will be with me forever. I pray that my feelings for you are shared and that you have been thinking of me even a tenth as much as I have about you, and I will be truly happy. My yearning to see you grows every day and please write back with all haste to the address below.

Yours forever
George Villers xxx"

Chapter Five

Hope, Heartache and Hardship

1st November 1648, Sir John and Alice Borlase's House, London

Sir John came home, soaked from the downpour that had just inflicted London, and greeted his wife, Alice Bankes.

"My dear I have some grave news. Thomas Goodwin is gathering views on a proposal that Harry Coke has put to him to restrict lavish design in newly constructed buildings, which would ban, amongst other things, Purbeck stone. It is clearly motivated by Coke's feud with your family. You must write to your mother at once."

"As if this nation did not have anything else to worry about! Is such a ridiculous suggestion being take seriously?"

"Well, it is not much more ridiculous than banning festivities at Christmas. I would not put anything past the radicals."

"You have to stop it, John."

The following day Tom Harvey arrived, unexpectedly. Cromwell had summoned him to be briefed on a mission that he did not elaborate upon but was appalled by the news that Sir John and Alice shared about Coke's plan to ban the use of Purbeck stone. Tom's father had told him about the Lady Bank's idea to trade stone again and he knew what opening the quarry again would mean to the community of Corffe and surrounding villages.

"Sir John can you arrange for me to talk to Thomas Godwin?"

"Yes, Tom, I think so but what will you say to him?"

"I do not rightly know, but I must try to talk to him before it is too late."

Early the next day Tom accompanied Sir John to St Stephen's Chapel in Westminster where the Commons sat, and they waited outside for Thomas Godwin. It was a dull day with a dirty grey sky, which the two men hoped would not dampen the spirit of the minister. It was not long before he arrived, a man in his mid-thirties, with a pointed face accentuated by his triangular beard. Sir John introduced Colonel Harvey and requested ten minutes of his time. He agreed and they walked to the riverbank, where they could be alone.

"So, Colonel what can I do for you?"

"Mister Goodwin, sir, I come from a wonderful part of the world in Dorsetshire, where God has graced the community with a beautiful landscape, second to none, and the folk there work hard as custodians of it for the glory of God. As you look out from the rugged Purbeck limestone coastline to the sea, whether tranquil and turquoise or wild and grey with waves crashing on the rocks, you feel that you are closer to God, closer to Heaven, with the wonder of his creation all around. I am so grateful to have been brought up there, although it was without education or prospect. But thanks to the mentorship of another Colonel and devout Puritan, John Bingham, I worked hard and fought fiercely in the name of righteousness. I will be eternally thankful that God has sought to reward me as an officer in the Parliamentary army. Now I do believe he has called me today to be your witness of the needs of the community in Dorsetshire."

"Colonel, John Bingham is a man I know well and who almost single-handedly planted the Puritan philosophy down in Dorsetshire to become a beacon and stronghold for the faith. I thank God for his work and if you have indeed been mentored by him I look forward to hearing what you have to say. Please go on, Colonel."

"And I do believe he would convey the same message to you today as I am about to. London has lost many men in the war but in truth it has been saved from much of the brutality, and to be clear I praise God that it has, for I would not wish for the horrors that I have witnessed on any community. But the folk in the Purbecks has suffered immeasurably, as fathers, sons and brothers went to fight, on both sides of the conflict, and few came back unscathed if they returned at all. Furthermore, the community endured a siege on its very heart, the Castell at Corffe with five hundred men stationed there under the brutal command of Colonel Coke. He failed to abide by a single aspect of the Petition of Rights, drafted by his own father, that governs the rights that we all believe in and celebrate for both individuals and the army. I will not labour you with the detail, Sir, but the community was terrorised, needlessly lost its place of worship and then its Castell was slighted, I admit by forces under my command following a Parliamentary edict. The heart and soul of the community have been ripped asunder. Widows and orphans struggle to feed themselves with menfolk buried on battlefields across the nation, and they battle with the escalating price of food. They cannot even seek comfort in their place of worship, the repairs to which have stalled due to lack of funds. There is one glimmer of hope, and that is the prospect of reopening the quarry that produced the Purbeck stone that churches, halls and homes in London have traditionally been adorned with. The beauty of this stone is surely a gift from God and provides people with a connection to his wonder and the rugged beauty of Dorsetshire. Colonel Bingham always said that it symbolised the rock of Jesus Christ in our lives. I believe this stone should be shared and enjoyed, in the same way as roses or lilies. Why should such a gift from God remained buried and not be shared with God's children to wonder at the marvel of His Glory?"

"You make a compelling case, Colonel. I will reflect on your views, pray for guidance and let Sir John know how we will progress. I must go now, for I am due to deliver a sermon before the House convenes. We live in times where we have never needed more God's light to show us the path to righteousness."

15th November 1648, Kingston Lacey near Wimborne, Dorsetshire – Mid-Afternoon

Colonel Tom Harvey had returned back to Dorsetshire the previous week. He had just reached the gates of the Bankes estate at Kingston Lacey, north of Wimborne in Dorsetshire. Accompanied by a troop of five men, as was usual for now of a man of his rank, his black destrier led the way, bearing the name of Lightning, the same name of the horse that carried Tom's mentor, Captain Cleall. The lodge in front of them was a brick-constructed house of two stories and several rooms, but small compared with any of the Bankeses' former homes or Corffe Castell. Mary Hardy, the cook from Corffe, and a maid from Wimborne serviced the household, a far cry from the staff in service that Ralph Povington had previously orchestrated on the family's behalf. Tom smiled to himself at the memory of Ralph. With the demise of the Castell, Tom, as governor of the Castell and the Bankes estate, had found him a small cottage to retire to in Kingston, on the limestone escarpment to the south of Corffe. He could see the Castell and village from the cottage, but perhaps it had been too much for him. After enduring the seven-month siege and then the destruction of the Castell, he had lost his purpose in life, and slowly withered away, until he died the previous summer. But in the ruins of the Castell his spirit still wandered for sure.

It was the youngest member of the Bankes family, Arabella, five years old and as jolly and playful as ever, who had opened the door and came running out to greet Tom, jumping into his arms as he dismounted from Lightning.

'Colonel Tom, will you play hide and seek with me?" she cried, as she was lifted up in the arms of the tall military man, her hair blowing in the breeze.

"I need to speak to your mother first, dear Arabella, but I am sure we can have some time for play later, if you are good of course."

"I am always good," she replied making Tom laugh. Turning to his men, he gave some orders.

"Sergeant, take the horses to the stable to be watered. I will be a couple of hours with the Bankes family. I will ask for some refreshments to be sent out to you. Now lead the way young lady," he said as he lowered the girl back to the ground.

In no time at all Tom was being greeted by the whole family as the house became abuzz with the excitement of his arrival. Lady Bankes immediately asked Mary Hardy to arrange some tea and cakes for their visitor and send some leftovers from their lunch out to his troops. The cook was happy to oblige and went away humming a jolly tune, whilst Mary told her children to go out to play in the fields and promised Tom would join them shortly. They reluctantly agreed, and Edward led them out into the autumn sunshine.

"I am glad you are here Tom as I need to speak to you," she said as she led her guest into the parlour. The room hosted a few pieces of furniture from the Castell, which Tom had arranged for the Bankeses to acquire at a low price when he was entrusted with disposal of the requisitioned Bankes estate: two ornate French-styled chairs and a sofa, as well as highly polished ebony style sideboard with exquisitely carved and gilded features. On the wall was a painting of the Castell that had been commissioned before its destruction which Tom walked up to.

"Its memory is etched on my heart, but it is good to see the old Castell in a real form," he said. Beside it was a small glass cabinet on the wall, within which were displayed some keys, those of the Castell which Tom had given back to Lady Bankes on the day of its destruction.

"I wanted to talk to you about John," Mary Bankes said after closing the door behind her.

"Where is he? I assumed he was out riding," Tom asked.

"I wish he were. As you know his temperament has not been good ever since the war. But his melancholy has taken a turn for the worse over the last six months. He is upstairs in bed. He stays in his room most days and I have no idea how to help him. I sent him on a mission to London which helped his mood for a couple of weeks, but now he is back to the brandy. Will you go and speak to him, Tom?"

"Of course. I am sorry to hear that. The war has had its toll on many men and way after the last shots have been fired on the battlefield. It continues to rage in men's nightmares and eats into a man's soul. I will do whatever I can for as you know John is very dear to me. But I also have a favour to ask of you, Lady Bankes, if I may."

"Of course, Tom, and when will you start to address me as just Mary? I do not want to revert to Colonel, do I?" she replied with a smile as she sat on one end of the sofa and Tom followed her example, positioning himself upright at the other end.

"Alas you have always been Lady to me, and I have always been Tom to you. But I will try, Mary."

"Status is hard to achieve, Tom, and is worth more than money can buy. I have always grown up with it but have never taken it for granted. I have seen many people and families lose it through social or financial scandal. During the last few years we have been clinging on to our position and status, stripped of almost everything else. But I am committed to preserving it and rebuilding our family's wealth and reputation. My husband may have been on the losing side during the war, but even the Parliamentarians held him in high regard. My daughters are marrying well and in a few years' time we will have paid off our debts, God willing. But Tom, you have earned your reputation and status during the same period of time. You should be proud and ensure you preserve it at all costs. I know you are a man of integrity and so I have no concerns in that regard, but as a Colonel and a man of status, do not put yourself down."

"Of course, my La—Mary. I have two things I would like to discuss, both important, and one must be in absolute confidence and involves the King," Tom said with a slight blush of embarrassment.

"You have my word to secrecy, Tom."

"Thank you. I have been asked to escort the King from the Isle of Wight to London. It will involve me hosting the King somewhere on the south coast for a couple of days. To be honest the mission terrifies me. Its importance is one thing—I feel the future of the Monarchy and indeed the nation rests of its successful execution, but worse still is just knowing how to host a King. You know my upbringing and I have no knowledge of these things. I wondered if you would join me to act as hostess. I would hope John and Camille will also be able to join. It will mean perhaps a one or two-night dinner with the King, but please help me as I would have nothing to say to him other than condemn him for every lost Englishmen over the last five years. But that is for others to do, if not God, and certainly not me. However, I do not want him to look down on me and want to hold my head up for the memory of those lost. Your presence I believe will balance the social status. What do you say?"

"Of course, I will be delighted. It may also rouse John's spirits. It will give him something to think about and get him out of the house. Where and when will the audience happen," Mary asked.

"Audience? I have not thought of it as such. He is still the King but he will be in my custody. A strange audience but your understanding of etiquette and protocols will give me greater strength and courage to follow through with my orders. I am not sure what destiny awaits him in London, only history will tell, but I do feel what will be written will include his trip to London. There are many supporters of the King, including yourself, Mary, but I know your support has waned and I trust you would not want to take advantage of this situation. Equally there are many who would want to string up the King on the nearest tree and watch him dance in the air. I am committed to delivery of the King to London safely and that is what I am planning to do. I cannot tell you now where or when we will meet, but I will send you two letters in the next few days—the first will include a date and the second a location but in a text that does not disclose the event I have spoken about."

"I understand, Tom. You are right. I was a supporter of the King but I am not sure what I think now. But I would like to see him again and to hear first-hand what he has to say. My husband had lost all faith in him, but I sacrificed so much I need to know it was not all for nothing."

"The second thing I would like to discuss is perhaps some good news. Did Alice write to you about Coke making the case to Parliament to ban Purbeck stone?"

"Yes, I am furious about that. Why does he have to meddle? I am hoping Sir John will be able to persuade Parliament of the folly of such action."

"Well, I have news. Sir John and I went to speak to Thomas Goodwin, and he has since written to me. He has said that we made a good case and he will be discussing with John Bingham and others."

"Why John Bingham? What has he got to do with it?"

"I mentioned him in passing and he seemed to hold him in high regard."

"Maybe I should visit Mr Bingham?"

"Reading between the lines, Thomas Goodwin, seemed to be sympathetic to our cause but he also goes on to say that his committee is considering a programme of restorations for churches that have been destroyed or damaged during the war and this may benefit the church at Corffe." Tom handed Mary the letter.

"This is good news, Tom. I hope they can help with the church. It has been on my conscience for so long and seeing it in such disrepair is as painful as the Castell itself. Thank you so much," she said as she read the letter.

The pair continued to chat whilst tea was served, and Mary told him all about her children and grandchildren, whilst Tom shared his joy and tales of his two-year-old daughter, Emily, and newborn son, William, before he offered to go and see John upstairs.

Tom knocked on the door of John Bankes's room and heard a grunt in response. Tom opened the door to find his friend lying on a partially made bed looking in a bedraggled state, unshaven and gaunt looking.

"Hello John. It is good to see you," Tom said as he entered the room, which had a stale odour and was in a messy state, with clothes scattered around.

"Don't lie; I look terrible. I saw you arrive, Tom."

"So why did you not come down, John? You cannot barricade yourself in your room. Where is the Captain Bankes who smashed Waller and his men, including me, in Wiltshire? Come on, let's go outside for a walk," and he threw John's jacket at him.

The action, tone and words of Tom seemed to have an impact on his friend and he slowly rose from his bed, grabbed his boots, putting them and his jacket on.

"OK, lead on Colonel," he said as he stood up and faced Tom.

The friends walked out of the house and into the estate. They could hear the children playing to one side of the house and started walking in the other direction.

"John, it is sad to see you like this. You have this estate. Surely this is sufficient to keep you occupied, and there is so much potential."

"Tom, I know and it sounds selfish but the truth is I do not care for it."

"John, you have to have something that you do care for. You cannot dwell in the past. The war is behind us. We need to build peace and a reconciled nation."

"It is easy for you to say. You have a position and a profession, not to mention a wife and family. I always wanted to be an officer in the army, I trained for it and experienced it. But now I am barred from that world for being on the losing side, but I lost far more than the war. I lost something inside of me, my raison d'etre. Brandy helps to fill the gap and null the pain, but night after night I have the nightmares of the battles I fought: Cheriton, Roundway Down, Edgehill. I see the faces of the men I slaughtered, and I hold my dying friends in my arms as they slip away, the cannon blast that wounded me, the blood and guts, the shit and mud. It is still inside of me and I am sure you have the same. But you are a colonel and can fill your mind and dreams with your responsibilities and duties."

"You are right, John. I wake up sometimes screaming as I recap some of my experiences. Or Camille finds me sobbing in my sleep for the losses—Francis, Jerome, Joseph. But having a focus on something better, a new mission, as well as time helps to quell them and I am sure we will eventually put all this behind us. We will never forget but the experience should not define us. John, I have come here because I have a mission and I would like you to help me with it."

"Can you not offer me a position in the army, Tom?" John looked around with a glimmer of hope flashing across his face.

"No there are orders from Parliament preventing Royalist officers joining the army, otherwise I would without delay. And the army is not what it was. Many regiments have been disbanded, and the men have returned to their homes. There are no more battles to fight in Dorsetshire, thankfully. Guess what I have been doing for the last few months? Tracking down smugglers and arranging for every ship that docks in Poole and Southampton to be searched. The excise that was supposed to pay for the soldiers was barely collected but now this is our priority. The army was not paid for most of this year, but we have just resolved that thanks to our latest crackdown on brandy taxes. I have heard stories of ships dropping off brandy into remote coves like Lulworth or on the Isle of Wight to avoid the excise. I am organising watches to cut off these supplies."

"It is amazing the lengths people go to avoid tax, but Tom, even that sounds appealing compared to being stuck in this house," John replied, although he had to supress a guilty look for he himself had acquired a barrel of brandy in Wareham that was free of duty the month before.

"I do have a more exciting mission which you can assist me on as an aide if you are willing. I have to escort the King to Windsor. I cannot tell you the details yet but I need somebody to accompany the King in his carriage all the way. Somebody I can trust and somebody who will be able to protect him if we are attacked."

"You trust me, Tom. I fought for the King."

"I know, but yes, I would trust you with my life and I know you would not betray me, even at the expense of your King. But I also know the King and his cause is not something that is close to your heart anymore. This will be an army mission John, and I know you would play your part in ensuring its success."

"You are right on that count. I am more likely to throttle him than rescue him."

"John, there will be no room for brandy on this mission. You must be clear headed and alert to every eventuality. There are risks of attacks by militants on the Parliamentary side, former Roundhead soldiers, attacking us to string up the King, as well as Royalist plots to rescue him and smuggle him out of the country. But if we achieve this mission, then I might be able to have words with Cromwell or Fairfax to see if there is a way around this ban on Royalist officers in the army."

"Tom, I really appreciate this. I will do everything that is required and live up to the trust you are showing me."

"I also need you to escort Camille and your mother to the location of the first encounter with the King, as I have invited them to dine with the King."

"Ah, that is more challenging. Two very strong-headed woman to keep at bay. I will do my best, my friend," John replied, raising an eyebrow.

Tom gave his friend a warm embrace.

"I believe I have some little ones who I have promised hide and seek. Will you not join me, John?"

"Why not?" he replied with a smile, at last, and his demeanour was visibly lifting.

16 November 1648. A Visit to Corffe & the Purbecks

The next day, John came down to breakfast a different man. The prospect of Tom's mission had lifted him out of his melancholy as if he had been reborn. Tom had provided him with hope, when before he had none. He suggested to his mother that they ride to Corffe, visit William Harvey, and ensure everything on the estate was all in order. Mary was delighted and agreed straight away. Within the hour, mother and son were riding south towards the Isle of Purbeck. It was a grey day, with a stiff breeze, but it was dry, and the thrill of the ride enlightened them both. Mary, ridding side saddle, was wrapped in a warm black cape, followed her son who showed the way with as much purpose as if he was leading a calvary charge in a matching tailed coat that flapped behind him. By mid-morning they had passed Wareham and the ruins of Corffe Castell still commanding a gap in the chalk ridge that defined the Isle of Purbeck beyond. The Castell was in a sad state having been blown to destruction by Tom Harvey at the command of Parliament after it had stubbornly resisted a seven-month siege. But there was still something majestic and defiant about the ruin, the form of its keep and ramparts still very evident, as it sat on its chalk throne, with the village in its shadow below.

The Bankeses slowed to a trot as the road led over the bridge across the River Wicken, its meander having been a defensive moat during the siege, and on to the cobbled street that wrapped around the foot of the Castell into the market square. Stalls had been set up with wares of local produce and behind which the Bankeses recognised a few faces who greeted their landlords with polite welcomes and smiles. Across the square was the new street that housed the newer dwellings in the village, including William Harvey, the Bankeses' trusted estates manager and Tom's father. William as a younger man would rarely be found at home, for he would ride across the estate ensuring it was being well managed by its tenants, and that fishing and quarrying rights were respected, as well as managing maintenance and improvement works. He knew everything that was going on and would also ensure all rents would be collected fairly. Now in his fifties, he delegated much of the work across the estate to his step-son Daniel, who was as fair and hard-working as he had ever been, having been brought up by William since he was a baby. He was now being groomed to be his successor and he was assured that the estate would be, and indeed to a significant extent was already, passed into safe hands. He loved with a passion the Isle of Purbeck and thanked God every night for his position, but also recognised the importance of his role. Bad management or husbandry by tenants could have a devastating impact on livelihoods, as well as significant consequences for nature. The war had shown this when Colonel Coke and his thugs had stressed the balance to extreme, and three years later it was only starting to recover to any sense of what William would know as right. Woods had been destroyed to provide fuel for the army's fires and weapons; wildlife from boar to pigeon had been over hunted, and fields over harvested resulting in hunger for the locals, leading to scavenging and poaching which he had to turn a blind eye to. But the longest-term impact of the war was the loss of life amongst menfolk in the villages. Without men, the fields could not be ploughed, the stone quarried or the fish caught, nor the grain ground into flour, new trees planted or fences for livestock repaired. Francis Drew, Joseph Cobb, Jacob Vaggs, Harry Mason, Arthur and Jack Pitt were some of the sixty menfolk who did not return to the Isle of Purbeck, many buried hundreds of miles away and with them the future offspring that would sustain the communities.

Mary and John arrived at their estate manager's cottage, one of the few two-storey houses in the village made from the local Purbeck limestone under a reed-thatch roof with two bedrooms and a lumber room for wood and hay on the upper floor, and a kitchen and parlour below. As the rode up to the cottage Elizabeth Harvey was coming out of the door, armed with a basket on her way to the market square.

"Lady Bankes and Mister Bankes, so nice to see you," she said with a smile, beneath a bonnet that covered her grey hair, as she was still tying the strings of her cape to keep her warm.

"And a pleasure to see you, Mrs Harvey. Is your husband at home?" Lady Bankes replied.

"I am afraid he is not, my Lady. He is at Swanage today as I believe there are some repairs to the wharf ongoing," Elizabeth replied.

"Well, we can ride over there can we not Mother?" John said, enjoying the prospect of an extra few miles' ride. "We saw Tom yesterday," he continued to Elizabeth.

"We have not seen him for a fortnight now. Chasing smugglers he says and he has another mission that he is secretive about but which is weighing on his mind. Who would have thought our son a Colonel but we do miss him, and he has a lot on his plate," Elizabeth replied.

"Off to the market I see," Mary said.

"Yes, but it is not the joy it used to be. The prices are higher than ever since the war and there are still shortages as I am sure you will appreciate, my Lady. Folk around here are struggling to get by. Rents, taxes, and the cost of everything rising; it seems that the effects of the war will be with us for ever."

Mary and John wished Elizabeth well and set off for Swanage. The bay soon came into sight as they emerged from the woods at the base of Nine Barrow Down, and then followed the pathway down to the beach. Mary adored Swanage for it was where she spent so much time with Captain Cleall, riding across the sand that stretch across the bay. You never knew what the sea would be like for it changed constantly. Today they were greeted by a silver-grey colour with white horses whipping up the water as the waves and currents battled against an offshore wind, upon which seagulls glided. It was wild and refreshing. There were no fishing boats out today, for they were all pulled up on to the shore. The wharf at the far end of the bay that Mary Bankes had constructed to preserve her quarry income had a boat moored up against it. This was the boat that brought the marble looking stone from the Dorsetshire coast to the wharf to be uploaded on larger ships and taken to London for the development of new aristocrats' houses to the west of the city. It was not just the weather that meant the boat was idle for the war had destroyed the market for new development in London and the quarry had closed, but Mary was determined to see it thriving again.

Mother and son kicked their horses on and across the sandy beach, and in no time they were approaching the working men. William Harvey had seen them coming and had walked down the wharf to meet them, leaving the two other workers behind.

"My Lady. John. It is good to see you," he said, his voice raised so he could be heard over the wind, his greying hair and even the long whiskers of his wispy beard waving frantically in the breeze.

"See you are busy, William," Mary said.

"As always, my Lady. We need to get the wharf ready for the quarry trade. The next challenge is finding enough men to quarry the stone. The war took the lives of many of the men who had worked the stone, so we need to train others," William replied.

"Well, one step at a time. If we can demonstrate that the quarry is viable and there is demand from London, I am sure the prospects of good steady work will attract folks into the area. In the meantime, we have some good news to share, don't we John?"

"Yes, Mother. There are some orders in place for the quarry, so we can start mining. But also, there is the prospect of Parliament making a grant for the church in Corffe to be repaired."

"Other than my grandson's birth, that would be the best news of the year, John. I cannot tell you what that will mean to the folk in Corffe. I will pray to the Lord in gratitude."

"I think you should also be thanking your son as well, William, for I believe Tom along with John Bingham played a part in both the quarry and making parliament aware of the need for church repair. The grant is still to be confirmed but at least it is being discussed, " John added.

"He is a good boy, as good a boy a man could ever want for, and I thank the Lord every day."

"We are going to pop in to see Camille now, but please come in and see us when you have finished here and update us on estate matters," Mary said.

"Sure, will do my Lady," the estate manager replied and the two riders turned their horses back along the beach and up the path that led to the cliff to the north, where Tom and Camille had made their home, a newly constructed two storey stone house with a view over the bay.

John knocked at the door, and Camille opened it with a cheery smile, her green eyes sparkling with the pleasure of seeing her friends. She was looking as elegant as ever in a simple low neck dark blue robe over a white petticoat. She led her guests into her parlour where a fire provided some welcome warmth for the travellers, and Camille asked Nella to bring some cake and hot tea for her guests. They chatted and caught up with local and family news on both sides, Camille taking Lady Bankes upstairs to see baby William, who was twelve weeks old, asleep in his cot, whilst young Emily played happily with John and a wooden doll. Camille had been Lady Bankes' lady in waiting and endured the seven-months siege with her, through which they had built up a strong relationship, despite a generational age gap. Lady Bankes respected Camille for her ability to understand people and nature and to make sense of it all in a way that was way ahead of her years. She said she had acquired a sense from her grandmother and could see things clearly which many could not. She was an easy person to confide in and would often be able to see to the cause of people's problems and understand what needed to be done whether it was emotional or physical. Whilst they were with William, Camille asked again how Mary was, as if she had disregarded her previous response.

"To be truthful I am struggling, Camille. It is hard without a husband or a man in my life. I know Sir John was often away, but the hope and expectation of him returning was comforting and we always wrote to one another so he supported me from afar through his wise counsel."

Mary Bankes walked over to the window with its idyllic view of Swanage Bay, the sand forming a moon-shaped crescent around the sea and the limestone headland in the distance. This was where Captain James Cleall and Mary had ridden on her first visit to Dorsetshire. It was a wonderful day and in hindsight it was the day when her love for him had started to blossom even though she did not recognise it at the time. She had not been looking for love, for she had a good husband whom she did love in a different way, but her love for James just slowly grew without her knowing it, until she had lost her heart to a man who had gone to war to protect her son, to someone who had defended her and her home through seven months of siege, and to someone who would just listen to her as she lay in his arms. The limestone headland in the distance was where they spent some intimate moments on the top of a cliff surround by wild flowers and long grass with the waves crashing on the rocks below as if they were perched on a pedestal made by the Almighty. And then from deep in her soul something erupted, and her eyes welled up, as she choked up and fell back into the chair next to the window. Camille came over to comfort her.

"What is it, Mary?" she asked, as tears started flowing down her friend's face.

"Everything. Camille," she said looking up, struggling to find composure.

After a while she continued.

"Captain Cleall. I miss him so much. We had so little time together before he was taken from me, so cruelly. Everything here in the Purbecks, in Corffe, in Swanage, wherever I look is a signpost to our lost love. I did not recognise how much I loved him and how much I needed him until he was gone. God gave me love when I needed it most, during the siege when I had so many self-doubts, and it strengthened me. But it also exposed me, for without it, I am nothing. James came into my life and provided me with some of the best memories but that's all I now have, just memories. The sun is set on that love, and it hurts to remember it, but I keep telling myself that I must be grateful for it, just to have shared the moments we did. Tell me Camille, will I see him in the next life?"

"I am sure you will Mary. If you believe in God, you must believe in love reunited," Camille responded.

"You know I will never be able to live here again. I will have to stay in Kingston Lacey as it is just too painful when I am here, although I love this place more than any other. There is an irony of having an estate with so much beauty yet it brings so much heartache."

Mary paused and took a deep breath before continuing.

"But then there are many other things, Camille, and in truth I do not have anybody to talk about them with. I am very worried about John. He is melancholic and does nothing but drink. Then there is the business of finding husbands for Elizabeth and Jane. Girls are such a worry, for if they are not wed by the age of twenty they are unlikely to find a suitor. Then there is the Parliamentary fine to pay and running the estate to meet the debts. We need to open the quarry but William tells me now it will be difficult to find quarrymen. There are just not enough men to marry daughters, to work the quarry, farm the land, fish the seas. And the cost of food, it is just one thing after the other."

"My Lady, sorry Mary, I know there is a lot on your shoulders, but you are strong, stronger than anyone I know. My grandmother used to say, 'We can't choose the music that life plays to us but we can choose how we dance to it'. It must be harder without out anyone to share your life with, but you have family and friends, and we are all here to share the burdens. Just keep dancing and rejoice in the blessing of your wonderful family, whatever music God plays."

"Thank you Camille. You and Tom are indeed good friends and I am truly grateful for my family. Alice is doing so well in London and her children are so delightful. But as for me, I am not as strong as I once was now that Sir John and James are no longer in my life. They were both in very different ways foundation rocks for me. On top of everything I am also struggling with the changes in my body. I feel I am losing my mind some days, and at night I struggle to sleep. I am hot one minute and cold the next. It is an age thing I know, but something else to deal with."

"I remember my grandmother going through the same. She took flaxseed, ground down. It really helped."

"Where do I get that, my dear?" Mary asked.

"They often have it on the boats from the Netherlands at Poole Quay. I will ask the local peddler to get some. Leave that with me, Mary. It will give me a good excuse to come over to Kingston Lacey."

"That would be wonderful. Let's hope it can give me some energy to keep dancing as your grandmother said, my dear as I feel that the music is changing and that I am out of step."

Camille left Mary to compose herself and returned to the parlour where she started talking to John, telling him how she missed Tom who seemed to spend so much time away, now chasing smugglers which at least was safer than battling Royalists or the Scots. Parliament had finally paid all the army their back pay which had taken a big worry off his shoulders. John confessed to his melancholy and how he missed the camaraderie of the army. John felt at ease with Camille more than any other woman he knew apart from his mother and sister Alice.

"What about a wife, John? Love is a cure for many woes," Camille said, reaching out to hold his hand as they sat on the sofa.

"I fear I am not suited to the fairer sex, Camille. I have met a few ladies who would make suitable brides, but it never seems to be right for me and I always feel awkward and uncomfortable. I think it is just too early. I need some more time in the ranks of men on missions and adventures. I cannot sit at home managing an estate or bringing up a family. The army was my family and I miss it terribly," he replied.

"Well maybe you need to rescue the King from the Isle of Wight and raise an army to his cause. I will not tell Tom," Camille said with a laugh, which at least brought a smile to John's face.

"Yes, that would be a mission. I'm hoping Tom may have a task for me and a possible route back to a military role, but within his command. He said as much when he visited us at Kingston yesterday."

"Why, that is wonderful news John," she replied with a radiating smile and a warm tone.

"I cannot want for anymore. I would be so grateful if that could happen. Just the prospect of it has given me new heart. Your husband is a wonderful man, Camille," John said, as Mary returned back into the room.

"I know. I am so lucky. I wish I just did not have to share him so much with his country," Camille replied.

"I know how you feel Camille but great men have great causes, and their wives need to be strong and resourceful to compensate for their absence," Mary added.

The afternoon wore on and it was soon time for the Bankeses to ride back to Kingston.

20 November 1648, Poole

Mary Bankes arrived at Bingham's bank just off the busy quay in Poole. She was shown inside and was announced to John Bingham who was expecting her in his chamber. The two of them had a long history not least of which being Bingham's attempted capture of Corffe Castell when Lady Bankes dispatched him away with the aid of a cannon fire and made herself a celebrated Royalist heroine across the nation. In more recent years they had learnt to respect each other, recognising that they had different views on many things but were both strong characters.

"Lady Bankes, what a pleasure to see you."

"Mister Bingham, thank you for your time."

"And what can I do for you?"

Lady Bankes explained Harry Cokes' attempt to thwart her attempt to reopen the quarry in the Purbecks.

"I was wondering if you could speak to Thomas Goodwin and lobby on our behalf."

"Well, we have had our issues over quarrying in the past have we not Lady Bankes? But I believe our interests are shared in this matter. The bank has now a stake in a Portland stone quarry and so Coke's proposals will no doubt be detrimental to that investment, even if the stone is less refined. I do believe that we need to promote reconstruction of our towns and houses, and not put in place barriers. I will be returning to London tomorrow and discuss this matter with Mister Goodwin."

Chapter Six

Custody and Cooking for a King

1st December 1648 Hurst Castell – the Solent, Hamptonshire

The wind blasted Tom Harvey's face as he stood on the pebble peninsula beneath Hurst Castell, looking out on to the Solent, a bustling strait of water between the Isle of Wight and the coast of the English mainland. A mile-long hook-shaped shingle bank narrowed the Solent at this point, creating some treacherous waters as it was funnelled between the Hurst spit and the island barely a mile away on its far side. Henry VIII had built Hurst Castell to protect the Solent and its ports of Lymington, Southampton and Portsmouth from attack by the Spanish coming from the West. It was plain to see its strategic advantage as the split's reach into the water puts the cannons on the Castell's austere grey stone ramparts in range of any enemy vessel making its way into the Solent. But in its hundred years of history the Castell's armoury had yet to be called upon with the Spanish Armada not making it this close to the English coast before its defeat.

The Castell was the stage for history today with a ship anchoring a hundred yards offshore and the story was unfolding as Tom watched six men climb down the gantry into a rowing boat moored to the hull. It was a naval warship, with two decks of twelve cannons facing the Castell, sails reefed on its three masks and with Cromwell's flag flying from its bow. Tom knew how important the Navy had been in helping the Parliamentarians triumph in the Civil War for he had been part of the Parliamentary victory at Bristol, where the Navy's bombardment of the City as well as the provision of supplies for the Roundheads was a critical advantage. It was still playing its role today but the cargo that was being brought ashore was far more valuable as the rowing boat set its course to land on the shoreline in front of Tom and his thirty men waiting diligently on the beach.

As each wave crashed on to the shoreline it was followed by a roaring rumble, as the pebbles were dragged back with the returning water. A wave gave the rowing boat a last push towards the shoreline and it was beached on to the pebbles. Four of the six occupants got up, two jumping knee-deep into the sea, one carrying two bags, whilst the other helped the two men still standing in the boat, both with hooded cloaks that shielded their faces, make the jump into the water. The four men clambered up the shoreline as another wave crashed into the boat and soaked the men up to their waists. One of the men almost lost his footing as the same wave retreated, bringing with it the rumbling pebbles. Tom made his way down to greet the men.

"Colonel Harvey?" the leading man asked, the wind lashing his blonde shoulder-length hair around his face.

"Yes I am. Captain Armstrong I assume? I am to take the prisoner from here," Tom replied, his face stern and his voice barely able to be heard as another wave of pebbles rumbled back into the sea.

"I am handing you over to the custody of Colonel Harvey. Sir Thomas will also be staying with you," the man replied, turning to the smaller of the hooded men behind him, but all he got in return was a nod as the man had his hood pulled to the full extent over his face with his hand to shield himself from the wind. The fourth man had deposited the two bags onto the beach, before he and the Captain returned to the waiting rowing boat.

"Welcome to Hurst Castell. Please follow me," said Tom looking down on to the two guests, with his newly grown beard providing an air of authority, in addition to his height. He did not wait for a response but turned and led the two men up the beach around to the land side of the Castell. There the company found shelter from the relentless blustering wind and where the drawbridge was down over the moat that had been channelled into the shingle of the split allowing water from the salt marsh to drain around the fortification's walls. The portcullis was raised as the Colonel led them inside and to the circular stone keep. They continued through a large oak door, down a dark passage and up a central spiral staircase to the first floor and into a large circular room with windows overlooking the sea. A large fire roared from a stone hearth providing warmth for the two guests to dry themselves and recover from being barraged by the Solent's bitterly cold wind. Their faces were revealed as they let down their hoods. The taller man turned to Tom; his dark eyes were authoritative, set in a face that was shrouded by long, flowing locks that disappeared in to his cloak and with a matching moustache.

"I am Sir Thomas Herbert," his said in a deep voice, which Tom recognised as having a Northern accent.

"Please to make your acquaintance, Sir. I am Colonel Tom Harvey and I will be responsible for your welfare between here and Windsor. I am still awaiting the return of my Captain from Windsor who is inspecting the security arrangements at the stops along the way. Security is of utmost importance and I am sure you will appreciate the risks that we face."

The smaller man sat on a wooden chair next to the fire and Tom watched him as a pool of water started forming on the floor beneath him, dripping from his cloak and britches that had been soaked by the sea.

"So how long do we have to stay in this godforsaken place?" the smaller man asked without looking around to Tom, his eyes fixed on the fire, slightly stammering over the word 'forsaken'.

"We appreciate the risks, Colonel, and need to be assured of His Majesty's safety," Sir Thomas replied, nodding to the man sat on his newly adopted throne.

"I cannot provide you with a certain date of departure but I would hope to be leaving in three to four days' time. I can, however, assure you of your safety at Hurst, and I will do everything I can to make Your Majesty as comfortable as possible, but the facilities are extremely limited," Tom answered, finally getting to see the face of King Charles, as he looked at Tom raising an eyebrow at the word 'limited'. So this was the King, the man who had brought the nation to ruin, the man who believed he had a divine right to rule and only answered to God. The man whose actions and attitude had caused the death of his friends Francis, Jerome, Joseph, Captain Cleall and Agnes. In stature he hardly looked majestic, only chest height to Tom, but there was something about him that still managed to give him an aura of the extraordinary. Or was it Tom's imagination? Maybe it was just a masque that hid the man, fuelled by the expectation of common folk. Many of his features were similar to Sir Thomas, although in miniature scale, but he was looking tired, his beard showing traits of grey and rather unkept for a man of such status.

"This room is for you to use during the day. You will be free to make use of the Castell grounds. On a nice day the ramparts do provide a wonderful view which I hope you will have the opportunity to see before you depart. I will show you to your bed chambers, but they are very basic I am afraid. We will be dining in about two hours. I have arranged for a cook from Winchester Castell to be stationed here and she will hopefully ensure that we can at least eat well."

The wind had dropped, and the sun started to peer through a break in the clouds rolling in from the direction of the Needles, a row of three chalk rocks that projected from the westerly corner on the Isle of Wight. Tom invited his guests for a tour of the Castell and to see their bed chambers. The King was underwhelmed by the Castell and dismayed by his bed chamber. In truth the Castell was more of a fort and hardly compared with Corffe Castell, where Tom had been brought up, or presumably Carisbrooke Castell, the home to the King for the last year. Hurst only catered for its garrison, with a small keep, and three bastions that provided the vantage points across the Solent for its cannons. In the keep, the first floor was divided at the front into a semicircular room where Tom had received his guests and behind it were two rooms for the garrison officers. Both were very basic, comprising a single bed, a small table and chair with a water jug, two shelves for clothes to be stored and a small lead-lined window looking out on to the small baileys behind the fortress walls. The walls were cold and bare apart from a single sconce with a candle.

"Well you will not be escaping out of that window," Sir Thomas jested, but the King was not amused. He was appalled by the basic room.

"I thought Carisbrooke was basic. I am still the King of this country and should be treated with dignity and respect," he said, venting his anger at Sir Thomas.

"Your Majesty, the Colonel has already explained that our priority is your safety. We could find a far more elegant room in a nearby Lymington tavern, but how do we protect you there? You will be soon in Windsor where you will have both safety and comfort but until then we can only offer you the former."

"I only briefed people in the Castell an hour before your arrival of your visit. Security has been of paramount importance," Tom added.

Despite his disgust the King said he felt tired and would rest in his room for a while, leading Tom to continue the tour with Sir Thomas. His room was the adjoining one and Sir Thomas asked for their bags to be brought up.

"May I ask your position, Sir Thomas?" Tom asked.

"Why of course. I am the King's gentleman of the bedchamber. Can you believe it?" he said with a laugh. "I was appointed by Parliament last year and have been looking after His Majesty ever since."

"And before that?"

"Well, originally I am from Yorkshire, but most of my life I have travelled as the nation's ambassador to Persia. I returned to my estate in the Wye valley and Parliament asked me to look after the King."

"I would love to hear about Persia."

" That would take some time to tell as it is truly a fascinating place and we have so much to learn from. Perhaps over dinner."

"I have invited some guests to join us. They are friends of mine but also acquainted with the King. Lady Bankes and her son John. Do you know them?"

"I met Sir John Bankes when I was at court but not his wife or son. He was the King's Attorney General," Sir Thomas replied.

"Yes, the very man, but unfortunately he passed away a few years back."

"I will look forward to meeting his family, but first let us complete the tour of Hurst Castell."

Tom showed him the rest of the Castell. Sir Thomas was most interested in the kitchens where Tom introduced him to the cook, Clara Peppercorn, from Winchester Castell. Tom informed him that Clara would be travelling with them on the road to Winchester, which would be a staging post, and she would be the King's cook in both Castells.

"Well planned Colonel. I am fearful of poisoning and I guess as you and I will be sharing his dish then we need to make as many safeguards as possible."

Tom took his guest to the western parapet and they could see the coastline of the South Coast and just about make out the Isle of Purbeck in Dorsetshire, the home of Tom and his family. He also pointed out the Priory at Christchurch and its quay and on the inland side the port of Lymington, where the Bankeses were staying. A few masts of tall ships harbouring there could be seen, and between them and the Castell were the salt marshes and salterns that provided a living for local folk in their huts along the marshes. Lymington provided much of the salt needed across southern England for preserving fish and meat, and alongside the evaporation ponds were windmills that were used to pump the brine into boiler rooms where the water was boiled leaving the salt crystals. There was no activity today, for it was too wintery, but normally the marshes would have been full of people washing the sand and silt out of the salty water. Tom explained as best he could the process and both agreed it was a hard way to make a living, although on the backs of the salt collectors the merchants who owned the salterns made a handsome profit.

As the tour finished, the sound of the gates opening and the portcullis being raised could be heard.

"That must be my guests from Lymington. I arranged for one of the captains to take the Castell boat with a few men to pick them up," Tom said.

"Well Colonel, please excuse me so I can prepare myself for dinner and also arouse the King." With that, Sir Thomas walked back to the keep, whilst Tom went to greet his guest.

Dinner with the King

When Tom arrived in the west wing of the Castell, Camille rushed to the Colonel and embraced him. They had not seen each other for over a month and inviting Camille along with the Bankeses was Tom's plan to be able to see her, whilst carrying out his duties and before he departed with the King to Windsor.

"My love. I am so pleased to see you. How are the children?" he asked as they kissed.

"Both well, hopefully resting in the tavern in Lymington with Nella."

Tom turned to greet his other guests, who were wrapped up in warm coats and capes to keep the bitter wind from the Solent at bay.

"And it is also great to see you my Lady and of course John," Tom declared, taking first Mary Bankes' hand and kissing it, and then embracing John. He had worked for Lady Bankes for much of his life, and indeed his father still did. He still felt a little awkward receiving her in this way, but over the last five years he had developed in gravitas and etiquette to socialise amongst the higher echelons of society. He could see that she had dressed for the occasion, the sparkle of her earrings, the rouge on her lips and a glimpse of the red silk dress beneath her cape.

"And we bring good news Tom. Yesterday I received a letter from John Bingham. Parliament has decided not to impose any restrictions on the use of any building products in new buildings. We have something to celebrate tonight because that means we can open the quarry again."

"That is good news. Folk at home will be delighted. Let's go in and celebrate, we have a hearty fire to warm you up."

"How is the King?" John asked, as he and Tom led the way across the stone courtyard.

"He has slept much of the afternoon and so I cannot really tell you, truth be told. I do know that Hurst Castell would not top his list of royal abodes," Tom replied.

"It does look austere, Tom. Perhaps not becoming of His Majesty? Not quite up to the Banqueting Hall at Whitehall Palace," Lady Bankes remarked, recalling the last time she had seen the King at a Masque Ball in the newly created masterpiece of Indigo Jones adorned with a Reuben's painting of his father, King James, on the ceiling, ascending to heaven surrounded by angels. The painting reinforced the belief in the Divine Right of Kings, something that the King and Lady Bankes had stood up for ever since, and the primary reason for nearly a hundred thousand people losing their lives during the war.

"Lady Bankes, it is secure and safe, and frankly that must be the main consideration for the King at this time, given the mood of the country and the tensions that are apparent," Tom replied and opened the large oak door that led into the keep. They climbed the spiral staircase which led to the circular room on the first floor where a table had been laid in its centre. It was lit by two candelabras providing sufficient light in the dusk to see the array of basic cutlery and chinaware on a white cloth. More candles had been lit in sconces on the walls, and on the table in the window a vase displaying an array of yellow winter jasmine flowers, contrasting with the austerity of the chamber with its harsh and cold stone walls. It was clear that somebody had made an effort in recognition of the status of their guest, but with limited means to impress. The fire had been stocked up with more wood and roared in anticipation of a jovial evening's entertainment. Camille and Lady Bankes took off their capes and went to the window, but the light was fading fast; the water was grey and Yarmouth on the far side of the Solent had been transformed into just a few twinkles in the diming light.

"I am told this is a treacherous piece of water for those who are not familiar with it," Tom remarked but before anybody could answer, the door to the room opened and in came the King and Sir Thomas. The King was dressed in a relatively modest velvet black doublet, knee-length breeches, and a lace-trimmed ruff, partly concealed by his long dark hair. His face was expressionless, but his striking, brown, heavy-lidded eyes and pointed beard were his characteristic features.

"Your Majesty, and Sir Thomas, may I introduce our guests. I believe you may already be acquainted with Lady Bankes, the wife of the late Sir John Bankes," Tom said, and Mary stepped forward making a small curtsey.

The introduction seemed to waken the King, and he managed a smile.

"My Lady, it is always a pleasure to see you. I was saddened to hear of the loss of Sir John. He served me and his country as well as any man."

"Thank you, Sire," she replied. "I would also like to introduce my son, Captain John Bankes, who has also served you well over the last few years."

John stepped up and bowed to the King "Your Majesty, alas no longer a Captain, but still keen to serve my country and King."

"I recall your father talking to me of your presence at Edgehill, John. That did not go as I had expected but thank you for your service."

"And finally, I would like to introduce my wife, Camille, to you, Your Majesty," Tom said, and Camille followed Lady Bankes' lead, and also curtsied.

"Votre Majeste."

"Ah vous venez du Royaume de France, Camile, comme ma femme," the King responded.

"C'est vrai, that is right," Camille replied.

"My Queen is with her nephew, King Louis. Alas I have not seen her or my son, Charles, for over three years now. I am sure they are being looked after well by your King and in a better comfort than we find ourselves tonight. But I have good company and I am grateful for that. Shall we eat? This sea air has made me famished."

Tom organised everybody around the table, with the King at one end and Sir Thomas at the other, Lady Bankes and John next to the King, and he and Camille next to Sir Thomas. As they sat down he realised that they had been divided Royalists at one end and the Parliamentarians at the other end, but he was hopeful of an evening that would transcend these differences. Camille smiled at him. She was pinching herself under the table, in awe at how her husband had risen to a position where he could host the King of England for dinner, even if under his protection. Only a few years ago she had been the lady in waiting to Lady Mary Bankes and her husband was just a pikeman who went off to fight for a cause against the very King he was now hosting.

John Anderson and a foot soldier entered the room with plates of sweetmeats and a decanter of burgundy wine. They were both clearly nervous, having no experience in etiquette at the dinner table of the aristocracy, let alone with the King present. John Anderson's hand was visibly shaking as he poured the wine into the glass for the King.

"Soldier, thank you for the wine. With just one arm you are very proficient. You would be welcome in my Court any day," the King said, easing the tension and surprising Tom with his apparent empathy.

"Thank you, Your Majesty," John Anderson responded.

"I would now like to make a toast to Sir John Bankes," the King continued looking at Lady Bankes and John in turn. "Sir John was a trusted aide and counsel to me for many years. John Bankes, remember what I have to say about your father for history should know it. I have had much time to mull over my reign whilst detained in Carisbrooke, and I frequently thought about Sir John and regret that I did not listen to his advice more often. Being a King is a lonely position and one with many dangers. My grandmother was beheaded, my grandfather blown up, and my father and elder brother almost met the same fate during the Gunpowder Plot. As a King you are not short of advisors, but many have self-interest at heart, or are following other agendas, or even plotting against you. Sir John was genuinely selfless and had only the well-being of his King, the nation and justice for its people guiding his counsel. He was a light when all these troubles started, a light that potentially shone on a route that may have

106

avoided the war and brought the King and Parliament together. His legal mind and his ability to build understanding between people were second to no one. When Parliament served that remonstrance on me, I must confess I did not even read it. I was so angry at the insult on the Monarchy, God's appointed King, by those Puritans and radicals," the King said stuttering over the word 'angry', but he continued his toast.

"I could not stomach even contemplating entering into discussions let alone a compromise. Most of my advisors at the time just supported this view as they knew I could not or would not hear of anything else. But Sir John advocated a different route. He was the one who was closest to Pym, Hampden and the rest of them, as he made it his business to try to understand both sides. He advised me that I should respond in part and show some humility and respect for the remonstrance, agreeing to some of the demands. He said that it would appease many of the Parliamentarians, and then later I could take action against Pym and Hampden, who, he advised, were the more radical. When he first suggested this to me I had him thrown out of the Court. Nonetheless he returned the next day pressing his case once more and facing my wrath again. He eventually wore me down and a few months later I agreed to allow him to enter into dialogue again. It is easy to see with the benefit of hindsight but there was an opportunity to avoid the war at that time, and on my part I was opening up to it. However, timing is everything and by then Pym and Hampden were entrenched and had already amassed an army. I do wish I had listened to Sir John a little earlier and maybe things could have been different. So I started planning for some kind of confrontation, although I never expected this to lead to war across the nation. I thought there would be a battle yes, but you, John, and my followers would deliver a decisive victory and we could bring to justice the warmongers. How wrong was I, but I am sure the Parliamentarians were equally misguided."

"I am sure you are right, Your Majesty," Lady Bankes reassured him, with a warm smile, her broach sparking in the candlelight.

"Sir John was also the first to advise me of the power of the printing press. It took me a while to believe him but in hindsight he was not only right but I believe the printing presses had as much impact as Fairfax's foot soldiers and Cromwell's cavalry on the outcome of the war."

The King was getting flustered.

"Fabrications and manipulations." He stuttered on both words with pinched lips. "That is what they produced. Fibs and myths shrouding me, the people's King, in a cloak and the mask of the devil who was the route of all wrong with the country: taxes, bread shortages, the plague and even the weather. The peddlers and town criers amplified this false news nationwide. I eventually agreed with Sir John that we should produce our own pamphlets, but in that he was the wrong man for the job. He told the truth and only the truth, when the lies that the Parliamentary filth produced were far more appealing to the people. He was too honest. The printing presses are the cause of a plague of information that has destroyed truth and men's ability to think for themselves."

Sir Thomas decided to intervene detecting the King's growing anger.

"Your Majesty, I do believe the Parliamentarians were producing more entertaining pamphlets as well with John Milton's pen and some very amusing sketches. I still chuckle when I think about those about Prince Rupert and his monkey. The peddlers and the people loved it, and I have seen you laugh a few times when I have shared some," he said with a warm smile.

"Indeed, Sir Thomas, humour is a powerful weapon as well. It would be funnier if it were not so serious. Back to Sir John, my Lady: more recently I have desperately missed his advice as I know no person who had a better understanding of the complexities of the nations I rule, their religious and political differences and how to bring them together. I seem to have made another poor decision, relying on the Scots to help my cause, but in the summer Cromwell and Fairfax brought that uprising to an end. I am now being summoned to London to discuss the current state of affairs with Cromwell and no doubt to be questioned by Parliament's representatives. The prospect riles my blood. I am the King as I am anointed by and accountable only to God. But I am the King without a court, without my Queen and I do not even know where my crown is. I suspect Cromwell has it, but people like him do not understand its importance and symbolism. The jewels in the crown belonged to Edward the Confessor, and I am sure he, along with all the other saints, will be fuming as they look down on the mess in this country. Parliament may have won on the battle fields but they cannot rule without me. Did the people of England not rise up in my name? Now Parliament must understand that my authority is never-ending and my power eternal. I am God's anointed King and the country knows this, even if I have made a few mistakes. And who are these representatives in Parliament anyway and who do they account for? I dismissed Parliament for more than ten years and the country was a better place for it. We had peace and prosperity, new innovations and great works of art. For the last few years they have been ruling without any account to a Monarchy and we are already in a mess. Food prices are going through the roof; Ireland is in total turmoil; nothing has been repaired or re-built and many people have left the country to find a better future in the New World. Christmas is banned and every disagreeable or unusual woman is accused of magic and ends up at the stake. What are they doing to my country? They should be the ones being held accountable, not their King. I am sorry, I am getting angry. I will take a deep breath to calm myself down," and the King did exactly that, quelling his rage, before continuing. "Soldier, who is the head of the nation's Parliament?"

John Anderson had just started to clear the plates at the other end of the table, and almost dropped them when he realised he was being addressed by the King. He looked up, and then at a couple of the other faces around the table before responding

"Oliver Cromwell, Your Majesty."

"C-Crrrrromwell Cromwell," the King stammered as his rage returned. "He is a nothing. Jumped-up Puritan from Huntingdon. Why does everyone refer to him? He is just a general but not even head of the army. Lord Fairfax is in charge right, Colonel?"

"That is correct, Your Majesty," Tom confirmed.

"So what about Whalley and Pride, or Hampden and Pym when they were alive? Do these names mean anything, soldier?"

"I have heard the name Hampden but not the others, Your Majesty," John replied.

"And who am I, Sergeant?"

"Why, the King, Sire."

"How do you know?"

"Well, everyone knows. Your face, it is on all our coins; your statute is in our churches and market squares, and we see your picture on paintings and pamphlets."

"Thank you, Sergeant. And Colonel, who built this Castell?"

"I believe Henry VIII, Your Majesty."

"King Henry. All the castells across the land were built by kings, as were the cathedrals. And Lady Bankes who gave the charter and money for the Minster at Wimborne?"

"I believe it was you, Your Majesty," she replied.

"And when you worship there, what Bible is used?" As the King continued to make his case with confidence, he seemed to be calming down.

"The King James Bible. The one your father translated for the people."

Mary was getting where the King was taking the discussion.

"Yes, that is correct, translated for every man and woman in this country to read. What greater gift could a King provide. And do not forget the Book of Common Prayer as well. And my father and myself, which nations do we rule over Sir Thomas?"

"England, Ireland, Scotland and Wales, Sire."

"And Parliament?"

"Parliament only represents England and Wales, Sire."

"So the power, the money and the faith is vested in the crown and it is I who have built churches and great buildings and promoted the faith. Just take a look at the glory of the Queen's House in Greenwich or Whitehall's Banqueting Hall, buildings that will be celebrated for generations. I have even married a French Queen, and betrothed my daughter to the King of the Netherlands to build relationships, promote trade and protect this country. And what has Parliament done? Nothing. It is just a bunch of self-serving aristocrats who try to stop me at every juncture. If I try to raise taxes to protect and develop this nation, they object. Why? Because they will have to pay them? And why should they not contribute as it is their wealth that is protected and even grows from my actions? They promise the Garden of Eden to the people, taking advantage of the Levellers and other groups. Yes, we will give you the rights to vote, land and education. But mark my words, these will all be broken promises. As soon as it comes to losing power or paying for any of this they will backtrack on everything. I understand they are even struggling to pay their own army because it means more taxes. Is that not true Colonel?"

"There have been some delays, Your Majesty," Tom Harvey replied.

"Self-servers, the lot of them, whilst I am the King of the people and have never broken a promise to my subjects nor my oath to God. As a King

I would never not pay my army, and all around the nation is physical evidence of what I have done for this nation and the real difference I have made to people's lives."

"Well said, Sire," Lady Bankes said.

"Thank you, my Lady. Yes I have much to be angry about but that is when I most needed Sir John by my side. There was no one better I had met for clarity of thought and good counsel. Please, a toast to my most valued and trusted advisor. Sir John Bankes."

"Sir John Bankes." The King toasted and the rest of the table raised their glasses in unison.

"Thank you, Your Majesty," Lady Bankes responded, dabbing her eyes with a tiny handkerchief trimmed with lace. "We all miss him."

"I know how much time he spent in my service and away from you, Lady Mary, and your family. So I must thank you both tonight. The last I heard was that you were defending my name down in Dorsetshire in that Castell of yours and brought about a humiliation to the Parliamentary cause. Sir John published pamphlets about your heroism I recall and sent them across the nation."

"My King, you are making me blush. It was nothing, but it is true that Camille here, myself, a Captain in your cavalry and four other servants did hold off an attack from the Parliamentarians of Poole. But alas the forty or so men we fended off retuned with over five hundred. The very same Captain, James Cleall recruited and trained men to defend the Castell and organised us to withstand a seven-month siege but we were totally outnumbered and outgunned. I would like to also toast his memory, for he is also no longer with us. Captain James Cleall."

"Captain James Cleall."

Lady Bankes felt emotion welling up inside her as they had just toasted the two men she had loved in her life. Her eyes were watering and she felt Camille's hand take her own under the table and give it a gentle squeeze. The two women looked at each other, and Mary managed a smile.

"But pray, my Lady, how did the siege end?" the King asked

"You had better ask the Colonel," Mary responded.

"Your Majesty, Corffe, where the Castell was, is my home. What the Parliamentary forces did to my village under Colonel Coke I cannot defend. The very worst of war was played out there in the endurance of the siege that Lady Bankes and my wife here suffered but also in the ways my family and friends in the village were tormented; destruction of their homes and their place of worship, theft of their property, torture and murder. Fortunately, my commander at the time, Colonel Bingham, and myself, when I was a mere lieutenant, took over command of the Parliamentary forces and we were able to bring matters to an end, although my good friend Captain James Cleall lost his life," Tom informed the King.

The King was about to ask a further question, but before he did so, John Bankes butted in.

"Colonel Harvey plays down his role. It was his plan which he devised, led, and executed, that brought to the end the siege with very little loss of life. He was faced with the situation of his wife and many of his friends being inside the Castell he was charged with defeating. As a Captain on the Royalist side, I have seen unnecessary trauma, death and destruction instigated by commanders representing Your Majesty and it sickens me in the same way as Coke's exploits have disgusted Tom. We have lost many great English people through this war, and Captain Cleall was one of the best. I believe you met him at Nottingham just before you raised the standard."

"Why John I do recall your father introducing me to a cavalry captain," the King remarked.

"It was that Captain that instigated the recovery of your Royal Standard at Edgehill. The Greencoats in the Parliamentary forces had seized it and were running back to their lines with it, spotted by Captain Cleall who devised a plan to recover it. Captain John Smith was credited with the deed, and I believe you knighted him for it. I am not undermining the bravery of that man, but it was Captain Cleall's plan and his own bravery that led the force that cleared the path for John Smith to recover it. I was behind the Captain all the way; indeed he was there to protect me as it was my first conflict. He protected me all right and recovered your standard, but at a dreadful cost for as we returned we cut through a line of Roundhead foot, men from Corffe including Tom here and our mutual friend Francis Trew, who is now buried at the foot of Edgehill. May I suggest a toast to Francis Trew."

"Francis Trew,

"A finer young man you will not find and a loss to this nation," Lady Bankes added.

New plates with a crusty pie of beef and potatoes were brought in by the waiting men, and glasses refilled.

"I am seeing how this war has torn friends and family apart," the King stuttered again. "I wish I had listened to Sir John Bankes more. As your sovereign I need to learn and understand the trauma to enable reconciliation and a new nation to emerge. Where else did you fight, Captain Bankes?"

"Too many places to remember and many I am trying to forget as they still haunt me. I guess most notably from a Royalist perspective Roundhill Down in Wiltshire but that is where I was once again facing Tom here."

"Ah! One of our greatest victories; tell me more."

"Perhaps you should hear what it was like from my side," Tom intervened. "I lost many good friends that day, and hundreds if not thousands were pushed over a cliff by your charging cavalry. A mass of broken bodies which, if they were not dead from the fall, were shot at by your musketeers from the clifftop. And it is by God's will that John and I are both sitting here tonight for we both had chances to kill each other and could have done had we not recognised the other at the last moment. We had been friends since childhood and this is what the war did, friends fighting friends, family fighting family. As you say Your Majesty, you need to hear these stories and reflect on them."

"Colonel, I am listening. Sir Thomas here has also been providing me with a Parliamentarian perspective, which has been insightful. I must confess, other than Sir John Bankes and my dear Queen, I have been surrounded by people with, shall we say, a narrow perspective. Yes, despite the Parliamentary lies, Queen Henrietta always advised me to find out what the people were thinking and feeling. I do miss her." The King looked forlorn.

"But Your Majesty, if you had been listening to Sir Thomas and your people, you would have known that they have suffered greatly and peace is what they wanted. So why did you secretly conspire with the Scots and commence the second war? More killing and more death and to what aim?" Tom asked, determined not to let the King get off the hook.

"To the aim of ensuring I could rule these nations as God's anointed King. I was actually crowned and anointed twice, in Scotland and England.

And as the anointed King, the aim was clear; to stop Cromwell and the usurpers. That was the aim, Colonel. I am the King of England, Wales, Scotland and Ireland, and the English Parliament should not dictate what the King of these nations is or is not allowed to do!" The King raised his voice and banged his fist on the table, looking sternly at Tom.

"But there are many and better ways to rule than just the sword. Too many people have died and for no reason," Tom responded, feeling the anger raging inside of him and determined to stand up for his lost comrades. It was the actions of the man in front of him that had caused so much suffering. He wanted to drive his sword into the King's chest but Camille reached for his hand under the table as he spoke, to quell his rising temper. He looked at Camille. She and his two little ones were the only reason not to take action and to despatch justice there and then.

"And Colonel do you think I do not know that. As King I am not just the ruler of the Kingdom but I am also Defender of the Faith, our Faith in God. And I for one have defended faith in all its forms whether Protestant, Puritan, Presbyterian or even Catholic. My Queen is Catholic, as a boy my tutor was Presbyterian, and my father practically defined Protestantism and so it is engrained in me a belief that as a nation we need to be more tolerant of different paths to our Lord's Kingdom. But Parliament only promotes its own self-interest, which is the Puritan mantra, and imposing it on the rest of the people. They have even banned Christmas."

Lady Bankes intervened.

"I am sorry Your Majesty; we have all lost so much. I have stood up for your cause as much as any man, Sire, but in truth I would not have done so if I had known the suffering and destruction that would follow this decision. But may I suggest we discuss some other topic?"

"It is difficult to discuss anything else when all our lives have been consumed by this war. You should know that, Mother, better than anybody," John intervened.

"Well let's try, Captain. I feel like I am on trial here tonight. Sir Thomas tells me many are demanding that I should be tried and this is a potential fate that that awaits me in London. But how can a country put on trial its King? Of course it is not possible, so let's move on. How is life in Dorsetshire, Lady Bankes? I must confess it is a county I have not visited but have heard a lot about your Castell and the countryside from your late husband," the King asked, as the main course plates were cleared, and more wood put on the fire.

"Your Majesty, my Castell was blown up on the orders of Parliament. It had been my home for over ten years and where I had given birth to five of my children. It had been home to the Colonel here all his life, yet he was charged by Parliament to slight it."

"I am sorry to hear that, my Lady. You see Parliament cannot be trusted and it is not always serving its people. The country needs its King to work with Parliament to refrain it from acts that are not lawful such as acts of theft on the nobility. Have you returned to your home in Middlesex?" the King asked.

"All our estates were taken away from us after the fall of Corffe but we have managed to negotiate recovery of them in return for paying a very large fine. I had to sell Ruislip to repay some of the fine. We had been staying with Robert Boyle at Stalbridge in the heart of Dorsetshire when the Castell was destroyed. We have now moved to a lodge back on our own estate, at Kingston Lacey, near Wimborne. It is nothing compared to Robert's wonderful grounds and he has been so kind to us, entertaining us of tales of his amazing travels and the fascinating scientific studies he is doing."

"In my youth I travelled to France and Spain, but as a King it is far more difficult. I had to send people like Sir Thomas here to represent me as my ambassador. You have certainly travelled afar, Sir Thomas," the King remarked, as the waiters brought out an apple tart and started serving it.

"Yes, I have had that privilege: Persia, India, Africa. I have started to write an account of my travels."

"Pray, Sir, what was your favourite place?" Camille asked.

"Well that is a question that has many answers. Madagascar or Mauritius for their beauty, but Baghdad on the Tigris River has a special place in my heart, being one of the most important cities in the Mohammedan world. It is an oasis of culture and history, as of course Florence, Venice and Athens are, but from a very different world, one which developed many centuries ago and with which we are less familiar with."

him. John coughed and looked like he was going to say something, but the King then continued.

"The truth is I have never known how to be a good father. I hardly knew my own and as a child had very few role models. The death of my elder brother Henry meant that my main priority was on becoming a king, without any help from my father. He actually wrote a book on the role of Monarchy for my brother and mentored him up until he died at the age of nineteen, but I think his death hit my father badly, as it did us all. He seemed to just immerse himself in his studies and writing poetry and forgot entirely that he had another son, eager to learn and understand. I read his book as a teenager but the subject of kingship is not the easiest to study without hands-on guidance. I was frightened of becoming king and yet my father remained aloof. And the same applied for fathership. When my son Charles was born I had even less guidance on how to be a father. I had lived with my mother at Clarence House in a separate world from the court and paternal influence. So I had little chance to learn how to bring up children as a father.

"I hardly saw my father either, but that was because he was in your service," John intervened, in a sorrowful tone. Mary looked at her son. She was taken aback by what he had just said. Was he criticising the King or his parents or was there something deeper?

The King responded. "John, he served me well, but looking back on my reign and that of my father, the Court was the be-all and end-all for so many good men, and women…" he nodded to Lady Bankes, "… but to the detriment of their families. Indeed, court life kept my father away from me, and for myself it was a barrier to my own children. I know children can bring you so much joy, something which I fear I have sacrificed for the position I hold. As a King I am serving the country every day with no respite and little time for family or even oneself. The eyes of the court, if not the nation, are on you constantly. Queen Henrietta was a natural mother, reminding me of my own, Queen Anne. She was Danish, you know. Such a sweet woman. But I would not know what a natural father was. This is something I dwell upon and regret." He seemed to be speaking to himself as much as anybody in the room and his voice petered out into inner thoughts, and another long silence.

"I would like to retire; please excuse me. I will see myself to the room if I could have a candle," the King said. All the guests stood up. John Anderson handed him a candlestick and the King made his way to the door.

"I do feel sorry for him. He seems to be genuinely misguided and oblivious to what has been happening in his country," Lady Bankes said a few moments after he had left.

"But surely a good King would not have his head in the sand," Camille replied.

Sir Thomas added, "That is a good point Camille. I have spent much time with him over the last eighteen months. To be honest I do not know what to make of him. There is a side to him that genuinely wants to be a good King, believes fervently in his right to rule and is concerned for the welfare of his people. But his naïvety is extreme. As he says, he has lacked good counsel in recent years and from his childhood was brought up in an unreal world with no guidance or help. He is famed for the extravagance of his masquerades, hardly something to be proud of, but his life does seem to be one big masque. He often seems to be still searching for the real Charles, the man and King within and you saw some of that tonight. Without his Queen he seems to be lost. Indeed, he is lonely, a man who was surrounded by his family, his Court, and his Royal household has just had me and the bare minimum of servants and guards for a year and a half, stuck in a small Castell on an island. But what he has lost is nothing compared to many. The question is, will he lose his Kingdom?"

"Is that possible? How can Parliament take away his Kingdom?" Mary asked.

"Well, I have no idea. I am not trained in law. This is where we would need your husband, Lady Bankes. However, we have received several delegations from Parliament at Carisbrooke over the course of this year. In my discussions with them it is apparent that views against the King are hardening up. I am told that Cromwell was furious at the King inciting the Scots to war again in his name. He apparently promised the Scots support to establish Presbyterianism in England. He told me that he was as much a Defender of the Scottish Faith as the English, but he must have known how much that would have riled the Puritans. Further religious division is the last thing this country needs. But I am told that after Naseby, the King's tent was captured and in it they found his correspondence. This showed how he had been colluding with the Irish, the Dutch and the French to support his cause. And more recently Colonel Ireton discovered a letter being smuggled to the French encouraging them to support the Irish and invade the country. How could he do that? The man is politically naïve and lacks judgement. He is easily misled, is a poor judge of character and acts in a knee-jerk way. The Parliamentary delegations are fed up with him. They have been lied to and are totally frustrated that he will not negotiate with them. I think there could be a face-saving compromise like a hand over of the Crown to Prince Charles, but he will not even have discussions about having such negotiations. As you say Camille, a man with his head buried in the sand. Will he keep it is the question?"

"What do you mean, Sir Thomas?" Lady Bankes asked.

"Amongst the last delegation we received there were at least three who openly discussed the prospect of putting the King on trial for treason."

"The very thought of that is treason in itself," Lady Bankes replied.

"I cannot comment, my Lady. My job is just the King's Bedchamber, but perhaps I should be looking for another job soon," Sir Thomas replied.

The dinner came to an end and the guests returned to Lymington in a small boat accompanied by four garrison guards and the boatman. It was a dark winter's night, but the water between the Castell and the town was calm, protected by the shingle spit.

The next day, Tom arranged for Camille to be escorted back to Dorsetshire with two trusted soldiers, whilst Mary stayed in Lymington for a few more days, and John joined the garrison at the Castell. Lymington was a bustling town, with a lively quay that shipped away all the salt that was produced in the neighbouring salterns, whilst barrels of olives and wine were offloaded for the merchants in the town who had prospered in the salt trade. This was a town that had escaped the post-war economic malaise of the rest of the nation and people carried on with their daily lives unaware that just over the water their sovereign was in custody at Hurst Castell and history was in the making.

Chapter Seven

Purges and Preparations

December 1648, Westminster London

The radical wing of the Parliamentarians, spurred on by Colonel's Ireton's revelations of the King's treachery and provocation of the Royalist uprisings of the second war, had one goal in mind, a trial for the King. John Bingham was amongst them and to him it was clear-cut: the King had colluded with the Scots but Colonel Ireton had evidence to suggest that he had been requesting foreign powers to invade and for that he must stand trial and answer a charge of treason. Once the King had made his defence a verdict could be reached and a sentence proclaimed. A charge of treason would normally result in a death sentence but John Bingham could see alternative solutions although Charles's reign must end. However, Bingham knew that amongst his Parliamentary colleagues there was little agreement about what should happen after a trial, but even to get to that stage was incredibly difficult. Parliament was totally divided on the issue, ranging from the radical view that the King should be tried and executed all the way to those who felt that the King's powers and privileges should be reinstated, and the focus should be on healing the nation. The Presbyterians were also backing the King to promote their interests. A cocktail of religious, political, moral and self-interest fuelled the open debates and secret discussions between different factions, but without any conclusion or direction. Parliament's power was paralysed.

Behind the politics were individual relationships amongst family members, former comrades-in-arms and business ties. Sir Walter Earle had been a long-standing ally of Bingham in Dorsetshire, having been a Colonel during the war, and an officer he had fought alongside on many occasions. He was now the representative for Weymouth in Parliament and with the development of Bingham's bank in the borough had many mutual business interests. Bingham had been invited on several occasions to Sir Walter's estate at Charborough House, north of Wimborne, but on the issue of the King's punishment their views differed, with Sir Walter fearing an execution of the monarch would make him a martyr for the Royalist cause and provide an excuse for the French to rally behind the Prince of Wales. He feared an invasion at a time when the nation was at its weakest and advocated imprisoning Charles and replacing him with the boy Prince Henry as a puppet monarch to Parliament.

The radicals had a trump card, the support of the army after having ensured they had received their back pay. Ireton had orchestrated that the army draft a remonstrance, a list of demands to address their grievances, and serve it on Parliament, and top of the list was that there should be a trial for the King whom the Roundheads blamed for the war. The army's leaders, Generals Fairfax and Cromwell, were much more guarded in expressing their views, despite the power that they yielded, and remained focused on quelling the uprisings in the North rather than the politics in Westminster. However, neither did anything to stop Colonel Ireton, Cromwell's son-in-law, and Colonel Thomas Pride, who had recently returned from the victory over the Scots in Preston, from flaunting the power of the army in the House.

The radicals had arranged for the King to be transported to Hurst Castle but would not transport him any closer to London until there was more confidence of the outcome and it was to Colonel Pride that they turned. Ireton had drawn up a list of Parliamentarians that were definitely opposed to the radical view and on the morning of the 6th of December the Colonel stationed his troops outside the entrance to St Stephen's Chapel, the house of the Parliamentary commons. As the representatives turned up, Pride ticked them off a list and in the process arrested forty-five Members for a variety of trumped-up charges. A further 186 were excluded and told not to appear again including Sir Walter Earle and his son Thomas Earle, the young representative for Wareham.

Bingham was considered by Ireton to be sympathetic to the radical view and so was allowed into the chapel hall for a much less crowded session with the expectation of starting a motion that would lead to the trial of the King. But many representatives were not in a mind to be cajoled in such a way. Shouts of 'disgrace' and 'coup' were heard. John Bingham sat with fellow Dorsetshire representative, William Sydenham, Member for Melcombe and John Pyne, Member for Poole, and watched in dismay as shouting and bickering across the Hall turned the session into chaos. It was not until Hugh Boscowen stood up and declared that he would take his leave from this disgraceful House and marched out, followed by over eighty representatives, Francis Chetel from Corffe, Richard Rose from Lyme, Viscount Cranbourne, as well as Sir John Borlase amongst them.

Bingham and the remaining members, just about half of the tally the previous day, set to work in the 'Rump' Parliament, as it was to be called in the news pamphlets the following day, to start discussing the passage of a statute to establish a court to bring the King to trial. The Monarch would finally pay for the suffering he had caused, but Bingham could see a wider perspective. The King's removal would open the door to the Puritan movement's continued growth and remove the threat of popism once and for all, not least from the King's own wife sat in her brother's court in France.

Hurst Castell

Each day Lady Bankes took the boat to Hurst to walk with the King, accompanied by Sir Thomas, as well as a half a dozen guards who followed out of earshot. They would wander along the pebbles of the stony spit that joined the Castell to the mainland. Colonel Harvey was happy that the spit was secure with water on either side, and a guard of ten men at the far end. He had visibility of every step that the King made and from the Castell ramparts had a good vantage of the sea and the full length of the spit. Tom was certainly pleased that Mary provided a distraction and company for the King, for he was at a loss at other ways to occupy him given the meagre facilities of the Castell.

The ever-changing Solent provided a backdrop for the walks. If the south westerly wind had not blown in a new skyscape, the current and tides of the sea would be changing the seascape. On some days the waves would roll up on to the spit throwing pebbles on to the shore and dragging them back as the water retreated with such ferocity that the three could not make themselves heard over the clamour. The white horses of the waves would be thrashing around in a turmoil that reflected that of the nation in the depths of the war, and the wind would chill the walkers to their bones. Another day it would be like walking next to a mill pond, with only the gentlest lapping of water against the shore, and the sun's rays glistening on the sea between the Isle of Wight and the spit. On the land side of the spit, the tide could be out revealing beds of seaweed filling the air with a pungent odour, until the sea covered them again and made the spit once more feel fragile as the water threatened both sides. Boats of all sizes and types could be seen navigating the waters: the smaller vessels carrying barrels of salt from Lymington and the larger ones, with their tall masks and array of sails, bound for Southampton or London if they were sailing east. Sir Robert would speculate on where the westward ones were bound: La Rochelle, Lisbon, Venice, or the new lands on the other side of the Atlantic.

The King found the changes and contrasts fascinating for he had spent little time by the sea and certainly not with so few people that he could indulge in nature's wonder. Mary suspected it was a good distraction for him, as she was sure he must be thinking about what would happen to him when he arrived in London. But he also seemed genuinely interested in Mary and her life asking questions about each and every one of her children. They found common ground in their view that marriage was a good way to build bridges across the divided nation as Alice had done with Sir John Borlase and her daughter Mary with Sir Robert Jenkinson, mirroring his own marriage at a country level to Henrietta Maria, a Catholic princess from France. Mary also provided him with more insight into the current troubles of his people: the shortage of men to farm the land, the closure of mines and quarries, the escalating food prices, the hunger of families who had lost their bread winners. This was all enlightening to the King who had little idea of any of the daily challenges faced by his subjects, living in his bubble in Carisbrooke on the island across the water from where they walked. On her third visit, whilst they were walking along the split, the King started talking about a message he would like to send to his subjects for Christmas. Sir Robert doubted whether he would be allowed to but as he spoke the King brushed up alongside Mary, his hand finding her hand, and a small, folded parchment of paper was exchanged. Mary realised that the King was using her to send a message presumably to some of his supporters. Back at the Castell whilst alone she looked at the parchment which was addressed to John Ashburnham and informed him the King would be travelling to Windsor via Winchester imminently and requesting that his followers rescue him along the road. Mary knew John Ashburnham through her husband: he had been the King's Bedchamber and before the war was a member of Parliament. She recalled the King saying the day before that he was at Hampton Court. But how could she fulfil the King's request? It would put her son John at risk and would betray Tom Harvey, who had put his trust in her. She had been loyal to the King throughout her life, putting her own life on the line and losing her home, Corffe Castell, in his name. But how could she risk the life of her son, whose mission was risky enough as it was. Mary went back to Lymington where she was staying in the Solent Inn, a small tavern at the bottom of the main street which rose up the hill on which the town had grown. As night closed in the traders closed their stalls, and many found their way into the tavern in the rooms below Mary. But it was not the sound of their revelling that kept Mary awake for even in the depths of the night when the town and tavern were still and quiet she wrestled with what to do with the letter the King had passed to her.

The next day Mary announced that she had to return to Kingston Lacey but not before the King made her promise to visit him on her way to see Alice with whom she was staying at Christmas.

"Mary, I hope you can help me with my Christmas message," the King said as she prepared to say goodbye.

"There are many considerations in such a message, Sire. I am and will think carefully about it."

"If you are unable to help, I will understand, Lady Bankes, I have very much enjoyed your company and you and Sir John have served me as much as I could ask any subject," Charles replied.

John Anderson was charged to chaperone Mary home. The small boat that ferried them back from Hurst dropped them at the quay, a short walk from the inn. Along the quayside, the sound of the fenders of the ships rubbing up against the quay, the clicking of the sheets against the wooden masts and the squawking of seagulls was the backdrop. But Mary was oblivious to it all and had not spoken a word on the boat as she wrestled with the King's request. She could feel the King's letter burning in her pocket and the weight of the future of the monarchy on her shoulders. As they walked, and now alone, Mary wanted to gauge John's view on the King, a man who had also fought for the Royalist cause at considerable cost to himself.

"John, what do you think of the King, now you have met him? Was he worth fighting for?" Mary asked, quietly and ensuring she could not be overheard.

"My Lady, to be honest I have not thought much about the King. I went to fight because they were offering a good wage and I had a family to support when the war meant there was not much labouring work to be found. I took a risk and live with the consequences. I do not blame the King or Cromwell. I just pray they can agree to something in London to stop this madness and bring back some peace and stability. That is what most folk want."

In her room back at the Solent Inn, Mary reflected on what John had said 'peace and stability – that is what most folk want.' If she did what the King had asked and his supporters enabled him to escape, she would be stirring up a hornet's nest. She would pray for a safe and uneventful journey for the King and that Parliament and the Monarchy are able to be reconciled when he arrives in London. It was time to bring the nation together, and if the King were to escape this would result in more war and bloodshed. She placed the parchment of paper in the fire, watching the flames end perhaps the King's last hope of keeping his throne as God's anointed monarch.

Much of the preparation for the trip from Hurst Castell to Windsor had already been made secretly before the King had arrived. Captain Arthur Morris, the man Tom had entrusted in planning the route, had been all the way to Windsor and back and had made all the necessary arrangements at each stop, under the guise of the visit of the Colonel, and so maintaining absolute secrecy about the plans for the King. Tom knew the Captain was meticulous in his planning, which would be critical to the success of this mission. Tom now went over the plan with Captain Morris and John Bankes who was impressed by its thoroughness, knowing the area around Winchester well from being stationed there and the battles he fought in the locality during the war. John suggested to avoid travelling through

Lymington, the direct route from Hurst Castell, for it was a thriving community and no doubt would include some Royalist sympathisers. Taking the King through towns would send ripples of gossip through the shire which could put the plan in jeopardy. They needed speed and stealth on their side and so John suggested a back road via Milford and Sway and then picking up the main road again at Brockenhurst. John was sensitive in making his suggestions as he understood he was not part of the command and did not want to upset Captain Morris who had otherwise devised a very robust plan. But he went on to make a further suggestion that the King travel in a carriage rather than on horseback. It would slow them down but they could still make the schedule and if there was to be an attack by either side it would be easier to protect the King in a carriage and equally harder for any attackers to escort him away.

"But where do I get a carriage from, John?"

"I have a suggestion. My good friend Henry Sandys' estate is just north of Romsey. I am sure if I ask his widow, Jane, she will lend me a carriage. Indeed, we could rest and water the horses there en route as it would be about the halfway mark on the first day.'

"The Sandys are well-known Royalists," Captain Morris interjected.

"Is that so, John? How can we trust them?"

"You have to trust me, Tom, and I am sure a widow and her daughter will not be a threat," John replied, with emphasis on the 'me'. He continued, his hand on Tom's shoulder. "The sons I believe are in France and what harm can two women do?"

The Captain and the Colonel looked at each other. The Colonel nodded and it was agreed that John would test the alternative route with the Captain the next day and return with a carriage for the journey to Winchester.

"Tom, thank you for this opportunity. I am already feeling reborn. I will not let either of you down," John declared.

"Tom and I have been talking about travelling after hearing Robert talk about his adventures. I must show my husband my home land of France but I dream of Florence," Camille said.

"Listen to your wife, Colonel, for I very much encourage it. Getting to see and understand different cultures provides you with a whole different perspective when you return. I will arrange for you to get a copy of my book and perhaps it will encourage you," Sir Thomas replied.

"Thank you, Sir," Tom answered with a polite nod.

"Tom, perhaps you could take John with you as well. I cannot have him moping around at home any longer. There was a time when I could not stand him being away but I am sure a trip would do him the world of good."

"Mother, I am quite capable of making my own plans," John replied.

"How many children do you have Lady Bankes?" the King asked.

"Eleven, but only five little ones plus John still with me at home. I lost one to smallpox but the rest are away at school, living in London in search of good matches or are already married."

"I recall your daughter married the Borlase boy."

"Alice, yes. She is in London and looks after two of her sisters."

"I miss my children, but like you it is difficult to keep track of them as they grow up. Queen Henrietta Maria and I had nine, did you know? We also suffered some tragedies and only five live today. Charles, my eldest, is with his mother in France. He fought alongside me until 1645, but with a heavy heart I sent him away to join his mother so I could ensure the dynasty would survive whatever happened. I have been told he has recently been joined by James, the Duke of York, who escaped from Parliamentary custody earlier this year. My eldest daughter, Mary, married William of Orange and sits on the Dutch throne. My two youngest, Elizabeth and Henry, are still under guard in London. Sir Thomas will confirm how much I have pleaded with Parliament to bring them to me or at least send them to their sister, Mary, for they are still so young, but alas it falls on deaf ears. I do hope to see them soon, for it has been nearly two years now, and I dare say I will barely recognise them. I fear I have not been a good father and wish I could make amends. Will they even know me? Or me them?"

As the King spoke, he seemed to cower and shrink into his chair, and now he paused in reflection. Silence filled the room. Everyone felt uncomfortable, as the King looked at his apple tart on a plate in front of

Mottisfont, near Romsey in Hamptonshire – December 15, 1648

John and Captain Morris arrived at Mottisfont, his old friend's house, which had been crafted from a medieval priory into a Tudor mansion. The River Test babbled by to one side, with willow trees draped into the fast-moving clear water. It had been Henry Sandys' great-grandfather, a noble in Henry VIII's court who had transformed the building, and he had chosen to adapt the chancel into the great hall of his new home, with new wings either side providing chambers, and a chapel to the rear. The original large arched oak door provided the focal point in the centre of the building and Lady Jane Sandys happened to be coming out of the door as he arrived, with her daughter Hester.

"John, what a pleasure to see you," Lady Jane said with a welcoming smile. Her warm grey-blue eyes matched her lavender blue modest dress and her grey hair was tied up in a bun. She had aged since John had last seen her and was now supporting herself with a stick. Hester was fairer than her mother, with mouse-coloured hair, but her eyes were walnut-brown eyes like her father's. She was also modestly dressed for one so young and of such social standing.

"Lady Jane, and Hester, the pleasure is all mine. May I introduce you to Captain Arthur Morris? I have something of an urgent nature I would like to discuss with you. Would you have a few moments?" he asked.

"Welcome Captain, and John of course we can talk. Hester and I were just going for a walk, but that can wait, and as you can see I cannot go far anyway. Come on in. You must be tired from your ride if you have come all the way from Dorsetshire," Lady Jane replied.

John and Captain Morris dismounted and followed the ladies into the grand hall, as they both removed their identical blue bonnets which were delicately trimmed with white ribbons. This was the hall that had received Queen Elizabeth on more than one occasion and large paintings of the Sandys' ancestry adorned the wood panelled walls. Under the glare of her ancestors John felt awkward in the company of Hester, for he had not followed up from their walk together shortly before her father's fatal injury at the battle of Cheriton. John had taken shifts with Lady Jane and Hester to be by Lord Sandys' bedside during his final days at Basing House, but he had avoided all but the barest polite conversation with Hester. He just did not seem to know what to say.

John addressed Lady Jane, avoiding eye contact with Hester. "You have been fortunate to keep the house. I am sure you heard what happened to Corffe."

"Yes, we are sorry, John. Many castells and houses have been slighted – I think the Puritans are trying to wipe out our heritage," Hester interjected.

Lady Jane continued, "Since Henry's death it has been extremely difficult with just myself and Hester looking after the estate, and my younger children. My three boys have continued to fight for the King but have now fled to the continent. Hester and myself have been fighting to retain Mottisfont and the Vyne ever since the Parliamentarians defeated us at Cheriton. We thought we had lost everything at one stage, but our family connections within the church helped us in the end. The Bishop of York is a good friend of Lord Fairfax, the Parliamentary army commander. But we are paying a very large fine and have had to lease out the Vyne. Then they have fined us again for being late on a repayment. It is a total nightmare."

"Have you had a visit from Coke?"

"Yes, that is his name. A horrible man. He imposed the fine on us."

"We know him only too well. He led the siege on Corffe and ransacked the village. He has also fined us. You need to be very wary of him."

"John, if you can help us at all we would be so grateful. We are running out of ideas on how to meet the payments, let alone any additional fines. Would you believe who is our tenant at the Vyne? Lord Fairfax – it is now his southern residence, no doubt paid for by the very fines that are being imposed on our families. My husband would turn in his grave if he knew but what are we to do?"

"We have no money for fine clothes and maintain a skeleton staff. We are counting every penny to get by, and the cost of everything is so high these days," Hester added.

"I know how you feel, for we are in the same situation. I live in a small lodge with my mother and siblings. But perhaps I can help in a small way. I need to hire a carriage for a few days and can pay a guinea a day if you would so oblige."

"Are you in the service of Colonel Harvey, John?"

"Yes, I am. He is a good man and a very good friend of mine, the very opposite of Coke. We need to bring people together and rebuild our nation, and he is one man who can help do that. I know that is hard when you have lost loved ones but we need to think about the future."

"I am sure you are right, John. What do you need the carriage for?"

"We are not at liberty to say, my Lady, but it is a noble cause. We would also like to request that myself and a troop of forty men can water and rest our horses for an hour here over the next couple of days but all this must be in total discretion. Nobody must know. I will send word ahead when the exact day is known."

"Well, I must say it is difficult to say no to a few guineas for so little on our part," Lady Sandys said with a smile.

And so the arrangements were made, before John and Arthur escorted Hester Sandys for a walk around the estate, at the insistence of her mother. Captain Morris seemed very familiar with many of the plants in the walled garden and struck a repour with Hester on how they flowered during the seasons. The Captain was much more at ease with Hester than John had been on their first walk, and his enthusiasm and character was infectious and relaxed John who enjoyed the company as they toured the gardens, looking somewhat unkept, a victim of the Sandys' financial cut backs. A robin tracked the three of them, darting between bushes and tree branches, many of which were masked by cobwebs still glistening with dew.

With some ale and a good slice of ham pie from Mottisfont's kitchen in their bellies, the two Captains harnessed the four-seater enclosed carriage up to the horses. It was perfect for their mission. The two men jumped up on to the coachman's bench and waved goodbye to the Sandys. John Bankes cracked the whip, the horses strained against the harness and the wheels started to roll, back to Hurst Castell. The road took them through the forest that had been the king's hunting ground ever since the days of William the Conqueror. There were a few cottages that could be glimpsed amidst the assortment of oaks, beaches, ash, elms, and the browning foliage of the forest floor. Lush green ferns, yellow celandine flowers and holly bushes, adorned with clusters of red berries, provided a relief of colour in the otherwise brown and grey hues of the sleeping landscape. The common rights in the forest belonged to individual cottages or holdings and dated back to Norman days. There were many different rights related to grazing, collecting wood or charcoal burning that enabled people to make a living in some format underneath the forest canopy. Periodically they would spot where charcoal burners had cleared some patches of trees, and thick grey smoke funnelled from the wood pile kilns coated in moss and peat.

The two men had plenty of time to talk, and they took advantage of it sharing their wartime stories and delving into each other's past, as they caught glimpses of deer running for cover as the noise of the carriage disturbed the calm of the forest. Overhead a hawk hovered seeking prey. The two men discovered that they had been on opposing sides at the Battle of Cheriton and had both lost close friends in that conflict. As they talked, they discovered that they had a lot in common and their shared experience created a bonding, despite having fought on different sides during the war.

"And so now you are fighting for Parliament? The Colonel must trust you given the nature of our mission," Captain Morris asked.

"Captain, my father served the King, but really he was driven by service to the nation and justice. I was young when I rose to the King's call, driven by a desire to be in the cavalry more than anything. I have learnt much since and have a similar outlook to my father. I would like to serve my nation and the cause of justice with my skills as a cavalry officer. I enjoy the camaraderie and excitement of the army and I would die if I were left to run my family estate or even take up law, following my father's footsteps," John replied.

"I understand, John, and please call me Arthur. It sounds like the law is as far from your idea of a good life as the church is to me. I am the son of an archdeacon and observed my father's preparations for different types of services. I apply the same mindset to the army for I may not be the strongest in battle, but the planning for it is something I love. Thinking ahead and ensuring all the provisions are in place, weapons, uniforms, food and medical supplies is a big and complicated task. The right provisions, at the right time and in the right place, not to mention at the right cost. Too few provisions, and the army would not be ready to fight, too many and it will be slow and cumbersome," Captain Morris explained.

"I totally understand. It has been the planning that gave the New Model army the victories in many battles. A good friend and mentor of mine, Captain Cleall, always told me, 'In the heat of battle it is the plan that gives you the edge, not the sword', and of course that means planning for the battle as well as in it. But alas he was one of the many fallen comrades."

"I am sorry, John," Arthur said and he gave him a comforting pat on the shoulder. John welcomed the gesture with a smile. The time seemed to fly, but it was dark by the time they had returned to the Castell and reported back to the Colonel, mission accomplished.

15 December 1648, The Purbecks, Dorsetshire

Camille had returned to Swanage with her children and Nella, knowing she would not see Tom until Christmas. The weather since she left Hurst Castell had been grey and wet with a mist choking the bay, but today she awoke to a bright and clear day which was irresistible. Nella blew the embers back to life in the kitchen whilst Camille fed William, and then she left the house and went for a ride in the crisp morning. She set out for Worth Matravers where Tom's step-brother Daniel Spear lived, who managed the Bankes estate along with his father William. He was her closest relative and she was keen for some adult conversation beyond the subject of household chores and the size of the Swanage catch that day. Daniel's job meant he knew everything going on in the Purbecks and even further afield. But the visit was an excuse to be out and for the pleasure of a ride which she knew would be invigorating. The bracing air soon cleared the cobwebs in her head, as she rode across the sandy beach of Swanage bay and up on to the limestone ridge following the rugged cliff line of the coast with waves dancing on the ledges below. The fresh breeze from the turquoise-blue sea swept through her long flowing brunette locks which she had left down for the ride. She rode up and down the valleys along the ridge that had been formed by streams running into the sea before she came to Worth Matravers, the village where Daniel lived. She found him chopping wood outside his cottage, a limestone thatched house in the heart of the community.

"Camille, my favourite sister-in-law, what a pleasure to see you," he said resting his axe on the log stack and coming over to greet her as she pulled up her horse to a stop, joined by his liver-coloured spaniel which was barking with excitement.

"I am your only sister-in-law, as you well know Daniel," she replied with a warm smile.

"Can I tempt you to a mug of ale—alas it is all I have?"

"*Merci*, that would be perfect." Camille followed him into the cottage. It was not a small house, with two good sized rooms downstairs, and a bedroom and hay store in the eaves of the thatch. Daniel's wife, Jane, was preparing food in the kitchen, with a large bucket-shaped pan hanging over the fire. She came over to greet Camille. The scent of baking bread filled the room, and Jane pulled out a loaf from the bread oven that was created within the brick of the chimney breast to the side of the fire. The three of them sat with mugs of ale around the kitchen table and started to chat. Camille told them about meeting the King and her time at Hurst Castle. Her story was interrupted with lots of questions about the King.

"I felt sorry for him. He seems to me like a person who is lonely and lost, but tied to convictions that are uncompromising and which may well see his downfall. Tom has now taken him to London, to what fate we do not know."

"Well, someone needs to be held accountable for what has happened. If anybody else made so many mistakes they would lose their job; why not the King? His son, Prince Charles, should take over," Jane said.

"Yes, it seems like everyone everywhere is suffering as a result of the war. But I doubt now whether the King is entirely to blame."

"Times are really hard, Camille," Daniel confirmed. "But we have some good news. The quarry has just had an order which will be the first work for years. It will take a while for us to get up and running again but it means the quarriers, stone cutters and marblers can start to do the work they know best and will earn a decent wage.

However, that will not help the rest who are really struggling. The pound at Corffe has been full of sheep and chickens we have had to confiscate for rent not paid, and that is with us being as lenient as possible. And it is not just the farm workers, as all trades are suffering; shoemakers, ropemakers, flaxdressers, claycutters, millers and even publicans. Folk have no money to spend so everyone is suffering. The quarry will bring money into Corffe, Worth and Swanage but it will be too late for some people to benefit. Families do not have food on their plates or wood in their fires, and that is causing sickness. It will not long before people are dying."

"Where, here in Worth?"

"Yes, and in Corffe. The people in Swanage have fish but there are families here who have lost men during the war and so have no money, and the cost of food has gone through the roof. Much of the food in the shire still goes to feed Cromwell's army and the corn for his horses. We share a lot of what we have, but it only goes so far, and there are several people who are now ill and they are too week to fight sickness. Take Eleanor Greystone at Lavender Cottage here in Worth, widowed during the war and four children to feed, I am not sure when she last ate anything and she is looking very frail. Everything we give her I am sure she gives to the children."

"And others think the hard times are the devils work," Jane intercepted.

"I am sure the King is not the devil," Camille replied with a laugh.

"No it is not a laughing matter, Camille. Eleanor knocked on John Stockley's door, begging for food last week. He turned her away and the next day his pig died. His wife, Mary, is going about saying Eleanor cursed them."

"What nonsense. But you need to stop that talk Daniel. It is dangerous. Remember what happened to Agnus."

"How could I forget, Camille? I have spoken to John and told him in no uncertain terms that this talk must stop straightaway. His wife is the village scold and I reminded him of what happens to them if he cannot rein her in."

"You mean the ducking stool? You would not do that Daniel?"

"Of course I would not, Camille, but sometimes you have to threaten people to get them to abide by your words."

"So what can be done about Eleanor and her family and the other families who are short of food, Daniel?"

"I do not rightly know. If you had a magic wand you could produce grain, some fruit and vegetables. The harvest has passed and is collected, but the yield was low as there were not enough people to sow the seed in the first place because of the war. Now it is winter and nothing can be done until next year. Prices will remain high until there is more to go around."

"So there is food but it is too expensive. Where can it be brought?"

"Well people are shipping it into Poole from France and the Netherlands but charging an arm and a leg."

133

"Daniel, we cannot let people die, not here in the Purbecks. Look, Tom has some money from his reward for taking Corffe. He said he would never spend it because he was just saving me and should not be rewarded for that. I know Tom would be more than happy to use it to buy food for the people. If I gave it to you Daniel, would you arrange for grain and fruit to be purchased from Poole, and then distributed to those who really need it."

"Camille, that is a wonderful gesture. If we can get people through the next few months, then hopefully the opening up of the quarry again will help to bring work back for folk."

"You are so kind, Camille. Everyone will be so grateful," Jane added.

The three of them put their plan into action, and by the end of the week food was being distributed to the people of Corffe, Kingston, Worth and Langton.

Chapter Eight

December 16th, 1648, the Road to Winchester

The day finally arrived to leave Hurst and set off on the road to Winchester and then on to Windsor. The importance of the mission could not be overestimated with so many risks and challenges on the way, that it had kept Tom awake many nights over the last few weeks. He had, with the help of Captain Morris and John Bankes, planned every step of the way and gone over and over the plan. He was hopefully that secrecy had been maintained and the remoteness of Hurst Castell ensured that the identity of its prisoner remained unknown. John personally vetted everyone who was allowed into the Castell. Mary Bankes had left Lymington a few days before and had returned to Dorsetshire escorted by two of Tom's men. Whilst John trusted Mary he had not disclosed any aspect of the plan to her: not when, how or what route the King would be taking to London. John Bankes remained at Hurst, whilst a message was sent to the Sandys at Montisfont to inform them when they would be travelling to their estate.

It was a horrible day when they left the Castell, with a dirty, heavy cloud cover and incessant rain, but Tom was glad for there would be fewer travellers on the road or curious people in villages they would pass through. The King had insisted that Tom travel inside the carriage with himself, Sir Thomas, and Clara Peppercorn, the cook from Winchester. The bitter wind showered them through the drenched curtains hanging on either side of the open windows and, although it was a novelty to be in a carriage, Tom had already realised it would be a long and bumpy journey and he was regretting he was not on his horse. Clara was a woman in her thirties, with mousey brown hair under a plain white maid's bonnet, green eyes and a warm smile. She felt uncomfortable travelling with such esteemed company and wrapped herself in a shawl avoiding eye contact and saying nothing. They were accompanied by forty cavalry: twenty at the front under Captain

Morris's command, accompanied by John Bankes. To the rear, the men were led by Captain O'Kelly, the Irishman who had fought with Colonel Bingham, and Tom Harvey leading up to the fall of Corffe Castell. The King was well protected, for Tom had insisted he had some of the best men in the Parliamentary army in the South. With the fall of Oxford in June 1646, the notorious Prince Rupert of the Rhine, who had commanded the Royalist army on behalf of the King, had fled the country with his pet monkey and poodle, and in his wake the cavalier forces had been disbanded. Many of the New Model army soldiers were also demobbed as the war had been won and Parliament could not afford to feed and pay the soldiers. There were still minor scuffles and unrest to be dealt with but the residual army was well disciplined with well-trained officers promoted on merit rather than birth right or wealth.

The King had managed to escape Oxford when it fell but was captured by the Scottish, fighting for the Parliamentary cause. They took him North, for he was also the King of Scotland, and grandson of Mary Queen of Scots, but even so they soon released him back to the English in return for a ransom. The English had assumed that the King would agree to some conciliatory terms, but found he was stubborn and resolutely refused to negotiate with Parliamentary representatives. And so they imprisoned him at Carisbrooke Castell on the Isle of Wight, so they could focus on rebuilding the country and in the hope that he would come around in isolation from his family, court and Royalist supporters.

When the King had arrived at Hurst Sir Thomas had told Tom how Charles was allowed considerable freedom initially, with many of his household coming to join him and he was even allowed to travel around the island in his coach. But then it was discovered that the King had negotiated and formed a secret agreement with the Scots again, resulting in a Scottish invasion of England and the start of a second war. Whilst Cromwell led the New Model army north to meet them, the King had been confined to Carisbrooke, and all correspondence would be vetted before it was sent or received by the King. But the King's supporters did not give up and Tom was amused as Sir Thomas had continued the story. A plan was devised for the King to escape the Castell and presumably flee to the continent, with horses and a boat made ready to enable him to escape. All Charles had to do was to lower himself down from his bedchamber window to a horse waiting below. But the King got stuck between the window bars, and could not move forward or backwards, until he cried out to the guards to rescue him. As Tom sat there in the carriage he started to chuckle at the tale while looking at the King opposite him.

"What amuses you, Colonel?" the King asked.

"Ah nothing of interest Your Majesty."

"Please share, for we need something to help raise our mood on this dreary day."

"If you insist your Majesty, but you must pardon me for it is at your expense."

"Anything to raise our spirits, Colonel."

"Well, your Majesty, Sir Thomas informed me why the small window in your Hurst bedchamber had been a wise security precaution. Captain Morris has made sure that your room in Winchester has a similar feature to ensure Your Majesty is not put in such a tight situation again."

Sir Thomas laughed, but the King dismissed the comment.

"Colonel, is that all you have to amuse you?"

"I hope you do not take offence, Your Majesty, but there has been little to laugh about in your Kingdom for so long. I am grateful for this incident, whilst at your expense, has given some of your subjects at least a smile. Would you mind if I shared the tale with Clara?" Tom asked.

"Ha! If you must, Colonel," the King replied looking at the cook sitting next to Tom, still awestruck by the company she shared and had not said a word yet.

"Clara, a good friend and Royalist who was lost to this war, Captain Cleall, taught me when I was a boy about the importance of a plan in battle. It was his advice that enabled me to end the siege of Corffe Castell, freeing my wife and sixty others. But the King's Royalist conspirators demonstrated what happens if the plan is not well thought through and every detail checked and rechecked. They wanted to free the King from Carisbrooke, where he had been imprisoned. The plan was for the King to lower himself out of his bedchamber window by rope, where horses were awaiting, and they would take him to a ship and off the island. Everything was prepared with the utmost secrecy and was executed in the summer of this year. Guards had been bribed, horses and ships were ready. But alas the plan failed at the very first step: the window of the King's Bedchamber.

Our King became stuck between the bars of his window. He could not move forward nor backward. The conspirators had to ride away, leaving the King hanging out of the window and calling for the guards to rescue him."

Sir Thomas and Tom started to laugh. The King, pretending to ignore the tale, looked out of the carriage window, while Clara was not sure what she should do.

But the King himself smiled and said, "I should not have had that extra portion of chicken for dinner that night. I thought it would sustain me on my journey, but it detained me literally in mid-flight," he said and this brought more laughter from them all.

Tom had taken a risk, making fun at the King's expense, but Sir Thomas had told him he liked to laugh, and the ice had been broken.

"Sire, it is a sign of greatness to be able to laugh at yourself and allow others to laugh with you," Tom said.

"Colonel, I think that you gave me a complement, thank you. But you are a brave man. There was a time when a King could have punished, even hung, subjects for making fun of him," the King said.

"That is why I have put my life on the line so many times against you, Your Highness. Even a King appointed by God should not have such authority, and the rule of law should be respected."

"This carriage is too small to start such discussions again, Colonel. I fear it will not end well. One thing I have learnt at Carisbrooke, other than I need to lose a little weight and plan better my escapes, is that I was living my life surrounded by a moat. Inside the moat was the King, his family and court, and outside the moat were the people I ruled over. In my reign I barely got to know these people, my subjects, the ordinary people of the Kingdom, the people we call 'Commoners'. People like you, Colonel, and Clara here. Although I suspect, Colonel, that you are not just an ordinary person, but an extraordinary one. I understand that you come from a humble background but are now a Colonel and indeed responsible for my protection. Yet you are still young, mid-twenties I guess? You also have a beautiful wife and have befriended the Bankes family as if you were one of them. Yet, as I understand it, it was you who captured and slighted their home. I am interested to learn more about you, Colonel, and what drives you," the King said, surprising Tom. He was not sure how to respond, as the wind blew the curtains open on his side. He could see the carriage was passing through a village which he recalled from Arthur's plan was called Sway. He could see a big manor house set back from the road and several cottages but the rain had kept all the folk inside. He let a few moments pass as he reflected on the King's request but decided to be open and not antagonistic, giving the King the benefit of the doubt. Would he listen?

"Sire, thank you for the compliment. I will be frank with you, but there is nothing extraordinary about me. I have just tried to lead an honest hard-working life for the glory of God. I have been influenced by the Puritan and New Model army's approach that people should be rewarded for the hard work that they put in, and the Leveller's view that all men in the country should have a say and a vote in electing representative to Parliament as well as religious freedom. But I also listen to others and keep an open mind. There is an old man in a village near Corffe who has wisdom from his years and he says there are men put on this earth to be kings, and others to plough the fields. But why can men not learn to develop beyond their status to the glory of God and their families?

Family is, I believe, the foundation for good. I was touched by what you said the other night about your childhood, Sire. You had all the comforts and education that I lacked, but without the strong family support that I had. I would not swap what I had and lacked for your situation, even although I lost my mother at an early age. My father and step-family are still a rock to me.

You asked what drives me? In a few words what motivates me is curiosity, and what I fight for is tolerance and a better fairer life. You need to be curious to learn and understand different peoples' views and you need to be tolerant to accept them and live together in harmony, which I believe will create a better fairer life. I believe there is a pathway to a better world through all these apparent opposing views, but it is a long journey for which curiosity and tolerance will provide the necessary sustenance and it may take many lifetimes to achieve."

"As I said an extraordinary man with radical views but strong principles. No wonder you befriended the Bankeses. I can hear Sir John in your voice," the King said with a warm smile.

"Your Majesty, you talked about being the Defender of the Faith on our first night together, and the need for a more tolerant approach."

"Yes Colonel; from what you say, we do have more common ground in that area. This was one area in which I can say my father provided me with good advice and guidance. Both he and I believed that the role as Defender of the Faith is more important than being King. Indeed, what could be more important than defending the faith, but also interpreting that role in the broadest sense and as you have just said being tolerant of different paths to God's Kingdom. There is only one God, and he is the same God whether you are Protestant or Catholic, or even Jew."

"Or even Mohammedan," Sir Thomas added.

"Tolerance is something we can agree is an important foundation for the nation, then Colonel?"

"Yes, we have a common ground there, Your Majesty."

"And Clara, tell me about yourself," the King asked.

"Nothing to tell Sire. I just love cookin'."

"Food along with faith is the sustenance of life and brings pleasure to us all. It is a good passion to have. Where are you from?"

"A village just outside Winchester, Sire, by the name of Hursley. But I have been a cook at the Castell in Winchester for ten years now. I do not know about politics or anything like that. I stick to what I know and that is cookin'," she replied.

"And that has been appreciated by us all at Hurst Castell. You have certainly provided us with food that is as they say fit for a king, and I will testify to that."

"Thank you, Sire," she replied blushing with the complement. "I have been planning tonight's dinner at Winchester since I arrived at Hurst and was told by the Colonel that I would be cookin' for the King. Venison I understand is one of your favourites and I will be pleased to be back in my kitchen preparing it. The Colonel sent a note ahead requesting it on his behalf."

"You are right, Clara. I do love venison, especially from the New Forest. This is a place I have often enjoyed hunting and I pay tribute to William the Conqueror for finding and protecting such a place. I cannot recall the last time I visited Winchester—it was before the war, that is for certain."

"It will be ten summers next year. I had only started work at the Castell six months prior, and was just one of the cook's assistants, but I remember the thrill and excitement of your visit like it was yesterday, Sire. We cooked venison for you then, after the Royal hunt. Although we did not see you, we did hear that the food was well received. I cannot wait to tell the kitchen staff whom they will be cookin' for tonight."

"Alas, Clara, the Royal moat would appear to extend within the Royal Castell itself. Since Carisbrooke provided me with more time and no courtiers to distract me with their feuds and romances, I have tried to build bridges and meet more people. Sir Thomas has been helping me. Would you introduce me to all your kitchen staff after dinner tonight, so I can say thank you?"

"Of course, Sire. They would be over the moon," the cook replied, and Tom thought that this was definitely a different side to the King.

"I will arrange it with Clara, Sire," Sir Thomas added.

By midday the rain had stopped, and the sun was intermittently peeking through the patchwork of clouds, as the carriage arrived at Mottisfont. Lady Sandys was overwhelmed and flustered to find the King in her carriage. She treated the King to a walk in her gardens, accompanied by Colonel Harvey, closely tailed by ten soldiers. John had been right as the garden walls made it easier to safeguard the King. The horses were refreshed and the troop tucked into the bread, cheese and ham that Clara had prepared for the journey. John Bankes was brushing down his horse by the stables when he encountered Hester Sandys in a lavender blue dress, with her mousey coloured ringlets framing a stern-looking face.

"Where are you taking the King?" she demanded without even a greeting.

"Hello, Hester; I hope you are well. Our mission is to keep the King safe and to take him to a place where that can be assured. There are many in this country who would want to string him up, so I must ask for your discretion. Please do not speak to anyone of our visit. The Colonel will ensure his safety," John replied.

"And then what?" Hester asked.

"I do not know beyond that but I believe his fate is in his own hands. He needs to show some remorse and be prepared to negotiate with Parliament, but my job is to keep him safe for others to decide," John answered.

Hester's demeanour changed. Her expression softened.

"And why do you avoid me, John? You have hardly acknowledged me or said a word since our walk here in Mottisfont two years ago. I know my father thought highly of you and I am sure this is not in your character? Do you not find me agreeable?"

"Hester, you are a very beautiful woman and a fine person but I think this war has taken its toll on me and I would not want to burden you or anyone with my company," John replied.

"I am sorry, John, but we have all suffered and we all need to rebuild, and that means supporting each other," Hester said in a softer tone.

"I am afraid I have been melancholic ever since the disbanding of the Royalist force and have turned to brandy for my support. I am not a good person to be with. I need the army and missions like this to give me purpose."

"But what about family, John? I am going to be direct and unladylike, but I have had to be since Father died and whilst my brothers continue the fight. I have had to manage the estate with my mother. I am twenty-one, and time is against me. During the war there was no opportunity to socialise and meet people. But I did meet you and I know you are a good person, John. My father was very keen on us getting to know each other better. I would like to have that opportunity."

"Hester, I am sorry. I am just not the right man for you, or at least not the right man for you at this time. These men to me are family, and I cannot even help my own mother manage our estates. I am sorry."

Their conversation was interrupted by Captain Morris coming over to let John know he was summoning all the troops back together. Captain Morris thanked Hester for her assistance and confirmed he would return the carriage in a few days' time.

Before long they were back on the road and on to Winchester, leaving the Sandys women with a lot to talk about. This time John took his place in the carriage with the King whilst Tom led the way at the front on horseback.

Winchester

The light was beginning to fade as the carriage drew up to the West gate of Winchester Castell. Captain Morris had already ensured that the guards had been pre-warned of the impending visit of Colonel Harvey, but not his prisoner. They recognised the Colonel as he led the procession to the gate. It was opened in no time at all, and as the carriage pulled up inside, Tom ordered the guard to find the Alderman of the city and the Captain of the Castell. Both gentlemen had been expecting the Colonel and were already coming out of the castell keep as he dismounted.

"Colonel, what a pleasure," the Alderman said.

"I have an important guest for you for whom we must provide the highest levels of security and comfort. The room you have prepared for me will be his tonight. He is the King and he awaits you in the carriage."

Both men looked shocked, but without any further words were led over to the carriage by Tom. Captain Morris was already in attendance opening the door of the carriage to allow the King to first get out, followed by Sir Thomas, Clara and John Bankes.

The Alderman was a portly man, dressed to impress in a dark blue short, unstiffened jacket with a chain around his neck and wide breeches hanging loose to the knee.

"The Alderman of Winchester, at your service, Your Majesty," he said and he bowed. "Welcome to our city, a total unexpected pleasure. As is customary I will present you with the keys of the city."

"That will not be appropriate on this occasion," Sir Thomas intervened.

"Why not?"

"Because His Majesty is under our protection and we could not risk anything happening to him. Captain Morris has already set out which rooms he will be assigned to within the Castell and he is to remain in these and not venture out further," Tom answered.

"Your Majesty?" the Mayor asked, assuming that he was the ultimate authority.

"Sir Thomas and the Colonel are right, but it is with much regret. Winchester is one of my favourite places in all England. My son Charles and I always dreamed of building a palace here, and we still may yet. It could be a gift to my Queen on her return from France, something in the French style. What do you say, Alderman?"

"A truly fantastic idea Your Majesty."

"In the meantime, I do insist on a visit to the Cathedral to pray. I have been locked up for over two weeks, and the Cathedral will make up for this, at least in part. Perhaps Sir Thomas and the Colonel would let me spend a short time in prayer there tonight before dinner?"

"It is out of the question, Your Majesty, and Alderman please do not try to arrange anything else for the King. We are here to eat, and Clara has plans for a venison meal. We will then sleep and leave first thing in the morning, nothing more," Tom replied assertively.

"I am sorry to inform Your Majesty that the Cathedral is not in the best condition, and for that you can hold Waller and his Roundheads to account, who wreaked havoc in the city when they rode their horses into the cathedral and ransacked the place after the siege of the city. They pried open the royal caskets of the early kings and threw their bones at the stained-glass window above the main entrance. We have reburied the bones and gathered all the broken glass but need money and expertise to reassemble the windows and continue the repairs."

"This is sacrilege. I insist I see the crime," the King asserted.

Sir Thomas gave Tom a nod, and against all his better judgement, the Colonel conceded to at least consider the request. Tom knew Winchester had a strong Royalist contingent, but safely barricaded inside the Castell with no pre-warning of their visit he was sure he could protect the King. He was sure he had achieved the element of surprise, for he could see the shock on the Alderman's face when they arrived. The officer inside him knew he should not risk it, but the King had got to him over the last few days. He did feel some compassion towards him; he was just a human being and had needs like everyone does after all. So he and John went to inspect the Cathedral to determine if they could risk it, leaving the King under the guard of Captain Morris.

The Cathedral was in a sorry state, with its main window above the entrance boarded up, but it still stood tall in defiance over the city streets, and the warm glow of candles inside could be seen from windows that remained intact, sufficiently enough to allow the building to radiate somewhat against the night sky. Both Tom and John had been to the Cathedral before but its magnificence always left them in awe, with its stout buttresses and vaulted ceilings on a scale that was out of this world. It was difficult to believe that this was man-made, a feeling reinforced by the splendour of the crypt and ornate chantry chapel.. This is where Kings and Queens of England had been married, and others buried. From a military perspective the good thing about the Cathedral was that it was relatively easy to protect, with a single large oak door at the front and two much smaller ones on either side to the rear. The two men agreed that if they sent ten men in initially to conduct a thorough search, and then stationed ten men at the front and five on each door on the rear, with muskets also trained on each door from outside they should be able to let the King have a few moments of prayer.

They returned to the Castell and sent Captain Morris back with some men to conduct the search of the Cathedral whilst Tom went to inform the King in his chamber. Captain O'Kelly was preparing the rest of the men for the planned mission, leaving John alone at the West gate where he was approached by the Alderman.

"Captain, it is good to see you in Winchester again. I recognise you from the days when you were barracked here with General Hatton and Lord Sandys," the Alderman said with an artificially warm smile.

"It is true I was a Captain in the Royalist regiment, but you will see I have no colours on my arms. I am now just an advisor to Colonel Harvey and hold no military position."

"But once a cavalryman, always a cavalryman; once a Royalist, always a Royalist," the Alderman stated.

John wondered where the conversation was going and so played along.

"Of course, Sir."

"You do realise they are going to take the King to London and try him. He will lose his throne and be replaced with a Parliamentary puppet. Some say they may even execute him."

"I am sure that is not possible, Sir. He is the King," John replied.

"That is why we need you tonight, Captain. It is your destiny. The King will go to prayer, and this is the chance to save him."

"How?" John asked.

"Where will you be positioned and with how many men?"

"To the rear door of the south transept, opposite the deanery, with a handful of men."

"We will have a dozen men. You will see them, and ensure the door stays open. From that point, it will be a quick route to where the King will be in prayer and we will escort him out and away on a horse that will be awaiting him."

"You have only a dozen men, Sir?" John whispered.

"A dozen will enter the Cathedral, plus yourself, and you will have the benefit of surprise. There will be another half dozen, including myself, waiting outside and we will take him away, whilst you and the rest will ensure the Colonel's men cannot follow. At such short notice I cannot gather any more men, but you provide us with the upper hand. We will take him to France where our Queen is at court."

"Sounds like the bones of a plan and it will save the King. What signal should I give?"

The two men continued to develop the plan in whispers, and the Alderman was impressed how John improved it, addressing some flaws he had not considered. That was why he was the Alderman and John the cavalryman, he mused, and he went away ready to put the rescue in operation.

A few moments later, Tom returned from his meeting with the King.

"Is he happy; are we still doing it?" asked John, conscious that the Castell walls might have ears.

"I still do not like it, but yes we are. We leave as soon as the King is ready and I have told him if that is not in a few moments it will not be at all. I just need to know that Captain Morris has searched the Cathedral thoroughly."

"Let me go ahead and take another look at the rear doors."

"All right but you go alone. I need as many men as possible to protect the King between here and the Cathedral. I will conscript a few of the Castell guard but I cannot trust more than say ten."

John set off to the Cathedral. He had to think fast but had to ensure his plan that he had been developing in his mind in parallel with understanding and adapting the Alderman's plan would work. Then he had to get a message back to Tom. The Cathedral was quiet when he entered, with one of Captain Morris's men guarding the door. He headed over to the rear door, across the stone slab floor, his footsteps echoing across the nave.

John found the door, large iron bolts on the inside of heavy oak panels, and studs on the outside. Yes it was as strong as he remembered. He looked outside into the darkness. The South gate to the City, the Deanery and the Bishop's house were lit up by torches that levered off their respective walls, but their light did not stretch this far. Any attackers would have at best a partial view of the doorway, which was shielded by shadows cast by the Cathedral. Cloud blanketed the night sky, denying any starlight and suppressing the moon into a haze to the east. He could see how his plan would unfold to his advantage: create the chaos and execute the plan. Yes, the words of Captain Cleall came back to him In the chaos of battle, a plan is more important than the sword.

There were some things he needed to do so he remained at the Cathedral but he would need Captain Morris to relay the plan back to Tom. He found his new friend walking back down the nave and about to leave the Cathedral with his men He called out to him, caught up and then ushered him into the side, where he could whisper without being overheard.

"There is a plot Arthur, to abduct the King by Royalists. The Alderman is behind it. I need you to warn the Colonel and let him know I have a plan to foil it," John said.

"If there is a plot, surely the King should remain in the Castell? And John how do we know you are not involved. You were – or maybe are – a Royalist?" Captain Morris replied.

"I first thought we should keep the King safe, but if they do not take him now then they will attack us on the road tomorrow. We now know their plan and can foil it, killing or capturing the plotters and safeguarding us tomorrow," John whispered forcefully.

"Yes, that is true but what about you. Can we trust you?" Captain Morris asked again, intensely staring into John's eyes.

"Yes, of course," John replied, returning the stare unflinchingly, his face so close that the two men could smell the other's breathe. It was a moment of closeness and intensity, with not only personal trust but lives and history at stake.

"Tell me the plan, John." And so it was shared, but with instructions for the Captain to only tell the Colonel en route. They had to ensure that the Colonel would have little option but to go through with it. Once they had left the Castell knowing there were plotters en route no doubt watching them meant it could be riskier to return to the Castell provoking an attack, rather than going through with John's plan and surprising the Royalists. John knew that when balancing the risks, trust in John would be the deciding factor. As Arthur left, John realised he was now having to trust the Captain. He could tell the Colonel straight away, the King remaining in the

Castell leaving John to the royalist frustration and possible revenge. But something told him that Arthur was someone whom he could trust. There was little he could do now but to prepare, pray and have faith in that trust.

John had just finished his preparations when he heard the King, the Colonel and his men arriving at the main entrance. He raced up the chancery and met his friend, the Colonel, whilst the King was looking at the damage that has been caused to the Cathedral.

"Are you sure?" Tom asked in a tense voice. "You know what is at stake?"

"Yes, trust me," John replied.

Tom ordered ten men to follow John, and then spoke to the King. He would be allowed to pray but not in the main chancery; rather, at the very rear in the Lady's Chapel. This would be furthest away from the southern entrance which would be where the Royalists would come from and could easily be secured for it had its own internal door and no other access. John Anderson and four other guards were positioned in this chapel which was separated from the rest of the cathedral by a semi-open timber frame that incorporated a set of doors. It was not the strongest defence but could keep attackers at bay for a short while, and when the doors were closed Captain Morris and the other four men charged with guarding the King were instructed to barricade it from the inside.

John had already bolted the Cathedral rear door to the east. He was not expecting the attack from this side anyway, but by closing it off more men could be freed up to defend the other side which is where he was now, preparing and explaining the plan and roles for each of the men.

It was time to put the plan into action, and so he headed out to the west rear door with ten men and a bottle of the Bishop's sacramental red wine he found behind the altar. Two of the soldiers were splashed with the wine, and John also coated his blade with it. He then positioned the remaining soldiers, five behind the open door and two hidden amongst the pews and handed a rope John had pulled off the curtains to the vestibule and had secured to the pews on the other side of the walkway. The final one was ordered to kneel in front of the altar in prayer mode. John returned outside with the two men with blood stains on their tunics and added some wine to the ground for good measure. He now had to wait for the sign that had been agreed with the Alderman, the waving of the torch on the South gate wall.

The bustle of the city on the far side of the Cathedral had died down as amongst the narrow streets the tailors, shoemakers, apothecaries, victuallers and chandlers were closing their stores, and market traders had returned home or to the taverns where behind closed doors they were keeping warm with fires, ale and gin. There was nobody on the western side of the Cathedral. It was eerily still but John knew that in the shadows somewhere were a group of Royalists who were expecting to pounce at any moment. An owl could be heard in the distance, starting its first hunt of the night. John could feel the tension in the air as well as his own heart pounding with apprehension. The Colonel was right, there was a lot riding on this, and as he waited he started to have his own doubts. Maybe the Alderman was playing him for a fool and was at that very moment about to launch an attack through another door. This was just like before a battle, the anxiety and fear, but what was required was a cool head and to channel that fear into planned action. He was relieved to see the signal when it came, a torch on the southern gate being lifted and waved by a man on horseback. John immediately raised his sword and then started a mock battle with his two guards, ducking in and out of the shadows. One fell immediately, clutching his chest and falling into one of the pools of the wine on the ground. The other held out a little longer but as John could hear footsteps running across the yard he gave the signal for him to follow his comrades example. John looked around to see a dozen men running towards him, swords in hand. John ushered them across, and told two to stay on the door, and the rest to follow him. He ran down the aisle between the pews, closely followed by eight men at his heels. Ahead of them was the altar, and the Royalists could see as expected a lone figure in prayer. But at that moment their world turned upside down as two ropes were pulled up to knee height, one just behind John but in front of his followers, and the other in the middle of the Royalists, catching two men at the front and two others in the middle of the pack and sending them flying. They hit the ground and their comrades ran into them and in turn went tumbling. Simultaneously the western door had been slammed shut, and out of the shadows came seven Roundheads with swords at the ready. John as well as the soldier who had been acting as the kneeling monarch turned and joined the fray. Only one Royalist had managed to keep his footing, but before he knew what was happening he felt two pointed blades in his back. He dropped his sword. The men on the ground were also greeted by blades before they had time to gather their senses or weapons. That left only the two guarding the door, who had turned and started banging on the door when it had been slammed in their backs, only to find the blades of the two roundheads who had risen from the dead from the bloodied floor behind them ordering them to surrender their weapons.

Moments later, Colonel Harvey ran down the nave and was relieved to see the total success of John's plan. He ordered one of the ropes to be cut up and used to bind the hands of the captives, and then the other to tie then together in a line ready to be led to the city gaol. Leaving John to oversee this task, the Colonel ordered all doors to be secured and guarded, before going to the back of the Cathedral and to the Lady's Chapel. Once the guards had removed the barricade of pews, he entered the chapel to find a table with a wooden cross and a sconce, its six candles providing the only light in the room. Knelt in front of the table was the King, his head bowed and his hands together. He must have had heard the noise of the confrontation in the Cathedral as well as the Chapel door being opened and cleared but had remained still, deep in prayer. He looked humble as he worshipped the God he believed had appointed him to be King and sought guidance and comfort for the road ahead.

"He has been like that ever since we arrived, Colonel," John Anderson said.

Tom stepped up the aisle towards the kneeling monarch. He gave him a few moments more before interrupting him.

"Your Majesty, we must return to the Castell. It is not safe here. There has been an attempted abduction."

The King slowly turned his head, looked at Tom and the nodded.

"I am ready, Colonel. Thank you for this time." Tom was struck by the King's apparent serenity and acceptance of Tom's request. The King stood up and led the way out of the chapel without a further word, and Tom thought he had detected a pooling in his eyes. Had the King been weeping? It was difficult to read his expression in the poor light. Was he sombre or fearful of what lay ahead; was he repenting for his actions or mustering strength for the next steps? One thing Tom was sure was he would not want to be in the King's shoes.

The King was escorted along with the captives back to the Castell. The Colonel ordered Captain O'Kelly to lead a search party for the Alderman and his accomplices, but he knew the chances of finding them were slight. Another day they would be brought to justice and could join their co-conspirators in the city gaol. But in the meantime, thanks to John, Tom felt any immediate risk in Winchester had been allayed and so everyone was looking forward to Clara's venison pie.

"Well, with no Alderman to feed, that will mean more venison pie for us all," Tom said to his captains.

Chapter Nine

The Road to Windsor, 17 Dec 1648

At daybreak the following morning, the Royal carriage left the East gate of the city. There was a hint of the sun rising behind the mass of grey clouds that filled the sky. As they left the city the entourage passed a gibbet hosting the remains of a hanged man, a few tatters of clothing holding together the remains of what the birds had left behind and the bones of the skeleton. Tom and his officers knew that this was the most dangerous leg in their journey for news of the King's journey would have seeped out of the castell walls to the vengeful parliamentary supporters, and the royalist were no doubt also considering what to do after their failed attempt the previous night. At least they could travel at pace as there was a good road from Winchester to Windsor, picking up the old Roman Road at Silchester, just north of the city, and that would take them directly to their destination. However, it was at the very limit of a carriage's distance in a day. Captain Morris had arranged for a fresh pair of horses halfway, and to reduce the strain further, both Tom and John rode alongside the carriage just leaving the King and Sir Thomas inside.

Tom thanked John again for his loyalty the night before and for such a well-executed plan.

"I told you, just trust me, Colonel," John said.

"At least I have something to tell Cromwell now. I am sure I can persuade him to bring you back into the army as an officer. We certainly need you," Tom replied.

"It is what I yearn for, Tom, more than anything. I am really enjoying being back in the camaraderie of men, with a mission to accomplish. Nothing else seems to get me out of my melancholy."

"Perhaps you need a wife John. Lady Sandys' daughter seemed like a very fair lady."

"I do not think so, Tom. I did walk with her before the death of her father but found the whole encounter difficult. I really do not see the attraction of womenfolk and their small talk, other than my mother and sisters. Oh, and of course Camille, who is delightful. But even they do not understand soldiery and the military. Is this not just great, Tom? The two of us and a bunch of trained and disciplined soldiers on a mission to defend and escort the King to Windsor. There is danger and risk, but also excitement and purpose. Anything can happen, and we need to be prepared for it."

"Of course you are right, but if you found the right woman, there is much joy is sharing a life and having a family."

"Maybe, but I cannot see it at the moment, Tom. I just want to be in a saddle with a sword in my sheath and enjoy the spirit of the army."

By mid-morning they were passing the ruins of Basing House, the former house of the Marquess of Winchester, who had been loyal to the King during the war and endured three sieges by Parliamentary forces over two years. John knew the house well for he had brought the injured Colonel Sandys here after the Battle of Cheriton. The House had been a symbol of Royalist resistance, although the Parliamentary press had made it out as a vipers' nest of Catholics, the Marquis being of that faith. Oliver Cromwell himself, with over eight hundred men and a heavy siege train, finally defeated the Royalists ruthlessly and the house was destroyed in the resulting fire. John told Tom of some of the skirmishes and how he had finally fled with half a dozen men before the final defeat.

The King called out to Colonel Harvey requesting the carriage to stop when he saw the blackened ruins. He got out of the carriage and was clearly taken aback by the devastation.

"Colonel, I have stayed in this house on many occasions. It was one of the few that was large enough in England that it could accommodate my entire Court. It was as sumptuous as Hampton Court and I have many memories of good times here. It is a tragedy to see such destruction. Cromwell is reckless. He is the one who should be brought to account for his actions." The King looked genuinely forlorn. He started to wander around the ruins.

"Your Highness, we need to be making tracks. We have a long journey and we must make Windsor before nightfall."

"Yes Colonel. I understand but it is important for me to understand what has happened to my nation," the King replied and Tom detected a slight watering of his eyes. He was genuinely upset and Tom allowed him to wonder for a while amongst the ruins, accompanied by the cawing of the crows that had made the ruin their home.

The King was climbing back into the carriage when a commotion was heard at the front of the convoy and Captain Morris called for the Colonel. Tom trotted to the front to find one hundred yards further up the road a barricade being created as men pulled together two large logs from either side of the road, and around it there must have been forty men with pikes, muskets and swords. They were being organised into a three-line-formation behind the logs. Some wore turtle-shaped helmets and breastplates, others in just farm hand or labourer clothing.

"Who the hell are they?" Tom asked.

"At least some of them look like former Roundhead soldiers," Captain Morris replied.

"Well let's find out. You and your men come with me," Tom said and then shouted to Captain O'Kelly, "Stay with the King."

The twenty riders pulled up a short distance in front of the line that had formed across the road. The men opposing them had been organised into a recognised formation, men with pikes at the front with their weapons anchored to the ground and the shafts angled towards the approaching horses, whilst behind every two pikes was a musketeer with weapon raised and aimed at the cavalrymen. Their tunics were old and battle weary, colours of blues and red faded to dull greys and browns,

"In the name of Cromwell, clear the way immediately, or else we will run you through," Tom commanded.

A pikeman in the middle of the formation stood up, the band on his arm that of a sergeant.

"We will let you through in exchange for the King. We are going to give that bastard what he deserves. We want to see him dance from a tree and send the tyrant to hell. He needs to pay for the suffering and destruction he has caused to this country."

"And if I do that you will dance the same dance, as Cromwell's orders are to take him to London."

"So the King can be protected by his court and royalist scum?" the man responded.

"What is your name Sergeant?" Tom asked, recognising the need to create some kind of connection with the men opposite.

"Sergeant John Brown, sir," the man replied. He was a well-built man, with a barrel chest, most probably in his mid-thirties with a full beard that was starting to grey.

"Thank you, Sergeant. And you hail from these parts?" Tom asked.

"I do. I have a tavern not far from here, and me and my comrades here all fought for the Parliamentary cause and lost many friends. Then we came home to destruction like this, and without Basing House many have lost their livelihood. We want to see justice."

"I understand and know how you feel, believe me. I fought for the same cause. I was part of God's army from day one at Edgehill. I sang the psalms, and marched to the beat of the drums, wallowed in the mud and guts, a pikeman with no training and barely any armour. I learnt what was worth fighting for, and what was not, and I learnt the importance of discipline and a just cause to drive you through hell. I was promoted to sergeant, then lieutenant, captain and now colonel. And I have fought, won and lost many battles including one which resulted in the same destruction of my home. I led the force to take the Castell which had been my home since I was a child. I was charged with slighting the Castell into a ruin, amidst the devastation of the church and the houses in the village, including my father's. And the friends and comrades I have lost on the way are too great to number, but including my best and childhood friend, Francis Trew, who lies buried at the foot of Edgehill.

"Sergeant, I am not a man of breeding or education, and certainly no aristocrat, yet the King is under my protection. Every time I see the King part of me wants to drive my sabre through his chest. But it is the memory of those battles, whether we won or lost, and the death of fellow Englishmen on both sides – mostly good honest folk leaving behind families to struggle in grief and hardship – that holds me back. I am taking the King to London, to the justice of Parliament and the cause I have fought for. It is critical that the nation sees justice being done, and that the King is tried and answers to the people. It would be an awful miscarriage of justice if he saw an end in an ambush on the road to London. But be assured, if you still want to string him up, it will be at a dire cost, for my men are handpicked for this mission I am leading from the finest in Cromwell's ranks, and very few of you will see another day."

"I say trust in me to deliver the King to Cromwell's justice and go home to your families and then when the time comes, make the trip to London and see the King answer for his crimes against this nation."

John Brown was not expecting this, nor were his men. He looked around at each of them and could see from their faces that Tom's words had resonated and they understood what he said.

"We will let you pass Colonel," the Sergeant said raising his pike.

Tom jumped down from his horse, marched over to the Sergeant and shook his hand.

"You have made the right decision, Sergeant. Justice will prevail," Tom said, and then shook the hands of each and every one of the men lined up across the road.

In no time at all, the trees had been removed and the royal carriage was on its way, with some jeering as it passed the men of Basing, but their arms remained at ease. *The King will have to get used to that, and most probably a lot worse, as we get closer to London*, Tom thought, and he nodded to Sergeant John Brown as he kicked Lightning on to follow the carriage.

Windsor Castell

Tom had not been to Windsor before but had heard about the magnificence and might of the Castell. As they approached the town, it was dark but the silhouette of the Castell walls and the Norman bastion within lived up to his expectations. The main street of the town nestled beneath was quiet, its traders and merchants having closed up hours before. Few would witness the completion of Colonel Harvey's mission, and none would realise its historic importance nor could identify the passenger in the carriage. The two taverns along the road had attracted many of the locals out of the cold of the night with fires and beers, laughter permeating through their walls as the carriage trundled over the cobbled stones, with its weary but ever-alert escort. Inside the carriage the King looked out on to a street he had known well, for Windsor had often been the home to his Court. He would stay at the Castell for months on end, with his family and would have always been received by a jubilant crowd when he returned to the town, with lots of fanfare, but not today. What saddened him most was the memory of his family, his beloved Queen Henrietta and their five children as he recollected many times of joy and happiness spent here, and feared he would never experience them again. He missed his Queen more than he could say. What he would give just for one more moment with her. Her beauty and grace, her kindness and understanding, her smile and laugh, her scent and the touch of her smooth skin. Everything about her, he longed for so much that he had an ache in his stomach.

The guard of the Castell had been expecting the Colonel and his troop, opening the heavy oak gates to receive the guests, but few inside the walls had knowledge of anything more than that a troop of men from Hamptonshire with their Colonel would be staying overnight. Amongst them, Oliver Cromwell knew the significance of this hour and the potential ramifications for the nation. God had delivered the King to him, and the Almighty's hand would guide the next steps, but first he must welcome and play host to the man who had been his arch enemy for so long. He heard the trundling of the carriage and the echo of the horse hooves in the courtyard below his chamber and set out to greet the King. Sir Thomas and the King had already disembarked from the carriage by the time the General arrived downstairs.

"Your Majesty, Sir Thomas, welcome to Windsor. I trust your journey was comfortable and without incident." The General forced a slow unwilling smile.

"Cromwell. Are you my new guardian? I am desperately looking forward to some more appropriate accommodation than I have experienced over the last weeks. I would also dearly love to see my children, Elizabeth and Henry. Please can they be brought to me at the earliest opportunity?"

"Your usual chamber awaits you, Your Majesty, and a hearty dinner is also being prepared. I have already arranged for Princess Elizabeth and young Prince Henry to be brought to you tomorrow."

"Thank you, General. And thank you, Colonel for your service in getting me here. I have also written a letter to Lady Bankes, which I would appreciate it if you could see arrives to her safely." He handed a sealed envelope to Tom.

157

"Your Majesty, it has been a pleasure. John will ensure the safe passage of your letter to his mother," Tom replied, passing the envelope to John. "General, I would also appreciate some time with you to provide a full report once His Majesty is settled."

"Of course, Colonel. Your Majesty, I think you know the way," and the King and General led the way into the inner keep of the castell.

Shortly afterwards, Tom was summoned to see General Oliver Cromwell in the Round Tower. He walked through the middle ward and into the Tower where the General received Tom in the Castell Guardian's room. Sconces on the walls held several candles, their light flickering as Tom closed the oak door behind him. Six-foot Tom was taller than the General, which made Cromwell feel slightly uncomfortable, as he stared at the young man before him, his silver breastplate dusted by the journey, and his hair and beard still matted with sweat from the ride.

"Sit down, Colonel,' Cromwell said to Tom, pointing to a large wooden chair, with a leather back. "Pray, provide me with a report of the journey to Windsor."

Tom recounted all that had happened over the last few days chronologically and with as much detail as was appropriate as Cromwell paced the room.

"You have served your nation well, Colonel. And what of the King's mood?" Cromwell asked, combing his fingers through his long hair as he sat down opposite Tom.

"I did get to know the King and talked to him over dinner and en route. To be honest his mood changes and he is difficult to read. As a boy I hunted boar in Dorsetshire. A trap is set of willow fencing amongst the trees and the dogs drive the boar into it. The boar turns and realises it has no option and so charges at the hunters to its death. Half the time the King is like a boar: his Queen, family, court, privileges and power have been taken away, and he feels like he has nowhere to go, so will come out fighting to whatever fate awaits him, dogmatic in his beliefs and his Divine Right to rule, accountable only to God. Other times he is downhearted and has barely any fight left in him, full of regrets and resigned to whatever London has in store for him. I think he is expecting a trial of some sort and an attempt to remove his crown but how he will respond is unclear to me and may change depending on his mood."

"Interesting," Cromwell said, scratching his reddened nose.

"I do have some empathy for him, which I thought I would never say. But I also want to see some justice for the loss of so many lives."

"Well, we will have to see what God plans for him. Ultimately retribution lies in his hands, and we will be guided by Him."

"General, I do have a request. John Bankes is a trusted friend of mine, who distinguished himself in service of the King during the war as a Captain. I have already told you how he devised and executed a plan to foil the attempt to seize the King in Winchester. He is first and foremost a soldier, and dedicated to the protection of this nation, with little interest in the politics beneath. I know it is prohibited to recruit Royalist officers, but I would like to make the case for an exception to be made."

"I will consider your request and discuss it with Lord Fairfax. We have to be careful not to create a precedent, but you have made a strong case, Colonel. I assume you will return to Dorsetshire now, but in January I would like you and at least two hundred men to return to London to reinforce the capital. I will be bringing in similar numbers from Buckinghamshire, Hertfordshire, Kent and Essex. There is a risk of trouble and we need to safeguard the city. It will make a change from chasing people who avoid paying the excise, which is of course important as it pays our wages, but I dare say not the most exciting mission. I will write to you with more detailed instructions before the end of the month."

"Of course, Sir. I assume you are expecting a trial of the King in the new year then?"

"We will see what God brings us in the new year, Colonel, but we must be prepared," Cromwell replied, but as Tom opened the door to leave, a familiar face greeted him. It was Harry Coke, the son of the previous owner of Corffe Castell, Sir John Coke, a man of great honour and virtue, but his son was his nemesis and had ransacked Corffe during the Castell's siege, causing death and destruction, from which the community was still suffering. The two men stood opposite one another, frozen in a state of recognition with hatred fired in both their eyes. Harry Coke detested everything and everyone from Corffe. He had been humiliated as a young man by the villagers and the place was a reminder of his inability to live up to his father's expectations as a young man. The failure of the siege of Corffe after seven months under his command had been a tarnish on his standing amongst Parliamentarians ever since. And the siege had ended a few weeks after he was removed from that command. Tom Harvey, the man standing a head taller than him in that doorway, played on all his insecurities in so many ways, not least because it was his heroics that ended the Castell's siege. Tom's last encounter with the Colonel was as a mere Lieutenant having just seen what he had done to his home village, and the suffering to his stepmother and sister, as the man lost his command. Despite his rank he had told the Colonel what he had thought of him then, and almost drove a sabre through his chest, something he had often regretted ever since. Hatred filled the doorway from both sides.

"Ah, Colonel Coke, do you know Colonel Harvey, perhaps from your days at Corffe?" Cromwell said.

"A Colonel now? I believe we have been acquainted, General," Coke replied.

"Good, then Colonel Coke, Colonel Harvey has requested that a former Royalist captain – I believe Bankes is his name – be appointed a Captain in the army. On all accounts he has demonstrated loyalty to our cause, and indeed helped to ensure the King came to Windsor in safe custody. What are your views?"

Coke winced inwardly whenever the name Corffe was mentioned but the name Bankes topped it up with fury and he had to do everything he could not to show his anger.

"Once a Royalist always a Royalist, General. I think it was a mistake to risk his involvement in bringing the King to Windsor and on no account should he be trusted to serve in the army." Coke's voice had risen but he knew he was getting one up on Harvey which was helping to quell his rage.

"You obviously feel strongly about it, Colonel Coke."

"And of course so do I, General. Is the success of the New Model army not built on a foundation of recognising and promoting ability, not prejudice or position?"

"This is true. I will consider the matter further and discuss with Lord Fairfax as I said I would and let you know, Colonel Harvey. Have a good evening."

Tom's morose face assumed a look of cold contempt for Coke. Tom wanted to say more but thankfully held his peace for he was not sure if he could control what he would have said about Coke—or indeed do to him, so he turned and left the two men to their discussion, no doubt with Coke spitting more venom on the prospect of John Bankes becoming a captain again.

Chapter Ten

Christmas, Contriving and Court

23 December 1648, Windsor Castell

The King had invited Lady Bankes to Windsor, and her son John had accompanied her and his younger siblings on the journey as a stop prior to spending Christmas with the rest of the family at Alice's house in London. Much of the prospect of the joy of the festive season had been put under a vail of Puritan prohibition but like many families they were determined to celebrate behind closed doors. They had arrived in Windsor the day before and the children were delighted to be staying in a castell. The older ones recalled their childhood memories of Corffe Castell and were in no time at all playing games on the ramparts, although they were severely restricted on where they could play. The Castell had been turned into a jail stronghold, with guards everywhere, male residents with known Royalist tendencies having been turned out and with them much of the vibrancy of the place. It was only through Colonel Harvey's advocacy that they were allowed to stay.

Lady Bankes's audience with the King had been arranged for midmorning and she arrived to find another woman waiting to be received in the anteroom to the King's chamber. She was a little younger than Mary for she could not see any signs of grey in her light brown hair styled with similar ringlets; the beauty in her face was emphasised by rouge on her lips, and she wore a silk navy blue dress, as decorative and stylish as one would dare in Puritan circles. She was introduced by the King's valet as Lady Anne Fairfax, somebody whose husband Lady Bankes knew by reputation. Lord Thomas Fairfax was Commander-in-Chief of the New Model army, having built a reputation in the civil war battles in the north of England over the last three years. He had led the army to the decisive victory at Naseby, the turning point in the first war, and subsequent victories. Given her husband's reputation, Lady Bankes was surprised to find her seeing the King. Both ladies introduced themselves, Lady Bankes fanning herself from a hot flush, but before they could say anything else to each other the valet opened the door of the chamber, announced the two waiting guests to the King and led them in.

"Ladies, such a joy to see you both, I trust you have been acquainted?" The King welcomed his guests, standing up from an ornate mahogany chair and stepping forward across the decorative rug on the floor, as the ladies entered the room together and both curtsied in unison.

"Your Majesty. Yes, we have been introduced but we do not know one another," Lady Fairfax replied, in an authoritative tone. She certainly was not intimidated by her audience with the King.

"Please ladies, do take a seat and make yourself comfortable. Would you like a drink? I wanted to see you both together which you may find surprising, but I have my reasons, which will become apparent with time."

The King seemed to be in a good mood, even bubbling with a little excitement, and very different from when Lady Bankes has seen him at Hurst Castell.

"Thank you for your invitation, Your Majesty. My children love the Castell, and I can see you are in much more appropriate surroundings than our last meeting," Lady Bankes said, continuing to fan herself as she looked around at the splendour of the chamber, a room adorned with French-style furniture, royal portraits and tapestries. A large arch-shaped clock, its glass face set in the finest walnut case beneath which were the most intricate of workings partially hidden by two gilded angelic figures, stood on a cabinet on the far wall next to an armillary sphere of the world. Behind the King the embers were crying out for attention.

"Yes indeed, a place fit for a King at last, but it is a travesty what the Roundheads have done to the Castell whilst occupying it. Have you seen St George's Chapel? But most importantly I am with my two children and have had a wonderful few days with them Lady Bankes. Your children should meet them later; I am sure they will have lots of fun together. I have been subject to a couple of inquisitions by Parliamentarians including Lady Fairfax's husband on one occasion, but I am limited on numbers of people I can see. There is no prospect of holding court that is for sure, but apparently I am allowed to have audiences with wives of respected people, and so I am delighted to see you both," the King said, pacing up and down the floor in front of his two guests, both sat next to each other on a chaise longue. The King was animated and restless, dressed in a long silk turquoise jacket and matching fabric footwear, with white hose. What was all this about and what did he have on his mind, Lady Bankes wondered.

"So ladies, there is lots I would like to talk to you about but top on my list is love."

"Love?" Lady Fairfax said.

"I am afraid I am past that at my stage of life, Your Majesty," Mary added jokingly.

"One is never too old to love, my Lady. But it is certainly a subject that has been neglected over the last few years. It involves a man who is very dear to me, George Villiers. His father was a close friend of mine, the Duke of Buckingham, but he was murdered twenty years ago, leaving George, my godson, a baby. I brought him into my court with his younger brother and he was treated on a par with my own children. He is now a grown man of good temperament and indeed a poet, but he had also supported my cause in arms throughout the conflicts. The initial battles he served under Prince Rupert, although more as an observer for he was still very young. But during the summer uprising he was still fighting in my name at Surbitan and St Neotts."

"You mean he was fighting against my husband?"

"Yes Lady; indeed, it is said that he held off five Roundheads singlehandedly at the battle of Surbiton before fleeing to the Netherlands. He has just written to me and he is now with my eldest son, Prince Charles, which is a joy to my heart."

"Why are you telling this to me, Your Majesty? He is an enemy of my husband," Lady Fairfax asked.

"Ah but not your daughter," the King replied.

"My daughter, Mary? What has she got to do with it?"

"At the start of the summer, he became acquainted with Mary and found her more than agreeable. They have seen each other several times and have written to each other enthusiastically."

"She has not told me of this, Your Majesty," Lady Fairfax replied.

"Perhaps she is worried about what your husband would say and indeed his reputation," the King replied, "On these types of matters, my good Queen Henrietta Maria would have provided good counsel, but alas she is in her brother's court, and so I thought I would invite Lady Bankes to help on this matter."

"What has she got to do with it, Sire?"

"Nothing directly, but I do know that she has a number of daughters and has been remarkably successful at finding good suits for them. Is that not the case, Lady Bankes?"

"Well certainly two are very happily married but I am still working on two others currently,' she replied, raising an eyebrow.

"Well, of course I do not know your daughter, Lady Fairfax, but I do know that George has many admirers amongst the ladies of my former court and frankly he could have chosen his pick from the most beautiful and eligible women of the realm, not to mention courts across Europe. But he is head over heels in love with your daughter. What I do know is that love is the best foundation for marriage and if the two subjects do love one another and there are no other reasons to object then why should it not be encouraged?"

"I would want my daughter to marry for love, but I am not sure my husband would support it, not that he would want to upset Mary, but because of the political sensitivities of such a union."

"That is why I invited you both here as I suspected Lord Fairfax would be less inclined. My Queen Henrietta Maria has a phrase, 'what a woman wants, God wants.' I am sure, ladies, that if you both support this union, then you will have means to bring Lord Fairfax around. If he feels that I have anything to do with it then I would suggest the idea would be a dead duck. I do not know what fate awaits me, but whatever it is I will be happier knowing I have helped, through your good services, to make my godson happy."

"I hope I can help you on this occasion, Sire. It was much to my regret that I could not help you with your Christmas message when we were in Hurst Castle but as you would have appreciated a mother cannot put her children at risk."

"Of course, I understand, and I should not have asked," the King said with a nod.

Lady Fairfax led Lady Bankes out and they made their way along a corridor lit by candles. They heard footsteps ahead, and as they turned a corner a well-known face confronted them with its red nose and dry skin, wearing a high-crowned, broad-brimmed black hat of the Puritan style, and a grey tunic, simple but the quality of the cloth suggested status and wealth. It was Oliver Cromwell.

Lady Fairfax introduced Lady Bankes to the General.

"I know you by reputation, my Lady. You showed more fortitude than most of the Royalist leadership. Colonel Coke still has sweats when anyone mentions your name. Down somewhere in Dorsetshire was it not?"

"Yes, that is correct. I also believe you knew my husband, Sir John, who spoke highly of you before the war."

"Sir John was a man respected by all who dealt with him, my Lady. I am sorry to hear of your loss and I am sure he is reunited with the Lord. What brings you to Windsor?"

"I am on my way to London to see my family. I have daughters to find husbands for, and they are in short supply with the war, aren't they Lady Fairfax?"

"Fortunately I only have one to find a husband for and a number of suitors."

"Sir John Borlase is married to one of your daughters I believe Lady Bankes—a fine match."

"Yes, and another has just married Sir Robert Jenkinson. But I have two more of marrying age, Elizabeth and Jane. Both are fair and of good character but Elizabeth is too much like me for her own good. She is strong-willed and I will struggle to find a husband who will be able to cope with her character. Jane is more mellow and will be an easier match."

"Indeed, Lady Bankes. I am looking for a match for my son, Richard. He lacks my strength and takes after his mother, who has many godly qualities. He is of very good character but I believe needs a stronger wife to make up for some of his own weaknesses. Perhaps we should arrange for Elizabeth and my Richard to meet?"

"You would contemplate a marriage to a Royalist?"

"The Lord guides me to recognise the diversity of strength in people and bringing them together with others of different capability, and that has included people across many different divides. It strikes me that you may be similarly guided Lady Bankes.— Perhaps it is a sign from the Almighty that we meet in this corridor at a time when we are both seeking suitors for our   offspring."

"Well thank you for the compliment, General, and a Royalist one at that. Queen Eleanor is an inspiration to all women. Elizabeth would be delighted to make an acquaintance with Richard Cromwell and if they are suited I would be more than happy to foster the relationship between our families."

The two ladies said farewell to the General and then found a room to develop a plan for both their daughters. The son of a General and a Duke were certainly catches of unparalleled status for their daughters. Lady Fairfax confessed that she had known that there was something that her daughter had been hiding, ever since the summer. She sensed it, but all her questions and investigations had revealed nothing. She needed to find out what her feelings were for the Duke, and if she did love him, then she would support her, but tackling her husband was another thing.

"I have not met your husband, but perhaps I could help you if I had the opportunity. The King is right, I do enjoy matchmaking, but it is much more difficult at the current time. Why do you not both join us for dinner over the Christmas period, so I can meet your husband?"

"That would be a wonderful idea, thank you, Lady Bankes."

Lady Bankes realised that if she befriended Lord and Lady Fairfax, that would help her prospects of Elizabeth being considered an appropriate suitor for Richard Cromwell.

25 December, Whitehall

Puritans saw Christmas as an extravagant festival that threatened Christian beliefs and encouraged immoral activities and in 1645 they drove through a decree that made it clear that Christmas and other festival days were not to be celebrated but spent in reverent contemplation of their religious meaning. And so after a simple service and time for prayer, the core of the radical wing of Parliamentarians were still busy on Christmas day drafting the ordinance which would set up the trial of the King. The challenge was to give legality to a court that would try the sovereign for starting the war and treason, when the definition of treason was an offence against the sovereign. The debates and discussions continued to go around in circles, and the numbers of members of Parliament continued to reduce as more voted with their feet rather than be part of the group that was determined to bring the King to trial. The challenge was to find the common ground even within that group, for it reflected a wide range of views and opinions, some wanting to see the end of the King for religious reasons, fearing his sympathies with popism and the threat of the Irish Catholics, whilst others were more nationalistic, for the King had raised Scottish armies and requested French forces against the English. There were others who just saw him as a bad King, a tyrant that needed to have his crown removed, recalling before the war the original Grand Remonstrance, a list of over two hundred grievances Parliament had with the King, a number that would be tenfold now. Others just saw him as the enemy of the civil war who was responsible for the death of so many. Within all of these groups there were those who saw the opportunity for personal gain and changed their views according to how they saw events turning out. The discussions on principles and the detail of words and their meaning continued throughout the day, compromises were made, and lines of negotiation redrawn. To keep the frustration of the more radical members at bay a more straightforward edict was passed towards the end of the afternoon which reduced further the King's estates, servants and privileges. Another spear into the monarch's side, as the trap around him became tighter. And finally, in the late evening, a form of words was agreed for the legal basis of a trial for the King. More members had been lost along the way, but the Rump Parliament was determined to get what it wanted, and so the scene was set.

25 December 1648, Sir John and Alice Borlase's house – the evening

The dining room was alive with conversation and merriment as the Borlase guests enjoyed the festivities of the season. Parliament had banned Christmas church services and open festivities, citing the catholic and pagan roots of the occasion, but the Borlase and Bankes families, like most others across the land, were even more determined to celebrate the occasion behind the closed doors of their homes. In the dining room the large mahogany table bearing three sets of candles hosted seventeen guests and an array of dishes with every vegetable one could think of, and on a side table the remains of a goose. Sir John's coachman was the waiter for the night and would take food and dishes to and from the room, for the housemaids to ferry back to the kitchen, whilst he ensured glasses were kept topped up with the finest wine and brandy. The fire had a Purbeck stone surround, something Alice had insisted upon when they first moved to the house, with decorative tiles within, reflecting the flames that licked the two large logs that were laid across the hearth.

At one end of the table was Ralph Bankes, Mary's second eldest son, dressed in his finest, befitting of a lawyer with a growing reputation. 'A chip off the old block' many commented who had known Sir John and his legal mind. Ralph had his mother's blue eyes and red hair, but similar facial features and mannerisms as his father, and certainly his aptitude for law. He was sitting between Lord Fairfax, with his dark hair and swarthy complexion that earned him the nickname 'Black Tom', and his mother, who was elegantly dressed in a new red silk dress, a present from her daughter who wanted to ensure that she was living up to her status level. She in turn was sitting next to Lady Fairfax, her dress less lavish and in line with her Presbyterian values but the midnight-blue fabric was of equally high quality. The invitation to dinner and the places around the table were the first steps in the two ladies' plan to rise to the challenge the King had presented to them at Windsor. Lady Fairfax had confronted her daughter Mary in the previous days and had discovered that she had met George Villiers, the Duke of Buckingham, whilst staying at Clyveden House. She had told her mother that had been charmed by him after nursing him to recovery, before he set off again to battle at St Neots, near Cambridge, which resulted in another Royalist defeat. He had been forced to flee the country. They had been writing to each other ever since, and Mary assured her mother that she had indeed given her heart to him. Lady Fairfax first suspected that the relationship was just a romantic dream featuring the dashing cavalier in a Romeo and Juliet play, but her daughter shared the letters and she could see that she was truly in love with this man. She was pleased for her daughter, for she had always said that she would want her to marry for love and she had been worried about finding a suitor before she was too old, but she had fallen for an extremely challenging match.

How would she convince her husband of the merits of it? Tonight the plan was just to plant a seed of an idea, one that would become his own, and to plant it she had the formidable help of Lady Bankes, who loved to rise to such a challenge, and was already in full flow.

"Lord Fairfax, you may see me as a Royalist, and it is true that I stood up for the King when my home was attacked. But the nation has to rebuild and move on. The country needs leaders who can bridge both sides, surely?'

"My Lady, you are right, we do need to reconcile differences and rebuild." The General's expression certainly looked sincere as his glass was topped up.

"If you consider how the wars across Europe were settled it has often been through marriage. Indeed, the King and his father, with the support of Parliament, ensured that the royal family were married to both Protestant and Catholic monarchs across the continent and that helped avoid the prospect of England entering into a war with the French or indeed the Spanish," Mary continued, Lord Fairfax was nodding, surprised by such a such a political conversation with a woman.

"But it is easier said than done," she continued. "You will see my own family around the table is trying to build the bridges: Alice married to Sir John, and Mary married Sir Robert."

"Yes, I can see that, Lady Bankes."

"Would you be happy for your daughter to marry a Royalist, Lord Fairfax?"

"Well, my Lady, I have never considered such a thing."

"What about you, Lady Fairfax?"

"I would hope she would marry for love, not politics, but if she did love a Royalist I would not be against it," she replied.

"Really, my dear? But I agree. Mary's happiness should be the primary consideration."

At the other end of the table sat John Bankes, Captain Morris, Alice Borlase, John's sister, and two close family friends, Charlotte Coke and Dr John Coke, who were the siblings of the dreaded Colonel Coke, but both could not be more opposite in character. The group were chatting away, with much laughter. John had truly left his melancholy behind in Dorsetshire. The mission to bring the King to London had been the catalyst, but his friendship with Captain Morris was now the lifting force. He just seemed a natural companion, somebody who understood him and who was so easy and enjoyable to be with. Being with someone who understood military life was as close to be part of it as he could hope for. John Coke was describing the outfit and protection he had to wear when he had to visit patients in Southwark, the area of London on the south side of London Bridge that was closed to the rest of the population because of another outbreak of plague. He described the long robe, coated in beeswax, but what made his listeners laugh was him describing the beaked mask he wore, as if he were a heron.

"Are birds immune from plague, Doctor? Is that why you dress in this way?" Captain Morris asked.

"There is some medical science to the dress. The beak is stuffed with herbs so I do not inhale the pestilence in the air."

"I guess your dress is no stranger than the turtle heads of the foot soldiers, and you are just fighting a different war. We pray for your victory and that the plague can be contained," the Captain continued.

"Maybe the Royalist armies would have been more successful if we had worn animal costumes," John Bankes said, resulting in laughter at that end of the table.

"I am so proud of my brother. There is nothing he would not do for people in need, whether the poor in the city or those inflicted by the terrible plague" Charlotte added, as the laughter died down, making her brother blush.

In the middle of the table was Sir John Borlase, Tom and Camille Harvey, Elizabeth and Jane Bankes, John Bingham, and the recently married Sir Robert and Lady Mary Tomkinson, the Bankeses' second-eldest daughter. The conversation ranged from London society topics to politics, and obviously the fate of the King. John Bingham had witnessed the purge of Parliament and continued his representation. He confirmed that Parliament was losing patience with the King and that it was hardening its position. In contrast, Sir John had felt alienated by the radicals and had refused to attend any sessions after the purge in protest at the treatment of the members who had been excluded or arrested. A little tension between the two men could be detected across the table, whilst Sir Robert, barely twenty years of age, aspired to become a member of Parliament and was fascinated by everything that was going on.

"So what does that mean for the King? Will they try to depose him some way and make one of his sons the
king—no doubt young Edward who has not be tainted by the war and whom they can manipulate whilst he is young?" Sir Robert asked, seeing both men as champions of his aspiration.

"You are very astute, Sir Robert. That is an avenue that is certainly being considered. But the challenge is on what grounds can you depose a monarch, one appointed by God. There is no precedent for it," John Bingham replied.

"There is no precedent for anything before the first time," Sir Robert pointed out.

"Of course, but when it comes to something so fundamental as the crown of the country it is important to act with respect to all customs and tradition, recognising that the foundation of this country is a belief in its monarch. God has provided us with strong and weak monarchs, good and bad. If the people could overthrow them on a whim and select a more favourable one in the same bloodline, or worse, of non-royal blood, then where would we be? The symbolism of the monarch is all around us, on our buildings, on our coins, in our artwork, and from the day he is anointed with God's holy water to the day he dies. He is the head of our Protestant faith as well as our armed forces; he approves our taxes and our laws. There is a lot at stake," Sir John replied.

Tom Harvey joined the conversation.

"Sir John, that is all true, but I have also spent much of this month with the King. I was originally of the view that he should be brought to justice as a traitor. I still believe he has a case to answer and I would like to see him face the questioning of the court. However, I now appreciate the King is just a human, whether appointed by God or not. He has faults like the rest of us and admits that he has made mistakes. Who of us is perfect? But who else has so much resting on their shoulders, and with nobody really to share that with. I wonder whether a mere mortal should have such responsibility especially as the King himself admits that he had very little preparation by his father before taking on the role and indeed no inclination to be King at the outset. It is only a twist of fate that we have Charles as our monarch. Is this not the time that both sides recognise this, and craft a new agreement, a Magna Carta version two, which shares more of that responsibility with Parliament for the well-being of both the monarch and the nation?"

"Tom, you always were a radical, but those views are sounding much more mainstream now. Matters I am sure are intensifying and reaching a time when resolution in some format must happen. Let's see what the new year will bring," John Bingham replied.

"But what will be the charge if there is a trial? If it is for treason, then the punishment is death." Ralph Bankes chimed in from the far end of the table.

"Ralph, that is the very reason why I and so many representatives are excluded from Parliament. Like Tom says, there are many of us who would want to see the King answer for what he has done to the country, but far fewer, myself included, who could stomach the execution of the King," Sir John replied forcefully.

"And equally many who believe the King a tyrant, who has recently called the Scots to arms against this nation and could do the same with France. Too many people have died because of his actions, and we need to see justice and an end to this tyranny," John Bingham interjected, with a raised voice, momentarily stopping conversation across the table.

"I very much doubt that the King will get justice with a Rump Parliament selected to execute the King, Mister Bingham," Sir John declared.

"Many years ago God taught me a lesson about justice. As a magistrate I thought a boy from Corffe was guilty of stealing a horse and sought to hang him for the crime. He was a friend of Tom's and yes he had taken the horse but there were extenuating circumstances that I was blinded to. Fortunately for the boy, your father-in-law, Sir John Bankes intervened, a man who believed passionately in justice and God used him to show me the error of my ways. I had been blinded by self-interest rather than my duty to uphold justice. That is why, Sir John, I have remained in Parliament. I recognise that there are forces at play which may try to flaunt the laws that we have to protect the people of our nation, and to me that must include the King. I believe he has a case to answer, but it is essential that the nation sees justice being done. He must be given the opportunity to answer the charges against him and make his case."

"I respect your position, Mr Bingham, and pray that you are able to influence from the inside the road to justice, but I fear that the writing is already on the wall," Sir John replied.

Back at the other end of the table, Lady Bankes had been telling the Fairfax's about their life in Dorsetshire, ever since the slighting of Corffe Castell.

"How do you cope with no real home of your own? You have lost so much Mary," Lady Fairfax enquired.

"You just get on with it," Lady Bankes replied.

"You need a new house I think. A house for the family to recognise as the Bankeses' house," he suggested.

"I agree, Lord Fairfax; it has been on my mind for some months. Once I have established my career in London, I would like, with mother's permission, to build such a house in memory of my father, Sir John Bankes," Ralph said.

"What a wonderful idea, Ralph, at Kingston Lacey rather than Corffe," Lady Bankes replied.

"Yes, we could make a wonderful garden, and we could use stone from Purbeck," Ralph replied.

"Plans for a new future, new homes and new relationships, reconciliation with the past and rebuilding our nation. Let's drink to that!" Lord Fairfax raised his glass and the other guests followed.

The men retired from the table for brandy at the far end of the room, and whilst they were away Lady Bankes and Lady Fairfax agreed that they had sowed a seed with Lord Fairfax, but they had a long way to go before it started to grow into a proposal that he would support, especially given the notoriety of the Duke of Buckingham.

At the other end of the room, Colonel Harvey was talking to Lord Fairfax about his journey with the King to London and asked him what he thought would happen to the King.

"They are planning a trial that is for sure, but I still cannot believe it will happen. I understand that they are still struggling to agree on what charge he should be tried," Lord Fairfax said.

John wanted to continue to explore this subject, but then caught John Bankes' eye and called him over, introducing him to the General and explaining how he had foiled the attempted abduction of the King in Winchester.

"Ah, John then you must be the Royalist captain that General Cromwell and Colonel Coke mentioned to me. You want to join our army, is that correct?" Lord Fairfax asked.

"My passion has always been the army, and I am very eager to serve my nation, Sir," he replied.

"I understand. It is a difficult one, and I am worried about setting a precedent. Colonel Coke is certainly adamant that such appointments should not happen," Lord Fairfax responded.

"Colonel Coke has a personal vendetta against the Bankes family and indeed anybody from Corffe, including myself, Lord, and so please be wary of his counsel," Tom interjected.

"Well, I still need to be convinced, but I will think on it some more. However, we do have a lot on our plate at the moment and I am not minded to make a quick decision, Colonel."

The dinner came to an end, and the guests started to leave, Captain Morris amongst them. John Bankes said that he would join the Captain for a walk as he was in need of some air. The two men set off down the Strand, this lavish part of the new city still played host to carriages returning the wealthy from Christmas gatherings and a few drunks singing merrily and making a stand against the Puritan festive ban. As they got to the magnificent Somerset House, there seemed to be a commotion ahead which they decided to avoid and veered off down towards the Thames. The river was more tranquil. In normal times, there would have been many taxi boats ferrying folk to and from Southwark, but the plague south of the river had been contained by restricting any passage either by bridge or taxi boat. London Bridge in the distance was a dark silhouette devoid of life. There were still a few boats travelling up and down stream, but there was a bracing breeze on the water which was another deterrent to travel. John and Arthur settled on a stone bench and watched the far side of the river gradually put itself to sleep, as candles were snuffed out behind windows.

"Lord Fairfax was quite dismissive about me joining the army when Tom pressed him," John said breaking the silence.

"I am sure he will come around, John."

"I honestly do not know what I will do if he says no. The army was, *is*, everything to me. I really enjoyed escorting the King to London, with you and the others. It was like old times, and I cannot face going back to Dorsetshire to deal with estate matters. Before that mission, I was seriously thinking about ending it, Arthur."

"What do you mean?"

"Ending it, ending my life. I just want the last month to continue and be in the ranks of men with a mission. If I am on my own in Dorsetshire, I am just haunted by the battles of the past, the death of comrades and friends. It sounds crazy, but I need the army to save me from that past. Without the army, John Bankes is nobody, nothing but a melancholic drunk plagued by nightmares, an unwanted embarrassment to everyone."

"John, John, John. You must not talk this way. It breaks my heart," Arthur said, looking into John's eyes, and putting and arm over John's shoulder. He could see that John's eyes were watery, and knew it was not just the wind.

"My world has changed since meeting you, John. I really enjoyed every moment of the last month, not because of the Royal mission, but because I was sharing it with you. I will do everything in my power to get you the commission you deserve. My father has some influential friends and I will write to him. But Colonel Harvey is a man who is tenacious and between him and your family I am sure Fairfax and Cromwell will come around. Your mother seems like a woman who gets what she wants. I have prayed for you to be granted this wish every night." Arthur gave John a gentle kiss on the forehead.

"Thank you," John said, giving his friend a warm smile.

"John, why don't you stay with me tonight? My family house is just around the corner. It is empty and has a guest room made up."

The next morning the bustle of the city aroused John as the winter sun announced a new day. He had overslept but found himself in the arms of Captain Morris in his bed. It took him a few moments to gather his thoughts and realise how he had arrived there, but he soon became conscious of an inner warmth, a feeling of contentment and joy, a sense of finding himself whilst at the same time discovering his true feelings for Arthur Morris. He was in love with another man. How could this be? But the more he thought about it the warmer the inner contentment glowed. Snippets of the night

176

before returned to him, and he soaked up the pleasure of each memory. What would this mean to his life and his future he did not know but for now he would just enjoy the moment.

That joy was soon disrupted with a loud battering on the door below, which awoke Arthur with a jolt.

"Morning John," he said with a smile. More knocking and some shouts of 'Open up'.

"That does not sound good," Captain Morris said getting up and putting on his shift then going to the window and leaning out to find out what the clamour was all about.

"What do you want? You had better have good cause for this racket. I will be down in a moment."

He told John to get up and go into the guest room.

Captain Morris unbolted the door and three constables barged in and started searching the house, followed by their Sergeant.

"What is this, Sergeant? I demand an explanation."

"We are under orders from Colonel Coke to arrest you and a Mister John Bankes for crimes under the Buggery Act."

"The other one is in here, Sarge," one of the constables shouted from the top of the stairs.

"This is an outrage, Sergeant."

"You can tell that to the Magistrate. Our orders are to take you to court for the early morning hearings. We can take you as you are, or you can get dressed without any more dissent."

26th December 1648, The Sessions Court, the Old Bailey

The court was located in a street about a hundred yards northwest of St Paul's Cathedral, just outside the western wall and near the infamous Newgate Prison, which John and Arthur were grateful that they had avoided, being escorted straight into a waiting room for the sessions. It was a dark room, with just one barred window, stuffy and full of people awaiting their hearing, perhaps nearly twenty men and three women. From their dress it was clear that they reflected the social strata of London: two other gentlemen, a merchant, a couple of apprentices, with labourers and the poor making up the majority, all looking very apprehensive and several looking the worse for wear from too much drink. The only door was guarded by two constables and a further four were positioned in each corner. The smell of alcohol and body odour intensified the oppression of the air.

"How did we end up in this hellhole?" Arthur whispered to John.

"I am sorry. I am sure it is Coke's doing. He has a vendetta against my family."

And as he finished the sentence, the very same Colonel Coke walked in with the Sergeant.

"What a pleasant festive surprise; you have been busy, Sergeant."

He walked over to the two gentlemen who were closest to the door. They talked in hushed voices, and the gentlemen took some coins out of their money pouches and then were escorted out of the room. Coke looked around and caught the eye of John.

"John Bankes, I am surprised to find you here. What would your father say?"

"I hardly think you are surprised when you have obviously set us up in the first case, Coke."

"Address me as Colonel. And who is your friend?"

"I am Captain Arthur Morris, Colonel. And this must be some mistake. Please can you sort this out and release us at once."

"That is for the Magistrate to decide. But this situation is hardly going to help John's request for an officership is it? Now I may be able to get you out but my constables have expenses that need to be covered. A half-guinea contribution from you both would help to meet those expenses."

John and Arthur looked at each other in disgust.

"Bribery. Blatant bribery. We have nothing to hide, Colonel. We are happy to face the Magistrate and make our case," Captain Morris replied.

"As you wish, but there will then be a record, whether you are successful or not. Let me give you the dignity of going in first. I understand buggery is the charge. Nothing like a spicy case to start proceedings."

The courtroom was a much larger room, with two huge windows at one end, in between which was positioned the judicial bench with three imposing throne-like chairs. The room was a breath of fresh air compared with the anteroom, with just four constables positioned around it, and a few other people sorting out papers in the middle. John and Arthur were led to the bar on one side, accompanied by two constables. As they stood there, they realised that light was being reflected on to them from the window by a mirror above, making them very much the focus of the proceedings.

"All rise," shouted one of the officials, and in came a man in his forties, in a black gown, looking like he may have had a rough night, his head bowed down as he settled down in the middle chair. He took a deep breath and looked up at the court room.

"Court in session!" The judge banged his gavel. "This is an initial hearing to determine if there are cases to be answered before imprisonment and a full hearing once all the evidence is collected. Depending on the crime this may involve a jury. What have you dragged in today, Colonel Coke?"

"Your Lordship, the first case is one of buggery."

"Buggery. Well that is a serious offence. This is a crime punishable by death. Who are the accused?"

"A Mister John Bankes and a Captain Arthur Morris."

The judge eyed up the accused.

"John Bankes. Are you the son of Sir John Bankes, former Chief Justice and General Attorney?"

"That is correct, Sir."

"There are not many finer legal minds and men more committed to justice that this nation has known. He would turn in his grave to find you here today."

"I believe he would turn in his grave to know the manner in which I have been dragged into this court, Sir."

"That is for me to find out, Mister Bankes."

"Sir John Bankes was a Royalist and convicted of treason, my Lord," Coke added.

"I believe he may have been accused of such a crime and a warrant issued for his arrest, but he was not convicted. Innocent until proven guilty, Colonel. I would have thought you would know that given your father was also one of the finest legal minds that this country has known."

The Colonel could feel the shadow of his father again, and he stared at the Judge, anger inside growing but he gritted his teeth and refrained from responding.

"And Captain Morris. Who is your commanding officer?"

"Colonel Harvey, Sir."

"If there is substantive evidence against you, Captain, I will refer this matter to Colonel Harvey. Buggery is a military as well as civil offence, and as a serving officer you should face that jurisdiction."

"I understand, Sir."

"Well Colonel, what is the evidence against these men?"

"I will call Mr Derry as a witness."

A small scruffy man with rat-like facial features entered the room and was escorted to the witness box, opposite the two accused.

"Mr Derry, this hearing is just to determine if there is any evidence against the accused. I will not be asking you to take an oath but I would expect you to be saying exactly what you say today under oath at the full hearing. Failure to do so will be treated as you acting in contempt of court. Do you understand?"

"I believe so, my Lord. I will just tell you what I saw." He had a blend of an Irish and London dialect.

"Exactly, nothing more and nothing less. Please go ahead, Mr Derry."

"Wellz, I saw those two gentlemen," as he pointed to the accused, "leaving a house just off the Strand about an hour before midnight, and I followed them up to Somerset House, and then down to the River."

"Why were you following them?" the Judge asked.

"Colonel Coke asked me to. He pays me to find people who are law breakers."

"To be clear, he asked you to specifically follow these two men?"

"Well, anybody coming out of that house."

"I had intelligence that there were festivities planned at the house of Sir John Borlase last night, my Lord," Coke interjected.

"Thank you, Colonel. Please carry on, Mister Derry."

"Well by the river the two men stopped, and they were talking. I was too far away to hear what they were saying. They then sat down on a bench and continued talking. Then one of them put his arm around the other, and they looked, shall we say, intimate. They then got up and I followed them to the house just off the Fleet. I sat and watched. Both men went inside and only one room upstairs was used, as I could see only one with lights in it. This light was shortly extinguished and I reported back to the Colonel first thing. He sent me with the Sergeant and constables to the house this morning."

"What did you find there?"

"They took some time to open the door. The man on the left came down in his shift. We found the man on the right still in bed."

"Thank you, Mr Derry. If you would remain with us in case I have any further questions. I would just like to ask the accused to respond. Gentlemen, would you like to tell the court what happened last night?"

"Mister Bankes and I had been serving together on an important mission for the army, under the command of Colonel Harvey. There was a family dinner at Sir John Borlase's house last night; he is Mister Bankes' brother-in-law. I and others were invited, including General Fairfax, and Colonel Harvey."

"A celebration of the success of the mission, Captain?"

"You could say so, Your Lordship. Mister Bankes has several brothers and sisters who were staying over that night and so I made the offer for him to stay at my family house. We left together. There was a disturbance of some sort on the Strand so we took a diversion down to the River. Mister Bankes had been a Captain is the Royalist forces and was hoping to join the army as a commissioned officer as reward for the success of the mission. But General Fairfax had suggested that this was unlikely. This upset Mister Bankes, and yes, I put my arm around him to console him, as any comrade would do. We went to my family house. I slept in the front room, reading with a candle before I slept, apparently observed by Mr Derry. John was in the back room, where he was found this morning."

"Captain, thank you. That is very clear. Colonel, unless you have any further evidence, I can see no case to answer here. The case is dismissed."

Captain Morris House, off the Fleet, London

Arthur took John back to his house. The two men were immersed in their own thoughts oblivious to the city's vibrancy and activity, hardly saying a word as they walked. They regularly glanced back over their shoulders, the thought of having been followed overshadowing them. John now realised the lengths Coke would go to in his goal to destroy his family's reputation as well as financial standing. But so much had happened to him in just the last twelve hours his head was still spinning, and he was uncertain what to think or his own feelings, let alone what course of action he should take and the wider ramifications.

Inside the safety of the house, the two men embraced.

"You were amazing in the court today, Arthur. You handled the questioning brilliantly and ensured our freedom."

"A freedom that is God-given. Our feelings for each other and what we do in our own houses should be between just us and God, and nothing to do with Parliament or Coke's constables."

"Are you sure, Arthur? I hope you are right but I must say I am all confused. I woke up this morning and felt wonderful, but are our feelings for one another godly?"

"John, I am the son of a preacher, and know the scriptures inside out and back to front. Christ's message is one of love, and that is for us to share with all of mankind and sees no distinction related to race, colour, religion or gender. And did he not himself surround himself with men as his disciples, many of whom declared their love for him?"

"Well Arthur, I certainly feel good when I am with you. But how do we have a relationship when the world will be watching us with accusing eyes, or with Coke's cronies, arresting us for just being together?"

"The first step is to get you your commission in the army and then I believe that will provide us with a lot of opportunity and cover to be together. I know it is not right that we cannot be more open but one step at a time."

"Do we tell our family and friends? What about Colonel Harvey?"

"One step at a time, John. We need to be patient. Let's focus on your commission and let's be careful. We cannot afford to risk anything yet."

The Sessions Court, Old Bailey

Colonel Coke was feeling pleased with himself after the morning's work. His purse was a little heavier, Newgate prison fuller, and his reputation in London a little more fearsome after his festive crackdown. The only disappointment was that Bankes was not amongst the squalor in Newgate with the rest awaiting trial. But just bringing the bitch's son to court was satisfying enough and a charge of buggery had made him laugh inside all the way through the proceedings, despite the Judge's putdown with reference to his father. And although the case had been dismissed, he knew mud could be made to stick. It just needed a little help, and he would ensure that it stuck all right. He sat down and started to write three letters, one each to Colonel Harvey, General Fairfax and General Cromwell, informing them of the events of the morning, and that he would recommend not risking the reputation of the army by commissioning John Bankes. 'No smoke without fire' was a phrase he used in the letter to Colonel Harvey. He was going to enjoy fanning the flames of that fire by spreading some rumours about a Captain Morris within its ranks and his homosexual relationship with a former Royalist Captain, the son of a traitor, convicted or not. The Puritan gossips would love this one.

Then he had an even better idea and ripped up the letter to Colonel Harvey and wrote a slightly amended version of the letter to the two Generals.

Chapter Eleven

Romance, Scandal and Remorse

Oliver Cromwell's House London, 27th December 1648

Following their encounter at Windsor, a meeting had been arranged between the Bankes family and Cromwell's to introduce Mary and Richard, the former accompanied by Lady Bankes and the latter by Oliver and his wife Elizabeth, a woman of similar age to Lady Bankes with an attractive although plump little face. Puritans believed in ensuring that there was a mutual liking between couples in an arranged match so love could flourish on fertile ground, and the Cromwells had invested much time in ensuring the happiness of all their offspring with suitable matches. Richard was a boy of softer features than his father's, with a rather timid expression, but he was handsome and his father clearly cared for him. Following the loss of his older brother Oliver during the war in 1644 from typhoid fever, Richard's parents were protective over their remaining son. Elizabeth Bankes had the looks as well as the character of her mother, and was dressed in a dark blue dress, which was not too lavish to offend a Puritan admirer. The families chatted in the parlour of the General's house, a modern three-storey building located at the western end of the Strand, with a garden that led down to the river. Elizabeth sang a song, her sweet voice captivating the parlour audience, whist Richard recited a poem, before Richard suggested escorting Elizabeth for a short walk in Hyde Park.

"You have a wonderful daughter, Lady Bankes, and I can tell that she takes after you," Cromwell said sitting back in his leather-upholstered chair with a reassuring smile and a twinkle in his musing eyes above his distinctive nose.

"You must also be very proud of your son, who is handsome and a true gentleman. But let's see how they get on without us."

"Yes indeed. I also understand, Lady Bankes, that your son wants to become an officer in my army and has the backing of Colonel Harvey. However, we have agreed not to allow former Royalists into our ranks. I hope you and he will understand," Cromwell replied in an assertive voice.

Lady Bankes was not going to give up so easily, despite his dismissive tone.

"General, what has driven you to so passionately to lead the Parliamentary cause?"

Cromwell was taken back by the question, and his demeanour changed.

"Why do you ask?"

"Because I held out for seven months in my Castell and home against a siege by five hundred men, with just forty on my side, enduring hardship, physical and emotional, and learnt that one needs belief and purpose to make a stand and lead. My stance was nothing compared to what must have been on your shoulders over the last few years."

"My Lady, I believe in the Puritan values of hard work and clean living for the glory of God. I pray for guidance and God provides that, and I act with vigour and relentless planning to be able to respond in whatever direction God should direct. I and my soldiers are fighting for God's glory, nothing more and nothing less."

"And has that always been the case? What was your life like before the Puritan cause and the army?"

Cromwell took a moment to respond, and Mary could see that he was contemplating whether to dismiss her or to disclose his thoughts. She gave him a reassuring smile.

"There was a time, a time before I found my faith as you say, when the world was dark and indeed I was melancholic." He paused for reflection. "But that was a long time ago… what has that to do with your son, Lady Bankes?"

"Everything, General. My son is in a similar state without the army. His passion is the adventure and camaraderie the army provides and in return he offers self-less commitment, courage and loyalty. He wants to serve God and work hard for his glory in defending this nation in the same way as you, General."

"That is helpful, Lady Bankes. If he has your strength of character he would indeed be an asset to our cavalry. Having said that, I will still need to discuss this matter with Lord Fairfax. There is a lot happening at present as I am sure you will appreciate and so it is likely to be several weeks before we can make a decision on this matter. Maybe I can write to you on it and at the same time outline a structure for a dowry in anticipation of Richard and Elizabeth getting on. Of course they should meet several times before any decision is made, and I would only want to proceed with both their agreement, but I am aware of your financial situation, Lady Bankes, and I would not want that to cloud the issue. Of course, if you are happy to proceed in this way?"

"Of course, General. This is very generous of you."

Sir John and Alice Borlase's House, 28 December 1649

The next morning Lady Mary Bankes was in the parlour when a servant brought in a letter. She opened it and saw that it was from General Cromwell and her heart jumped with excitement and anticipation, but as she read the letter, the words hit her hard, and she had to read the letter three times before she fully comprehended them. He was writing to her to curtail the relationship between Richard and Elizabeth on account of him being advised that John Bankes had been accused of having a relationship with an officer in his command. He would be looking into this matter further but it was a matter of sensitivity that needed to be resolved given his position and he was sure Mary would understand.

Mary went into the library where she found John reading a book, alone.

"John I have received a letter this morning that suggests there have been some charges against you. Well, you had better read it," and she handed him the letter.

"I wanted to tell you yesterday Mother but I did not get the opportunity, or perhaps did not know how to. I am sorry, and poor Elizabeth. But it is Coke's doing. They were trumped-up charges, with no evidence, and the officer was Captain Morris. The judge dismissed the charges."

"I am sorry John. What lengths will Coke go to destroy this family," Mary replied, holding her son's hand, for she also knew that would be the end of his chances to become an officer again.

"John, what is your relationship with Captain Morris?" his mother asked, as she absorbed his emotions and feelings.

After a few moments of silence, John stood up and paced the room. He was still coming to terms with everything that had changed in his life over the last few days and was now facing his mother. He wanted to be honest but was still struggling to be true with himself.

"We are good friends, Mother. We worked closely together in bringing the King to London and he is supporting me in my request to become an officer. That is what I really want more than anything and this mess now seems to be destroying any hope of that. If Coke was here now I would strike him down with one blow of my sabre. Please excuse me; I need to go for a walk."

As he headed out the library door, Mary called out, "We are here if you want to talk about this more, John."

An hour later, Colonel Tom Harvey and Captain Arthur Morris arrived. Alice and Lady Bankes received them in the parlour and called John down from his room.

"My Lady Mary, my Lady Alice, would it be possible to have a moment alone with John?" Tom asked.

"We have received a letter from General Cromwell about Coke's trumped-up charges against John, so if it is about that then there is nothing to hide, Tom," Lady Bankes replied.

"Yes, I am afraid it is. I was summoned to see the General this morning. I apologise in advance for being crude, Mary and Alice, but I have no option. He had received a letter from Colonel Coke that informed him that John appeared in court yesterday, accused of having a relationship with a serving officer. The implication was that it was one of the officers who had brought the King to London, which would be myself, Captain Morris or Captain O'Reilly. Captain Morris has informed me that it was himself and John who were taken to court, but all charges were dismissed. But in the eyes of the General, Captain O'Reilly and I are also under suspicion."

"Tom, Coke must have deliberately worded his letter to implicate you. There are no depths that man will not sink to," John said.

"There is more I am afraid. On the way over, one of my troops handed me this news pamphlet," John replied and handed over the pamphlet to Mary.

"This is outrageous. Who wrote this defamation? We must stop this," Mary said angrily, passing the pamphlet to John.

"There is no doubt that Coke is behind this as well, but how do you prove it?" John said.

"I will ask Ralph to secure records of the hearing and then we can take it to Cromwell," Mary replied.

"Whatever happens, you will continue to have my support, John," Tom said.

"Thank you, Tom, but you need to protect your position. My dream of a new role in the army is dead now I am sure," John replied, his face distraught.

"John, do not despair. You and I must visit your brother and get a copy of the hearing as Lady Bankes suggested. We must plan a way out of this mess and take action against Coke," Arthur intercepted.

"The man needs to be strung up, but in good time. Arthur is right, we need to take action," John added.

John Bankes and Captain Morris left for Ralph's chambers in Temple Inn at the other end of the Strand, leaving Tom, Alice and Lady Bankes to comprehend what had happened and what to do. They agreed that they needed to move fast and see the General that day.

"Do you think Arthur and John do have a relationship?" Mary asked Tom.

"I wish you had not asked me that; it is something I have been asking myself. They are no doubt good friends and Arthur does seem to be able to bring the best out of John. Is there a relationship beyond that? I would not know, and who am I to judge anyway? I know what the law says and I know the army's view on such things, but how can loving another human being be wrong?"

"It is a forbidden love," Alice said.

"How can you find happiness in a forbidden love? I just long for John's happiness but feel for him in everything he is going through. And even if all his prayers were answered, he became an officer and comrade of his friend Arthur, would he be happy? Look at this pamphlet. This is the abuse he would get, if not fear, all his life. Or he could marry, and live a lie, a life of unhappiness, no doubt making his wife equally unhappy. How can I comfort him?" Lady Bankes asked.

"Alas, I have no answers, my Lady—sorry, Mary, but I will return here after lunch and the two of us can visit the General."

"And what about my sister Elizabeth? It is so difficult being a woman with your entire life resting on a few moments to match make or spend your whole life as a spinster. I know her hopes were high in meeting Richard Cromwell. She will also be distraught," Alice said.

"Let's console her as best we can, Alice, and see what can be done," Mary replied.

The Sessions Court, The Old Bailey

Ralph Bankes led his brother and Captain Morris into the Sessions Court, a building he was familiar with in the course of his legal duties. He soon tracked down the clerk and asked for a copy of the proceedings of the session a few days earlier. The clerk was reluctant as he was a busy man, but a silver sixpence helped to smooth the way to him reprioritising his workload, and an hour later the three of them emerged from the Old Bailey with a certified copy of the document.

On the way back, they walked down Ludgate Hill, out of the old city and on to Fleet Street. This was the home of many of the printing presses that produced the pamphlets that had fuelled the divisions on both sides of the war with information, both false and true, and no doubt the source of the article on John Bankes. Ralph Bankes knew many of the printers for it was the legal profession in the four nearby Inns of Court that was the main consumer of printed material. A couple of apprentices came out of one of the printing shops, one of the less respected ones. The young men had ink-covered aprons and hands, with the distinctive 'Roundhead' haircuts, for the apprentices had been the mainstay of the Parliamentary forces during the war. One recognised Ralph and made the assumption that the man he was with was his brother whom they had read about that very morning.

"Ah, is that John Bankes, the Royalist scum, with his lover boy?" one of the apprentices called out, waving a pamphlet he pulled from his pocket.

John immediately reached for his sword and was ready to confront the two men but was held back by Ralph and Captain Morris.

"Do not rise to their taunts, John. They are not worth it," Captain Morris said.

"Yes brother. We do not want to give them more ammunition to make more false claims."

The three men hurried on down Fleet Street, heads down and collars up, hoping for no more confrontations as printers, peddlers, lawyers, paper producers and ragpickers hurried about their business.

Oliver Cromwell's House, London

Mary Bankes arrived at the door of the General's house for the second time in two days, this time accompanied by Colonel Harvey, who knocked on the door. They were fortunate, for he had just returned from Parliament and the footman said that that he would see them in his study. They were shown into a room that had a large desk, behind which sat Cromwell, a quill in his hand and partially written letter in front of him. He stood up to welcome his guest and offered them each a chair, two matching walnut armchairs with brown leather seats and backs positioned in front of the desk, before sitting down again. The room had dark wooden panels, a bookcase full of leather-bound titles, the largest of which appeared to be the Bible, and a portrait of his wife, Elizabeth.

"General, it seems like yesterday was such a long time ago, having received your letter this morning and Colonel Harvey having informed me of your earlier conversation. I wanted you to know that Coke has a personal vendetta against my family and this is the latest attack. He framed my son with some false accusations which were thrown out of the court, but he is still using that to defame his character and my family's reputation, and even throwing into question that of other officers in your command."

"I dearly hope that is the situation, Lady Bankes, but we live in tense times and we must be sure of our standing and maintain our reputations."

"Of course, General. And so we wanted to clear this up with you. My son and Captain Morris were falsely accused of a crime, but it was dismissed by the judge."

"Here is a copy the court hearing, General," and Tom handed over a two-page document to Cromwell, who read it, whilst his guests remained quiet.

"Well, I am glad you have come and shared this with me. I will speak to Colonel Coke personally about this matter. I would suggest your son leaves London for a while, until this matter blows over. I am happy for Richard and Elizabeth to continue to get to know each other but let them take their time over it and see what God's will is. There are plenty of other matters to keep us preoccupied and with time this will all be forgotten."

Borlase House, London, 30 December 1648

The Bankes family had decided to stay for a few weeks longer in London, for the children loved being with their big sister Alice who spoilt them all. They had been happy to see the sights in the capital, especially the exotic animals in the Tower, their favourite being an elephant. But John Bankes decided to leave London and return to Dorsetshire, heeding the advice of Cromwell. He did not want to be alone in Kingston Lacey fearing a return to a meaningless life as well as the nightmares that haunted him at night, but he feared staying might have an impact on Elizabeth's prospective courtship with Richard Cromwell and his brother's reputation in the Inns of the Court. He had no choice but to leave and informed his mother of that fact.

"I am not sure I can stay here anymore, Mother, and so much has happened to me in the last few days I think I need to return to Kingston Lacey and think through it all."

"John, you know whatever happens and whatever you want to do I will be here for you."

"I know, Mother, but I do not know what I want or to be honest who I really am anymore."

"Well, you do know that you want to join the army, and I will do everything I can to make that happen, that I can assure you."

"But what Coke has done makes that impossible now."

"Nothing is impossible. It may be harder but that means I will have to put more effort into it. I will stay here for a few more weeks and continue

191

to press both Cromwell and Fairfax, and of course pray to God every day. You are right, returning to Dorsetshire will give you time to think things over, and I will write to you as soon as I have the news that you yearn for."

"Thank you, Mother. I will return tomorrow. I believe Arthur will be returning to Windsor in the next few days as well."

"Well perhaps you can see him there, John, if his duties allow. I am sure time with him will also help. Then let things die down and give yourself time. I could accompany you to Windsor tomorrow because I want to see the King anyway, and you can continue your journey west."

Windsor Castell, 31 December 1648

The next day Lady Bankes found herself in the presence of the King in his chamber in Windsor Castell. He was looking smaller than the last time she had seen him, or was she just imagining it? He was certainly more sombre, with barely a smile as he offered her his hand to kiss.

"Thank you for seeing me, Your Majesty"

"It is always a pleasure, Lady Bankes."

"How are you, Your Majesty?"

"Oh, I am fine. They have reduced my privileges, and my household staff, but it is still much better than Hurst Castell."

"You must be under a lot of pressure Your Majesty. There is talk of a trial, indeed I am told it is almost a certainty. Is there not a compromise that could be made?"

"My Lady, yes I am sure they will bring me to some court but it will have no authority. I am the King and above the common law. Anyway, how can you compromise? I am the King appointed by God to rule in his name, and the Defender of the Faith. There can be no compromise. I cannot give up being King as God appointed me, nor can I give up any rights of the Monarchy as they also came from God. What will be will be determined by God."

"And so I ask again how are you, Your Majesty?"

"I am spending a lot of time in prayer and with my children, Elizabeth and Henry. Both are comforting. I have missed my family immensely locked up on that Island, and over the Christmas period it has been wonderful to be reunited with the two of them. Elizabeth is so sweet; she is thirteen now, and so gifted. She can sing and paint. And Henry is so funny. He is eight but I have missed nearly half his childhood."

"Time is so precious when they are young, and it seems to disappear as quickly as the sand in an hourglass."

"It is so true. And how are you, Mary?"

Mary told her about the incident with John and her worries about how he would react.

"I do not get these Puritans. On the one hand they take away what they call the religious practices that are barriers to Christ, freeing people to read the scriptures and sing hymns, but then they manacle society with rules on social behaviour that put in place barriers to God and making Christian life sombre and restrictive. My own father, King James, appointed by God to rule this nation, a man who did so much for religious freedom, was quite open in his love and feelings for other men. Where is the sin in true love Mary? As King and also Defender of the Faith and Head of the Church, I should have a voice on these issues to balance the radicalism of Parliament. You can hardly call it a representative House now anyway as it is now a Rump of what two hundred men? How can such men say they represent this nation, when the majority of the commons have been arrested or are banned from the chamber? The use of the army to enforce their will is appalling and that is something else a monarchy should have the power to prevent. And if they have authority, should they not be focused on the big issues of the day? I understand the price of food is causing starvation whilst there is plague again in London, and the country's representatives are focused on concocting proceedings for a trial for their King, preventing Christmas festivities or determining who we can or cannot love. If it was not so serious and causing so much harm and hurts, you would think we are living through a Shakespearean tragedy."

"Your words are truly spoken with wisdom, Your Majesty. I was hoping to come here to give you some comfort but it seems like you are providing that for me. John is so precious to me, and I am determined to help him and get him what he wants, an officership in the army, but every step I take to do that I seem to get pushed back two."

"And as a King I should be able to grant that wish as well, an officership in the army that should be defending King and country. Indeed, as King I should be in charge of the army. I am so frustrated by my powerlessness when there are so many obvious wrongs to put right. I have been King for nearly twenty-five years, one of the longest-serving monarchs since William the Conqueror, and I know I have made some mistakes, but I have the benefit of experience and constancy over this time, in contrast to most of the Parliamentarians. Many of them were not even born when I came to the throne. In contrast I was born into politics, my mother and father leaving me in Scotland at the age of three to unite the English and Scottish Crowns. Before I was King I had travelled to the courts of Europe and I know all the rulers of the major European nations. But the Parliamentarians are blind to this and what I can offer to the nation. They only have their self-interest at heart. They asked me to stand down so my young Henry could be King. Of course, a boy of eight would be just a puppet, and they would yield all the power, not for the people, but for themselves. The very notion is ridiculous for I asked them if they thought the Scots would accept this position when they have their own Scottish Parliament. Even if it was agreed that I stepped down, the Scots would insist on my heir becoming King, my son Charles who is old and strong enough to stand up against Parliament. And in all seriousness, how could little Henry be Defender of the Faith, given the diversity of the faith we have today?"

"Your Majesty, everything you say is right. We are living in very turbulent and strange times, and it seems every day there are fewer and fewer Parliamentarian representatives taking this nation on a course which is less and less what people want. I wish there was a way to stop this madness," Lady Bankes said.

"My Lady, I am honestly at the end of the road. Some of the Parliamentarians are looking for a compromise as I have explained, but there can be no compromise on principles in my mind. They have called me 'pig-headed' and I plead guilty for there is only right and wrong in this case. I will be damned Mary, if I let them win, and if that means I am a martyr for the cause of Monarchy, then so be it. And let my more enlightened followers rise up and put my heir Charles on the throne in the name of righteousness."

"It is with news of one of your most ardent followers, Sire, that I came to see you, the Duke of Buckingham."

"Ah yes, please tell me, my Lady."

"Well, as you know I have been conspiring with Lady Fairfax on this matter. She has discussed this with her daughter, Mary, and it is true, Mary Fairfax did meet the Duke in the summer, and they fell in love with each other. She has had sight of the Duke's letters and believes he is genuine in his feelings to her daughter. Lady and Lord Fairfax were invited to dinner with my family a few days ago, and we sowed the seed of a marriage of his daughter with a Royalist in the General's mind. It will take some time to nurture that seed before he is confronted outright with the prospect of Mary marrying George, but I am very hopeful that our plan will succeed."

"Oh, thank you, Mary. I knew you would know how to bring this about and whatever happens to me, I am comforted that there is hope of happiness for my god son."

Chapter Twelve

A New Year

2 January 1649, River Thames

Oliver Cromwell walked alone along the bank of the River Thames below the ramparts of Windsor. He needed space to think. He sensed that this was a turning point in history and he had found himself at its pivot and, whilst he was a man of strong character and authority who had been instrumental in driving the Parliamentary cause so far, it was a lonely place to be. He would be fifty in a few months' time and would need all the experience and wisdom he had accumulated over his lifetime as well as the drive and passion of his faith to take him through the next few months. He prayed frequently each day for God's guidance and was now convinced that God had chosen him to lead this nation out of the darkness of the Civil War. He remembered the enlightenment of his own life when he found the grace of God, before that time being a man lost in a depressed state of mind drowning in his own melancholy.

Of course there was the national picture but there was also his family to think about. He was still worried about finding a suitor for Richard and was hoping that Elizabeth Bankes would be that person as long as the situation with her brother died down. He thought about Lady Bankes' son. He feared that he would be sucked into a similar melancholic dark state that he experienced twenty years before if he was not given his commission. Cromwell was minded to grant the request, but again in time when any risk of a scandal had passed. He liked Mary Bankes, she had been a Royalist, but she was a woman of principle like her husband and not driven by self-interest. Unlike other women, she was opinionated and challenged men in their views. Her question to him came back to him – as a leader what is your cause?

His faith was the answer. He was a Puritan through and through and worked hard for the glory of God. He was guided by God ever since his conversion twenty years before. He believed that God had chosen him and his troops to perform His will as they marched into battle singing psalms to His glory. Now after the war there was the opportunity to reform society in the same way as he did with the New Model army. That would mean providing society with opportunity and education, particularly in the teachings of Christ, whilst clamping down on drunkenness, immorality and other sinful activities. He also believed in the freedom for a range of Protestant groups and faiths to practise their beliefs undisturbed and without disturbing others, for he recognised the common views of Puritans, Calvinists, and Presbyterians, rather than the differences. Catholics were a different matter; his view on their faith was largely coloured by the Irish Catholics' treatment of Protestants, something that he knew had to be addressed but first the focus should be on peace and rebuilding of England. He recognised that after six years of fighting, and a decade of confrontation between King and Parliament before that, the nation needed reconciliation, not more division, as Lady Bankes advocated. But to do that there was the important issue of what to do with the King to settle and this should result in an end to the Royalist uprisings. Negotiations with the King over the last eighteen months, ever since he had been imprisoned in Carisbrook Castell, had led nowhere. Indeed, the King had lied to Parliament, gone back on commitments and colluded with the Scots to uprise again. Cromwell had spent much of the year in the Northwest of England, fighting the Scots, which finally resulted in their defeat at the end of the summer, in Preston. He had captured most of the second war uprising leaders, Hamilton, Lord Chapel, the Earl of Holland, Lord Norwich and Sir John Owen. Their fate could await but it was unlikely to be pleasant, and very likely to be short. Many others had fled, but mainly those with no backbone and they would not pose a threat individually or collectively. There were one or two, like the Duke of Buckingham, who could rally behind the King's son Charles and who could still prove to be a thorn in his side, but he felt that their cause was weakening. A final solution to the Monarchy he was sure would strike a fatal blow.

The letter that Colonel Ireton had discovered which demonstrated in the King's own hand his treacherous soul confirmed to Cromwell that he had to bring the matter to a head. He could see that someone had to grab the situation by the horns and move the country forward, building a peace with a resolution to the question about what the future of the Monarchy should be. On Christmas Day, a day when work continued to the glory of God, Parliament had agreed to put the King on trial. This was a step forward in determining the issue, a step that he had played no role in and let God determine the direction. But what would be the outcome? He would again let God guide this but he needed to be prepared for the possibilities so he could implement God's will.

Cromwell could see a number of different outcomes. The trial itself may bring the King to his senses and agree to a Monarchy with reduced power. But the more radical wing that was starting to dominate Parliament after Pride's purge, wanted Charles removed, and replaced with one of his sons, or wanted to see the end of the Monarchy altogether. The Levellers were driving this last scenario, with John Lilburne its inspirational figurehead, who had roused many to fight for the Parliamentary cause in the first place. Many in the ranks of the army were of this mindset. They wanted a reward for what they had been through and favoured more rights and a greater say through a Parliament for the people. And if there was no Monarchy what should happen to Charles Stuart? Amongst the radicals there was little doubt. He should suffer the consequences of his treachery, and there was only one punishment for traitors. They were really contemplating the execution of a King. There was no precedent for this and Cromwell struggled with the notion of Regicide. He no longer believed in the Divine Right of Kings to rule, but surely God had given the nation Charles for a reason. Could the nation reject the King and execute its sovereign? It was a question he asked himself many times. On the one hand he had personally witnessed so much bloodshed that there was no doubt in his mind the King's actions had caused. But even now there was still a lot of support for the King throughout the country, and the monarchy was engrained into the country, symbolised everywhere you looked from the coins, to statues, to the names of taverns and paintings in churches. On the anniversary of his coronation in March last year London had been full of music and cheer, perhaps for some just needing an excuse after such a period of turmoil. That was before the Scot's uprising but there was still an undercurrent of Royalist sentimentality.

Cromwell was not a man to be rushed into a decision and preferred to let events take their course under God's guidance but being prepared for all outcomes. However, he was now of the opinion that God was curating events in such a way that he was in a pivotal position. He was a man who had the support of the army as well as a Parliamentarian who was seen as somebody who could bridge many of the factions given his experience and standing. Yes, Cromwell needed to be prepared and ready to lead, but he was equally certain that at this point in time he should not be driving any agenda, and so be as impartial as possible. He had ordered Colonel Harvey to bring the King to Windsor last month, and here the King awaited his trial. He had not talked to the King since he had arrived but sensed his presence. He had been informed that the King was spending time with his children and in prayer, and that he was in a sombre and contemplative mood. He had known the King since he was a boy, and had never liked him, but he still felt some sympathy for the man whom he felt was alone, lost and misguided.

Events were moving quickly, and now the ordinance setting up the court that would conduct the trial of the King was approved. But that was just logistics; making the case against the King in the court was much more difficult. The question of the legal basis to try the King was another issue that vexed him, but he would leave to the other Parliamentarians. Even the radicals recognised that they needed to be seen to be acting in accordance with justice, and absolutely not pander to or be part of some mob rule. Parliament was the maker of the laws and had to be seen to comply with them. The main claim against the King was that he had started the war, which they needed to prove, but even if they could there was no law that they could use to claim this was an act of treason, for this crime was defined as an act against the sovereign, and so the King could not be accused of a wrongdoing against himself. Cromwell would let others deal with the complexities and God would dictate the outcome. But he needed to think beyond this, to be in a position to bring the country together in the aftermath of the trial and help the country heal itself. He could see that God could have a role for him in this as a man known for his tolerance and with the backing of the army he would be a strong and powerful reconciliatory force that has not been seen as an agitator, radical or reactionary. He had been in the North when Ireton, Pride and others had purged the House of Commons from all members who favoured continuing to negotiate with the King, and so had not been tainted by such agitation. He was even contemplating marrying his son to the daughter of a well-known Royalist family, a prospect he had shared with a few influential Parliamentarians who were broadly supportive. He had proved himself an excellent military organiser and fighting man, but was he a man who could build a peace, and in what aftermath? If this was the path that God had laid out for him, he had to be prepared.

Cromwell also knew the importance of planning and preparation for whatever outcome God determined. The New Model army had taught him that. He had ensured the Roundheads were well trained and had equipment, uniforms and food which meant his soldiers were better prepared for the battles and the events that God would direct. It was the small things that all mounted up and made the difference. One of the most important had been the news pamphlets that John Milton and other Parliamentarian supporters had recognised even in the early stages of the dispute between Parliament and the King. The printing press was as powerful a weapon as a dozen saker canon in firing up the power of the people, recruiting soldiers and maintaining morale. Cromwell sensed the next couple of months would be definitive for the nation and so he had to prepare behind the scenes and be ready. He would bring troops into the capital, men who would be absolutely loyal to him to deal with any unrest during the trial and strengthening his position. He would ensure that the people were informed across the country about events that unfolded, but through a Cromwellian perspective. If the King was to be tried then his subjects should know and he suspected many former Roundhead soldiers would travel the city to see justice carried out, which again would play to his advantage. Yes, he would let others drive events and be ready for whatever outcome God willed, strong and prepared, and if that meant leadership, he would lead.

2nd January 1648, The Vyne, Hamptonshire

The Vyne, near Sherborne St John, in Hamptonshire was transformed from a cluster of medieval buildings into a Tudor palace just over a hundred years earlier by William Sandys, the Lord Chamberlain to King Henry VIII.. The warm red-brick building was one of the most modern and eloquent buildings in southern England and had hosted kings and queens ever since and was now rented by General Fairfax from the Sandys to help pay for their war fines. Today a Puritan preacher rode up its long drive, dismounted and approached the large oak doors set in its portico. He handed a note to the servant who saw that it was addressed to Mary Fairfax. The preacher then returned back down the drive.

An hour later Mary rode her horse out of the Vyne estate, her long, hooded cape keeping out the chill of the January morning, and headed for a crossroads two miles away, where she pulled up and waited. A few minutes later the same Puritan preacher emerged on his horse from a copse of pine trees nearby, greeted Mary, and then led her back into the cover of the trees. They both dismounted and then embraced.

"George, I hardly recognised you."

He kissed her, passionately, once, twice, three times.

"If you could not recognise me then nor will my enemies, so this is good."

"But it is still not safe for you. My father says they have captured most of the Royalist leaders, but there are a few he wants to ensure are brought to justice for the outbreak of the second war and named you amongst them. And you ride up his drive, passed the guards and knock on his door. You are crazy, George Villiers."

"I am in love with his daughter, and the risk is far outweighed by the prize of being together now."

They kissed again. Mary's body tingling all over, her eyes closed, but every other sense absorbing the moment, his scent mingled with the pine, the sound of their breathing and the feeling of his body pressed up to hers.

"But George, it will be certain death if you are captured. You should stay abroad until the situation dies down. I will wait for you, and in the meantime my mother aided by Lady Bankes are slowly working on my father to bring him around. The King himself asked Lady Bankes for help after you wrote to him."

"I know of her. I understand she is a formidable woman and hopefully she can have some influence over your father, but I fear this is an insurmountable challenge. What father would agree to marry their own daughter to their declared enemy?"

"Well, I believe she has a plan, but it will take time."

"I also have a plan and it is to take you to the Netherlands where we can get married."

"George." They kissed more. Mary was a-tingle, he wanted to marry her. Was she dreaming? But how could this happen?

"There is nothing in the world I would want more than to be married to you but let's give Lady Bankes a few months. If her plan works and we could be married in England, then all my dreams would come true."

"My heart wants to take you now with me but my head is telling me that you are right. I would not want to take you away from your family and all that you cherish if there is a chance of avoiding it. Let's pray that Lady Bankes can influence your father."

"George my father has guards all around the estate. It is really not safe for you here. You should get out of the country as soon as you can."

"I have a small mission to complete and then I will be gone and I will write to you as soon as I arrive in Amsterdam." "You do look funny George. You will never be a Puritan. Go, my love and do what you have to but be careful and come back to me soon through your letters, but hopefully in person soon."

They kissed again and he helped her mount her horse. He watched her ride back out of the copse. A few moments of reflection passed before he mounted his horse but set off in the opposite direction on the road to London.

January 3rd Kingston Lacey

John awoke to tapping from the window. Morning light was seeping into the room from behind the curtain. He had slept late, which given his long ride yesterday and late arrival was not surprising. His thoughts that tracked him from London, had also caused a restless night. His feelings for Arthur Morris, a love that could not see the light of day yet had already led to many tears being shed by John. He reached over and pulled back the curtain, revealing the cause of the tapping, a sparrow on his frosted window sill. The bird stretched out its wings, ready to fly to safety, but appeared to have second thoughts. John starred at the creature, so perfectly formed, striped brown and black feathers, white cheeks and a black bib. The bird stared back at John, turning its head perhaps to make senses of the strange being behind the glass, and tweeting, a song John could just about make out as he slowly backed up and returned to the warmth of his bed. John remembered he had taken some bread and broth to bed, and turned to find some crumbs still on the plate beside his bed. He got up slowly, not wanting to frighten the bird, and took the plate to the window.

"Hungry my little friend. Not many worms to be found with that frost?"

He opened the latch and tentatively started to open the window, but the sparrow was startled and flew away. Nevertheless, John scraped the crumbs on to the sill, closed the window and started to get dresses, although he wondered to what aim. What was he going to do alone, other than the staff, in this house? He buttoned his shirt, and pulled on his tunic and as he did so he noticed his friend the sparrow had returned.

"Well at least I have made one person happy today, little sparrow."

After breakfast, he told Mary, the cook and housekeeper, about the sparrow and asked her to put something out for the little bird. Mary reminded him of how Jesus used the sparrow as an example of God's love, and so it was right to care for them. This enthused John and it occurred to him that it was perhaps a message that he should feel less sorry for himself and God did indeed care for him. Things may work out after all. He decided to write to Arthur and tell him about the sparrow.

January 10ᵗʰ 1649 Kingston Lacey

Arthur had persuaded Colonel Harvey that he should ensure the garrison were well stocked whilst he remained in London, and this meant travelling to Winchester, Poole, Salisbury and Southampton. It also allowed him to take a small detour to Kingston Lacey where he found John grooming the horses. John was delighted to see Arthur who brightened up the grey and heaviness of the winter's day. It was noon and so John asked the cook to make lunch, whilst the two men went for a quick walk around the estate.

"Arthur, I have missed you more than I can say."

"Me too my friend. But at least you have your little friend the sparrow," Arthur replied, sensing he needed to raise the spirits of his friend.

"Alas, he became the victim of our cat. I found the body yesterday in the garden. So much for God caring for his smallest creatures."

"I am sorry John, but that is just nature's way. We should not read too much into that."

"Give me something positive to read into, Arthur. The more I am apart from you the more I need you, and the more melancholic I become, but I know we cannot be together."

"John, I know it is difficult. I feel the same way but I will work something out."

"At least you have the army to pre-occupy you. Anyway, what is there to be done? Our love is forbidden. There is no place for us in this world.'

"Our love is precious and should not be denied, even if it has to remain hidden. I will come up with a plan that will enable us to live at least close together, just given me time." Arthur said with his arm around John's shoulder and bringing him closer to him with the intention of a kiss.

"Closer together, but not together," John retorted, pushing Arthur away.

The two men walked silently back to the house for lunch, which was eaten amidst a heavy and awkward atmosphere, with few words being spoken.

Arthur had to depart after lunch, and John walked him to his horse.

"I am sorry for my melancholy, Arthur. I should be so happy that you have come to see me, and indeed I am, but it is difficult to shake off my malaise. You are leaving now and I have wasted our time together. I am just stuck in this place, too much drinking, too much thinking and doing nothing. Before the mission to take the King to London, I was in a similar state, but then the mission for the King and meeting you changed everything. I felt I had a purpose, and our friendship blossomed into love without me even knowing it. I thought I was walking the streets of heaven for a short time in London. There was at least the prospect of enlisting with the army, and the joy of our time together, only equalled by the cruelty in which everything was taken away."

"John, come here my friend." As John took a cautious step towards him, Arthur took his friend in his arms, his horse shielding them from a view from the house. "I am going to find a way for us to be together, somehow, somewhere, so we can talk together, laugh together, ride together, go on missions and adventures together, grow old together, feeling alive together and die together. I promise."

"Oh Arthur, that sounds wonderful, but how can it be. Spending one night together we were almost tried and hanged. We need to be real, but the pain is insufferable. When I am awake at night, here alone, my tears only dry up when sleep finally takes me into my nightmares of battles lost and won, gun shots ringing in my head and the faces of friends gone and foes that I have despatched to God knows where. It is endless Arthur, and I do not know how long I can take it."

A sob escaped John's throat, and he took Arthur's hand "Arthur, please be back soon."

"I will be John and I will write to you even before then as soon as I have news or even the bones of a plan for us. Do not give up hope, my friend. I know you are going through hell my love but keep going for we will find the promised land at the end of the journey. We will be together." His hand stroked his face and brought their heads together, their lips brushing against each other's, before sharing a tender kiss. But he had already stayed longer than he had dared and needed to get back to Winchester by night fall and so the two men parted company again.

17 January 1648, Winchester.

Tom had returned to Winchester with Captain Morris to focus on ensuring the peace and no more Royalist outbreaks in the South. He did not know what to think about John Bankes, his friend, and Captain Morris, a trusted officer. He knew there was a strong friendship and he suspected it had developed beyond that. He knew that this would create considerable difficulties for them both and he was at a loss at what to do or advise. Cromwell and Fairfax would be much less inclined to support John being an officer now, and he could understand why as the army frowned on such relationships. But he was worried at how that would impact his friend. John was so passionate about the army, he was not sure how he would cope being barred from it, whether on grounds of his Royalist past or a suspected relationship with Captain Morris. He had discussed John's state of mind with Captain Morris en route from London, and it was clear that he was also worried about his friend.

Captain Morris had returned from a ride to Mottisfont and knocked at the door of the Colonel's office.

"I have some news Colonel; I am to be married. Hester Sandys has agreed to be my wife," he declared as he came in.

"Well, that is news. I did not know that you knew the Sandys that well."

"I have been acquainted with them through John over the last months and have seen Mary a few times now. She is of good character and fair complexion. They need a man to help them."

"I am sure that is all correct, Captain, but are you sure you are marrying for the right reasons?"

"Of course I am. I will continue to serve as an officer but will have a wife and family to support."

"And what about John?"

"John? He will be happy for me, and it will quell the rumours about us, and open the way for his officership."

"Captain, you must marry for the right reasons as your happiness and that of your wife will depend on it. There are other obstacles in the way of John's commission."

"I know Colonel, but one less now."

Chapter Thirteen

The Trial, 22 January 1649

Westminster Hall, London

Tom had been summoned back to London in mid-January, with his troops, for trouble was expected with the impending trial. Four weeks ago, Lord Fairfax had told Tom a trial of the King would never happen, but here he was escorting Lady Fairfax along with Lady Bankes into Westminster Hall, the symbolic powerhouse of the capital next to the Palace of Westminster and south of the Abbey. The Hall has been built by King Rufus, half a millennium before, and it was the venue for grand events and celebrations, banquets for coronations or hosting foreign monarchs, but it was also the centre of the nation's government and legal system, hosting the Courts of the King's Bench, Common Pleas, and Chancery. The building was impressive in scale with a vast wooden frame that spanned an area of 17,000 square feet and said to be the largest hall in the world. It was ornate in decoration with symbols of the monarchy inside and out, including the stories shown in its stained-glass windows and statues of every king since Edward the Confessor and crowns and corbels sculptured into the wooden frame. As Tom walked in, he was proud to see the floor laid out in Purbeck stone and pointed it out to Lady Bankes.

Lord Fairfax had refused to attend as he wanted nothing to do with the trial. It was he who, along with Cromwell, had been the celebrated leaders of the Parliamentary army that had defeated the Royalists. They had remained united in managing the demands of the army, fuelled by the Leveller influence of John Lilburne and others, against Parliament who did not want to meet the cost of the soldiers' salaries. But in the last few weeks the two generals had formed different views about what should happen to the King. Fairfax had originally been appointed as the leader of the commissioners who would act as judges at the trial but soon realised that most of them had already decided the outcome. Whilst he was not against some form of justice for the King, he could not contemplate a path that would lead to the death of the monarch, and so he resigned his position. Cromwell had sat on the fence until the turn of the year, at which time the Commoners had successfully mastered the Act which had created the authority and means to bring the King to trial. Cromwell claimed that it was God's will if the law had been passed, and so he would now play his part in bringing it to a conclusion. He was being directed by providence and necessity. Fairfax argued if it had been God's will then why had it necessitated a purged Parliament to make it a law, and he was convinced there would be severe consequences in this life or the next for those who had royal blood on their hands. His wife, Lady Fairfax, was even more determined that this façade of justice should be stopped and was adamant that she would attend and indeed make her voice known. She was a Presbyterian and the King had agreed to support the spread of their faith across England in return for the last Scottish uprising. Lady Bankes was equally committed to standing up for the King, for she believed in the Monarchy and a fair trial for the man she had got to know over the last two months. Tom Harvey had agreed to escort the ladies partly as a favour to Lord Fairfax. They were both dressed in red, the colour of royalty and blood, but also the passion which both women oozed for their respective causes.

The entrance to the Hall was surrounded by guards not from Tom's command but clearly sharing the same mind as many in the army, for as he and the two ladies arrived a number started to chant, "Bring the King to trial, Bring the King to trial." Tom ordered them to be quiet and to pay attention to guarding the Hall and look out for anything suspicious. Royalist sympathisers could stage some kind of attack and the capital was very tense. He led Lady Fairfax and Lady Bankes into the stand on the north side of the central square so they could get a clear view of proceedings in the enormous Hall which was nearly three hundred feet long. The room oozed history and had been the stage for the trials of William Wallace, Thomas Moore, Guy Fawkes and many more heroes, patriots and villains. Above them the vaulted ceiling of the Hall with its oak beams reaching up to the heavens, but below which all hell was to be seen and heard as the hoards pushed, argued and even came to blows as they drove into the standing area of the central square in front of them to find a spot to view the spectacle. The galleries behind them were bustling with people trying to squeeze another body in, and the oak stanchions creaked with the weight. The public were positioned at the north end of the Hall whilst the court sat to the south, an area that had been cordoned off by a wooden partition along which armed guards were stationed. Tom and his party could see that the court comprised commissioners who would act as judges: sixty-eight of them sat in four rows. In front of them was the Lord President, John Bradshaw, the man who had orchestrated the Parliamentary edict of the 6 January, which accused the King of treachery. He was at a magnificent table draped in a colourful Turkish tapestry. The Lord President was a judge from the North but few people had heard of him before he had been elected president of the Parliamentary commission. He had long grey distinguished-looking hair and wore a scarlet robe, with a sword at his side, and broad-brimmed beaver hat. Tom had heard that the hat was reinforced with steel to make it bulletproof and that he wore armour under his robe, a man clearly expecting trouble. Looking around Tom suspected that they were wise precautions, as anybody in the audience could have a weapon despite the checks the guards were making on entry. Anything could happen in the atmosphere of the Hall, tense and disorderly. Bradshaw faced an oak chair, with a red velvet seat and backrest, standing alone, opposing the president and judges in an air of isolated defiance. This would be where the King would make his stand, equipped only with a paper, quill and ink set out on a side table. Tom could see the lay of the battlefield and it looked like the odds were against the King, a view reinforced by the display of the Royalist colours captured in battles of Naseby, Marston and most recently, Preston, as a backdrop to the commissioners.

"He is being tried like a common criminal," Lady Fairfax said.

"But I suspect without the rights of the common man," Lady Bankes added.

"There is still time for it to be called off," replied Tom, but his words were followed by the sounds of trumpets that brought everyone to attention, as the Sergeant at Arms rode into the Hall from the southern end, away from the crowds, carrying a mace and sword, accompanied by six trumpeters on horseback. Drums joined the proclamation, as the mace and sword were presented to the Lord President who positioned them on the tapestry in front of him. The trumpets sounded again, announcing the King who stepped into the Hall from a side door and necks strained amongst the audience to get a better glimpse of the accused. He was dressed all in black, apart from the Order of the Garter on his chest, and his white lace collar. The performance was about to begin, and the lead actor entered the Hall slowly, his head focused on the centre stage. His wide-brimmed hat was cavalier in style and he used his cane as a prop to emphasise his presence. He reached the enclosure that surrounded the chair, stopping in expectation of someone opening the gate, but nobody moved, so the King opened it for himself in a somewhat awkward manner, but reaffirmed himself as he strode to the velvet chair and sat down with composure. This would be his throne from which he looked on to the Lord President and judges. They were his subjects after all, and he was their king and he would be defiant in his stand.

Amongst the commissioners behind the Lord President was John Bingham, Parliamentary member for Shaftesbury, local magistrate and banker, being now called upon to act as one of the sixty-eight judges in the trial of the King of England. He, the son of a ship's mate, had come along way he thought as he sat amongst the likes of Oliver Cromwell, Sir John Lisle, and Colonel Ireton. But status was not important to him as he was determined to remain focused on why he was there; to ensure justice prevailed. He wanted the King to face this trial but it must be conducted on the principles of justice. He understood that the situation was unprecedented and strictly that there was no law governing the King, as had been discussed and debated endlessly in Parliament over the last few months, but that did not mean that justice should not prevail. His fellow commissioners were largely Parliamentarians, and many had already made up their minds; the King was guilty and should be executed. John Bingham was not averse to this outcome, but the King must be given the opportunity to have his say and justice must be seen to be done. He was determined to listen intently to everything that was said and the arguments on both sides. He could see the public in the other half of the Hall and was sure there were many there who would be happy to hang the King there and then but he was also sure there would be supporters of the King amongst the two or three thousand people. Justice, properly conducted and fair, was the only cause that could bring the sides together or else he feared violence would erupt. He was comforted by the many hundreds of guards that had been stationed throughout the Hall for he suspected trouble would be inevitable as proceedings progressed.

From the balcony Tom looked down on the sovereign, a man he had got to know whilst at Hurst Castell, just two months ago, but in that time he saw that the King had aged, and his demeanour lacked the calmness and steadfastness he had known, replaced by a hint of nervousness and uncertainty. Was this a defeated man facing his last act, or was he just putting on a show, and had another trick up his sleeve? As he faced the Lord President, the sixty-eight judges, as well as at least fifty Parliamentarians with Cromwell, Ireton, and Ludlow amongst their ranks, the odds did not look good, but there were men amongst those ranks that looked equally uncomfortable. They knew they were in unchartered waters, and their own individual reputations and futures were at stake, as well as the nation's. Tom looked at Lady Fairfax, who exhaled a deep breath and shook her head. But before she could follow up her gesture of disapproval with words, the Hall was filled with a rush of apprehension as the King suddenly rose to his feet. Many in the crowd stood, including Tom and his escorts, in habitual reverence, removing their hats. What was he doing? He turned his back to his prosecutors and looked around the Hall, at the common people. Tom felt his gaze, as the King's eyes scoured the northern stands, and indeed it appeared that everyone in the Hall sensed the same feeling. There was a clear sigh of relief across the faces of the officials in the centre when the King finally sat down again.

"Who is that?" Tom asked as a man stood up and addressed the Lord President.

"His name is John Cook. He is the Prosecutor. The Attorney General is apparently not well and they could not find anyone else. He is just a lawyer from the North-West, totally out of his depth," Lady Fairfax replied.

The man was reading out the charges, facing the Lord President and with his back to the King.

"Charles Stuart is accused of a wicked design to erect and uphold in himself an unlimited and tyrannical power to rule according to his will, and to overthrow the rights and liberties of the people. In carrying out this strategy, he has traitorously and maliciously levied war against the present Parliament and the people therein represented." His back was still to the King, clearly a breach of royal etiquette, and whilst many recognised this, nobody said anything. But it annoyed the King. He first gave a cough to interrupt proceedings, to no avail, and so tried again, but this time using his cane, poking the prosecutor in the back but the prosecutor continued.

"The King renewed the war after his defeat with the soul objective of the upholding of a personal interest of will and power for his personal benefit against the public interest, common right, liberty, justice and peace of the people of this nation. On behalf of the people of England, the King is impeached before this court today as a tyrant, traitor, murderer, and a public and implacable enemy to the Commonwealth of England."

John Cook received a second harder thrust on his back. This time the silver tip at the end of the black ebony cane came off and fell to the floor. Silence filled the Hall as the heavy thump was followed by the clatter of the silver cone rolling to a standstill. The prosecutor, the court and the entire audience in the Hall watched, mesmerised.

Nobody moved. There was not a sound in the Hall, all eyes on the King. Everyone was thinking the same *Never in his life had the King had to pick up anything*. Lady Bankes started to rise from her seat with the intention of going to the King's aid and stopping the embarrassment, but Tom held her arm. Somebody had to do something, surely. The silence was deafening, and everyone felt uncomfortable. The prosecutor just two feet from the object remained statuesque, and to his side the judges, Parliamentarians and officials resolutely still. This was round one, and the King slowly accepted defeat, rising from his chair, bent down and picked up his cane tip.

"You should have let me go," Lady Bankes muttered under her breath.

The prosecutor continued finishing his statement of charges which was followed by a roll call of the Judges. Halfway through, Lord Fairfax's name was called, and there was no answer, but then Lady Fairfax called out, "He had more wit than to be here."

This outcry caused many in the crowd to show their true colours.

"Shame on all of you," cried one and, "God save the King!" another. General mayhem followed and the guards were ordered into the crowd to quieten things down. When order returned, Bradshaw called upon the King to answer the charges and this riled Lady Fairfax again.

She stood up and shouted, "It is a lie. Oliver Cromwell is the traitor."

Colonel Axtell, who was in charge of the guard in the hall, ordered muskets to be trained on the stand where Lady Fairfax was sitting, and then sent a guard in to make an arrest, but Tom pre-empted them.

"That is enough, my Lady. You have made your point. We must leave, and I suggest you join us, Lady Bankes, for your safety." And, holding Lady Fairfax's arm, he led both ladies down the steps and out of the Hall, followed by a dozen troops.

Cromwell felt even more uncomfortable now that Lady Fairfax had shined the spotlight on him. He had planned to take a back seat and let Bradshaw and Cook drive the proceedings, but now all eyes were on him, as Lady Fairfax was escorted out. The mutterings in the Hall, although indistinguishable, he was certain echoed his name. Why did she have to interfere? Could Fairfax not keep her under control? Bradshaw finally brought proceedings to order again.

The King was about to answer, and he waited for absolute quiet to reinforce the point he was to make, his trump card.

"Mister Bradshaw, by what authority have you brought me to this court? I mean lawful authority for there are many unlawful authorities including thieves and robbers along our highways. Remember I am your lawful King, appointed by God. I see no Lords here who would make it a Parliament. And any other courts in the land are by royal appointment. I do not recall appointing this one. I will not answer to a court with no authority," the King said, almost with a casual air, to underline his own authority. His dress, his manner and his demeanour indicated that he indeed was above the justice of the so-called judges in front of him. His words were followed by some supportive murmuring around the Hall, but at least this time order prevailed.

"It is by the authority of the people of England, by whom you had been elected King," Bradshaw responded.

"Mister Bradshaw, I inherited the crown, and did not receive it by any election. I do stand more for the liberty of my people, than any here that come to be my pretended judges, I cannot see that this court has any authority and so will not answer your questions. Let me see a legal authority warranted by the Word of God, the Scriptures, or warranted by the constitutions of the Kingdom, and I will answer. Think what sins you bring upon your heads, and the judgement of God upon this land. Think well upon it, I say, think well upon it, before you go further from one sin to a greater. I have a trust committed to me by God, by old and lawful descent; I will not betray it, to answer a new unlawful authority," the King responded calmly with a cold smile.

This was not going well, Cromwell conceded, as Bradshaw continued to confront the King, but his stance was robust and he would not concede anything. It was a relief when Bradshaw adjourned the court until the next day. The Hall emptied and there were mixed mutterings amongst the crowd, with many seeming to have heeded the King's words and worried about God's wrath on the nation if indeed the King was found guilty.

The next day Tom returned to the Hall, but this time alone. As the proceedings continued, Tom thought that it more unlikely that the judges would come to a guilty verdict, and if they did they surely would not have the courage to sentence the King to death. The King maintained his defence and simply continued to deny the right of the court to judge him, speak to him or even exist, and certainly would not answer the charge against him.

"I do require that I may give in my reasons why I do not answer," the King demanded in a raised voice.

"It is not for prisoners to require,' the President responded.

'Sir, I am not an ordinary prisoner,' the King retorted.

Well that is true, thought Tom. He was not a subject within the Common Law, and the prosecution was struggling to progress with the charge because of this. However, in the afternoon a flabbergasted Bradshaw simply instructed the clerk to record the King's default in response to the charges. John Bingham, sat amongst the judges, was concerned that he was not going to see the justice he wanted. The King and the court could endlessly argue about the validity of the proceedings, but would the King have the opportunity to defend his case. From what he had witnessed so far he feared not. Worse still this did not seem to concern many of his fellow judges who seemed to already have a clear view on the verdict as a second day in the Hall came to an end.

The court did not sit on the next day, Tom assumed because of disarray in the camp of the prosecution. This seemed to be compounded by news that the Scottish Parliament had denounced the trial. Tom reconciled himself by writing to Camille and told her that he was convinced the King would fight another day. In his letter, he declared that part of him wanted to see him executed, to bring some closure to the loss of his friends during the war, which he still believed the King was at least partially responsible for, but he was increasingly wondering about the part the Parliamentary representatives played in the lead-up to the war. The King had already sown a seed of doubt in their integrity and this seemed to be reinforced from what he had witnessed in the last few days. He had also got to know Charles the man after spending so much time with him. He understood his weaknesses and also that he was like any other man: he made mistakes, he had self-doubt, he loved and yearned for his family, and had never asked to be King, nor even been prepared to wear the crown. And Tom admired the King's stance and how he was standing up to them, and for the principles he believed in, especially given that the stakes were so high.

The next day, witnesses were brought into the Hall and questioned to build on the case against the King. They included men who had been at Nottingham and seen Charles raising his standard against Parliament and the elected representatives of the English people, and others seeing him on the battlefield with his sword drawn. Tom did not really think these facts were in doubt, for he himself had seen the King at Edge Hill rallying his troops before the first battle, and his friend John Bankes had witnessed the raising of the standard in Nottingham, along with tens of thousands of soldiers and civilians. Bradshaw seemed to be making the case that Charles Stuart had levied war on his own people, and therefore broke the contract of trust with his subjects. This seemed to wrap up proceedings in the eyes of the President, and Bradshaw directed the court to proceed to sentencing. John Bingham sat in dismay. He was not going to hear any case for the defence and the King would be sentenced without explaining his actions to his nation. He wanted to understand why this war had really happened and why the King had raised the standard in Nottingham but he was now less clear about this than before the hearing.

In the balcony, Tom also yearned to hear both sides of the case as was expected in any court of law, and disappointed to hear that again the court was adjourned. The King remained defiant as he was led away, although Tom felt he detected the first sign of uncertainty in his step as if his childhood limp was returning. What would a man be thinking, knowing he could be returning to the court tomorrow to face the ultimate punishment?

Chapter Fourteen

The Sentence

Westminster Hall, 24 January 1649

The King did not return the next day, for when Tom arrived at Westminster Hall he found a crowd gathered around the entrance, and a notice on the door saying there would be no proceedings today. As he turned away, in the distance he saw Oliver Cromwell and two men heading towards the Privy Gardens, with six guards following them. Tom ran after them and quickly caught them up as the Cathedral bells chinned ten o'clock.

"General, Sir. Please could you spare a moment of your time?" Tom called out when he was in earshot of the three men, who stopped and turned around. John Cook the prosecutor was one of the other men, but Tom did not recognise the third.

"What is it Colonel?" Cromwell asked, his nose having reddened further in the crisp January morning, puffs of vapour filling the air as he spoke.

"I need to speak to you for a few moments, in private, on a matter of importance. Can we speak in the gardens; it will not take long?" Tom replied.

"We have a meeting with the President shortly, but I can spare a few moments. Gentlemen, I will catch up with you shortly," Cromwell said, nodding to his two colleagues.

"Thank you, Sir," Tom responded, as the General joined him, and the others carried on a head, four of the guards following, whilst two waited for Cromwell. "General, I have fought for the Parliamentary cause since Edge Hill convinced that the King had done wrong. I was at Roundway Down when we lost so many men, and I led the band of men that captured Corffe Castell from the Bankeses. I have lost many friends to this cause, and as

216

time has passed, I have been less convinced of the reason for fighting. I have witnessed atrocities on both sides, and have seen the nation ripped apart, father fighting sons, brothers fighting brothers. Whilst the King was in my custody I talked to him and asked him many questions, but of course I am not a man of the law. I expected the hearings over the last few days to provide me with answers and an understanding of what we were fighting for but I confess I am at an even greater loss of why there was such a terrible war. If anything I can see the King's case more clearly now, and less our own. I need to know, General. I must know what was this all for and what is to happen next and why?"

"You asked for just a few moments Colonel? Well, what will happen next is clear." He pulled out a document from his pocket. "Here is the sentence for the King. Execution by severing his head, and the warrant has been drafted, with my own signature as one of the first on it beneath President Bradshaw's."

Tom gasped. "He will be beheaded! Surely not!"

"Yes, and I will try to justify this, but it is not easy. I was at many of the battles and also suffered much loss including my own son and ask myself similar questions to you. I believe what is happening is God's will, and my role is to ensure that will is executed as effectively as possible but not judge his will and the direction he has set. I was not one that initially confronted the King in the years that led to the war, but once war was declared I fought as fervently as I could for the cause and remodelled the army to ensure victory as quickly as possible. Since then, I have kept an open mind as what should happen to the King and believe me have tried to make an agreement with him that would preserve his position as well as life. But he connives and lies, raising the Scots against us and even conspiring with the French and Irish. The Act was passed by Parliament earlier this month to put the King on trial. I believe this was a clear sign of God's will, and I am now ensuring that it can be expedited as soon as possible. God must have a reason for this, and I am sure this will be revealed to us as soon as this dreadful matter can be brought to a close. I think closure is indeed what God wants for this nation, and then to take us to a place where we will be stronger and better reflect God's glory. Indeed, I pray for peace and an opportunity to rebuild the nation, but it would seem this can only happen after the beheading of the King, and I am thankful that I can see the beginning of the end, for there are still challenges beyond his execution. I am certain that we must not cower away from what God wants or I am sure there will be consequences. With the King's death we can bring this sad chapter in our nation's history to a close. If he lives, before long he will have rallied some followers again, or worse, brought the French onto these shores, and more blood will be shed. One man must die to save many and bring closure for this nation to so many that have died. Just listen to the ranks in your own regiment Colonel and you will hear the calls for the King to be brought to justice. This must happen whatever the legality or individual justice of it, for the wider cause, for it is God's will. I have known the King ever since I was a boy and he cannot be trusted. The decisions he has made have directly resulted in the grief of so many families in this land and he is not apologetic in any way. We must expedite God's will as soon as possible and move this nation on. I hope this makes sense?"

"At one level, but it does not answer the question of why we fought and what will be the benefits for the ordinary people. These are the people who have really suffered and lost the most. Indeed, they continue to suffer, many half-starved with the price of food and the loss of the breadwinners in their families," Tom replied.

"I am sure it will be revealed by God in good time and I have been praying for such enlightenment. A new Commonwealth of England perhaps, with more Parliamentary determined rights. We may even have a new King, but Charles Stuart has too much blood on his hands and must meet his end. I must go now, Colonel as I need more signatures on this warrant," Cromwell said, waving the paper in his gloved hand.

The Privy Gardens

Tom was left in the Privy Gardens to contemplate what he had heard. He had wanted to kill the King personally at one stage but hearing now that he would be executed by Parliament was a shock. He knew the man himself now but had also been influenced by what the King had said to him. At least he had been clear about the role of the Monarchy and the importance of it in balancing power and governing the country. In comparison, Cromwell seemed to be much less clear, having absolute faith in the hand of God setting the direction, but that did not answer the question of what the war was all about. Yes, the King had made mistakes, abused his power, but did the people of England have the right to execute the anointed King of England?

Tom decided he needed a drink and found a local tavern. He was delighted to find Ralph Bankes inside who was having lunch with Robert Boyle, the Irish noble who had housed the Bankeses temporarily after the slighting of Corffe Castell in his house in Dorsetshire. He joined them and told them about the trial.

"My father will be turning in his grave at the lack of justice," Ralph said.

"I am not sure what is driving it. As you say certainly not justice, as evidenced by the absence of Fairfax and so many other Parliamentarians in the process. Cromwell believes it's God's will and he is just following the Lord's direction but anyone can say that anything is God's will to justify their actions. What do you think, Robert?"

Robert was in his early twenties, with a quite expressionless face, dark eyes and he was wearing a shoulder length mousey wig which was unusual for someone so young but reinforcing the impression of a wise head on young shoulders. A few years older than Ralph he become a friend and helped him with his studies when he lived at his house in Stalbridge and his passion for science and the studies and experiments he was doing. Robert always spoke slowly and intensely.

"Well, I have more views on the world of science and substances, than men and motivations. In nature it is simple, as I would apply inductive reasoning and logic to determine cause and effect. But men are not logical or rational in the same way for God has given us freedom of will. There are those who think the King should be executed and those who think the King should continue to rule with his divine right, and the third set are those who are unsure. Rational thinking would look for common cause but the freedom of our human will means that it is often driven by irrational thinking and emotion which cannot be quantified. Cromwell is an example of the irrationality as he is saying that whatever he thinks it does not matter, it is God's will that is important and this is driving him. At one level, you can see why he is adopting such an approach, because he can use it to counter all other arguments. He is rationalising all the irrationality."

"So that is clear then!" Ralph said with a laugh.

"Please excuse me, I must relieve myself," Tom said standing up. He found at the back of the tavern a door that led to a small courtyard, divided into two by canvas tents, one for the men and the other women. In the men's tent he found a trough, and he pulled open the drawstrings of his trousers to answers nature's call. As he was finishing up he heard the door of the tavern open behind him, and two men outside the tent conversing in irate whispers. They were speaking in French and he could only hear and understand words and phrases here and there. They were talking about the King and one sentence was clearly distinguishable, "Cromwell must be killed tonight if we are to save the King."

Tom was careful not to make a sound and continued to listen behind the canvas as he heard the door open again, heralded by the amplification of the din inside. Before the door could be closed he peered through a gap in the canvas and saw the back of the second man as he disappeared within. He was wearing a cloak, a distinguishing rouge in colour, and a black hat with large drooping brim casting a shadow over his shoulder. Tom made his way to the door and opened it slightly ajar. The two men were disappearing into the crowd but he could see the first man was taller and a Puritan preacher.

What should he do? Maybe he should let them assassinate the General and save the King? What was he thinking? Was he losing his rationality and letting God's will dictate events? No of course he should take action for he had always believed in justice and the rights of man, and he was a Colonel in Cromwell's army. He had to do his duty. The King's life was a separate matter. He decided to keep a watch on the men and send a note to Cromwell warning him and requesting his guards to help arrest them. The bones of a plan emerged in his mind and he would need the help of Ralph and Robert, but neither were experienced in military activity. He had no choice but to trust them and hope they would come through. He saw that the two men were stood at the far end of the tavern and could be seen easily from where Ralph and Robert were, so he returned to the table, sat down and whispered what he had heard, nodding in the direction of the two men. Ralph looked around but Tom pulled him back.

"Ralph, do you have a quill and parchment?"

"Of course; I am a lawyer," and he pulled them out of his bag.

Tom quickly drafted a note for Cromwell, and then sealed it with wax from a candle. He addressed the note to "General Cromwell, God's Will."

It was decided that Ralph was best placed to take it to Cromwell as he was well acquainted with several Parliamentary representatives and would be able to run faster.

"Well, this is stretching my legal skills but I hope I am up to the task. I will make sure I get to Cromwell," Ralph whispered and left. Robert and Tom made stilted conversation keeping an eye on the two men. Tom thought they must be waiting for somebody or something and sure enough another man entered and joined them half an hour later. This man's shifty eyes seemed to dart around the room, looking out for trouble. A large scar on his forehead testified to past troubles. He was dressed in a large brown coat and was clearly a man of many battles, but more likely in the streets of Southwark than Naseby or Marsden. Maybe he was a hired hand. John was feeling outnumbered, but then he realised that in the corner behind him were four men, Roundheads, no doubt in the capital to see justice done as many had travelled to London. Tom told Robert to watch the three men, but discreetly, and signal to him if they tried to leave or anything out of the ordinary happens, for he would not be able to see them from the corner of the tavern. He left Robert fiddling with his wig, clearly feeling uncomfortable in the situation he found himself,

"Everything is out of the ordinary to me, Tom. I am just a scientist," Robert complained.

Tom approached the four men, who looked like hardy foot soldiers, precisely the help he needed, although they had had perhaps a mug of ale too many.

"May I join you for a few moments, men? I am Colonel Harvey," Tom asked and pulled up a chair before they could respond.

"I may need your help. There are three men you cannot see from here but they are at the end of the bar. I may have to arrest them as they are conspiring to kill Cromwell."

"Royalist scum?" one of the men asked.

"Yes, precisely, although one is dressed as a Puritan priest, the other dressed as a gentleman in a red cloak and the third in a large overcoat with a scar above his eye. It may turn out nasty, but I assume you are all armed?"

"Sure thing, Colonel. Ready for action," the same man replied, tapping the hilt of his sword.

"Well, I want to take them alive as we need to flush out their co-conspirators to ensure the plot is foiled. I am expecting shortly an armed guard to arrive but if they attempt to leave beforehand, I will need you to follow me, and my orders. I will be at that table from where I can see them. Is that clear?"

But before anybody could respond, Robert turned and signalled to Tom.

"Something is happening! Follow me, men."

Tom and the four men left their chairs and rushed towards the bar where Tom could see the three conspirators making their way to the door. He pushed his way through the crowded tavern, followed by his new recruits. The three men had made their way out of the tavern before Tom could reach the door, but when he opened it he could see them walking together towards the Priory Gardens. Tom and his four followers with their drawn swords chased after them, Robert a safe distance behind

"You three, stop," Tom shouted, and the men looked around. All three drew swords, and Tom paired up with the man in the big coat, whilst the other two men were drawn into duels with two each of the foot soldiers. Swords clashed, and it soon became clear that the odds were shortening against Tom and his men. The priest had already disarmed one of the foot soldiers, whose sword clattered on the stone street and was now nursing a nasty cut to his forearm. The priest was now battling two others with fast strokes and agile moves. He was no priest that was for sure. Tom's opponent was a good match in sword craft, as well as physical strength. A few bystanders and Robert watched on, but the sound of boots from further up the street could be heard. Tom and his opponent both turned to see a guard of about twenty men running towards them, accompanied by Ralph Bankes. Tom was quicker to react and used the momentary pause in fighting to thrust at the big man and his sword found flesh in his sword arm, the man dropping his weapon. Tom pointed his sword soaked in blood at the man's chest as he held his arm. The guards were only fifty yards away but Tom realised that the priest was running away in the opposite direction, having somehow disarmed one of the foot soldiers and pushed the other to the ground. The third conspirator was still in battle with the remaining foot soldier. Tom judged he could hold his opponent off until the guards arrived, and scar face was not going to cause much more trouble.

"Robert, grab that sword and guard this man," Tom ordered, as he set off after the escaping priest, leaving an unprepared scientist to step up to the mark for a few moments before the guards arrived.

The priest turned into a street on the left. Tom followed to find his opponent had turned to face him, for there was nowhere to go. It was a dead end that serviced the rear of Westminster Hall, the service door bolted shut. Tom advanced. The priest held his ground. Tom thrusted his sword, parried by his opponent, who then countered. Blades clashed at an increasing pace. The priest was good. They struggled. Tom feinted another attack hoping to draw in the man in black, but he was too wise for that, and Tom only just recovered to parry a counterattack. The priest spun round, surprising Tom with his agility and it would have exposed him to an attack from his left had the priest not tripped, his foot caught in a hole in the street. It was Tom's chance. He brought the hilt of his sword down on the priest's back as his opponent fell to the floor.

"Throw away your sword," he ordered, the tip of his own sword pressed into the black jacket of the man splayed on the ground. The sword was thrown a few yards away and Tom pulled the man to his feet, tearing his collar and breaking a chain around his neck as he did so. But then the man kicked out like a horse, his boot finding Tom's crotch and propelling him backwards in agony. Before Tom knew it, the priest was up, had recovered his sword, and was running away. After a few deep breaths, Tom recovered and staggered after him, but by the time he had made his way to the main street, there was no sign of him, although Tom still clasped the chain that he had pulled from the man's neck. He looked at it, a gold chain with a pendant on which was an elaborate coat of arms, certainly not that of a Puritan priest but maybe a clue to the man's true identity.

By the time Tom had returned to the tavern, the captain of the guard had the injured man with the scar and the other Royalist disarmed and hands tied behind their backs.

"Captain, the priest escaped, but let's get these men to Cromwell and see what they have to say." He turned to Robert who was still holding scar face's sword. "Well done Robert, we will make a soldier of you yet."

"Alas, science is much more predictable and safer for me, thank you, Tom."

Cromwell was delighted to hear about the capture when Tom and the Captain of the Guards presented the two prisoners.

"Colonel, it appears you have been as busy as me protecting the future of this nation in the last few hours. Thank you for your note. Addressed 'God's will' ensured it got my attention, and it appears I must thank another Bankes member of the family for bringing it to me. You Bankeses seem to get everywhere," Cromwell said, smiling at Ralph.

"So, John Ashburnham. You were plotting to kill me to save the King," Cromwell said to the captured Royalist. "It is God's will that the King should be executed and that is clear. Even if you killed me, do you think that God's will would not prevail? Somebody else would just step into my shoes."

"God appointed the King, and there are plenty who would step into my shoes, Cromwell, to ensure that our anointed monarchy is not murdered by your treachery." The cavalier with furrowed brows spat out the words in defiance from gritted teeth behind his groomed goatish beard.

"And I am sure with some persuasion, you will be telling the Captain here all the names of those people who would step into your shoes and whom you have been conspiring with. You and your hired thugs," Cromwell replied, pointing to scar face, who had a blood-stained cloth acting as a tourniquet around his arm, under the coat draped over his shoulder. His face was cold and empty, a man with little emotion.

"General, there was a third man who escaped I am afraid, although not without a fight. He was an excellent swordsman but disguised as a Puritan priest. I managed to pull this chain off his neck," Tom said handing the chain to Cromwell.

"The Villiers coat of arms. It must have been George Villiers, the Duke of Buckingham. He is indeed an excellent swordsman, for I hear he escaped the Battle of Surbiton after fighting five men single-handedly. Captain, take them away and let me know what they tell you."

The first sentence – Kingston Lacey near Wimborne 27 January 1649

John's despair continued in the Bankes' house. He was alone but for the maid and cook and it had been over two weeks since he had seen or heard from Arthur. The events of the last few months continued to spin around his mind without sense or meaning, the ups and the downs, the revelations and incriminations. He had written to Captain Morris, but he had never been one for writing at the best of times and in his current state found the medium just frustrating. His letter just asked questions – how could they spend time together? How could they be open about their feelings to one another with friends and family? How could they avoid living a lie? He found no resolution to his mixed-up feelings. Perhaps the response from Captain Morris would help.

The following day he did receive a letter from Captain Morris – their letters had crossed and so brought with it no answers but, to the contrary, the opposite. Captain Morris had proposed marriage to Hester Sandys. He had declared that this had been motivated by his love for John, as it would draw a line under the accusations about the two of them, and so this would help John's case to be commissioned. But it would also provide cover for the two of them to spend time together – Mottisfont and Kingston Lacey were thirty miles apart – not too far away but far enough. They could have a small, isolated cottage halfway distance and meet up regularly.

John read the letter several times before tearing it to pieces and throwing them into the fire. This was not what he wanted - meeting up in some kind of clandestine operation, a sentence to imprisonment in a secret illicit life. He wanted to share love and adventure with Arthur and he wanted to be open about it. John knew his love was forbidden but Arthur was sentencing him to a life of suffering and frustration rather than of joy. He reached for the brandy bottle and poured a glass.

That evening John Bankes staggered out of the house into the gardens and the dark of the night, a brandy in his hand. His melancholy numbed him to the bitter cold and in his stupor he was oblivious to the allure of the night's sky and the comforting scent of wood smoke that permeated from the house on the gentle breeze. The same questions raced around his mind chasing answers that he alone could not address. What was he going to do with his life and what was its purpose having his two loves, Arthur and the army, forbidden to him? He had tried to unpick these questions. Love and relationships for aristocrats was never straightforward at the best of times. Most marriages were arranged with fathers often focused on the negotiations over dowries and status rather than happiness, whilst mothers are eager to find suitable husbands before the ticking clock dragged daughters into spinsterhood. John's own mother in London was a prime example, for she had written that she was even entertaining the prospect of Elizabeth marrying Richard Cromwell. His own mother, the Royalist heroine of Corffe whom they called 'Brave Dame Mary', was now trading with the Roundhead General his sister's hand as if she were cattle at the auction. He had seen it so many times before, when two families determined that a couple was a right match for reasons of status and security with minimal consideration to the feelings of the prospective husband or wife. There were exceptions to these top-down arrangements. His sister Alice seemed to fall for Sir John and he was mutually attracted before any parental involvement, but even then John felt they did not really know each other before they made their way to the altar. The poorer classes were much freer to build relationships based on love or at least friendship. But his love for Arthur was real, built on a foundation of friendship, and their emotions and feelings for one another growing without either being conscious of them or embarrassed by them. It was a relationship that naturally developed into love and a desire not to be apart, a longing for one another. But as soon as John had realised what it was, a love for another man, it had been taken away from him.

He looked up at the dark of the moonless night sky, but to the east a few stars provided hope amidst the mass of black across the rest of the sky. It had been a long, depressing month for John and much of it had been a brandy inflicted fog. During more lucid moments he realised that he was grieving for the loss of the man he had wanted to be; the army officer and head of the family, married with the Bankes line continuing from his offspring. He needed to leave that person behind but he could not come to terms with the new John Bankes and he failed to understand him. He longed for Arthur, his mother, or indeed his sister Alice or friend Tom Harvey to help him rebuild his new persona. But he was alone with his new self and not knowing how to relate to it.

He lifted his glass to the last remaining star in the sky as a hidden blanket of cloud travelled east threatening to engulf it. He struggled to maintain the trajectory of his hand, as he staggered a step forward.

"My star of hope, I toast you."

But as he spoke, that star was snuffed out, leaving a sky of total blackness. Nothing.

January 27th, 1649, the second sentence

Whilst Tom had been foiling the attempted assassination, Cromwell had been collecting signatures on the sentencing and death warrant. It had been more difficult than he had anticipated as men reflected further on the action they were contemplating, but with much cajoling he managed fifty-nine signatories amongst the sixty-eight commissioners who were acting as judges. John Bingham and Sir John Lisle were amongst those who refused to sign.

"General, I cannot sign a death warrant for a man who has not been given the opportunity to defend himself," John Bingham told Cromwell, in a small room within St Stephen's Hall.

"But you have seen first-hand the tyranny of the King, the death and destruction his forces have caused on this nation."

"But I have not heard him explain how and why this occurred. Many years ago, I was a magistrate and had made up my mind that a young boy was guilty of stealing a horse in Wareham before the trial. That day God taught me a lesson in the form of Sir John Bankes, the Chief Justice at the time, arriving at the court and putting me in my place. Justice prevailed and I thanked God for the light he had shone on my short-comings. Since then, I have vowed to up-hold justice, and frankly I have not seen any form of justice in the King's trial. He has not even been given the opportunity to state his case."

"Because the King will not recognise the court. Mister Bingham, there are fifty-nine signatures on this warrant, a clear majority, and so the King will be executed. After the King's death there will be a world where those that have helped the nation draw a line on this war and move on and they will certainly benefit, and there will be those who did not."

"That sounds like a threat, Mister Cromwell, and what are the plans for government beyond your execution of the King?"

Cromwell did not like how Bingham was making it personal and him not using his title. "It is not my will, but God's will that the King should be executed, and as a General I am just an instrument of the Lord. Afterwards God will show us the path to a new commonwealth and how it should be governed, and I will make it happen."

"Easy to say, but it sounds to me like you have no plan for afterwards. You are about to do something unprecedented and as big as anything I can think of in English history and you have no idea what will follow. As a Parliament we have not even considered this. So the King will be executed without justice, and then we have no idea what next. What is certain, General, is that there is a world beyond this one where you and I will account for our actions to God. I know the position I am taking is the right one and I will go to my maker with a clean conscience."

"Be dammed with you man. You told me yourself that the King is a tyrant. It is without question the right thing to do. The end of the monarchy will bring more glory to God and freedom for the Puritan faith to flourish than all your efforts in Dorsetshire over the last thirty years. Your failure to sign will not save the King but it will be noted by those who will define the future of this nation," and Oliver Cromwell got up and left John Bingham.

Cromwell had enough signatures but was infuriated by those amongst the commissioners that did not sign. He wanted a unanimous verdict but it was not to be. Some just did not want the King executed, but that was the sentence for treason and for him it was clear-cut. Others, like John Bingham, had their own reasons that he could not comprehend. And so the King was summoned back to Westminster Hall and the crowds returned with much anticipation.

The Lord President was determined to get the session over as quickly as possible and was clearly impatient whist the judges, Parliamentarians and the King himself were seated. Tom Harvey had resumed his position in the gallery but this time with Ralph Bankes. On the opposite side of the Hall Tom spotted Colonel Coke and pointed him out to Ralph.

"That rat, no doubt he is in league with the Rump, concocting evidence again the King. He is the one who should be on trial."

Tom was about to reply, but the Lord President brought the court to order and commenced proceedings.

"Charles Stuart you are brought before this court to make an answer to a charge of treason and other high crimes exhibited against you in the name of the people of England," Bradshaw commenced. A woman in the balcony yelled out, "Not half the people!" but guards were stationed throughout the hall and she was silenced with threats, but not before the rest of the audience broke out in shouts and comments, some supporting her but many more opposing and angered at the interruption. The Hall was tense and even more guards were brought in and deployed amongst the audience.

Bradshaw continued as soon as the crowd was brought to order in the Hall.

"There is a contract and a bargain made between the King and his people and certainly, Sir, the bond is reciprocal. There is the bond of protection that is due from the sovereign; the other is the bond of subjection that is due from the subject. Sir, if this bond be once broken, farewell sovereignty! You do not recognise this Court, and so your defence to the charge will not be heard and you have not proved to be a protector of England but a destroyer of England, as judged by all England, indeed the world."

The King was offered a last chance to respond.

"I wish to be heard in the Painted Chamber before the Lords and the Commons. But that if I cannot get this right, I do protest that these hearings are a sham and the nation will know that their King has not been heard."

Bradshaw dismissed the request.

"They are not going to give him a chance to defend the case against him. They are just going to sentence him," Ralph muttered in the ear of Tom.

"You have been found guilty by this court of the charges and have been judged tyrant, traitor, murderer and enemy of the realm of England. I will now pronounce sentence. You will be put to death by the severing of your head from your body," Bradshaw declared, with a triumphant tone.

The crowd reaction was mixed, many cheers but mixed with shouts of 'murderers' and some in the audience were just stunned, anticipating some punishment and even his crown being removed but not his head! Could the nation really execute their monarch anointed by God and what would be the consequences? The King had just sat in his chair staring blankly but he was quickly removed from that throne as well and led away.

Chapter Fifteen

The Death of The King

Fairfax's House, Covent Garden, 27th January 1649

Ralph Bankes had dropped into the Borlase house on his way back to his legal chambers and told his family what had happened and the King's sentence. Mary Bankes had immediately left and set off to see Mary Fairfax for she felt she had to do something. She knew she had had the opportunity when the King had passed the note to her requesting the rescue mission from his supporters, but she had decided not to do so. She could not put her son at risk nor betray the trust of Tom Harvey. Nevertheless, she felt guilty for she had always been loyal to the Monarch. Would she had decided on a different course if she had known they would execute the King? She did not know, but for sure there would be many who would never be able to forgive those who were behind this treachery and she was one of them. She could not believe she had been hoping for her daughter, Elizabeth, to marry Richard Cromwell. She understood from Sir John Borlase and others that General Cromwell had not been involved in the purge of Parliament, the act that brought the King to trial, and she was hoping that his presence on the committee of judges would balance some of the more radical views and ensure a more compromising outcome. But Colonel Harvey had told her yesterday about his encounter with the General the day before that. He had told her that he seemed to be instrumental in gathering signatures to execute the King. She had been shocked, then reframed her views on the General and now Ralph had confirmed her worst fears. Time was running out for the King so she had to do what she could for him and then decide what to do about Elizabeth.

Her carriage drew up at the Fairfax's house, just off Covent Garden, in the drizzling rain. It was the King who had been instrumental in the development of this area of London, one of many legacies that he would leave behind. Indigo Jones, the Royal Surveyor, had designed and planned Covent Garden with its magnificent piazza as a clean and fashionable sanctuary for aristocrats and courtiers in contrast to the overcrowded and cramped city. She recalled what the King had said at dinner in Hurst Castle, what had Parliament done for this nation, when the King had done so much. Indeed, she knew the King and his Queen wanted to do even more, modelling the development of the west of the city on Paris, but had been frustrated by a lack of funds to initiate such a grand scheme. The Fairfaxes had rented one of the new arcaded houses to the north of the open piazza, opposite the roman- temple designed church that fronted the square with its magnificent stone portico. Many of the gentry had left their houses for the safety of the country in the lead up to the war, and few had returned. Whilst wealthy puritans had started to move in, the area still lacked the elegance and vibrance of the previous decade. In the last year, a small market had now been created in the centre of the piazza, which was starting to bring back some life to the area. It was devoted to selling flowers, fruit and vegetables, and even in this dreary day was attracting servants buying produce to cook for the aristocratic households from all across the capital, and sellers walking from the market with their wares in baskets swinging from the yokes balanced on their shoulders.

Mary's footman knocked at the door and informed the servant who greeted him of Mary's visit, before escorting her from the carriage to the house under cover of a parasol. She was shown into a drawing room, a bright room with large windows fronting out to the piazza, with wooden shutters either side. The room had two sofas as well as an abundance of other chairs and furniture, too much Mary thought, but she was glad to take a seat at the request of Lady Fairfax near the hearth from which a fire breathed warmth into the room.

"My husband will join us shortly," Lady Fairfax informed her.

"That is good but before he does, there is some news I wanted to share with you. Colonel Harvey informs me that there was an assassination attempt on Cromwell, which he personally foiled, and the Duke of Buckingham was one of the conspirators. The Duke escaped, but the others are in the Tower."

"How can he be sure it was the Duke?" Lady Fairfax asked.

"The Duke was wearing a necklace which the Colonel grabbed off him before he escaped, and it has his coat of arms on it. Apparently, he was disguised as a Puritan priest."

"Well, I should not hold an attempt to kill Cromwell against him. I am sure he has been conniving in the background to bring the King to trial, whilst letting others do the public dirty work."

"I know he is taking a much more active role in driving events now."

The door opened and in came Lord Fairfax, dressed in a fine black jacket, with the modest white lace of his collar and cuffs complementing his dark facial features.

"Lady Bankes, it is good to see you. I so much enjoyed your family's company at the Borlase dinner, a wonderful idea. And to what do we owe the pleasure of your visit today?" He greeted his guest with a warm smile, sitting next to his wife on the opposite sofa.

"I wish my visit was for happier reasons, my Lord, but I am sure you have heard the verdict and sentence of the King at Westminster Hall in the last hour."

"Yes, we were informed. I am shocked although I had been expecting it. The Commissioners had largely formed that view before the hearing started, and that is why I resigned as its chair a couple of weeks ago."

"I know neither of you want to see the King executed, despite the injustice he may have caused to this country. I just wanted to plead with you, General to speak to Cromwell and save the life of our King. Strip him of his power, put one of his children on the throne, fine him, give him a humiliating penance, but do not execute the anointed sovereign of our nation. You are the commander of the army and so must have some sway."

"Commander of the army but not a politician, my Lady. I am commander because Parliament made me, and so it is a complex relationship and frankly my position is not strong. Amongst the ranks many will be celebrating today's news and will be making their way to the capital to see the end of the King whom they see as the tyrant who started the war and caused the death of so many comrades. Within the leadership of the army are many politicians, Cromwell, Ireton, Pride, who have the political power in their new Rump Parliament to relieve me of my command at their will. So please do not have any false hope of my influence, but I will do as you request, Lady Bankes, for I was minded to do that anyway."

"Thank you, General. We cannot let this injustice happen without any attempt to alter events."

"We are living through a defining moment in history and so you are right my dear to be seen to be on the side of justice. As you know my dreams of Presbyterianism being supported throughout England will be lost with the King's death, and I am sure the Scots will also be dismayed," Lady Fairfax added, tapping her husband on the knee.

"I will go to Westminster now, my dear, and see Cromwell. He is the snake that has conspired behind the scenes. I have heard that he will chair a committee that will govern the nation after the planned execution."

"How can you govern by committee? A nation needs a figurehead, someone that we can look up to and who will lead us through good times and bad, someone that is a symbol for the national identity, and represents stability and continuity. The King has been our monarch for nearly twenty-five years, and has delivered many things for this nation, even your own home here as part of his vision for London. He is the Defender of our Faith. How can a committee do any of these things?"

"Your views are well made, Lady Bankes, and you are preaching to the converted. I will take your message to Cromwell and any others who will listen to me in Westminster, but I am not hopeful."

"Thank you General, and I will return home to write to Cromwell saying that his son and my daughter can no longer see each other given his actions in recent months. But first I have to tell Elizabeth, and she will be upset."

"Why do it then, Lady Bankes?" Lady Fairfax asked.

"Yes why? I know Richard Cromwell. He is a man of good character. Not as strong or savvy as his father, but generous of heart," the General added.

"Maybe I will not be so hasty and think on it. Our children's happiness should be upmost in our thinking and maybe Elizabeth could find contentment with Richard. His father will be too busy with his committee to interfere at least."

St James's Palace, London January 28th, 1649

Mary was received by the King, sat in his chamber on a two-seater chair with Princess Elizabeth and Prince Henry cuddling him on either side. Both children looked sombre, although exquisitely dressed. Elizabeth wore a cream silk dress and she had ribbons in the ringlets of her golden brown hair, whilst Henry had a royal blue suit also made from silk with a lace collar. They both stared at Mary with much sadness in their eyes that did not respond to the smiles she gave them.

"Lady Bankes. Thank you for coming to see me."

"I am so sorry, Your Majesty. I am not sure what to say."

"What will be will be, but I am truly grateful for your visit. There was a time when I was surrounded by courtiers and would pray to be alone. It appears that the nation has deserted me, and whilst I am savouring every moment with Elizabeth and Henry, I feel very alone."

"God is with you, and the prayers of many of your subjects. Even on the Parliamentary side there are many that see what has happened a travesty."

"It is heart-warming to hear that, Lady Bankes. I have told Elizabeth and Henry not to grieve and that they should obey their elder brother Charles, the lawful sovereign; is that not right, Lady Bankes?"

"Yes children, and your father will still be with us all in our hearts."

Elizabeth started to sob.

"She has been crying ever since I told her of my fate. It is hard."

Mary could see the King struggling to hold back his own tears as he stroked her hair.

"I hear from my son in-law, Sir John Borlase, that the Duke of Buckingham and a few followers did make an attempt on Cromwell's life in order to stop this madness. It was foiled but he escaped."

"He is a good man, as loyal and devoted as any son. I do hope you and Lady Fairfax will have success in helping him to marry his true love. His actions no doubt make that more difficult."

"Be rest assured, Your Majesty, it may take time but the will of the two of us will prevail. Lord Fairfax himself is one of those who believes the sentence on you is unjust and argued with Cromwell on your behalf."

"Lady Bankes, we have only really had the opportunity over the last two months to get to know each other, but I have very much enjoyed your company and you have provided me with much to think about and reflect on, as well as strength to carry on over that time. You have been the most loyal of subjects but also a great friend. I only wish we had more time together."

Lady Bankes was now welling up. She had sacrificed so much for the man before her, and he had made mistakes, but was not the villain or tyrant that people made him out to be. He was a good man and loved his country and family. He had been appoointed by God for good reason, and the world would be a worse place without him. She had lost her home, her husband, her lover, her daughter, Bridget, and would now lose her King. She could not face losing anything more. She gave the King a farewell kiss on his hand, but could not look him in the eyes, before leaving as the King's chaplain, Bishop Juxon, arrived.

The Vyne, Hamptonshire, January 28th, 1649

Lord Fairfax had been rebuffed by Cromwell, Ireton and anybody else in the Rump Parliament he spoke to in Westminster. He had argued with Cromwell intensively, but he knew the weight of the army opinion sided with Cromwell, as the General reminded him, and despite being technically higher ranked, he felt powerless to do anything about it. He was disillusioned, not just by the rebuttals but by the whole conspiracy against the King. He wanted nothing to do with the execution and so he and Lady Fairfax returned to Hamptonshire. The mood was sombre at the dinner table.

"Apparently the Royalist had a conspiracy to assassinate Cromwell. I must confess I wish they had succeeded. The man has become power crazy. The plan was foiled by Colonel Harvey whom we met at the Bankeses' dinner. The lead conspirators were John Ashburnham and George Villers."

Mary squealed.

"Are you all right my dear?" Lord Fairfax asked his daughter. Lady Fairfax exchanged glances with Mary and felt her pain.

"What happened to them, my dear?" she enquired of her husband.

"Oh, they are in the Tower, being questioned. Well actually just two of them. I believe Villiers escaped, the slimy devil. But Cromwell has ordered

Coke's men to find him. You are looking pale, my dear. Are you not feeling well?" he asked his daughter.

Mary looked at her mother, but she could not maintain her composure anymore. She burst into tears and left the room.

"What was all that about?" Lord Fairfax asked, looking dumbfounded.

His wife took a deep breath before responding.

"My dear, we, Mary and myself, have been waiting for the right moment to raise something with you, a matter of utmost importance but also very sensitive. Last summer, whilst staying at Sir Edward's, an injured Royalist officer sought refuge at Clyveden. He had been at the Battle of Surbiton. He was gravely wounded, indeed close to death, and Mary nursed him back to health. The two of them inevitably got to know each other and formed a relationship. They fell in love. He then fled to the continent but has been writing ever since. The officer was George Villiers, the Duke of Buckingham."

"My daughter in love with Villers, one of the most prominent Royalists I have been fighting against. Nonsense. Impossible. I forbid it."

January 29th, 1649, Banqueting Hall, Whitehall Palace, London

It was a bitterly cold day and thousands were a massed waiting for the final act of their King. They had started to arrive at first light in front of the Banqueting Hall at Whitehall Palace, the building in which King Charles had held his infamous extravagant masques before the war, beneath the ceiling with the Rueben's painting glorifying his father and portraying the divine rights of kings to rule. It was seen by many who saw the King as an insensitive profligate tyrant to be a fitting backdrop for him to meet his end. But it was a mixed crowd, rich and poor, young and old, standing shoulder to shoulder, soldiers eager for justice who had travelled from afar, as well as Londoners, some curious and others thirsty for the blood of an execution. There were some who sympathised with the King and wanted to show their support to the end, and amongst them was Lady Bankes. Tom Harvey had escorted her to Whitehall at lunch time and used his influence to secure a good position with a clear view of the scaffold that had been erected: the stage of death, dressed in black cloth. On it were the three executioners masked by their menacing hoods. The heavy, intimidating charcoal bladed axe and thick wooden block awaited their victim, and behind them the enormous glass windows of the Palace reflected the scene of execution, beneath the heavy clouds of the wintery day. Looking around Tom recognised in the crowd the Sergeant and his men whom he had encountered at Basing House. They were clearly yearning to see the end of the King. He scanned around, the soldier in him looking for potential troublemakers, and the organisation of the guards protecting the scaffolding.

"Look at the executioner at the back. Recognise him?" Tom asked Mary.

"How can I with that mask on? And I am sure I would not know such a person in any event."

"I am sure it is Colonel Coke, from his stature. The execution would have to be overseen by an officer and he would be the obvious candidate. The good-for-nothing scoundrel that does all the dirty work for the Rump Parliament."

"You are most probably right, Tom. If, sorry, when Prince Charles returns to the throne, I will make sure that Coke is at the top of his list of people to punish for killing his father. A corrupt rat, murderer and now a man guilty of regicide. Decapitation will be too light a punishment for him. I am not a vengeful person but I will gladly make an exception for Coke."

"I do not understand why Cromwell tolerates him. He is the most ungodly man I know yet is supposed to be the moral enforcer of London."

From the stage, it was Coke who looked out on the expectant crowd from behind his black hood. He did enjoy overseeing executions and had seen many a Royalist and popist monk see their end under his command; this had reinforced his reputation as a man to be feared across the capital. On such occasions he would not wear a hood, but indeed play to the crowd, for many in the capital would flock to be entertained by the spectacle of an execution. He enjoyed geeing up the crowd as if he was a showman, enticing them to throw rotten vegetables and hurl verbal abuse at the prisoner, and even demand greater cruelty and pain during the execution. But today was different. He knew the day was significant beyond any execution in his lifetime and it had to be conducted properly and respectfully. There were many in the audience who supported the King and many other Parliamentarians who were against the execution, and of course there were those in Parliament who wanted to see the end of the monarch but in a way that was fitting for a King, whatever that meant. Cromwell had briefed him, and it was he who insisted on him wearing the hood. It was he who had determined what would happen at every stage of the execution, although he would not be on the stage and only witness it from afar, behind the glass of a room across the street. Yes, Cromwell would be watching him now and he could sense his gaze, reinforcing the chill of the air that blowed on the exposed scaffold. He would follow the instructions and had fully briefed the two executioners he had selected for the role, two men both experienced in the act to ensure there could be no mistake, and the job would be done in a single blow, but only he and the two men would ever know which man had yielded the axe. He was chilled to his bones as he rehearsed in his mind once again the proceedings, and it was nearly time for the show to begin.

The church bells across the city tolled one o'clock, the publicised time for the execution and the buzz of anticipation intensified. Many had seen executions before but none like this. But it was not until the bells chined the quarter hour that the King finally emerged directly from one of the windows of the Palace straight on to the scaffold, dressed in a black cloak to keep at bay the bitter cold. The noise of the crowds amplified whilst the tension increased. He was accompanied by Bishop Juxon, wrapped in a cloak, wearing his biretta bishop's cap and clasping a bible. Tom had witnessed several executions, and most poor souls had to be dragged out, with hands tied, the faces ashen and their eyes terrified, as they were forced on to the platform to meet their fate. But not Charles Stuart. He was still the proud monarch and King of England, prepared for his final masque.

"Tom, whilst we were at Hurst Castle, the King passed a note to me which was to message his supporters of his intended trip to Windsor. Of course I could not betray the trust you had vested in me, and I burnt it, but I feel guilty now, looking at him facing the axe."

"My Lady, you have done more than anyone for the King. I am the one who brought him to London, and feel some guilt myself, even although I wanted him to face justice. But I also thank you for what you did, I mean not betraying me."

The mixed emotions on the thousands of faces could been seen – joy, sorrow, rage, curiosity, disbelief, anger. The King addressed the crowd, but few could hear what he said. From where Tom stood, he could make out most of the words, but not understand the meaning. He seemed to be ranting about the causes of the war, God and even a reference to Alexander the Great. He did hear him say "… I have forgiven all the world and even those in particular that have been the chief causers of my death. Who they are, God knows. I do not desire to know," and thought that was gracious and the King then added, "I go from a corruptible to an incorruptible crown, where no disturbance can be, no disturbance in the world."

There was a commotion at the back of the crowd, but even with Tom's height he could not see what had happened. But the time was due. The King removed his cloak so he was dressed in just a white shirt and knelt before the block, in prayer. The crowd respectfully hushed. He looked intense as he knelt there and Tom could see he was perspiring despite the cold. But he was dignified. Prisoners were usually chained and dragged to the block, but the King freely knelt awaiting the horror of what was to come. He was a brave man, Tom thought as he heard the King take a deep breath and say 'Amen.' He stretched out his arms and bowed his head. The executioner raised the axe high above his head and then with all his strength brought it down and the blade crushed its way through the flesh and vertebrae of the King's neck, beheading the nation of its Sovereign.

The crowd groaned as the axe fell. Mary turned away, burying her head in Tom's coat and prayed silently that the King's soul would find the way to heaven as his head found the planks of the gantry, painting them red. The crowd was silent and still. Tom felt sick inside. He had seen thousands of men die on the battlefield, but there was something revolting about an execution, heightened by this being the first time he had known the victim. He had often vowed to kill Charles Stuart himself, but his conviction of the King's tyranny had been undermined by getting to know him and the sham of his trial. And now the King was dead, and there was no King to follow. An emptiness seemed to fill the capital as the crowd in an instance realised the nation had no ruler and reflected on what had happened; the loss of a sovereign or the punishment of a tyrant for the loss of so many friends and loved ones. One of the executioners grabbed the head and held it high for the crowd, the gore bringing a wave of sickness for many in the audience.

A woman not far from where Mary and Tom stood fainted, but many others were elated by it, breaking their moments of reflection and cheering a just and rightful end. But the cheers soon faded, and a more sombre mood prevailed. What was there to cheer about? Those who had wanted justice had seen it done, those who were supporters of the King had been there to the end, but the emptiness touched them all. The nation had beheaded its King, and another husband and father was added to the death toll. The emptiness was fuelled by the loss of life that had touched everyone in the crowd. There was nothing to be celebrated. Those lives would never be returned and now the figurehead and sovereign of the nation for nearly twenty-five years was gone with them. For some in the crowd, the King's supporters, many in disguise, it was the end of their cause, there was nothing now to fight for. Over the intense last few weeks all the talk in the capital had been about the trial and the outcome. Few had expected such a tragic end but here they were. It had all been decided and there was no going back. There was just the emptiness and worries about what next? What would Parliament do and how would the nation be governed? Who would defend the faith and lead the country? What would be the consequences of what they had just witnessed? Would the nation face God's wrath?

St James Palace – the night of the execution

Two soldiers guarded the King's bedchamber where his body had been laid to rest, with many more stationed at the perimeter of the Palace. But other than the guards the Palace was empty, with a few flickering candles providing the only life. The King was dead, those few servants that were left to service his needs had been dismissed and his children sent away to the custody of the Earl of Leicester at Penhurst in Kent. It was well beyond midnight when the guards heard the footsteps of somebody approaching echoing in the emptiness of the hall leading to the King's bed chamber, and they both tensed as a man dressed in a black hat and cape approached, holding a two pronged candlestick. He stopped in front of the door and nodded to the guards. One of them leant across to open the door of the bedchamber, for it was a man they recognised, and he entered the darkened room beyond.

Inside the room was a bed on which a coffin lay, and to its side a chair in which a man snored peacefully. It was Lord Southampton who had been given the responsibility to protect the body, but the man entering the room decided not to disturb him and walked over to the coffin. Inside was the King, still wearing the bloodied white shift of his execution, with a necklace of stitches where his head had been crudely sewed back on. A sheet beneath the head was stained in royal blood. The man raised his candle so the light illuminated the face, its eyes closed but the horror that had been endured was displayed in the frown of the features. The King was clearly not at peace.

The man whispered under his breath.

"It did not have to come to this, but your actions gave us no choice. Your execution became a cruel necessity. You have God to answer to now for the lies you have made all your life, and for the suffering you have brought on this nation. I pray He has mercy on your soul."

Cromwell whispered a prayer for his adversary before leaving the room to lead and rebuild the divided nation as God had guided him to do.

Chapter Sixteen

Aftermath

30 January, Sir John and Alice Borlase House

Lady Mary Bankes was writing a letter in the corner of the parlour, while Ralph and Alice were chatting on a sofa. A knock on the door was heard and, shortly after, the Borlase footman entered the room to announce that Bishop Juxon had arrived.

"Please show him in," Mary said, rising from her seat.

The Bishop entered the room. "Your Grace, to what do we owe this honour. Please take a seat," Mary asked, pointing to an armchair in the corner.

"Thank you, my Lady," the Bishop replied, sitting himself in a velvet backed chair close to the fire., He was wearing a black robe the arms of which were white and he carried a small wooden box which he placed on his lap. The Bishop's gentle demeanour helped put everyone at ease, despite his status and standing.

"I hope you are well, my Lady," the Bishop said, his neatly trimmed beard and facial features portraying a warm smile.

"May I introduce you to my daughter Alice and son Ralph, your Grace. But we are all here mourning the loss of our King," Mary replied, taking a seat next to Ralph on the sofa.

The Bishop's expression sobered, "I believe most of the nation is mourning the loss of Charles Stuart, my Lady. I pray his death will be the last and draw a line under this nation's troubled times. I can tell you our King went to God with a clear conscience, and I am sure will be sitting beside his father next to our Lord Almighty. I also know that he held both you, Lady Bankes, and your husband, in very high esteem. You personally were a source of great comfort to His Majesty in the last few months, for which I thank you. It is also the reason I am here."

The Bishop opened the box on his lap. "Here I have a letter from the King addressed to you, my Lady." The Bishop handed the folded letter with a wax seal on its back to Mary.

"I believe the letter refers to the contents of this box. These are the private letters of the King and my instructions are to leave them with you." Mary glanced at Ralph and Alice before taking the box that the Bishop was handing over, and walked over to the writing desk where she found a letter opener and used it to break the seal. The letter was short, which Mary read to herself still standing.

"My Dear Lady Bankes

There are few words that I can think to say in these last moments before my death, but I wanted to write to you to say thank you for your loyalty, as well as that of your husband and the rest of your family. Your company has been a great comfort to me over the last few months, and the loyalty of your family steadfast and beyond reason. I am truly grateful, but I do have one last request if I may. I am passing to you the custody of my personal letters. Sir John always advised me to be more transparent and open about my views, and to use the power of the printing press to my favour. I am sure Cromwell's fake news presses will be churning out pamphlets portraying me in a bad light to the nation and justifying their treacherous actions. Please could you take these letters and publish them in an open and transparent way for my subjects to read and hear the truth and learn about their King first hand. Please take care in this act for I would not want you to face any danger. Sir John I am sure will be by your side so truth can prevail.

Thank you once again, my most loyal of subjects.

Forever your King

Charles R"

Mary's eyes glistened with tears, and she dabbed them with a handkerchief.

"What does it say, mother." Alice asked. Mary took a deep breath and read the letter out aloud.

"What are you going to do?" Ralph asked.

"As the King requested. Do you know a printer, of Royalist persuasion, that we can trust, Ralph?"

2 February, Colonel Coke's House, Covent Garden.

Doctor George Coke arrived at his brother's house in early afternoon, after having received a request earlier in the day. He had very little to do with his elder brother almost the whole of his adult life, for they lived very different lives and had little in common. George had dedicated much of his life attending to the poor of London and more recently as a military doctor in the Royalist forces. But now he was back in London, and there was plenty of need for his services, not least with another outbreak of plague south of the river. In contrast, Colonel Harry Coke had spent the first half of his life gambling, drinking and womanising, squandering his family fortune and wrecking his marriage. But from the depths of depravation he had been converted to Puritanism and appointed the leader of the London militia that enforced the Puritan doctrines of piety and morality on its citizens. A poacher turned gamekeeper if there ever was one. His network of spies, his band of thuggish enforcement officers and the harsh penalties he imposed made him a feared man across the capital but had also allowed him to rebuild his wealth and status. He even managed to entice his wife back to him, and it was the pale-looking and fragile Jane who greeted George when he arrived. She had lived a sad life married to Harry but had somehow managed to bring up her two sons into good men without any help or support from her husband, but the years had taken their toll on her.

"Good to see you, Jane. How are you?" George asked as he entered the hall, removing his coat and hat.

"I am well, and thank you for coming, George. You know I would not call you if it was not serious."

"Where is he?" George asked, and was led upstairs to Harry's bed chamber, where he found his brother with a fever and wrapped up in the bed. A fire warmed the room but the air was stale.

"Brother, you do not look well. Let me take a look at you," and George inspected the patient.

"I have caught a chill George, at the King's execution. It was a bitterly cold day and I should have wrapped up warmer."

"It was a bitterly cold day for the nation, and not just because of the weather. No doubt you were supporting the regicides in their crime?"

"Much more than that brother, I was overseeing the execution," Harry responded, coughing as he finished his sentence.

George pulled back from him, more in disgust of what he had heard than the coughing fit.

"Our father would—"

"Do not say anything about our father or I will…" but his words were lost in another coughing fit.

"Harry, it is difficult to comprehend that you are my brother. You represent the opposite of what I stand for in every respect. But I am a physician and have dedicated my life to the health of citizens of this city, mainly the poor, but that includes obnoxious individuals, criminals and tyrants. I will treat you, not as a brother, but as I treat them, out of duty to you as a human being, but believe me I would prefer to walk out of here and let you suffer."

There was silence, as George continued to make his diagnosis.

"Well Harry, perhaps God is punishing you for your crime against this country and the King. You have the winter fever. It is a serious condition and it is likely to get worse; the coughing, difficulty in breathing, fever, aching and chills. It is an illness that could take your life. I will leave with Jane some syrups and herbs with instructions, and I will visit you every day until you recover."

The Colonel was dumbstruck for a moment whilst he took in what the doctor had said. He started to say something but a coughing fit hit him again before the first word could be heard. George grabbed hold of his brother under his arms, pulled him up and repositioned the pillow behind him.

"Sitting up will help to reduce the coughing, as well as the syrup."

"Thank you, George, you are a good man. There is no doubt that our father is proud of you."

8 Feb Sir John and Alice Borlase's House

A week had passed since the King's death and Lady Bankes had felt very downcast, but she had woken that morning determined not to drown in the sombre mood of the capital. The King was to be buried in Windsor the following day and she hoped that would allow her and the nation to move on. She planned to attend the funeral and then travel back to Dorsetshire. She had also been mulling over what to do with Elizabeth and her relationship with Richard Cromwell, but God at least took that problem away from her. Two days after the King's execution, 'Dick', as he had become to be known, had invited Elizabeth for a walk in Hyde Park. He escorted her there by his carriage, but before they arrived they had started to argue about the rights and wrongs of the King's execution and the role of Richard's father. Elizabeth requested that he take her immediately back to her house and the couple never said a word to each other on the return journey. Lady Bankes had some consoling to do when Elizabeth returned, but she soon recovered and Lady Bankes was pleased that the family had nothing to do with the Cromwells anymore although it was clear from Sir John Borlase and John Bingham that Oliver Cromwell was going to be the most powerful person in the nation under the new order.

That morning the family had received some good news, and Lady Bankes was now writing to John Bankes to share it. She had received a letter from Lord Fairfax that confirmed he had agreed with Cromwell that John Bankes would be offered an officership, the rank of Captain, in the cavalry under Colonel Ireton's command. Mary had assumed he had secured the agreement just before Elizabeth and Richard had broken up and she was overjoyed for she knew what it would mean to John. She told John in her letter that she would be with him in three days' time and could not wait to see him. She also wrote to Lord Fairfax and said that she would stop over at the Vyne in Hamptonshire on her way to Dorsetshire to express her gratitude personally.

9th Feb Swanage, Tom and Camille Harvey's House

John had been drinking for most of the morning. He was in a state of despair for he was now convinced that he had no prospect of joining the army and his future, with or without Captain Morris, whatever direction he considered taking, just seemed to have no hope. The wartime nightmares haunted him after dusk and he was even getting flashbacks during the day. He missed his friends and family and was lost in the emptiness of his life in Kingston Lacey. The cook, Mary Hardy, who had known John since he was a boy, had politely suggested he needed to go for a ride to get some air and clear his head. He had responded angrily that it was not for her to tell him what to do, but later felt guilty for the way he had spoken to her and heeded her advice, riding to Swanage. He wanted to talk to someone and the only person he could think about who was not in London was Camille. It was mid-afternoon by the time he arrived at his friend's house.

"John, what a pleasant surprise. Come in," she said as she opened the door.

"Thank God you are here. I need to speak to someone; can I have a drink?"

"Perhaps you have had too many drinks already John," she replied, as she led him into the parlour, having caught a whiff of his breath as he kissed her on the cheek.

"Just one, please Camille. It has been a long ride," and so she poured him a glass of calvados.

"What is it John? You do not look well."

"Everything, Camille. I have been alone at Kingston going mad. I do not know what to do or where to turn," he replied taking a large gulp from the glass.

"This is not like you."

"Well, I do not know what is like me anymore or even who I am."

Camille told him to sit down and tell her everything. He recapped his feelings of loss from no longer being in the army and that he feared he would never serve again.

"I believe Tom and your mother are making representations at the highest level. Be patient, John, and I am sure common sense will prevail. Tom talks about troubles in Ireland and whilst I pray for peace every day, the country faces tensions in almost every direction and will need experienced officers if not this year, then the next."

"I cannot tell you how much I miss the army, Camille. But at the same time the trauma of my experiences in battle will not leave me. I wake up at night, screaming as I dream about a musket ball fired at me or a sabre cutting me into pieces. Then there is the noise of the cannons and the cries from my friends whom I have lost. Their faces and those that I have killed come back every night to haunt me. I am starting to get jumpy as well. The slightest thing can panic me."

"Tom has nightmares as well, John. It is only natural after what you have been through. They will pass with time."

"No Camille, not time. I have too much of that. I need action and my mind needs to be filled with new challenges and missions. When I was with Tom in December, I was a different man. I was able to cope and starting to enjoy life again. I was with people who understood. But sitting in Kingston, the memories and the traumas are just recurring day and night. I am so close to losing my mind. Maybe I have already."

"John, I am sure Tom and Lady Bankes will sort things out and you will get what you want, what you deserve. Your mother and family will be returning from London soon."

"I assume Tom has told you what happened in London; appearing in court and that pamphlet Coke produced?"

"Yes, I am sorry John, but I am sure people will forget that with time as well."

"Time, time, time. I do not think I have time, Camille." He paused, looking at her despairingly. "Can I tell you something Camille? You must not tell anyone, not even Tom. You must promise."

"If it helps, John, of course."

"Captain Morris and myself, well we do have some kind of relationship. I mean more than just friends. I have never had such a friendship before."

"Is it love?"

"What is love? I keep asking myself. I was never expecting this, but I am certainly extremely happy when I am with Arthur, and melancholic when I am not. I have not felt that about anybody else and I believe I may be in love. But if it is love, I cannot declare it for either of our sakes."

"And what do you want to do about that John? Love is a precious thing and should not be denied."

"And how can it not be denied if it cannot be declared? Arthur has a plan but it is not what I want. He wants to marry Lady Sandys' daughter and live in Mottisfont. He calls it a marriage of convenience, as it is not far away and we could see each other regularly, secretly as well as socially, whilst the Sandyses need a husband for Mary."

"And what do you think of this plan?"

"I wish he had discussed it with me first. Frankly I do not know what to think about it. I believe it is deceptive to Mary, of whom I am already jealous which is not a good feeling. But equally I cannot think of any better options. My mother would die if she knew the truth for she is so concerned about the status of the family. 'We may have lost our wealth, but we can earn that back. We must maintain our status, as that cannot be earned', she always says. This scandal would destroy the Bankes name for ever."

"I think your mother would be much more understanding than you give her credit for. You are her favourite son, and there is no end to a mother's understanding and, I was going to say forgiveness, but what have you done wrong — love another human being."

"Which just happens to be a crime punishable by death!"

"John, I suggest you talk this through with Arthur as soon as possible."

"Camille, I do not even know what to say. I am just going around in circles. When I served with Colonel Sandys just before the Battle of Cheriton we whipped two men for being together. One of my fellow Captains strongly argued that they should be hanged and at the time I could see the sense in what he was saying, for it was important to set an example. After being whipped the two men were discharged. I suspect that the New Model army, with its Puritan values, is even more strict. There are two things I want in life: to be with Arthur and to be in the army. Each is difficult, both are impossible. My love is a forbidden love, Camille, and perhaps I need to forget it, bury it somewhere, and try to live a normal life. But it hurts and what is the point of a normal life without love once you have tasted it? There is no way back."

Camille suggested that John stay for supper and spend the night in Swanage, for it was nearly dusk, and John was pleased to accept. He continued to drink and the calvados soon disappeared, but after supper he fell asleep in a chair in the parlour. Camille retired and left him there.

In the depths of the night John got up after more nightmares recapping horrors of the war, with a hangover that had sent the world spinning around him. He staggered about and felt a need to escape, so with his coat found the door and ventured out into the night. He struggled to find the stable in the dark but soon his eyes adjusted and he lurched over his horse with his saddle and led it out into the night. He set off to where he knew not. The cold air from the sea breeze seemed to help to soothe the throbbing in his head as his horse carried him down from the Harvey's house to the main road out of Swanage. He could see his horse's frosty breath ahead but little else. Overhead the waning crescent of the moon followed him. John slouched in his saddle, letting his horse carry him at walking pace, feeling utterly in despair. A big chunk of his life had been bitten away, just like the moon and he was struggling to keep what was left together. How could he go on, with his love forbidden and his passion for the army barred from him. He had been alone for five weeks now, a loneliness that just amplified the pain of not being with Arthur or enjoying the camaraderie of the Army. Life was meaningless and he had no hope. He felt tears make their way down his cheeks, and that bitter emptiness in his stomach that seemed to be sucking the life out of him; his energy, motivation, happiness and reason to exist. He whispered a prayer for an end to this existence. He thought of the short time he had with Arthur in London, but the memories seemed to be foggy. The darkness of the woods along the road threatened to engulf him as he struggled to see the road ahead. As he rode on, he came to Corffe, quiet and asleep. He passed the partially repaired church and as he entered the market square the dark silhouette of the castell ruin stood before him. This had been his home for so many years, a place of joy and happiness. Perhaps he could find peace and serenity here again?

Camile awoke through the fog of a dreamworld to the cry of William and a bitterly cold dark morning. With the aid of the remaining embers of her bedroom fire, she lit a candle and cautiously retrieved her little one from his cradle. After snuggling him in a cozy blanket, she offered him nourishment from her breast, a task that usually brought her pure delight, although this morning she was still half in her dream and a tad dazed. She closed her eyes attempting to reconnect with her dreaming oddity, gradually capturing disjointed images of trees, moonlight, Corffe village, the ruins of the castell and the distraught face of John Bankes. A sense of unease began to build within her. Something was not right and the dream's symbolism did not bode well. William had finished feeding and appeared to be comforted, but she knew that he would not return to sleep anytime soon. Nevertheless, she settled him back down in his cot and, with a candle in hand, exited her chambers. She saw that the guest room door was open, and poking her head inside found the bed empty and un-disturbed. As she crept downstairs to the creaks of the stairs, she found the parlour door ajar, and inside the sofa where John had fallen asleep empty. John was nowhere to be found, and her sense of anxiety enveloped her. She peered out the parlour window into a still-dark morning, noticing a faint beam of light emanating from the eastern sky. She wrapped herself in a warm cloak and went outside, making her way to the stables. To her bewilderment, she discovered that John's stallion was missing. Why had he left in the depth of such a cold night? Who knows what may have befallen him? He had been in such despair and her concern was intensifying.

She found Nela in the kitchen, stoking up the fire.

"Morning, Nela. Would you go upstairs and look after William. He is in his cot. I need to ride over to Daniel's house."

"It I still dark, my lady. Wait a while. Or if it is a message, I can take it."

"Thank you Nela, but it is John Bankes. He disappeared in the night and I fear for his safety. I must go now. The morning light will be with us by the time I have saddled up and I need to ask Daniel to look for him. I will not be long, but I need to make sure he goes straight away."

Camille wasted no time in dressing and saddling her horse, before setting off to Worth along the road out of Swanage via Langton, the direct route rather than the scenic one over the cliffs she would ride at her leisure. The ground was hard and the branches of the bushes and trees along the roadside glistened in their frosted coats as the sun's light heralded the start of the day from the bay behind her. Diligently scanning both sides of the road through the morning mist as she rode, meticulously on the lookout for anything unusual or any signs of John's presence, but to no avail. At Langton, houses were coming to life and she could smell the smoke of wood being burnt from the hearths of the fires within. Here the road forked and she took the high road up to Worth Matravers, rather than the low road to Corffe. When she reached the top of the limestone ridge she reined her horse to a stop and looked down into the valley, hoping to see John Bankes riding along the road to Corffe. But the frosted fields and naked trees in the woods bared no sign of life and it was hardly surprising on such a bitterly cold morning.

Camille arrived in Worth to find Daniel hauling an armful of wood towards his cottage.

"Camille, what crazy reason could bring you here so early on such a cold morning?" Daniel asked, misty puffs emanating from his mouth as he spoke.

"Daniel, it is John Bankes." Camille answered breathlessly, dismounting her steed and rushing towards Daniel before continuing. "He came over yesterday evening and was in a very melancholic mood. He was drinking but fell asleep in the parlour. But this morning when I awoke he had gone. Daniel, I am worried for him. Anything could have happened to him riding in the dark, half drunk. And I sense something is amiss. Please will you search for him and if necessary, ride to Kingston Lacey to make sure he is alright. I cannot rest otherwise."

"John Bankes is a hardened soldier and is made of sterner stuff than you give him credit for, Camille. He is used to being out in the cold. I may manage the estate but I am not his nurse maid."

"John, please. I know something is not right. He may have hit a branch and be on the road unconscious in this cold. Please do this for me."

"I must be mad. As if I have not got other things to do. But if you insist, Camille, I will do as you ask," he grumbled.

"Thank you, Daniel. But please don't dally and go now. I have already followed the road to Langton and you can pick up the fork from there. I am truly grateful." And she gave her brother-in-law a big hug.

9th February, Windsor Castell

Mary and her four children had travelled to Windsor the night before in a coach with its driver who had been hired to take them all the way to Dorsetshire. They had stayed in a tavern called the Two Brewers and enjoyed the fare of the hostelry. The King was to be buried at St George's chapel in late morning, but with a simple service and no formal ceremony. Mary left her children in the care of the innkeeper's wife whilst she attended. It seemed like the whole town came out to say goodbye to their sovereign, as his coffin, covered in flowers, was carried on a matt black funeral carriage up the long gravel drive through Windsor Park. Mary was on a list of mourners compiled by the King himself who were allowed into the chapel for a service amongst friends and family, and she was delighted to find that the list included Lady Fairfax.

"Did you see the crowds outside? There is to be no official ceremony, no gun salutes, no flags, no honour or celebration of the life of one of our longest-serving monarchs. But whatever Parliament decrees, the nation will come out to honour its King," Lady Fairfax said.

"Yes, but they do seem to have already stripped him of his crown for I remember it being on his father's coffin. And this chapel, so much of its grandeur has been removed, presumably by the army that occupied the Castell during the war," Lady Bankes replied.

"My husband tells me initially there was a lot of looting by Parliamentary forces, particularly in places of worship that were considered too high church, before he and Cromwell imposed the discipline of the New Model army. But now Parliament is trying to sell everything royal to pay for the debts of the war. I heard in the town that they are even trying to rent the Castell."

"Henry VIII and many other monarchs will be turning in their graves in this very chapel."

The two women silently watched the coffin enter the chapel escorted by the guards of the Castell, and followed the ceremony, conducted by Bishop Juxon, the King's chaplain, and the Archbishop of Canterbury. At the front, Princess Elizabeth and Prince Harry, who showed royal courage and strength, their stern faces not betraying their grief. Both women felt for them and would have gladly taken them under their wing but were glad that

Lady Leicester, who had looked after them for the last two years, was comforting them and at their side. When the service was finished, Lady Bankes and Lady Fairfax followed the mourners out of the chapel, leaving the King to be interred with his father and amongst his royal ancestors. Whether he would be granted the glory of Ruben's painting in the Whitehall Banqueting Hall would be for God to determine, but both women had prayed for his soul. Outside the chapel a tent had been erected and a small book was being offered. Lady Bankes was overjoyed to see that Ralph and herself had managed to do what the King had asked and in time for his funeral. She picked up a copy. It was entitled *The Portraiture of his Sacred Majesty in his Solitudes and Sufferings.*

"My Lady, the manuscript has just been published today and is drawn from the writings of the King, which he passed on to Bishop Juxon," the man in the tent said.

"I know and thank you. I will take one, and I am sure Ann will as well," Mary replied.

Mary opened the book and read a few paragraphs and could hear Charles Stuart in the words. He had left something behind which painted a true and empathetic account of the King and his character, the man she had got to know so well in the last two months, in contrast to the image John Milton portrayed in writings on behalf of the radicals. She smiled to herself as she thought how mad Cromwell will be when he finds out. The King had finally listened to her husband who had repeatedly counselled him to embrace the power of the printing press. If only he had listened much earlier.

February 10th, The Vyne

Lady Fairfax had insisted that the Bankes family stay with them at the Vyne after the King's funeral and so they did. It was an opportunity for Lady Bankes to close ranks with Lady Fairfax and challenge her husband's dogmatic view of his daughter's relationship with the Duke of Buckingham, and after dinner when Mary Fairfax had retired, this is exactly what they did.

"Lord Fairfax, when we were in London, we spoke of marriages across the divides in our nation to help reconciliation," Lady Bankes said.

"Ah no doubt Ann here has requested you to ask if I should reconsider my position related to Mary and her Duke?" he replied.

"She may well have the interests of her daughter at heart, in the same way as I have in both promoting marriages for my daughters, Alice and Mary, and more recently when it came to Elizabeth and Richard Cromwell. Fortunately, Elizabeth argued with Richard on her own account, but if she had not and if she had truly loved him I would have supported her, even if it went against all my instincts since his father was instrumental in the execution of our King."

"You think I should follow such an example?"

"I think you should follow your daughter's example and her heart. From what Ann has told me, she is very much in love with the Duke, and I can tell you that love is a precious thing and should not be denied."

The next morning Mary Bankes and her family set off early from the Vyne on the next leg of their journey, and as they departed a messenger arrived with a letter for Mary Fairfax. She took it straight up to her room to read. From the handwriting she knew who it was from and so it meant George had not been captured. She took a few moments to compose herself sat at her dressing table before she opened it.

"My dearest Mary,

I have longed to write to you ever since our rendezvous in the woods, but until my business in London was over, it was not safe to do so. I have witnessed an almost indescribable tragedy in the murder of my god father and our King, something that is so heavy on my heart that only the thought of being with you again provides me with the strength to carry on. I can confess to you now that I was part of a plan to stop the madness, but it was foiled. My fellow conspirators were captured, but I managed to escape and go into hiding. I believe we must have been betrayed somehow, but with the thwarting of our mission, all hope of salvation for the King died.

I witnessed the trial in disguise, a total mockery of justice. The King repeatedly questioned the authority of a small group of Parliamentarians to bring to justice the King of England, appointed by God. Half of Parliament had been purged and the House of Lords disbanded so Bradshaw and Cromwell could proceed without due process. My heart jumped with glee when your own mother interrupted proceedings to demonstrate against the lack of justice. I felt a connection with her and wanted to shout for joy and run over to hug her. It was also noted by the court that your father was not present, presumably because he did not support it. I pray that this means there maybe hope for us in the eyes of your parents.

I also witnessed the King's execution from a window in a building opposite Whitehall Palace. He died with dignity, and I hope to pay my respects at his tomb in Windsor when it is safer to do so. I loved him, Mary, and have wept much since. He was the closest person to a real father to me, and he treated me as one of his own. He was always kind to me and encouraged me in swordsmanship and hunting. I believe he was also a good king and loved England and Scotland very much. Queen Henrietta will be mortified, as will Prince Charles. I fear for Princess Elizabeth and Prince Harry, father and motherless, and pawns of Parliament.

The King's execution was a martyr's death, from which I hope the Royalist cause can be rekindled supporting his eldest son Charles as King. I am about to embark on a boat to France to be with Charles, but I fear it will be some time before it is safe for me to return. There is a warrant for my arrest in London., I have become a master of disguise but I have had some close encounters with those after me and now need to give it some time to settle down and for people to forget about me.

I pray that you will not be amongst those who forget me, for I will never forget you and will write to you as soon as I get to France. I will plan somehow to see you and, in the meantime, send you all the love from my very broken heart.

Yours always,

George."

She reread the letter several times, before there was a knock at the door. Putting the letter away she said, "Come."

Her father opened the door.

"Mary, how are you?"

"I am fine, thank you, Father."

"I am sorry I have not talked to you about George Villiers before. Your mother told me of your acquaintance, and it angered me. His father was a tyrant who was responsible for some of the worst military campaigns in English history. He was the cause of thousands of lost lives. I am worried that his son may have similar characteristics. But your mother and Lady Bankes have shown me that perhaps I have been misguided and perhaps I should reconsider my views."

"Yes Father. Judge him on his own character and actions, not that of his father's whom he never even knew."

"I have always wanted the best for you, Mary, and I have always said that we would find you a suitable husband that you are fond of and could love. Whilst I have been distracted by the war, it seems like you have been finding love for yourself. Tell me about this man and what you feel about him."

"He is truly a wonderful person and a perfect gentleman, Father. I believe we both love each other. He is now in France and I miss him terribly. He came to see me last month but we only had a few moments together."

"He came here?"

"Yes, I told him he was crazy."

"It sounds like he is prepared to take big risks to see you Mary, but I can understand that. He has also taken big risks to save the King, which is more than any of the other Royalists have done. Mary Bankes asked me if ten years ago I would have been happy to consider a marriage of my only daughter to the Duke of Buckingham and godson of the King. The answer was yes. She then asked me in ten years' time, when hopefully this war has been forgotten, would I have been happy for my daughter to be married to the Duke of Buckingham, and I also answered yes. So why should I not be happy now, especially as my daughter is in love with this Duke?"

"Oh Father, thank you," she said and gave him a big hug.

"Mary I still need to meet him and I will also make some further enquiries about his character, but in the meantime I thought you might like this." He handed her a necklace.

"Why, it is his! How did you come by it?"

"It was recovered by the Colonel who tried in vain to capture him, for its seems that only the beauty of my daughter can entrap this Cavalier."

"Oh, thank you, Father."

11 February, Kingston Lacey

It was very late and dark when the carriage carrying the Bankes family finally arrived at Kingston. There were lights on in the house and the door opened as the horses were pulled up by the driver, but rather than John Bankes or Mary Hardy, it was Tom and Camille who came out to greet them followed by William Harvey. Lady Bankes knew that there was something wrong from their faces and how they sluggishly approached the carriage.

'Where is John?' she asked Tom.

'My Lady, walk with me." He led her to the side of the house, away from the children. "I do not know how to tell you this… John has taken his life. I am so sorry."

Mary abruptly halted, her face contorted with agony, drained of all emotion as she wailed, "No! No! This cannot be true." She turned to find Camille behind her. "Camille tell me it is not so."

"I am so sorry, my Lady," Camille said as she enveloped Mary in a comforting embrace. "Self-murder, why oh, why? We have the news he wanted. I wrote to him," Mary lamented.

"We know. Your letter arrived this morning but after he had ended it all," Tom said.

"What did he do?" Mary asked, her voice quivering and barely more than a whisper.

"He hung himself, my Lady. In the castell ruin at Corffe with his horse's rein."

"I wrote to you my Lady but the letter would have crossed with you on your journey. Daniel found him yesterday and Tom helped me bring the body over from Corffe earlier today. He is inside," William added from behind.

Mary was utterly at a loss, incapable of taking in the words, the colour drained from her face. She had been struck by a tragedy she could not comprehend or know how to deal with. She turned, looking at Tom, Camille and William in turn, hoping for one of them to say it was not true. She turned again as the rising, choking sense of despair and crushing loss overpowered her, and she sank to her knees and wept. She put her hand to her chest as she thought her heart would stop. Camille knelt beside her and tried to comfort her. She wrapped her arms around her, praying she could alleviate even a fraction of the anguish, but she knew how much Mary loved John. The sobs continued, as Mary buried her head into Camille's chest, like a helpless child.

"Let me see my boy. Can you watch the children in the meantime, Camille?" she asked through her sobs.

Tom took her inside and up to his room, where John's body was laid in a coffin on trellis legs. She wept.

"My boy, my beautiful boy. What have you done?"

13 February, Winchester

Tom was on his way back to Winchester, his heart heavy with grief and guilt. Another friend lost; another life wasted. He couldn't help but wonder what he could have done to support John in his darkest hours. Camille's account of John's final night only reinforced his sense of failure. He was approaching Winchester, the city where John had once shown his courage and officer credentials, but to no avail. The thought of having to break the news to Arthur made the last leg of his journey even more daunting.

When Tom found Arthur checking supplies in the storeroom, he tried to put on a cheerful face, but the weight of their loss was too great. "Something's wrong, what is it?" Arthur asked, his concern evident.

"It's John, Arthur. I'm so sorry, but our friend has taken his life," Tom replied, struggling to keep his voice steady.

"No, that can't be true," Arthur replied, in disbelief.

"I wish it weren't true. He hung himself amidst the ruins of Corffe Castell," Tom said, struggling to restrain his own emotions.

"That's impossible, John would never do something like that," Arthur exclaimed before kicking over a stool and charging towards Tom, his anger palpable.

Tom dodged the charge but wrapped his arms around Arthur as he passed. He was much stronger than the slender Captain and held him tightly. He could feel Arthur quiver and convulsively catch his breath before sobbing, unable to control his grief.

"We all shared a love for John, he was truly a great man," Tom declared.

Arthur continued to sob.

17 February, Wimborne Minster

The crushing loss of John to Mary was more than she could bear. She had lost her husband, but he had led a full life and she has nursed him to the end. She had lost her lover, Captain Cleall, and regretted how his cruel death had deprived them of a future together in the last moments of the fall of Corffe Castell but was thankful for the time she had spent with him during the siege. She had lost her child, Bridget, but she had been there every moment of her illness. But John was her favourite and the manner of his death was more salt to the wound. Taking his own life. He must have been so low, so lonely and in such despair and she, his mother, had not been there. And fate again had been so cruel, for she was on her way to him and she must have been so close to being there for him. The what-ifs and whys had circulated her mind until she became dizzy. She felt numb inside. An emptiness that was like a knife through her soul. Her life had just crashed into a wall and the lady of fortitude had no strength left, unable to care for her other children or herself. She had spent much of the last week in bed, for what was there to get up for? She was angry. How could this happen? Who was to blame? Cromwell for not letting him join the army sooner. Arthur Morris for breaking his heart. Herself for not being there. The anger was mainly directed at herself. Why had she not come back sooner? The King's funeral? Yes, she had grieved for the King but had he really deserved her compassion? She should have returned earlier.

She had been brought up in a world where self-murder was considered a sin against God. The Church and much of society had changed its views over the last twenty years and the Church now accepted that God could be merciful to those that suffered such fate. But many still held traditional views and would see suicide as a stigma on a family. What would be the impact of this loss on the Bankeses' family status, something she had fought so hard to preserve? She knew how important status was and how easily it could be lost, and so would John's loss have long-term ramifications for the rest of her family? She sobbed uncontrollably. She hardly slept and when she did she awoke to the loss of John even heavier than before. Alice and her other daughters came from London as soon as they received word, and the grief was shared, but it did not detract from the pain, the sorrow and the guilt that Mary endured. Earlier in the week Father Jerome, the former chaplain from Corffe who was now preaching in Dorchester since the destruction of St Edward's church, visited her and assured her that through Christ there was a path for all to God, irrespective of the cause of death. Yesterday Arthur Morris came to see her. Mary was still in bed and Alice accompanied him. When he stepped in through the door she felt anger rising inside her, but at the same time a cold draught seemed to blow over her and she sensed a presence, a calming influence in the room, beside her. She looked around in confusion, but there was nothing there. She stared unseeingly around the room.

"Mother, are you all right? Captain Morris has come to pay his respects," Alice said, holding her mother's hand.

"Ah, ah, yes, my dear. I am a little confused, but yes, Captain, thank you for coming."

"I am so sorry to hear about the loss of John, my Lady," but his own eyes were welling up.

"Captain—can I call you Arthur? I am grateful for your visit, because I know you share in our grief and John was special to you, as you were to him. Thank you for making him happy over the Christmas period."

The Captain took a deep breath.

"Yes, I am heartbroken. I have been in despair ever since I heard the news. It is such a loss, such a waste. He was such a wonderful person, such a spirit, so kind. We have all lost so much."

But today she found herself in Wimborne Minister for John's funeral, which she could barely comprehend. Camille and Alice had helped her get dressed and to the church, and Elizabeth and Mary had comforted and prepared her other children. The Minster church of Saint Cuthburga had been a place of worship, pilgrimage and religious study for many centuries and had received a new charter from King Charles before the war which granted it money to grow and develop, and so it bore his coat of arms which comforted Mary. And here the Bankes assembled in the front of the church, but the formidable Lady Bankes was absent; in her place, just an old despairing woman who was no use to anyone or for anything. She had insisted that Captain Morris sit with them and so he did.

The Saxon church in the heart of Wimborne has many famous limestone tombs, including that of King Ethelred, the brother of Alfred the Great. Today in Purbeck stone a new tomb would intern the body of John Bankes, son of Sir John and Lady Bankes, and to pay their respects were many mourners from across the nation who had buried their differences for the day. Lady Bankes was pleased to see such a presence as it would suggest perhaps her fears on the impact of her loss on the Bankes family status were unfounded as she turned around to see Lord and Lady Fairfax, as well as their daughter Mary, Sir Thomas Herbert, Lord and Lady Cranbourne, Lady Sandys and her daughter Hester, Sir John Borlase, Sir Humphrey Weld from Lulworth Castell, Sir Robert Boyle, John Bingham, Colonel Harvey and his wife Camille, Charlotte and Doctor George Coke and many folk from the Purbecks and Wimborne, including William and Elizabeth Harvey, Daniel and Jane Spear, John Anderson and his family, Josh Miller and his wife, and Mary Hardy. There was also a group of former Royalist cavalrymen at the back who had served under John and travelled from Hamptonshire as well as Captain O'Reilly, and soldiers from Colonel Harvey's regiment that had been part of the mission to bring the King to Windsor three months earlier.

After Father Jerome opened the service and the first hymn had been sung, Colonel Tom Harvey was invited to say a few words about John Bankes. Tom had never made a speech to such an audience, but Alice and Ralph had insisted, and John summoned all his courage to walk to the front. He turned to look at the expectant faces and pulled out a piece of paper, which he had prepared with Ralph and Camille earlier. He coughed.

"John Bankes was my best friend. His passion all his life had been to join the army, and he served the King well in numerous battles. Lady Bankes asked me to speak today because of my shared experience, although on opposite sides of the battlefield. There will be many in the room who will understand the spirit of the army, whether cavalry, foot or artillery, Roundhead or Cavalier, gentry, artisan or labourer, of the spirit and camaraderie and above all the honour of serving together. That is what John Bankes lived for and ultimately died for. There are many wounded soldiers across this nation, carrying mental scars, men who struggle with the return to a normal life, men who are haunted by trauma and memories of friends lost on battlefields. Like many in this church, I have almost forgotten what it is like to attend a funeral is such a place yet have stood by more graves than I can remember and recall just as many fallen comrades whose bodies were left to rot unburied. As we stand here today, to celebrate John's life, and as this nation hopefully moves forward in the name of peace, can we remember the needs of all soldiers, those who still wear uniform as well as those who have given up muskets and pikes, as they try to come to terms with a civil life rather than a civil war? I hope there are people in this congregation, including myself, within my regiment, who can help to ensure John's legacy can be to help men across the nation manage and overcome the traumas that they have experienced and adapt to their new lives. After the Battle of Roundway Down, John saved my life, and I never had the opportunity to pay him back. But I will commit to ensure the loss of his life will not be in vain, but benefit many in need, and I pray that others here today will join me."

Tom looked at Lady Bankes who was dabbing her eyes but managed an appreciative smile and then Lord Fairfax who returned a nod. There was a silence in the church as John walked slowly and solemnly to his pew whilst Ralph Bankes got up and took his place at the front of the church.

"My brother John was a Bankes through and through. He lived up to the values of the family and particularly our father, for he was honest and fair, trustworthy and kind. Our friend, Colonel Tom Harvey, has elaborated on his passion and skill as an officer, and I am sure he was respected by his men, as much as he was loved by his mother, sisters and brothers. As the eldest boy he was a role model for the family; he was kind-hearted and always liked to have fun. He will leave a big hole in our family, and his memory will be cherished as we pray for his soul and redemption whilst he joins our father and sister Bridget at Heaven's gate."

"We will always remember the wonderful times we had as children at Corffe, living in the Castell, riding in the hills, swimming in the sea and adventuring out to Green Islandm in Poole Harbour. John's jokes and pranks, his laughter and happiness will be memories for us all to cherish forever."

"I wanted to use this opportunity to look forward and celebrate the legacy of John, building on what the Colonel has said. Corffe was a home to my brother and a place that he dearly loved. The ruin of the Castell and the devastation caused to the church was something that filled us all with sorrow, and as a family we are truly sorry that we have not been able to contribute more to the repairs on the church. I am delighted to announce that thanks to John's friend Captain Morris and I believe the influence and lobbying of his father, a grant of £250 has been made by Parliament to repair the church. I know John would have been delighted with this news, as I am sure many here in the audience will be.

"I also would like to declare our family's intent to build a new home at Kingston Lacey, a fine house reflecting the family's status and tradition. We will commission an architect to build a house out of brick and stone from the Purbeck quarry and will call it 'Kingston Hall' in the memory of Sir John Bankes, my father and John Bankes, my brother. It will take us some time to fund and fulfil this dream, but I am committed to making this happen and building a new home right here in Dorsetshire."

As he stepped down there was a respectful round of applause.

The funeral service came to an end and the coffin was taken out for burial in the churchyard. Father Jerome blessed it, and with prayers it was lowered into the grave, Mary and Alice arm in arm, sobbing as they silently said their own prayers and goodbyes to John.

Mary and her family, along with the Cokeses and Fairfaxes, returned to Kingston Lacey. Meanwhile, the Harveys and the folks from Corffe made their way south towards the Purbecks. As they set off, Tom noticed two horses heading to the east, and one figure stood out to him. He spurred his own horse in pursuit and chased after them until he caught up with the riders.

"Good God, Harry Coke, what are you doing here?" Tom yelled as he pulled his horse between the two men.

"Calm down, Colonel, can't a man enjoy the beauty of your shire while witnessing the Bankes family's downfall?" Coke replied, bringing his horse to a halt.

"You're sick," Tom spat.

"Not as sick as the man who took his own life by jumping off a ruin with a rope around his neck. Come on, Colonel, we all know where his soul is now - in hell with his King," Coke said with a sneer.

John exploded with anger and hurled himself off his horse, tackling Coke to the ground. While John emerged unscathed and upright, Coke was on the ground bruised and winded. John drew his sword as Coke's companion looked on blocked from being of any assistance to his commander by the riderless horses.

"It's your soul that's damned for the evil you've spread every day of your life on this earth. I know you oversaw the execution of the King, and John Bankes' death is largely down to your lies and deceit. You have a lot to answer for when you face God, and I'm going to make sure you get there pronto," Tom growled, ready to put his blade through Coke's chest. As he raised his sword, Coke closed his eyes, a wet patch emerging from the crotch of his trousers. With all his might Tom brought down the blade but at the last moment directed it into the ground to the side of the cowering Coke. Something inside him, or perhaps someone, told him that there had been enough killing and God should be left to punish this tyrant.

"If I hear one word against the Bankes family in any pamphlet, I'll personally come after you and kill you. Mark my words." Then, addressing Coke's companion, Tom added, "Take him to London and make sure he remembers what I said. You wouldn't want to lose your master, now, would you?"

With that, Tom mounted his horse and rode back to Camille and his father.

Back at Kingston Lacey Mary Bankes had been heartened by Ralph and Tom's speech, as well as the attendance. Seeing all her children together was uplifting and showed her how much she still had to do and love to give to ensure all their well-being and development. She was so pleased to hear about the funding for St Edward's church at Corffe and taken aback by Ralph's announcement of a new house.

"Ralph, what is this about a new house at Kingston?" she asked later as she sat in the parlour, comforted by the presence of all her family, children and grandchildren.

"I have been thinking about it for a while, Mother. Would this land not make a fabulous house for the family. It is a perfect setting."

"But how can we afford it?"

"Mother, it is time that you took a step back and stopped carrying all the family's burdens on your shoulders. I have saved money to commission an architect to develop an initial design. Obviously, you and all of us will be involved in this process. But if we like what he comes up with, I and the rest of us will make it happen, somehow."

"The funeral reminded me that I still have my younger children to nurture, and I need to find the strength to do that, Ralph. I do not know how I will do it but I will. And I would very much appreciate your support, Ralph, in managing the estate."

"Of course, Mother. You have given this family so much, now it is time we gave back to you."

Doctor George Coke came over to talk to Mary and asked how she was.

"How long have you got Doctor Coke? My heart is shattered and my body is tired and suffering from the flushes. I cannot sleep and am struggling to find the will to live. I am just grateful for my family and friends."

"I have some tonics I can leave with you. They should help a little, but time will be the best healer. I am sorry I could not have helped John, he was truly an exceptional man, a trusted comrade in the army and a good friend."

"Thank you, George."

"Also, I know my brother, Harry Coke, has caused your family so much wrong, for which I am truly sorry. I never understood his personal vendetta against your family, and I fear he had a part to play in what happened to John. I believe God will be taking his vengeance on him, not least for his most recent crime, for he confessed to me that he oversaw the execution of the King."

"Colonel Harvey thought he recognised him on the scaffold. It troubles me to hope for the death of another human being, but I would truly like to see the back of him."

Lord and Lady Fairfax joined them with their daughter Mary. They offered their condolences, and Lady Bankes thanked them for coming.

"I am so sorry that I cannot offer you a room for the night. You have been so kind to me and my family, hosting us, but as you can see our house is very small. Perhaps you can come back in five year's time when Ralph's plans for a new house come to fruition," Lady Bankes said apologetically.

"Mary, do not worry yourself. We stayed last night in a tavern in Wimborne and Thomas loved it."

"Yes Mary, real living. Nothing like an English tavern. But Lady Sandys has invited us to stay with her at Mottisfont tonight."

"Well, that would be nice. Her husband will be turning in his grave, but it is wonderful to see bridges being built across the nation."

"Indeed, and in that vein, their daughter is now engaged to Captain Morris. Another marriage across the divide," Anne Fairfax added.

"And hopefully not the last," Mary Bankes said, looking at Mary Fairfax with a raised eyebrow.

"Yes, I am praying George can return to this country soon. Thank you for all your help, Lady Bankes," Mary replied.

Mary Fairfax went on to find Elizabeth and Jane Bankes in the adjoining room chatting to each other. She was eager to talk to two people of a similar age and so introduced herself.

"Our mother has told us of your love for the Duke of Buckingham, but do not worry, we are sworn to secrecy," Jane said.

"It sounds wonderfully romantic, I mean being in love with a Duke, although you must be worried for his welfare. I understand he is Cromwell's most wanted man." Elizabeth added.

"Yes, I am sick with worry but last I heard from him he was on his way to France. He takes such risks, but I think that is in his character." Mary replied.

"Well at least you have somebody to worry about. There seem to be so few eligible men around and those that are seem to be immersed in politics. Please tell us how you met the Duke," Jane asked, and Mary told the story.

"What a story. It is just like Romeo and Juliette, but I pray for a happier ending," Elizabeth remarked.

Behind the women John Bingham found Ralph Bankes and offered him his condolences.

"You are right to be thinking about the future. A family needs a home and now as head of the family you have the responsibility to provide it."

"Thank you, Sir. I can see how important it is too our family, but alas funding it will be more difficult."

"Well, I hope my bank can be of assistance when the time comes, but on that front I have some good news. Parliament has a plan to commission some significant re-building projects across the nation, the church at Corffe being just one. I have positioned Purbeck and Portland stone with the committee as key components for this initiative. I can see money starting to flow back into the shire."

Chapter Sixteen

A New Commonwealth

25th February , 1649, The Vyne

Mary received another letter from the Duke of Buckingham to tell her that he had arrived safely in France, and was with Queen Henrietta and Charles, the son of the late King, who had declared himself Charles II and held court in Paris. But he was not hopeful for he also said the Royalist cause faced oblivion with most of its followers flocking to foreign protection or plantations in the colonies. He was still grieving the loss of the King but suggesting a rendezvous on the island of Jersey, which remained loyal to the Monarchy and supported Prince Charles. Mary could not see how her father would allow this, but was delighted when her father said that he would see how he could make it happen. He suggested the island of Guernsey would be better for it was Parliamentarian but had a Royalist enclave in a castell there, but he understood no active fighting. He also said that he and her mother would join her to meet the Duke. It would take time to prepare for such a trip, but Lord Fairfax would ensure that such preparations were put in place and Mary could not wait, writing straight back to the Duke with the news.

26th February 1649 Oliver Cromwell – A nation to protect

Oliver Cromwell had just finished his morning prayers. Never in his life had he felt the need for God's guidance more than at the current time. He felt that nation was and had been on a knife edge the entire year, and God was helping him to do what had to be done to move it forward. The death of the King had helped. Many voices had been silenced, for there was no going back. But there were those declaring for his son, Prince Charles, to be made King. The heavyweights behind such views remained at his so-called court in France, their cause he believed was lost. Scotland had already proclaimed him King, but the Scots had only invaded England six months previously and had been humiliated by Cromwell's forces. They were now seen as the enemy by many Englishmen. In the short term, Cromwell did not have to worry about those north of the border. Matters in Ireland were much more concerning, with the Catholics presenting a vocal and untamed defiance, along with many Royalist English landowners. The Catholic uprising in 1641 and the massacre of many Protestants had been one of the main reasons that he had so enthusiastically supported the Parliamentary cause for he and many others were fearful that the King would leverage the support of the Irish to promote his cause, and that of his Catholic Queen, Henrietta. During the course of the war an alliance between the Catholics and Royalists had resulted in conflict with the minority Parliamentary English supporting forces on the island. The threat and fear were only too real for Ireland could provide a springboard for a Catholic-Royalist alliance backed by France or Spain. Many of the monarchs in Europe were shocked by what had happened to King Charles and would gladly back a viable endeavour to restore what they saw as God's order.

To Cromwell, God's guidance was clear: firstly secure the English Commonwealth and ensure that the people were fed and focused on rebuilding the nation, and then deal with the Irish. The Rump Parliament had already declared itself the ultimate authority in the nation and was now developing and drafting a new constitution which Cromwell hoped would be passed as a new law in the next month or so. It would be known as the Commonwealth of England and would involve formally dissolving the House of Lords as well as the Monarchy. There would be no move to put one of Charles's children on the throne, even as a puppet monarch. The monarchy was finished and had no place in the new Commonwealth, which would also see the end of the Privy Council and the Star Chamber. These bodies were no longer required, for Parliament had already delegated power to a small Council of State, a governing group of men who had elected Cromwell as its chairman. This was a matter of expediency and Cromwell took on the role as if he was commanding an army on the battlefield. He set out plans to eradicate opposition to the Commonwealth and remove the symbolism of the Monarchy. Any group that voiced dissent would be dissolved and their leaders faced severe punishment. It was also important to draw a line under the past and eradicate Royalist symbolism, everything from statues, the names of buildings and taverns. The removal of the King's head from the currency was the most symbolic act, but also it was necessary to maintain confidence and build back a peaceful England and Wales.

Cromwell recognised the importance of communication and recruited John Milton as his main propagandist, crafting messages that addressed different interest groups that included the Levellers demanding a fairer society; the agricultural workers concerned about enclosures and the apprentices in London, as well as the Puritans and Presbyterians. He also had to address the funding crisis created by the war. The property of the Monarch and Crown were sold off to the highest bidder to feed the exchequer, the increased taxes to pay for the army already causing a backlash given the high prices of food and other goods. Finally, he had to think about international relations, for the Commonwealth was not recognised by foreign states. New trading relations were essential because England was still suffering from a lack of production of grain and basic products which was fuelling further the rise in prices. European Monarchs would not recognise the new English Government and so he would have to look to the New World where the English had started to colonise great areas of land in the Americas and develop plantations in the Caribbean. If leading an army was complicated enough, leading a nation would require even more effort, determination and strength of character with God's guidance.

28th February, Winchester Castell

Tom was in his command room within the Castell, still digesting the letter he had received earlier in the morning. The fire in the hearth warmed the room, but not the chill within Tom which had been spread from the words in the letter. He was being ordered to prepare his regiment to join Cromwell and his forces to go to Ireland. This was news that he did not want and he dreaded telling Camille. He knew a campaign in Ireland would be long and no doubt bloody. There was a knock on the door and Captain Morris entered.

"Captain, please take a seat."

The Captain sat on one of the chairs in front of the table where the Colonel was positioned.

"I have just received orders to prepare the regiment to be sent to Ireland under the command of General Cromwell."

"Ah, of course, Colonel."

"I want you to lead the preparations, the order is to be prepared to move within six weeks and to be supplied for at least six months. But I suggest we need to be planning for a longer campaign and put in place appropriate logistical support to regularly re-supply the army. I am also not sure how the men will take it as I know there is a lot of apprehension about going to Ireland, but I wanted to talk to you about how this could affect you personally first."

"Yes Colonel."

"I know you have plans to marry Hester Sandys. I suspect that your proposal was based on a marriage of convenience rather than love. I would strongly suggest that you use this Irish campaign to put on hold your plans and use the months in Ireland as a period of reflection to do the right thing for both yourself and Mary."

Captain Morris took a deep breath, but before he could say anything, Tom continued. "What I have said is a lot to take in, Arthur. Go for a walk by the river and we can discuss it on your return. I am still taking this in myself and have a lot to think about as well."

28th February 1649, Kingston Lacey

Camille had ridden over to see Lady Bankes, leaving William and Emily with Nella. It was two weeks since the funeral and Camille was sure Mary would welcome some company plus she wanted to see how she was. The two ladies sat in the parlour around a small table that Mary's cook had prepared, with some cakes.

"How are you feeling Mary?"

"I do not really know Camille; I feel numb. I pray to God every day to ask him why. What plan does the Lord have that necessitates him taking from me first Bridget and now John? And I pray for both their souls. I have never recovered from the loss of Bridget, but the way John was taken from me, just hours before I arrived with the news that he craved and which surely would have saved him makes it so much worse. The last three years I have lost my husband, lover, my home, my wealth, my daughter, my King and now my son. But I cannot fester here in self-pity. I must find the strength to carry on for the sake of my other children."

"Your strength of character is admired by all, Mary. But to be strong you must share the grief and burden with family and friends who can support you. Tom and I are here for you, and will always be, for you have done so much for us."

"Thank you, Camile. As you say I am blessed with a wonderful family and Alice and Ralph especially have been so good to me this last month, only returning to London yesterday. I thank God to see my grandchildren so healthy and full of life playing with little Arabella, for that is certainly a joy. Alice will be spending more time here and will try to find a house nearby for she says she can see the benefit of the children being in the country. Ralph has also promised more time here. He really is serious about this new house. John Bingham is confident that the demand for Purbeck stone will rise rapidly. We just need to keep Coke off our backs."

"That would be wonderful. In the meantime, there is a more pressing building project in Corffe with St Edward's church. I am sure it would progress better with your involvement, Mary."

"Trying to keep me busy, Camille? But that is a good idea. Perhaps we can meet next week in the village with William Harvey and see how we can get the re-construction going again? And then go for a ride across the limestone ridge. I would like that, Camille."

"Yes, we can go to Worth and ride along the cliffs. It will be bracing but the air will do you good, Mary."

Camille was delighted that Mary had accepted her suggestion. It was another small step in her journey to deal with her grief but an important one. Maybe there could be a memorial to John within the church she thought? She would sow that seed next week. The door of the parlour opened and in came little Arabella and her brother Charles. Arabella ran over to Camille and gave her a big hug.

"Camille, would you teach me French?" Charles asked as his sister revelled in Camille's warm embrace.

"Of course, Charles, but why would you want to learn French"

"So I can go to France and support Prince Charles in the French court and help him to return as King of England."

"Well, there is plenty of spirit left in the Bankes family after all," Camille said smiling at Lady Bankes.

1st March 1649, Worth Matravers Dorsetshire

The air was filled with the scent of spring after the long harsh winter when Tom had set off from Winchester at the start ofthe day. He was accompanied by John Anderson and they had now reached their Purbeck homeland as the day started to close. They rode up to Worth Matravers, John's home but Tom was hoping to catch his step-brother, Daniel Spear, for an ale. The sun was disappearing behind the western flank of the limestone ridge trailing splashes of pink across the clouds in the dimming sky as John and Tom pulled up outside the small village tavern, which was no more than a house open to the villagers during the evening. The tavern had been owned by Agnes, a woman who had foresight and paid dearly for it, being burnt at the stake by Colonel Coke as part of his tyranny during the siege of Corffe Castell. Now a widow from Wareham, Charlotte Tristram, who had lost her husband and son during the war, had taken it over to provide some income for her and her two teenage girls. John and Tom went inside and found Daniel with his pals, old George and Ned Parfit, sat around am wooden barrel with a jug of ale each in front of them. Daniel's spaniel was lying on the floor by a small fire which was providing warmth and light to the dim room.

"Daniel, George, I thought I would find you here, and good to see you, Ned," Tom declared.

"Why, Colonel Harvey, and John, what brings you to Worth? Fed up with the smoke of London?"

"A jar with family and friends is far more appealing than anything London can offer," Tom said with a warm smile, patting old George on the back, while shaking Ned's hand and greeting Daniel with a big hug. One of the Tristram girls came out and Tom ordered an ale for himself and John, and asked for all the other jugs to be refilled. The local men were eager to hear Tom's news.

"Well things are certainly strange since the King's death. London, Winchester, Salisbury… wherever you go there is a sombre tone. Many people wanted to see the King punished for his treachery, me included, but now we are in a world without a King, people realise that perhaps something is missing in their lives."

"They should not have executed him, that is for sure. God gave us the King, whether he was good or bad, and we have no right to behead him," old George declared.

"Folk around here feel the same, Tom. What country has no King? What country would behead their King? People say that vengeance should be left for God to deliver when it comes to kings not common people," Daniel added. "And now people are saying we have done wrong and we will have to pay the consequences."

"I got to know King Charles well before he was executed. He was misguided, a poor judge of the situation, but he was not a tyrant nor a traitor. He wanted to be a good king and in many areas we did not appreciate what he did for the nation. Was he a cause of the dreadful war from which we are all still suffering the consequences? Yes absolutely. But I now believe Parliament was also to blame. I believe he should have been punished or locked up and then perhaps one of his sons should have been made monarch, and a compromise solution found that preserved the Monarchy. I saw his execution. He died with dignity, humility and even forgiving those that had tried him, and as soon as he was dead, there was a mood in the audience that changed and you could sense it spread across London. It was a feeling of loss and remorse, and it was something I felt quite deeply, and which I continue to feel. It shocked me that I would feel this way, but he had been King nearly all my life. and I had known no other. I bet even old George here can barely recollect his father?"

"True enough. Although I do recall his death. It was a sombre time. The passing of a monarch is a sad time for any nation."

"But this time the sombreness is mixed with a sense of guilt. The nation somehow executed the King, who had been appointed by God. Guilt and sorrow shared by us all, at a time when there is so much pain still being endured from the war," Tom continued.

"I was a lad when King James died. I remember it being declared – 'The King is Dead, Long Live the King' but now there is no new King," Ned remarked.

"I had always believed Cromwell to be a good man, and certainly a great leader, and I still have much hope for the changes he can bring to this country, but I know he was instrumental in the death of the King, and I am still struggling with that in my mind. There are those who say he wants the Crown, but that is not his way. However, power can change any man, I am sure. I am hoping he will lead the country like he led the army and provide us all with more opportunity and give us all more of a say in how this country is run," Tom said.

"That is Leveller talk again, Tom. I think you can dream on with that idea. The gentry will keep power to themselves, that is for sure, and without the King, who can stop them," Daniel retorted.

"Well, we need hope, that is for sure," John replied as the girl brought back the drinks.

"Yes, let's hope for peace and for prosperity in a country that can reflect God's grace. Let's toast to hope," and Tom led them to raise their jugs of ale.

"And look what I have, some of the new coinage without the King's head." Tom opened his money bag out on to the barrel. "See they have replaced King Charles's head with a shield containing the cross of St George and a wreath of laurel."

"It is the standard for the New Commonwealth," John declared.

Then men picked up a coin each and inspected it.

"T'aint right, is it. There has always been the King on the money," old George said.

"What is this talk about Commonwealth? I am sure it will make no difference to the likes of us. We just need our church re-built, orders for the quarry and crops in the field. That will give us commoners the wealth we need, not any political declarations in London," Ned said forcefully.

"Guess lots of things will be changing, and we will just have to get used to it, but as you say Ned we just need to carry on working hard to keep food in our bellies," Daniel added.

"As long as people accept it for what it is worth I suppose but I would prefer a King on my money that is for sure. It seems less valuable now," Ned said handing the coins back to Tom.

The men continued to talk about the prospects for the quarry as more orders had now been received from London and the re-commencement of the repairs and works to the church at Corffe, before Tom bade farewell and set off to his home in Swanage.

Swanage

Camille had rocked William gently to sleep, then lay him down in his cradle before joining Tom in their bed.

"It is good to be home, safe here in Swanage, all together in our house, away from the madness of London," she said as she rested her head on his arm.

"Yes, our peaceful little piece of England, amidst a headless nation. You know I was starting to like him towards the end, I mean King Charles. He was misguided but certainly not a bad man. I was so certain that he should be executed before I got to know him, I wanted justice, but now he is gone, I feel an emptiness. He did not deserve to be executed and now I do feel the country is missing something or someone. I am not sure that this committee that has been established can replace a king."

"My grandmother used to say, 'You do not know what you have got until you have lost it'."

"Yes. In Winchester, I was given some of the new coins, the ones with no King's head on it. I was reluctant to accept them at first but it will replace all our coins over time. I also picked up this pamphlet."

He handed the pamphlet that was headed: *'A Coffin for King Charles; a Crown for Cromwell; a Pit for the People.'*

"Inside it says they are selling the Royal Collection, the King's property and the crown jewels to pay for Cromwell's plans. Many see the Commonwealth of England, as they call it, the future for levelling up society. I have my doubts. I am not sure Cromwell shares that view at all, although I hope he can learn from what he did for the army and the opportunity he gave to men like me. My fear is that power will go to his head. He says he is guided by God's will, but I fear that God's will can be interpreted into what is good for Oliver Cromwell. I hope I am wrong. But his committee has already announced anybody opposing the Commonwealth will be liable to extreme punishment. I am sure they will have closed down the press that printed this pamphlet already."

Camille replied, "In France we say 'plus ça change, plus c'est la même chose' - the more things change the more things stay the same. I am sure it will not be long before the English are crying for their king to return, well at least his son."

The couple listened to the gentle breathing of William in his cot next to their bed.

"The main thing is we have peace. We need peace for William and Emily. No more fighting. I pray for it every day, whether it is with a king or a committee, that is what we need. I cannot stand the thought of you fighting any more, Tom."

Tom had not told Camille about the orders he had received from Cromwell to start preparing his regiment to be sent to Ireland. He did not know when the army would be sent to Ireland and what they would face over there, but the thought of it was foreboding, and he did not know how to tell Camille. For now he was relishing every moment with his family but how long would it last, and what would Cromwell's plans for the nation under his protection mean to him and the Harveys? Only God knew.

The Places in A Nation Beheaded

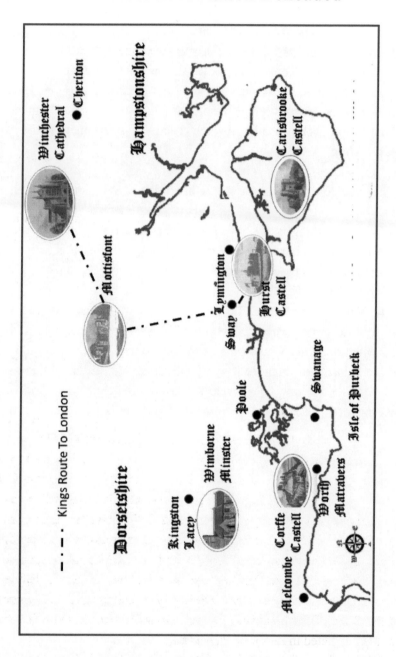

ACKNOWLEDGEMENTS

A Nation Beheaded stays true to events and people as far as possible, with some variation to the timing of happenings and supplementary characters for literary effect. The Bankes family names are real and the story is broadly true to their historical record, but characters, relationships and specific events are fictional. John Bankes, the eldest son, did die a few years later than depicted in this story as a young man after returning from travelling in Europe. He was unmarried and without heirs, but the course of death is not known so I used fictional license to explore the post-traumatic effects of the war as well as morality in a Puritan environment. His death left Ralph as head of the household.

The same applies to King Charles and Oliver Cromwell, the Parliamentarians John Bingham, Colonel Ireton and Sir John Borlase, the Fairfax family, the Cokes and the Royalist Sandys and Duke of Buckingham. The Harveys and Arthur Morris are entirely fictional and John Bingham was not one of the commissioners at King Charles's trial, although was still a member of the Rump Parliament and did sit amongst the common's representatives in Westminster Hall. The villain, Harry Coke character continues from a Nation in Ruins, the son of Sir Edward Coke. He was born Henry but known as Harry, and did have financial problems but otherwise all the portrayal in this book is fictional including his position as the Puritan enforcer, Parliamentary debt collector and role in the King's execution. The book is dotted with other historical characters, including John 'freeborn' Lilburne, Indigo Jones, John Milton, and Robert Boyle, all of whom are placed historically at the right time and location. Mary Fairfax and the Duke of Buckingham did have a courtship but it was a few years later than depicted in A Nation Beheaded.

John Anderson is a true historical person who lived in Corfe at the time, whom I discovered recently was a relative to me via a branch of my mother's family tree stretching seven generations. I will develop his character further in my next book.

Whether Charles and Oliver Cromwell played as children is possible but there is no historical evidence of this. It is a seed that was sown in a children's story book I read as a boy and the idea stayed with me. Cromwell and Ireton's discovery of Charles' treachery in the letter they intercepted en route to his Queen at a tavern in London, as well as Cromwell visiting Charles' body after his execution are stories that have been told for many years but are unlikely to have occurred and have no historical evidence to support them.

To many, Charles was seen as a martyr for his people and, to this day, wreaths of remembrance are laid by his supporters on the anniversary of his death at his statue, which faces down Whitehall to the site of his execution. The clock above the entrance to Horse Guards has a black mark between the one and the two – the hour of the death of Charles I. The value of monarchy to our nation was reaffirmed with the passing of Queen Elizabeth and I am sure was deeply felt by the vast majority of the population in 1649, those who were not political or within the army but had celebrated the anniversary of his coronation so fervently just the year before. The sequel, *A Nation Protected*, will continue the story of Oliver Cromwell, the Bankeses and the Harveys, as well as the Fairfaxes, the Duke of Buckingham and John Bingham.

I would also like to thank the Dorset History Centre which looks after the Bankes Archive including letters written from and to the characters in this book as well as Mary Bankes' detailed financial accounts and many invoices. Another thank you to my friend and former colleague, Tony Hutchinson, whose photography created the cover to A Nation Protected.

A big thank you to the National Trust, a wonderful organisation that tirelessly looks after the ruin of Corfe Castle, and the houses at Mottisfont, Kingston Lacey, the Vyne, Clyveden and Hinton Ampner (the Battle of Cheriton) amongst so much of this nation's heritage. I am equally grateful for the work of the English Heritage particularly in respect to Hurst Castle and Carisbrooke Castle. I have visited these places many times and I am grateful on each occasion as one is taken back in time, with the help of informative volunteers and living history events. I hope the experience will be enjoyed by many more after reading this book. Understanding how people dealt with the challenges of the past gives us strength and comfort to take on those of the present and future.